*Pages in the Wind*

## Testimonials for *Pages in the Wind*

"This is a mystery book about a family wrecked by violence, secrets, cruelty and tragedy. All of this contributed to Emily Quinn, a beautiful young woman, landing in prison for the murder of her sadistic father. She suffers anxiety, depression, and amnesia for key periods in her life. The prison psychiatrist is a compassionate combination of "Sigmund Freud, Dick Tracy, and the Pink Panther" who uses his superb skills to discover and evaluate an astonishing chain of events. The saga will keep readers glued to this clear, well-written, and surprising narrative. I recommend this gem to all interested in mental problems, human emotions, and survival under seemingly impossible conditions."
**—Rodrigo A. Munoz, M.D. Professor of Psychiatry, U.C. San Diego— President of the American Psychiatric Association 1998-1999**

"*Pages in the Wind* is one of those novels that had me guessing all the time. The author skillfully weaves a complex story entwining a web of family secrets that unfold into horrendous events. With many twists and turns, something unpredictable in the story would be revealed and kept me wanting to read on, right to the end. If you like psychological dramas, full of suspense, this is the book to read."
**—Linda Payne Smith, Creative Writing Instructor and Author of *Tin Tubs and Hollyhocks*.**

"I thought I was watching a movie! The author's imaginative descriptive words paint a picture of the characters and each scene. The psychological thriller is a real page-turner. A novel you will not want to put down and will want to read more than once as it fully grips you."**—Regina J. Farmer, Director, Los Angeles News Group, Digital First Media**

# Pages in the Wind

SALLY SAYLOR DE SMET

ISBN: 0996527605
ISBN 13: 9780996527606
Library of Congress Control Number: 2015910236
Greenly Publishing, La Mesa, CA

This book is dedicated to my daughters, Nicole and Julia, my inspiration for getting up every day—and to my brothers, John and Richard Saylor, for proving the everlasting bond of siblings. Thank you to my mother, Mary Saylor, whose loves lives on every day.

# Gratitude

I am grateful to Julia McVey for her editing talents. Thank you for taking the time to read my writing every day, catching every detail and giving me feedback. I could not have finished the book without your help. You are amazing.

Thank you to Regina J. Farmer for giving me the gift of confidence as only a best friend can do. Regina read the early pages and cheered me on. You are an inspiration.

Thank you also to Linda Payne Smith, a talented writer, for editing the final draft and providing guidance. To Marolyn Hayes, who read the early pages and encouraged me. Thanks also to JT, for making me laugh.

I am blessed.

# Contents

# One

## SHACKLED

I held the sketch back to admire my drawing. The girl in the picture was six months past fifteen. She started wearing makeup on her birthday—not much, just cotton candy lip-gloss, and pink blush to add color to her pale cheeks. Her butterscotch hair touched her slender waist with a single curl. She couldn't bring herself to cut it in the new short Twiggy hairstyle although she hadn't ruled it out completely.

"Quinn! Drop your damn pencils! Time to go!" The guard whipped out his restraints and had me in the hallway in less than a minute.

I glanced back at the picture and watched the pencil roll under the bunk. For the first time since my arrival fourteen days ago, I'm out of confinement and away from my make-believe world. I'm Emily Quinn, a nineteen-year-old murderer. I clamped down on my lower lip and braced myself for the long walk to meet my psychiatrist.

The chains around my ankles scraped the cement floor as I shuffled down the corridor of the San Francisco County Jail. Rumbling toilets, guards yelling, women shouting, and plates slamming against steel tables echoed throughout the jailhouse. I retched at the stench of urine, ammonia, and sweat blasting through the old ventilation system.

1

We finally reached the fifth floor. My shoulder ached, and my legs were numb from towing ten pounds of metal. I glanced at the officer, wondering if we might take a break, but his fixed expression told me otherwise. He led me into a small office and chained me to a leather chair. I twisted, trying to sit up straight with leaden shackles hooked to the legs. All one hundred fifteen pounds of me slid downward, leaving me flat on the seat, staring at the ceiling. I inched my way up, gripping the arms. Seated at the desk in front of me was my reason for being here, Doctor Daniel Lieberman.

He flipped through the papers without looking up. "I'll be with you shortly."

My lips began to quiver so I hung my head, forming a dark curtain around my face. The intake officer informed me early on not to show emotions. While being strip-searched and fingerprinted, I couldn't stop crying. She let me know I wouldn't "keep my baby face" acting like a two-year-old; the seasoned inmates would target me as a punk and trade me to other detainees for a pack of cigarettes. Besides, slaughtering a parent doesn't win you esteem among the prisoners, and no one buys the "amnesia" excuse. It's been used before.

I peeked through my long, dark hair at the doctor. I had done a little homework on him courtesy of a *Time* Magazine article I retrieved from the book cart. His work received a stellar review and touted him as a leading forensic psychiatrist. I expected a tall, professorial type in a three-piece suit. Not so. He was a short, pencil-thin man in his late sixties, wearing a wrinkled gray jacket and slacks.

He held up his "wait a minute" finger as he continued to fumble through the pile of papers.

I pushed a clump of hair behind one ear to look around. His office was twenty years beyond shabby, and not what I would expect from a celebrated doctor. The walls were putrid green; framed degrees and awards teetered in all directions, coated in dust. Empty candy wrappers and coffee-stained mugs covered his desk along with loose files and manila envelopes.

He stopped the paper shuffle and focused his attention on me. He stared, tapping his index finger against his mouth. "Glad to meet you, Miss Quinn."

"You…too," I mumbled. My hands trembled, and the knots in my neck made it hard to move my head. I didn't know how to talk to a psychiatrist, let alone one with the power to retrieve the lost memories of my life.

He leaned back in his swivel chair. "Emily, tell me something about yourself."

The shackles made me squirm like a trapped animal. "Um…"

I faked a cough to buy some time. Surely he'd read my file and knew that killing my father two weeks ago wiped out most of my life. Since the murder, hazy snapshots have flickered through my mind, fragments of an event or face. The visions have evaporated on impact, leaving nothing but the fact that I had a life—once.

The doctor ran his hands through his frizzy white hair. "Let's start with some basics that you know."

I opened my mouth, but nothing came out. It felt like I was playing connect the dots without the pencil. His tics made it worse. He rubbed his chin, shrugged his bony shoulders, and pushed his glasses up and down his skinny nose.

"Just say whatever comes to your mind."

"Well…" I bit down on my lower lip. *What was I supposed to say? Recite what others told me or what I remembered?*

They said I murdered my father, but I didn't know why. I had an older brother who hadn't come to see me, and a mother who shelled out a tidy sum to defend me but had only called me once. And that was only to apprise me of legal issues. For the first few minutes, I thought she was one of my attorneys. I had a fiancée I couldn't remember, sequestered at a boot camp cut-off from the outside world. I got the news from his mother; she telephoned me after my arrest, worried sick about her boy. He had no idea that while hiking through a simulated Viet Nam battlefield learning to be a good Marine, his intended bride was arrested for premeditated murder.

Now a psychiatrist was asking me to drudge up the lost details of my life to explain why I killed my father. Whatever comes from hypnosis, my father will still be dead, and I'll still be the one who killed him.

He held his stare; his brown eyes were intense and steady. "Relax, Miss Quinn. Tell me what you know about yourself."

"I was told...I mean, my name is Emily. I'm nineteen. I have a brother, Robert, and a twin sister, Penelope. But, um...they say she died in 1953 when I was five. My mother and..."

"Please continue."

I looked down, squeezing my hands. "My father...they said I stabbed him...twenty times. They found me...us...on the kitchen floor."

"Is there anything else you can tell me?"

I rubbed the sweat from my forehead. "No sir."

He leaned forward in his swivel chair. "Let's talk about what we're going to do here."

I swallowed hard, feeling like my throat had narrowed.

"You will be guided back to different stages in your life. I will be looking for patterns and progression in your thought process. We will start at eight years old because the brain's ability to recall detailed events is more developed after the age of seven. Once I have enough data to establish a thought pattern, I will progress you forward to another age. After each session, I would like you to keep a journal of your thoughts and memories, which will be sent to me prior to our next meeting. It does not need to be formatted, just write whatever comes to your mind."

I rubbed my sweaty hands on my jumpsuit, cringing at every word. Terrified to shine a light in what had to be an evil soul.

"Hypnosis is entirely safe. You won't do or say anything that you would not normally do. I will guide you into a relaxed state, and you will recall events as they occurred. When you wake up, you will remember everything that happened. You will be fully awake and aware of your surroundings."

"Uh-huh."

"Okay. Now I want to talk to you on a more personal level about what we're going to do."

I tried to hide my nerves, but my right eye twitched, and drool trickled down my chin from my mouth hanging open. I lowered my head and wiped the gunk with the scratchy sleeve of my jumpsuit.

He continued to explain hypnosis. "...And we'll work together for as long as it takes to retrieve your repressed memories. He paused, dragging a notebook across his desk. "Tell me what you hope to gain from hypnosis."

A hot sensation ripped through me, holding back the doctor's words. I shook my head, feeling damp hair tap against my face.

He rested his elbows on his desk. "Miss Quinn, I'm here to help you make sense of what now seems senseless. Do you have any questions?"

I opened my mouth and burbled a series of unintelligible sounds. "Uh...I...." I twisted my foot against the shackles.

His fingers formed a steeple as he waited for me to talk.

"I don't know!" The words sounded like I spit them out in protest. I rammed my ankle on the shackles hard enough to draw blood.

"I understand this is difficult for you. My role as your doctor is to help you. Think of this as a beginning, not an end. We'll do this together...we'll discover who you are, and what shaped you. Can you do this with me?"

I hid behind my hair and wondered why. It seemed like a morbid journey, traipsing through the mire and muck only to hear a dead man moan. *My own father.* There was no repentance worthy enough or defense strong enough to erase murder. The Ten Commandments were seared in my memory, and I had broken five and six: "Honor, your mother and your father," and "Thou shalt not kill." There was no going back from two mortal sins. On Earth or in death, I was damned to Hell.

My agony melded into low moans of sorrow. Finally, came the frightful silence. My lungs gave out, my tears desiccated, leaving the dread of nothingness. A chill traveled through me, cold and tingly, like the faint flurry of a desperate heartbeat. I hung my head, as my shoulders jerked in anguish.

The doctor stood up to move to the corner of his desk. He sat down, his head bowed.

I sensed his pity. He no longer prodded me to talk, and every so often he sighed. After a few minutes, I wiped my face and stared at the floor. My crippling anxiety left me exhausted and compliant.

I took a deep, quivering breath and spoke the two words he wanted to hear. "I will."

"Good, Emily." He began talking in a low, melodic voice. "... Close your eyes and imagine yourself on a cloud. The wind is gentle, and you are starting to relax. Feel your arms resting, your shoulders, and head. You are floating through the air where there are no worries or cares..."

My mind disengaged from my thoughts with each breath. The tightness in my muscles loosened. I clung to his words and felt myself wafting through a vast space. His voice was rhythmic and calm. "As you listen to my voice, that relaxed calming feeling will become deeper and deeper until you are in a peaceful state of hypnosis. The deeper you go, the deeper you will want to go..."

With each word, my body melted into a timeless stretch of tranquility.

"...Emily, you are going back to when you were eight years old. Tell me where you are and describe how you feel..."

# *Two*

## HEAVEN TO HELL

**August 1956. Seattle, Washington**

The faint glow of the late afternoon sun touched my face as I jumped out of the car. Birch trees quivered in the breeze, and the scent of damp pine needles and cedar reminded me of Christmas. The fruit groves, giant evergreens, and fields of wild clovers and moss surrounded the old wood and stone craftsman home like an enchanted forest. I gushed with giggles and short squeals knowing the day had finally arrived. I couldn't wait to spend a month with Grandma.

Clay pots filled with bluebells and daisies lined the weathered stairs leading to her arched door. Tiny yellow birds hovered at glass feeders, as long-beaked hummingbirds poked at nearby trumpet flowers. I straightened my straw hat as I dashed up the steps toting my Huckleberry Hound bag.

"You better damn well hope she wants you!" Father shouted, slamming the trunk. "Or I'll have to leave you by the side of the road!"

I turned to Mother. She grabbed my picture books from the back seat. My big brother, Robert, jumped up and down, shaking off the long car ride from San Francisco. Mother caught me watching her and shrugged as she fiddled with Robert's bow tie.

She put her hand on Robert's shoulder. "Come along now. Let's go see Grandma."

They met me on the porch. Father soon followed carrying my suitcase.

I pushed Grandma's doorbell. My tummy fluttered as I peeked through the glass door.

Wearing a blue shirtwaist dress and flour-dusted apron, Grandma swung the door open. "My deux grandchildren! Bonjour! And bébé Emily! How long I have waited!"

I snickered at her French accent; her words had a distinct 'z' sound with a rise at the end of each word.

"Grandma! I'm eight now!"

"You are? Let me see you! Emily is no longer a bébé!" She held her hands to her lips. "Oh, sweet chéri, you lost two teeth!"

I pointed to an open space in my mouth. "Look, Grandma! My big teeth are coming in!"

Father embraced Grandma and turned to Robert. "Son, what do you have to say to Grandma?"

"Hi, Grandma. We drove a long way!"

"And what a big boy you are! You have grown so tall!"

Father tousled Robert's hair. "And a smart boy, too. Tell Grandma how you skipped to the seventh grade and what you're learning."

He shrugged. "Algebra."

Grandma's eyes widened. "My boy is so bright!"

I bounced up and down. "Grandma! I can write my name in cursive now!"

Mother interrupted. "Okay, children. Run along so your grandma, and I can visit."

As soon as my family left the next morning, I ran up and down the hallway, peeking into bedrooms, pink tiled bathrooms, and a staircase leading to an art studio. Grandma called me the "princess of the manor."

I woke up every day to the sounds of birds singing and the smell of cinnamon raisin bread baking in the oven for our morning French toast. I thought the days would go on forever.

⟋⟍

But thirty days later, my visit came to an end.

Puffs of dirt brushed against my bare legs as I searched for a place to hide. Summer was over, or at least it seemed that way. The spring flowers that stayed through August had withered. The songbirds held their chirps, and only a brown buzzard lingered in the gray skies. Nearly noon, I knew my parents would be pulling into Grandma's driveway any minute.

I shook both hands, running in circles. "What do I do? What do I do?" My heart pounded so fast; it snatched my breath, but I had to keep going. I raced past rose gardens and shady pagodas covered in leafy plants.

My ponytail got stuck on an alder branch, knocking me to the dusty ground. I picked some broken twigs from my hair and rubbed my knees with my pleated skirt.

My eyes watered as I gazed at the porch swing on the south veranda. Every night, I sang for Grandma while the bullfrogs croaked in the background. When the song would end, she would ask for an encore and then another. Off to the side, on the grassy knoll, we picnicked every afternoon and played "hide and seek." A few feet away, I spotted a row of lemon trees and remembered picking fruit for her meringue pie. Everything reminded me of Grandma. I didn't want to go home.

If only the grounds had a moat with flesh-eating crocodiles with snapper jaws and scaly skin. The scary monsters would display their razor teeth and lunge from the water to stop the sedan from entering the estate and taking me away from her.

Father wouldn't care. He says there was something wrong with me and calls me a misfit.

"Emily! Mon bébé! Where are you?"

"I'm over here, Grandma," I shouted, waving among the pepper trees. "Are they here yet?"

I grinned at the sight of Grandma in her flower-print apron and her hair twisted in a bun. She maneuvered through the tall trees, carrying a plate of éclairs. "No, ma, chéri! I'm coming! This old dame can still dodge a leaf or two!"

We found a wooden bench a few feet away. "You're not one bit old, Grandma." I didn't want her to age and told myself that she would live another sixty years. That way we could die at the same time.

She handed me a pastry. "How is my bonne fille, today?"

I traced a heart in the powdered sugar. "I'm sad. I don't want to go home...I want to stay here with you."

"Then you'll stay with Grandma, ma chéri! Do you remember our signal?"

A smile crept across my face. "Of course I do!" It was a secret plan we used every summer. If I squeezed her hand twice that meant I would ask Mother if I could stay longer.

The fear and sadness I felt moments ago changed to cheerful talk of cave crickets chirping in hollow logs and a woodpecker hammering away at a pine tree nearby.

A motor rumbled in the distance. I turned to Grandma to see if she heard it too. She nodded and took my hand. "Mère est arrivé."

We met Mother, Father, and Robert on the porch. Robert waved and shouted a quick "hi" before running into the yard to jump on a swing.

"Ma," said Mother, with a warm hug.

She turned to me next and smiled. "Hello, Emily, did you have a nice stay with your grandma?"

I took a step back, twisting my hair around my finger. "Yes, ma'am."

Father greeted Grandma and cocked his head at me. "Did you behave yourself?"

I looked down, wondering if I did something wrong.

"Oui, Emily was a very good girl!"

Father raised one eyebrow at me. "So happy to see you, Ma. Last time I was here, the upstairs bathroom had a drippy faucet. Let me go check that."

Robert stayed outside, but the rest of us went into the house. Mother and Grandma sat at a table in the dining room. I waited in the foyer, watching and listening.

They chatted quietly, their fingertips touching. Mother talked about my grandpa, who died when I was a baby. He was a businessman and an artist. His artwork hung in every room with gold lights over each picture. Every so often, Grandma spoke in French, and Mother nodded.

Even after only a month away, I gawked at Mother like I was seeing her for the first time. Her full lips and turquoise eyes stood out against her milky skin, and her chestnut brown hair formed gentle curls around her shoulders. She wore a white dress, straw hat, and a single strand of pearls. She seemed more like a movie star than a mother.

Being near her again dissolved my secret plan to stay in Seattle. I kept my eyes on Grandma until she caught my expression. Her eyes softened, and she nodded. I think she knew all along I would go home.

Early the next morning, the family gathered at the front door saying their goodbyes. I stood back, dabbing my eyes.

Grandma sat eye-level with me. "My precious bébé. We'll be together soon. Next time I will teach you to make crepe cakes."

My chest heaved as I caught each whimper and reined them back to talk to her. I gazed into her soft blue eyes, already thinking about next August. She had no idea why going home was killing me—I didn't even know. "I'll write you every day, Grandma. My hand never gets tired. I'll draw you beautiful pictures too." I grabbed her hand, wondering if it was too late to squeeze it twice.

Father pushed me aside. "That's enough. Leave your grandma alone."

The feel of his broad hand on my back released pent-up tears. I stood beside Robert with my head down, wiping the teardrops as soon as they touched my cheek.

Father hugged Grandma goodbye and turned to Mother, Robert, and me. "Come on, we have a long drive ahead of us."

Everyone was already in the sedan when Grandma and I stepped onto the porch. I continued to the car door, then turned and blew a kiss to Grandma. She pretended to catch it and blew me one back.

Father revved the engine. "Goddamn it! Get in the car!"

I hopped in next to Robert and wiggled my fingers at Grandma. She followed us down the long driveway. I waved until we turned a corner, and I couldn't see her anymore. I pressed on my eyes, trying to smother the tears.

Watching out the window, I listened to the steady tick of the turn signal, and the occasional thump of tires hitting a bump. My eyes watered and burned as the smoke of Father's cigarette drifted into the back seat. I rested my head against the glass, feeling like I was going from Heaven to Hell.

Mother reached around and touched my knee. "It's good to have you back, dear."

I sat up straight. "Thank you, ma'am."

Sunlight beamed into the car, casting red streaks in Mother's hair. I studied the lilt in her voice, the way she tossed her dark hair, and how she gently blinked her eyes when my father talked to her.

We arrived home right after midnight. Mother and Robert quickly retreated to their bedrooms, as Father and I stood at the foot of the stairs, his head drooping. I hated myself for wishing flesh-eating crocodiles on him and calling our home Hell.

He gestured for me to climb the stairs to my bedroom. "Go to bed," he mumbled.

"Yes, sir."

He no longer looked like the scary monster I had imagined. I listened to his heavy footsteps behind me as we headed up the steps. As I turned the corner to my room, I saw him yawn and pat his mouth.

"Goodnight, Daddy." I promised myself that tomorrow would be the start of a new and better Emily.

# *Three*

## GHOST OF PENELOPE

Rain tapped my window with an occasional burst of windswept water. Grandma always said the angels were sprinkling her garden, which happened a lot in Seattle. I snuggled back under the covers, imagining white-winged cherubs tilting gold watering jugs on fields of wildflowers.

The summer storm paused, leaving the steady flow of water pouring from the rain gutters. I pulled back the coverlet, anxious to rush downstairs and help Grandma with Sunday's blueberry pancakes and fritters.

I had one foot on the floor when I noticed my hand clutching a yellow paisley bedspread. The walls were eggshell white instead of periwinkle blue. A sunflower print hung above a veneer chest of drawers. The house smelled like ammonia instead of Grandma's lilac soap.

*I was home.*

I pulled a pink shirt over my head, reciting the house rules. "Keep the door six inches from the doorstop, no elbows on the table, no running in the house…"

I could write the others down later. The house was still, so I grabbed the long Bloomingdale's box that once held Mother's winter coat. I found it leaning against a trash can a few years ago, and it's been with me ever since, carrying my art supplies. I picked out a sketchpad and pencils to go outside. I had at least an hour to draw without worrying about messing up.

I tiptoed down the stairs, careful not to step on the creaky third step from the top. That was one of the simple rules. I opened and closed the back door without making a peep. The crisp air of San Francisco hit my face like opening a freezer on a warm day.

I headed for the Adirondack chair next to an old oak tree. The yard was shaped like a rectangle with a round section of grass, a swing set placed near the fence, and a brick path. Father paved the walkway last year so we wouldn't track dirt in the house. For me, the trail was a place to skip in search of a magical world with candy castles, fairies, and rainbows.

Gray clouds sent goose bumps up and down my bare arms, as cool air fanned the pages of my sketchpad. I shivered and wondered how I would be able to draw in the bitter cold.

A few weeks ago in Seattle, it drizzled for three days straight. Every time I went outside to play, the blustery weather drove me back inside. Grandma suggested I run and sing to get warm, and it worked.

"I could do the same thing here!"

I dropped the pad and braved the frigid air, whizzing around the path. When the wind stung my face, I ran faster, waving to the clouds and singing a song Grandma taught me:

"Somewhere over the rainbow! Skies are blue…"

The back door slammed. I turned to see Father standing on the steps with his arms crossed. He wore a brown terry cloth bathrobe, his feet were bare, and his sandy hair stuck out in all directions.

He lunged from the stairs and gripped my forearm. "Goddamn you! I drove twelve hours to pick you up, and your shitty singing woke me up!"

I lowered my head. "I'm sorry, Father."

He squeezed my arm and then let me go. "Knock it off you little twit!"

The door re-slammed when he left.

I rubbed my arm and gazed at the back door before trudging back to the chair. I felt deflated, like a helium balloon that flies high until one day, it's just a blob of vinyl on the ground with all the air sucked out.

I tucked my legs under me and studied the oak tree. I usually drew girls and made up stories about them but decided to sketch the tree instead. I followed the pattern of the branches, one leading to another, thicker near the trunk. After awhile, I picked out five colors and started outlining the shape.

Father's words bubbled to the surface. I stared down at the pad, biting my lip. I brushed the tears away, and put the pencils back in the box.

The back door slammed again. Robert jumped into the yard carrying a toy airplane. He glanced at me. "Ooh! Emily got in trouble!"

He didn't wait for a reply. He hopped on the brick path, moving the plane up and down making "rum, rum, rum" sounds as he raced around the yard.

Father came out of the house wearing his khaki uniform. He pointed at Robert. "What ya doing, partner?"

"Watch this!" Robert squatted, thrust the plane into the air and caught it before landing on the grass.

Father lunged forward. "Now you're the airplane! Bet I can catch you!"

Robert held his arms out like the wings of a plane. They ran along the trail as my brother giggled.

"I'm gaining on you!"

"No, you're not!"

Mother cracked the door and announced breakfast.

"Okay, partner. Flight 152 has landed. Time for re-fueling!"

Father motioned to me. "Come on, time to eat."

They were several feet in front of me when the screen door slammed. A cloud parted, sending beams of light through the old oak. The leaves rustled, releasing a few from the branches. One twirled down to the damp soil as the other leaf landed on the bricks. I squinted, trying to see the road as bricks that Father had built to keep dirt from the house.

I couldn't. I still saw a magical road leading to enchanted forests, wild horses, and colorful rainbows.

I took my seat at the square Formica kitchen table and slid my sketchpad under the chair.

Mother gave me a side-glance. "Have some breakfast, dear."

She stood at the green tile counter of our small kitchen buttering toast, adding each slice to a plate of stacked bread. Her slender fingers aligned the pieces so all the corners lined up the same. She wore a white cotton blouse and black fitted pants tucked into slip-on velvet shoes. Her dark hair was pulled up on the sides.

Father often called her a blueblood. She graduated from a fancy college called Vassar, spoke five languages, and read books with long titles. After twelve years of marriage, my father still called her "Miss America" and bragged that he hit the jackpot when he married her.

I turned to my father, wondering if my mother hit the jackpot too. As a Naval Captain, he kept his shoes shiny and his pants creased down the middle. With wavy blonde hair, hazel eyes, and suntanned skin, Mother said he looked like Kirk Douglas. People called him "the wit." He liked to tell funny stories, and he laughed with his whole face.

But he wasn't always happy. I could tell by his eyes. If he walked through the door with raised eyebrows and a slight kick, he was happy. If he stared straight ahead, paced, and muttered under his breath, that meant he was angry. When he looked that way, I ran to my room.

Robert looked like Father with dark blonde hair, blue eyes, and light freckles. He was different though; my brother was calmer and harder to read. Father adored him; he called him "nine years of perfect" with his straight-A report cards and awards.

Mother listened to Father and Robert talk without adding to the conversation, which wasn't unusual. She had gone days without saying a word. Father called them her "quiet spells." I wondered if her silence had to do with the death of my twin sister, Penelope. She died mysteriously three years ago, but we were forbidden to talk about her. The secret of her death loomed over me like a ghost between Mother's silence and Father's anger. I thought of her every day and wondered if my life would be different if she hadn't died. Whatever happened to her changed everything, but I didn't know why.

Mother stood over me with a plate of evenly aligned bacon. "Another piece?"

I shook off Penelope's ghost. "No, thank you, ma'am."

Father paused his conversation with Robert. "Help your mother with the dishes."

I rose to clear the table, but Mother waved me down.

Father grabbed the last slice of bacon. He walked to Mother, who was at the dishwasher lining up the dirty plates by size and color. He leaned into her, put his hand on her hip, and kissed her cheek. "The new recruits come today, darling. Oh, Claire, is tonight our dinner party?"

"Yes, darling. The guests will arrive at six. I picked up your camel jacket at the cleaners."

He kissed her neck and turned. "Bye, kids. Behave yourselves." He winked at Robert. "See you tonight, partner!"

⟋

I sat cross-legged on my bed, sketching a girl with blue eyes and ringlets. As I grabbed a pencil to make her a pink sweater, Mother stopped by my room.

"Time to get ready for the party, dear. Wear the outfit I bought you at the Emporium last week. It's hanging on the left side of your closet."

"Yes, ma'am."

I ran to the small closet and found the dress. "Wow!" The gown was blue organza with tiny bows gathered at the bottom, revealing layers of white tulle. Mother had positioned white bobby socks and black patent leather shoes under the dress. Inside one shoe, she placed a butterfly clip for my hair.

Mother made dressing easy. She set my clothes out every morning, freshly washed and ironed. She even identified which sock was left and right. They looked the same to me, so I made sure not to mix them up.

I twirled out of my room like Cinderella on her way to the ball. I found Robert in the hallway dressed in a brown tweed suit and black tasseled shoes. His hair was slicked back with a thick gel. His brow creased and his lower lip protruded, dimpling his chin. He fidgeted with his clothes and rubbed his head.

He caught me watching him and stomped his foot. "Take a picture, it'll last longer!"

"What's wrong, Robby?"

He peered down the stairs and huffed. "I hate these things!"

I started to say something when Father entered the hallway wearing his camel suit and red tie. "Downstairs, Son," he said, motioning to Robert.

I stood up straight, primped my dark brown ringlets, and held out the puffy dress.

He examined me up and down. "When are you going to get ready?"

"Jacob," said Mother as she walked out of her room. "That's rude!"

He curled his upper lip. "Come on, Claire! I'm just kidding."

Mother shook her head as Father went downstairs to the guests. His booming voice rang out, along with the laughter that always followed.

"Emily, you should be downstairs with Robert. The neighbors are arriving. Remember, don't talk to the adults unless they ask you something."

"Yes, ma'am."

One glance at Mother and I understood why Father said I wasn't ready. She wore an emerald green strapless dress and high-heeled shoes. Gold drop earrings dangled in her hair and a strand of pearls rested at the bottom of her neck.

I twisted my hair around my finger. "Mother? Do I look okay?"

"Yes, dear. The blue matches your eyes. Now, come along." She motioned for me to follow her downstairs.

We entered the living room. Two guests sat on the green couch, and six neighbors were gathered around our small piano with my father. He had his arm around Robert, talking about how his boy had skipped to the seventh grade at only nine years old and won the Spelling Bee four years in a row. Robert stared straight ahead with his face puckered.

Mother greeted everyone with a handshake. Between the front door and the living room, a tiny walled foyer had a wooden bench, so I escaped there to watch the people.

I studied Mother, trying to imitate the whisper in her voice, and the way she tossed her hair before she laughed. I longed to be close to her like I was with my grandma, but we never played games, laughed, or watched television together. She spent her days cleaning, cooking, and reading, while I waited for her to talk to me.

My study ended when she excused herself to the kitchen to check dinner.

Father still had a crowd gathered around him. Mrs. Parker, a widow three doors down from our house, couldn't take her eyes off him as he shared a story. She had on a black dress with sequins and touched his arm every time he said something funny. She reminded me of Marilyn Monroe. Her platinum hair was teased and her eyeliner had a curl on the ends. "Oh, Jacob," she said, laughing. "You certainly did stand out at the promotional party a few weeks ago!"

Father tilted his head and laughed. "I'll let you in on a secret. It's easy to be an alpha dog in a kennel of runts!"

She poked her index finger on his chest. "Jacob," she said. "You're so bad."

I turned my attention to Mr. Wagner, the father of my best friend, Reid. His dad was the deputy chief of police for San Francisco. He usually wore a suit, but tonight he had on a tight shirt that was unbuttoned at the top, showing gold chains. His hair was light brown, cut short, and his dark brown eyes widened and narrowed when he spoke.

His wife stood by herself a few feet away. Mrs. Wagner was a quiet woman; Father always called her "mousy." She styled her ash brown hair in a pageboy just below her ears. She wore a navy-blue cotton dress with an eyelet collar and low black heels. She glanced between her husband and her wristwatch like she was waiting for the party to be over.

Reid's dad loved women. I'd overheard my parents whispering about his squad car being parked in strange driveways for hours and how he was up to more than police business. Father called it "monkey business."

I leaned closer to see Mr. Wagner nuzzle close to a lady wearing a red halter dress. He raised his eyebrows and nodded as she talked but couldn't seem to stay focused on her face. He touched her bare shoulders and ran his fingers down her chest to her bulging breasts and chuckled.

Mrs. Wagner twisted her wedding ring as she watched him. I started to think it was naughty to watch them, so I got up to find Robert.

I searched the living room, kitchen, and even the bathroom, but no Robert. He seemed agitated before the party and a bit like a boy-soldier later at Father's side.

I combed the upstairs. "Robby...are you here?"

I started to go back downstairs when I saw him crouched in our parent's closet.

"Shush," he said.

"What are you doing in there?"

His fingers pressed against his lips. "Quiet! I didn't feel good...that's all."

Mother announced dinner. I turned to my brother.

He stood up, wiping his forehead with the back of his sleeve. "Get behind me. We'll sneak into the buffet line."

I followed him downstairs. We easily filed into the line. Robert reached behind and patted my hand.

The brotherly hand-pat surprised me, reminding me a little of Grandma's hand squeeze. I took it as a secret thank you. It went without saying that I would never say anything about him hiding in the closet. As we stood in line waiting for a turn at the Beef Wellington and scalloped potatoes, I realized that Robert wasn't the always-happy boy I had thought.

# Four

## Secrets and Cat Doors

"Mother, does Father have the duty today?" I had no idea what "the duty" was except it had something to do with the Navy, and he wouldn't be home.

She continued to scrub the dish. Mother took a simple task, such as loading the dishwasher and fussed until it was "just right." All the bowls and plates had to face in the same direction with equal distance between them. She used her fingernail as a ruler. As she scoured the plate, strands of hair fell over her face and her peach angora sweater.

"Mother," I started again. "Does Father have…"

"Yes, dear," she interrupted, with a quick glance. "I heard you. He won't be home until tomorrow."

I curled my lips to suppress a smile. His absence meant no peeking around corners, or triple checking to make sure the door was six inches from the doorstop, or one of my dark hairs didn't find its way into the sink. I could run free with my best friend, Reid, without my stomach churning all day.

"Can I help you with anything?"

She picked up a new sponge and sprinkled Comet Cleanser in the basin. "No, dear. Robert went to a science exhibit at the high school. You run along too."

"Yes, ma'am." I smiled and turned to leave the kitchen.

"Emily? Will you be playing in the street?"

Mother asked me the same question every day. Odd, because I couldn't remember ever playing in the street. "No. I'm going to play with Reid and maybe go to the lake."

"Very well."

She walked into the living room and settled into her brown tweed chair with her latest novel. She seemed tired.

Last night, a scratching sound awakened me. I peeked down the stairs to find her scrubbing the walls with a cleaning brush.

"Is there something else?" she asked.

I jumped, embarrassed I'd been gawking at her. "Oh, nothing."

"Then please...run along."

I rushed upstairs and grabbed my sketchpad, still avoiding the third step in spite of the fact Father wasn't around. It was automatic, and at eight, I could easily skip it without tumbling.

I sat on the porch steps to wait for Reid. I flipped through my sketch-pad until I found a blank page and began outlining a girl's face. I gave her big blue eyes, dimples, curly hair, and named her Penelope. Most of the girls in my book were called Penelope.

Sadness shivered through me. I leaned against the porch pillar and closed my eyes, thinking of the real Penelope—my twin sister. I learned about her last fall after a spanking from Father for not putting the rake away after cleaning up the leaves. At bedtime, he stopped in to explain the importance of putting things in their proper place. When he finished, he called me Penelope. I remembered gazing at him and asking, "Who is Penelope?"

With stone-cold eyes, he had replied, "She's your dead twin sister. That's all you need to know." He turned and walked until he reached the door. He spun around, glaring at me. "Never—I mean never, ask about your sister, Penelope. Do you understand me?"

After he left that night, black drifted into the bedroom, devouring the shadows. I had discovered a family tragedy covered in secrecy.

I shook off the memory and began to count my breaths, "one, two, three..."

"Penelope, where are you?" I whispered. "Why can't I remember you?"

But one day last year, she came back to me. It happened an afternoon last spring at the playground. Girls were giggling nearby, and I swung around expecting to find my sister. I stood still, feeling silly and light, my body tingling. We must have laughed all the time until something terrible happened to her and the laughter stopped.

Whatever happened to Penelope made Father angry and Mother quiet. I believed her death altered my life and changed my parents.

One time, when they were away I flipped through their college yearbooks.

Mother was beautiful, like now. There were pictures of her smiling at parties and a group shot of the swim team with Mother wearing a bathing suit. Classmates scribbled on the back pages about boys, sorority parties, and going to the Palladium to see Frank Sinatra.

Going through my father's West Point Academy album had been embarrassing. The yearbook showed military events and serious-looking students and teachers. The album was boring until I found a few photos stuck between the pages. The pictures showed him at parties, holding beer bottles with half-naked girls hanging on him.

The albums hadn't helped me understand what happened to Penelope; she hadn't been born yet. Still, at least with Mother, she seemed different back then.

I doubled over, clutching my gut. This happened every time I thought of Penelope. Not a wallop but a sinking feeling. Not being allowed to talk about her made it worse. She was my twin, so I wondered if the sadness of her death shifted to me like I reminded them...

"*E*arth to Emily!"

Reid stood in front of the porch, grinning at me. He wore a plaid shirt, blue trousers, and a green windbreaker over one shoulder.

I slid my sketchpad to the side and sat up straight. "Hi!"

"Gee Whiz! I've been standing here five minutes!" He plopped down next to me with his elbows on his knees, chin in his hand, staring into space. "Let's have some fun."

I waited for him to come up with something, wondering for the millionth time why a ten-year-old hotshot picked me to be his best friend.

Reid redefined average. His hair was a common light brown but was stick-straight until it reached below his ears, forming curls around his neck. His eyes were dark brown, almost black. His lips were full, and his front teeth slightly crooked, in an interesting way. He walked with a slight strut showing confidence and a little conceit. He could be a block away, and I would know him by his walk.

"What should we do, Emmy?" His eyes had a mischievous twinkle as he surveyed the neighborhood.

"Well, what do you...?"

With a scowl, he pointed to the Hemet house. "Old Mr. Hemet told me to get off his lawn yesterday."

"Yeah?"

"Yep. He hollered to stay off his grass."

"Oh...yeah, he doesn't like kids on his lawn."

"And," he added with a long pause. "He has a cat door!"

I studied his face, wondering why it mattered.

"Come on, Emmy, let's head to Mallard Lake."

I shrugged off his chatter about Mr. Hemet. As we walked to the lake, the crisp morning air whipped through my shirt. I shivered and clutched my arms.

"Here, take my windbreaker." Without missing a step, he slid his jacket around my shoulders.

I pulled it closer. "Thanks, Reid."

When we reached the lake, Reid grabbed a long stick and began poking in the brush. I stood back, jumping up and down to shake off the chilly air.

"Found it!" Reid shrieked. "I found it! Quick! Fetch a bag out of one of the trash cans."

"Huh?"

He stayed focused on something near a tree. "Go! Get me a bag, fast!"

I ran to the first campsite and found a crumpled brown bag next to a bunch of empty beer bottles. I shook the bag open and carried it back to him.

He pointed about twenty feet away on the dirt path. "Get back! Stand by the water fountain!"

I backed up to the drinking fountain, giggling. He held his stick-weapon above his head as he clasped the paper bag below him. His eyes stayed focused on his target, ready to pounce.

"Got it!" He dropped something in the bag and squeezed the top. "Got it, Emmy!"

I clapped to show my admiration as I walked to view the prize. "What is it?"

"A snake!" He held the captured target over his head like he'd won a gold medal and playfully shook the bag.

"What! A snake? Like a rattlesnake?" I jumped back on the dirt path, almost falling into the brush.

"No, Emmy…a garter snake, it ain't gonna hurt you."

I took another step back. "What are you going to do with it?"

He raised his eyebrows and pointed to the bag. "Remember Mr. Hemet's cat door?"

"Yeah, so? What does that have to do with…wait! What?"

He jumped from the brush and signaled in the direction of home. "I'm gonna put it through Mr. Hemet's cat door. That's what!"

"What does that mean?" The bag darted back and forth as the captive reptile flopped helplessly. I stopped, hoping he would re-think the crazy idea.

He gestured for me to catch up.

I darted to my best friend, bringing a cloud of dust with me.

The daring hunter strutted with his chest stuck out and a big self-satisfied smirk. He didn't hesitate, not even when he stepped onto the sidewalk toward Mr. Hemet's house.

"Emmy, stand over there, in front of the house," he whispered, motioning with his free hand. "If you see anyone coming, cough loud. Not too loud, just enough for me to hear."

I stood like a skittish soldier, hoping someone would come out of the house. I cleared my throat, ready to cough.

"Oh no." I moaned, as I watched Reid shake the creature loose from the bag and into the cat door. He sprang to his feet, kicking and hee-hawing as he ran to me.

"I did it! That was so cool! Did you see me? Did you see me do it? Did you see me push the snake through the door?"

I put my hand over my mouth and stared at him.

"The snake slid right through the cat door! Did you see it?"

A few minutes later, a large hand cupped the back of my neck. Out of the corner of my eye, I saw the other hand on Reid. Two feet away the garter snake slithered back to the safety of the lake.

"Okay, wise guy. I know this is your doings. Turn around, boy. You too, Emily." Mr. Hemet demanded.

I swallowed hard, emitting a loud hiccup. Reid looked straight into Mr. Hemet's eyes, no flinching and no hand wringing. We stood side-by-side, two prisoners waiting for our execution.

"This ain't no joke puttin' a snake in my house. Somebody could 'a got hurt. You think this is funny, boy? Well, it ain't. The wife's scared to death of snakes and seeing that'a put her in a tizzy. Boy, this ain't the first time you've pulled some harebrained prank in the neighborhood, but Emily, I gotta say, I'm surprised to see you go along with such a dumb trick."

I nodded, surprised he acted more disappointed than furious. I'd seen him on the block quite a bit tending to his garden and mowing the lawn. He always tipped his hat and said hello. He seemed like an easygoing man in his sixties, plainspoken and casual in his button-down striped shirt and overalls. The word was he moved here a few years ago from Louisiana to be closer to his kids.

"I'm sorry, Mr. Hemet," I said. "I shouldn't have done that. I feel bad. Did Mrs. Hemet…you know, see it?"

"No, she didn't, and thank the Lord. The wife was in the kitchen, so I caught the varmint before he left the mudroom. Emily, you're a real good kid and you oughta think twice about hangin' with hooligans hot footin' around the neighborhood scarin' folks. You got anything to say for yourself, boy?"

Reid smirked. "Sorry," he replied, drawing out the first syllable to sound sarcastic.

Mr. Hemet shook his head. "Okay, youngins. Get on home and stop yer shenanigans. I'll be watchin' you, Reid."

Reid nudged my elbow. "Let's go, Emmy. Lecture over."

I watched the elderly man grab his newspaper and walk in the house. As the screen door slammed, I sighed with relief. He sounded more like a teacher than an executioner.

Reid picked up a rock and flung it down the sidewalk. "What a hick!"

I wrinkled my nose and stared at him. The man hadn't even punished us, and this wasn't a slammed door or a dripping faucet—it was a live snake! For me, the punishment was a gift wrapped in a "get out of jail free" bow!

He tossed another rock. "How dare stupid old Mr. Hemet talk to me like that!"

"What'd he say to upset you?"

"Didn't you hear him? He called me a hooligan!"

"Oh, well…I don't even know what that means."

"Me neither, but it ain't good. I think it's like a criminal or something."

"At least he didn't punish us."

"Big deal." Reid continued to spout off, chattering about awful Mr. Hemet, but my confusion pushed his voice into the background. We lived in different worlds where the lines between right and wrong differed. Reid didn't understand I'd be in serious trouble if Mr. Hemet told my father I put a snake in the man's house. I would be in for a terrible whipping or much worse.

He quit pitching rocks. "You mad at me?"

"Well…not exactly." I didn't know how to tell him it was dumb to put a snake in the cat door.

He stopped walking and faced me. "Listen, if you're gonna think it, spit it out! Say it, Emmy! Go on, say it!"

"Say what? What are you talking about?"

"Err…why do you always do that? You always do that!"

"Do what?" My stomach knotted up, and my eyes started to water.

"Stop it! Why don't you tell me the truth? You agree with Mr. Hemet! Admit it!"

"What do you mean? Agree with him about what?" My knees shook. I grabbed a tree to keep from stumbling.

"You agreed with dumb old Mr. Hemet when he said you shouldn't be hanging with me, that's what! Admit it! Just admit it! Tell me the truth!"

"I do not! I would never think such a thing!" I protested, fighting a battle between my tears and my hands, which were not fast enough to brush them away.

"You agree with him! Admit it!"

"I do not!" My voice cracked. "I don't!"

Reid's voice softened, and he started calming down. "You sure?"

"Yes, I'm positive! I would never in a million years think such a thing! Never!"

A half grin crept over his face. "Okay. Sorry, Emmy. It made me mad when Mr. Hemet said that stuff about me. I thought maybe you agreed with him."

I opened my mouth to speak and then stopped. It didn't matter anymore. Reid stuck up for me, sort of. He defended our friendship. It made me happy to find out Reid worried I wouldn't want to be his friend anymore. He had no idea how I fretted every day that he would drop me because he found a better best friend.

Once the prank faded, all I saw was my fearless Reid. I agreed with Mr. Hemet's lecture about the danger of putting a live snake in his house, but his warning to stay away from Reid was wrong. Wrong for me. I didn't feel jeopardized by Reid, I felt protected. I believed someday the fearless boy would become an adult hero. If my life were threatened, he would be the one to save me.

# *Five*

## THREE SQUARES

*I* stood at the bathroom sink and quietly turned on the water. Every day, I set my alarm for six. That gave me two hours alone to draw and not worry about the rules.

"Five," I said under my breath. I picked up the bar of Ivory Soap, twisting the soap five times around my hands. Five rotations. That was the rule.

I crept downstairs and onto the porch with my paper and pencils. The porch was just a slab of cement with two steps leading to our small blue Cape Cod house, but it was big enough for me to sit and draw. My sketchpad was a part of me, filled with colored-pencil drawings of Grandma's gardens, the rainbow fetterbushes that droop over the lake, and the blackbirds perched on the telephone wires outside my house.

I sat down and stroked the cardboard cover. The best parts of my sketchpads were my girls. I spend hours outlining their features, capturing the highlights in their hair, giving them names and personalities. I liked to draw girls and pretend to be them.

I gazed at a picture I had drawn yesterday. "Penelope," I whispered.

I closed my eyes and listened to Penelope and I giggling. The sound was like far-away echoes dancing in tune, two sisters finding their way back to each other. God turned up the volume; the sound was like angelic background music.

*Penelope was never far away.*

"Emily?"

I opened my eyes. "Mother?"

"You're two minutes late for breakfast. We have our lesson at ten."

"I'm sorry. I came outside to draw and…"

She interrupted. "Just grab your things and come along."

I gathered my pencils and pad and hurried inside. The scent of bacon overlapped a shrill, clanking sound coming from the bathroom.

Mother seemed frazzled. "The commode is clogged. Your father is trying to fix the pipes, so we don't have to call a plumber." She retreated to the kitchen, shaking her head at the "hells" and "damns" coming from the washroom.

Father charged into the living room wearing a white sweatshirt and loose dungarees. He waved the plunger, huffing. "Emily, come with me. You too, Son."

We both nodded and followed him into the bathroom.

He sat on the ledge of the bathtub. "Over here." He pointed to the toilet.

We stood beside him.

"I fixed the commode," he said. "It was clogged. Luckily, I shut off the water before the whole room flooded."

I glanced at Robert. "That's good."

Father shook his head. "You're clogging the toilet, Emily. These old pipes can't handle so much toilet tissue."

"Yeah," said Robert. "You're clogging up the toilet, Emily."

I smirked at Robert. "I'm sorry, Father."

He unrolled a long strip of tissue. "We have a new rule, to make sure this never happens again. Do you see the lines here, Emily?"

"Yes, sir."

"Those are perforations. Now, show me with your finger where on this strip you would pull."

I didn't know but pointed in the middle.

"No. That's wrong. Now, here is what I want you to do every time you use the bathroom. Start from the last piece and count three squares up and pull. You must use only three squares. That is a new rule."

"Yes, sir."

"Okay. Let's try it again. Show me how you'll tear the toilet tissue from now on."

I counted one, two, and three and tore it off.

"Good. Remember, one, two, three and pull. So, the rule is three squares and no more. Do you understand?"

"Yes, I do."

"Is that clear, Son?"

"Yes, sir."

"Okay, kids. Breakfast is ready. Let's eat."

I walked into the kitchen behind Father. Mother placed the sausage, bacon, and eggs on the Lazy Susan in the center of the dining table.

She sat down and turned to my brother. "Robert, would you like to say grace this morning?"

"Yes, ma'am."

"Do the one I taught you last week," Father suggested.

We bowed our heads as he recited the morning grace: "Thank you, Lord, for the food that feeds our hunger. For the rest that brings us ease, and for my home where pleasant memories linger. We give our thanks to thee."

He poked Robert. "Good job, partner. Let's eat."

Mother placed her napkin on her lap, so I did the same. The conversation started with the usual "please pass the eggs" talk, and then Father chatted about a movie he'd seen with Robert. Mother listened as she positioned the food on her plate with nothing touching.

All I could think about was toilet paper. I repeated "one, two, three and pull," in my head while Robert and Father talked, and Mother scraped her fork against the glass plate.

*I*dly flipped the corners of my sketchpad, waiting for today's lesson. Mother turned the pages of the French book. "Please stop fiddling."

"I'm sorry," I said, sliding the pad under the dining room chair.

"All right, dear. We'll start with the simple greeting we learned last week. I'll say the words in English, and you translate the words to French."

I leaned forward, poised for the first sentence. "Yes, ma'am."

"The first phrase is 'how are you,' dear."

"Comment allez-vous?"

"Correct. Now, if someone asks you your name, what do you say?"

"Oh! I know that one! Mon nom est Emily?"

"Very well."

After a number of translations, she glanced at her wristwatch and closed the book. "Well done, dear. Our hour is up."

"Already? I can do a lot more. Can we keep going? Please?"

Her long black lashes blinked slowly as she turned to me. "We've been translating for an hour. I'm pleased you are doing so well. You will be fluent in French when you visit Paris someday."

"But I want to learn more. Can't we go a little longer?"

She held up her hand. "Now, now, the lesson is over. Next week will be mathematics. We'll be going over long division." She got up, tucked the French book back in the bookcase, and walked to her brown chair with her newest novel, *Defeat into Victory*. "Keep practicing the new phrases you learned today for next time."

Her slender fingers removed the bookmark from her novel.

"Mother, is French the hardest language to learn?"

"No. Chinese is the most difficult," she answered, turning a page.

"Oh, really? Why is Chinese so hard?"

She stopped reading but kept her head down. "It's a tonal language. You need to learn the tone of words and alter your voice, as each tone has a different meaning. Also, Chinese has a complex writing system."

I moved closer to her. "Wow! That's so interesting! Do you know how to speak Chinese, Mother?"

She sighed. "Yes, Emily. I do, but you are far too young to learn Chinese. We'll be working on French again in two weeks. Now, please run along. Be home in time for dinner at six o' clock. Will you be playing in the street?"

I drooped, knowing this was always her last question. "No, ma'am."

She turned a page. "Good. Run along, dear."

"Okay." I stood in the doorway, hoping she would glance up and notice my hurt feelings. After a minute, I turned and walked outside.

The boys in the neighborhood were gathered on the street playing flag football. Reid was in the mix. I sat down on the steps, thinking about Mother and wondering when I first ached for a mother right in front of me.

I had to be about six because Penelope was gone. Every night, after watching *Lassie*, I'd race upstairs and wait for a bedtime story. Mother would come in, sit in a chair, and read to me in her soft, melodic voice. After she spoke the last words, "The End" she would say goodnight and get up to leave. I'd beg her to read it one more time. She'd shake her head, touch my blanket, and tell me to go to sleep.

As soon as I heard the door rub against the carpet, I would cry for her to come back. She never did. Eventually, I stopped calling for her. I'd lie in bed with a hollow ache, like now, and wonder why she wouldn't stay with me a little longer.

⌒

"*H*ey, Emmy," Reid shouted. "Wondering what trouble we'll get into today?"

He stood over me grinning, wiping sweat from his forehead with a hand towel.

"Huh?" I asked. "No, not really. Oh, great game."

"Relax, Emmy girl. I'll be good today, just for you. How about we go to Mallard Lake? No pranks, I promise."

I jumped up. "Sure!"

The sun was unusually hot even for an August afternoon. Reid continued to wipe his brow. "I got it! Let's do some fishing. My dad's got a new pole I've been dying to try out. You can use mine."

"Your father would really let you use his new pole?"

He frowned and gazed at me sideways. "Yeah, why wouldn't he?"

"Oh, I don't know..." I forgot that Reid lived by different rules. Anything belonging to my father was untouchable, so it was an obvious question, to me anyway.

"It's no biggie. Come on. Let's go get them. You like to fish?"

He didn't wait for an answer as he ran into his garage to fetch the poles and bucket.

We trudged through weed pockets and rock beds to find a good fishing location. Reid found an ideal spot where he claimed the water was moving and we were sure to catch fish. The ground was full of cape ivy, so he cleared a small area and used his hand towel to dust off a place for me to sit down.

I grinned, touched that he didn't want me to get dirt on my old gingham shorts. "Thank you."

He held the stick out like a prized sword. "Okay, Miss Emily Quinn. I award you my lucky fishing pole. Many a fish has been caught with this and not little fish either. This pole is legendary in these parts!"

I chuckled. "Thank you, kind sir. You know, if your dad's pole isn't as good, you can have this one back any time."

"Heck no. This one needs to be broken in."

"Well, okay," I said, wrinkling my nose. "Actually, Reid...I've never fished before."

He shrugged. "So what? You got me. I'll teach ya how to fish. I'll even bait the hook for ya. I'm sure this squiggly worm would make you scream," he said, holding a wiggly critter in front of my face.

"Ewe!" I screeched as he bounced the ugly crawler up and down.

He tossed the squirmy monster back in the bucket. "Good thing you're a girl, or I'd have to throw you in the lake and make a man out of you!"

"Okay," I said, gripping the pole. "Tell me what to do and I'll try."

Being with Reid made me forget about my troubles at home. I loved looking at him, especially his smile. When he grinned, little lines formed from the corner of his eyes to the tips of his mouth.

"Watch me, Emmy. I'll show you how to cast."

"Cast?"

"Yeah. You gotta throw the line in the water as far out as you can." He wrapped his hands around mine and adjusted the grip on my pole, and together we flung the line into the lake in one precise movement.

"Now what do we do?"

"We wait. Fishing's about patience. Stay still till ya feel a little tug in your hands. Don't reel him in right away, or you'll lose him. Ya gotta learn the difference between a curious fish and a biting one. Play with the bite till ya know he's hooked. It's all in the timing. Remember, slow and easy. Don't get too anxious."

What I thought was an easy sport was much more complicated. "Aren't you going to fish? Don't you want to try out your dad's new pole?"

"Nah, that's okay. This is your first time, and you need the help." He scooted a little closer, watching me like a patient teacher.

I gripped the fishing rod, thinking about all his instructions. I couldn't help but steal a few glances at him. He looked so darn cute resting one elbow on his knee with his tanned face focused on my fishing technique.

My pole started to bend. "I got one!" I yelled. I turned to Reid, who was shaking his head.

"No, Emmy. That's lake gunk. When ya land the real thing, it'll tug up and down. You'll feel it in your hands." He lifted the line to free the lake moss.

"Shoot! I thought I caught one!"

"Patience, remember? That's the key to fishing."

I wanted to impress him, but two hours had gone by without a single bite. "Reid, I'm not getting the hang of it. I think you should take over so I can see how you do it. That way, I will, you know...learn better."

"Ya sure?"

"Positive."

He took over the reins. "If you say so."

After only a few minutes, he jumped up. "I got one, Emmy!"

The line moved up and down with sudden jerks. In one quick movement, he pulled up a big catfish flip-flopping at the end of his line. He removed the hook from its mouth.

"Wow! You got one!"

Reid grinned. "You like fish?"

"Well, not really," I admitted. Being Catholic, Mother baked, barbecued, or fried fish every Friday. It was the one day I dreaded eating dinner.

He tossed the fish back in the lake. "Me neither!"

"But...why'd you throw him back? You caught him!"

He brushed the dirt from his pants. "Nah, fishing ain't about eating, not for me anyway. It's all about winning." He grabbed the poles and pulled me up.

I examined his face, wondering why he had so much confidence at ten years old. He seemed older, but still, he was only ten.

We headed home, walking side by side, talking about the best rods, fly-fishing, and the best places to catch trout. I didn't like fishing, but being with Reid was the perfect cure for my disappointing morning with Mother. I watched our shadows and fantasized that someday we would grow up and get married.

I touched the doorknob of my house and turned to see Reid lugging two fishing poles and an empty bucket down the sidewalk.

"Reid!" I shouted.

He spun around, his brows creased. "Yeah?"

"Thank you."

Reid stood at attention and did a quick salute, "You're welcome, Miss Emmy. Next time, I guarantee you'll catch a fish!"

"Thank you!" With a last wave, I entered the house knowing all-too-well I wasn't thanking him for the fishing lesson.

**San Francisco County Jail, July 10, 1966. End of Session One**

" . . . *I*'m going to count from one to five, and at the count of five you will awaken feeling refreshed, aware, and fully alert."

I blinked, adjusting to the room and watchful gaze of Doctor Lieberman. My long hair hung like a black sheet in front of my face. I sat up straight, dragging the shackles with me. *I remembered.*

Hypnosis had sliced me open. I remembered the sound of Penelope's giggle, the depth of Reid's eyes, Mother's beauty, Robert's freckled face, and Father's voice. They were no longer fleeting snapshots—they were real.

*And I had murdered one of them.*

I jerked at the sound of crackling plastic coming from Doctor Lieberman's desk. The brilliant man leaned back in his swivel chair and popped a Hostess cupcake in his mouth. He gobbled the cake up in three big bites and rubbed his thin lips with his veiny hand.

He leaned forward with his elbows on the table. "Good session, Emily. Let's talk about the details."

I felt far from relaxed or refreshed. I rubbed my temples, trying to ease a developing headache and figure out what to say.

"What do you remember about our session? Let's put it in context."

I tried to decide whether I liked him. It was hard to imagine liking someone that munched on a vending machine cupcake while I sat riddled in fear.

"Let's discuss this."

I opened my mouth; my lips moved, but all that came out was a series of vowels and consonants without the ability to form a single word.

He sat still and focused on me.

My voice trembled as I pushed the words out, "I...remember them."

"How do you feel?"

I didn't need to think. "Guilty."

"What do you mean exactly?"

A hot sensation rippled through me, like being hooked up to low-voltage electrical wires. My mouth gaped open, and my body vibrated.

His face relaxed, and he began talking in a deep melodic voice. "You are calming down, letting go of your fear. You are sitting here in complete safety. What you have learned today is positive, and as you continue with this process, you will have good results. I am here to help you, and together we will find clarity and understanding."

He continued to talk in measured beats as I clung to him like a drowning child reaching for a parent's hand. Every nerve in my body and mind shook as I gripped his words and embraced the rhythmic sound of his voice. I slowly released the terror, at least enough to return to a crippled state of stability.

I shivered as cold sweat clung to my hair. "S-sorry."

I poked my skin, trying to recover the sensations in my face. I felt like a refugee, looking for a sanctuary.

But jail was not a sanctuary. Jail gave the world a sanctuary from *me*.

The doctor poured a cup of black coffee from the crusty old carafe. "Emily, this isn't the time to discuss what you've remembered. We can talk about it next week."

He was right. I couldn't concentrate while my brain buzzed with my troubled past.

I took a deep breath. "Oh…okay."

"There is one thing I want you to think about over the next six days. You have been compromised by trauma and whatever events led you here we don't know yet. Our job is to find out and to use therapy to recover what you've lost and rebuild your life."

I nodded, wondering if he gave that speech to all the inmates.

A guard appeared to take me back to my cell. I listened to the clicking sound of handcuffs and glanced at the doctor. His hand tapped his chin as he watched me.

Doctor Lieberman nodded. "Goodbye, Emily. I'll see you next week."

"Thank you." I shuffled to the door, flanked by a sturdy officer with clanking keys.

"Okay, Quinn," the guard pronounced as she removed the cuffs and locked the cell. "Supper in one hour."

Supper—the word, synonymous now with the memory of Mother announcing dinner, and Robert and I waiting in line for Beef Wellington. How did I get from there to here? I held one hand over my mouth to choke the sound of my teeth chattering and the other on my knee to subdue my twitching legs.

I listened to the shouts of women, flushing toilets, and dominos hitting metal tables. With the clatter of each one, I cringed, knowing this was my life now. In the coming weeks, Doctor Lieberman and I would methodically put the pieces of my past together—until ultimately, the stack would tumble around me leaving nothing but the shards of a broken life.

# Six

## RULES AND REASONS

*San Francisco County Jail, July 17, 1966. Beginning of Session Two*

"*L*et's go, Quinn!" A guard unlocked my door and cuffed me. "You're on vacation for two hours."

I understood what she meant, but getting out of solitary was hardly a respite. My meetings were not to discuss a maladaptive condition or help me cope with incarceration. My visits were to retrieve my history and figure out why I became a murderer.

I kept my head straight ahead as we walked past several cells on the way to the stairs. My temporary hiatus from isolation created a ruckus with the inmates.

"Hey! Rich Girl! You in the ghetto now!"

"Where you going daddy killer?"

The guard ignored them. I supposed she dealt with that every day, so I had better get used to taunts every Tuesday. With my hands and ankles chained, all I could do was bite down on my lip to prevent the urge to break down and cry.

Jail officials allowed me to wear a thick sweater under my jumpsuit because I couldn't stop shivering. After a ten-minute interview, they agreed it was better than a trip to the infirmary. The smallest decisions were weighed here, including my body weight. At the last weigh-in, I dropped to one hundred ten pounds, twenty-five pounds underweight for my five foot seven height.

That's not why I asked to wear a sweater. I wanted to prevent the trembling I couldn't seem to control. Unfortunately, it wasn't working. I toddled into the doctor's office with stringy dark hair dangling in front of my face, towing twenty pounds of metal and shaking like a junky in withdrawal.

The middle-aged officer un-cuffed me and chained me to the chair. The doctor hadn't arrived, so we waited in silence other than the occasional clink of her keys knocking together. I looked around the somber room and rows of steel file cabinets. I could almost hear the clamor of sustained misery. I shuddered, knowing my pitiful story would be there soon enough, marked "Quinn" with a long series of letters and numbers.

I glanced at the guard and pressed my wrists against my eyes. Mother hiring this high-profile doctor to unearth years of memories seemed pointless. The lawyers wanted mitigating circumstances to spare me from the death penalty, but I was already dead on the inside. Last week, the doctor tried to convince me I was compromised by trauma, and therapy was vital to rebuilding my life. The words sounded good at the time, but sitting alone in a cell all week dispelled his words. I killed my father with a knife. I watched the blood pour out of him, draining his existence from the wounds *I* inflicted.

The guard moved, jolting me out of my thoughts. Doctor Lieberman came through the door, carrying several binders under one arm. The files were thick with loose papers, threatening to fall out. His white hair looked freshly washed, frizzing in a tangled mess. The rectangular glasses he wore had fallen to the tip of his long nose, and his gray suit was as crinkled as his lined face.

"Okay, now." He bounced the loose binders on his desk to straighten the papers. "How are you today?"

"I'm fine." My shackles scraped the tiles as I pulled myself up. Something made me wonder whether I'd left scratches on the floor. I tightened the grip on my chair and waited for him to say something.

"Fine is a banal word, Emily…a knee-jerk answer to 'how are you?' So, I'll ask you again. What is your mood today?"

"I'm nervous," I admitted.

"That's understandable. Remember, you're safe here. You won't say anything under hypnosis you wouldn't typically reveal. You are still in control."

I felt the opposite but nodded.

"I've gone through my notes from last week and your journal entries. This week, I am going to take you back to when you were thirteen. I will guide you into a relaxed place, and you will remember events exactly as they happened. Are you ready?"

"Okay…I mean, yes."

He began the same routine as the last time. With each melodic word, I found myself drifting back to my earlier life—this time, at thirteen years old.

⌒

*I* woke up to the sound of banging on my bedroom door.
"Open the door!"

I leaned against the headboard, flinching with each blow.

"Yes, Father?" I asked, rushing to the door.

"What took you so long? Church starts in an hour. Be downstairs in thirty minutes."

He didn't wait for an explanation. I listened to the click of his flip-flops as he headed to his room, running his hands through his uncombed hair.

I leaned against the door casing, wondering why I always thought the worst of Father. Everyone loved him, especially Robert. I wanted the same thing.

It was my fault. All he had wanted was to wake me up for church. As I closed the bedroom door, I wondered how to impress him. Father likes punctuality, so that's a start. I'll be the first one ready for church.

Mother coded my clothes by season and color. I chose a sunny yellow dress with an eyelet collar, black patent leather shoes, and white socks with tulips along the top. I dashed to the mirror and brushed my hair, keeping an eye on the clock.

I tiptoed down the stairs, avoiding the creaky third step. The final touch was a hat stacked on a shelf in the living room closet. I took a stool and chose the hatbox marked "straw hats" and picked a white hat with tiny rosettes. I quickly slipped on the lace gloves Mother kept in one corner, along with the beaded purse that held my rosary and hymnal.

I rushed to the foyer and the small bench, the perfect spot to hide. When he walked into the living room, I could yell "surprise!" I stifled a giggle and waited, eager to see the surprised expression on his face.

After a few minutes, Father's heavy footsteps pounded the stairs. I fluffed my dress, ready to jump out.

"Emily! Get the hell in here!"

I froze at the unexpected sound of Father's angry voice. My body tensed, wondering if he thought I was still sleeping.

"Emily! You damn-well better get in here…now!"

I followed the direction of his voice and found him standing next to Mother's reading chair. I stood wide-eyed, wondering why he was so mad.

"Did you leave this box here?"

I gazed at the black-and-white hatbox sitting on the chair with the lid tilted to one side. "Yes, sir."

"How many times have I told you to put things away? Are you that stupid?"

I fidgeted with my dress, hoping he would notice I was the first one ready.

"Answer me! Are you that stupid?"

I looked down. "Yes sir," I mumbled.

"Speak up!"

I put my head down and rubbed my watery eyes. When I opened my mouth, all that came out was a whimper.

He lunged forward and grabbed my arm, digging his fingers into my skin. "You numbskull! I've told you a hundred times to put things away when you're done with them!"

I tried to hold back the tears. "I'm sorry…I didn't mean to."

He yanked me to the hatbox, shaking me. "I'm sick of you leaving a mess!"

I crouched down, trying to hold onto my purse.

He released his grip on my forearm. I lost my footing and hit my head on the coffee table before falling to the ground.

"Damn it all! Get up and put the goddamn hatbox away!"

When he left, I couldn't move. Everything hurt. Most of all, I hurt—the kind of pain that has nothing to do with bones or tissue. My soul was in shock.

My beaded purse had opened, leaving the rosary spread out on the floor. I tucked it back in my purse along with the hymnal. I stared at the silver cross of Jesus sparkling against the black lining, picked it up, and held it to my lips. After a minute, I stood up, rubbing my head as I somberly grabbed the footstool and put the hatbox back in the closet.

The girl that rushed around twenty minutes ago, putting on a sunny yellow dress eager to surprise her father was gone.

I listened to the pleasant chatter upstairs. Mother, Robert, and Father barreled down the stairs ready to go. Mother was dressed in a navy blue and white suit with a big floppy hat. Robert wore a blue shirt and black pants, and Father was handsome in a beige suit with a brown tie. They were the picture-perfect family—all three of them.

I gathered behind them for the car ride to church, pretending to search for something in my purse so no one could see my face. I didn't want Mother or Robert to know I had gotten in trouble. Father hopped into the driver's seat, exchanging small talk with Mother, as I crawled into the backseat next to Robert. I stared out the window, watching the houses file by as I counted them one, two, three, four. I filled my brain with sculptured hedges, toddlers peddling tricycles—anything to ignore how stupid I was not to put the hatbox away.

The procession of trees and houses was over with a fast zip as Father pulled the emergency brake. A sharp wind swished through the backseat as he opened the door for Robert and me. I expected a smirk, a residual sign of rage, but his face was smooth, relaxed. The anger I saw ten minutes ago vanished faster than the time it took me to get ready for Sunday mass.

"Let's go," said Father.

Saint Mary's was a hundred-year-old cathedral with bluestone steeples, a marble statue of Jesus with outstretched arms, and arched wooden doors. Reid and Robert hated going to church, but not me. I loved the rituals, the music, the stained-glass windows, and the sermon.

After a few polite words to Father Flanagan, Father led the way to an empty pew. I stared at the dark mahogany cathedral, the inset colored windows, and the flickering candles glowing in crimson glass. Adults, singing in Latin, dressed in deep purple tunics lined the rear of the altar. Their voices and the organ music echoed like God's angels. I closed my eyes and wondered if Penelope heard the same sound every day in Heaven.

The music changed to a melancholic melody as the priest walked down the aisle. I clutched my hymnal and sat up straight, watching the holy procession. I was awestruck as he walked down the aisle in a long, white satin robe holding a gilded Bible. Altar boys marched behind him with tall pillar candles.

The priest turned to the parishioners and opened with, "May the Lord be With You." I knelt on the cushioned ledge, bowed my head, and recited the prayers I'd memorized in catechism. I recounted them quickly to allow time for a personal request. It was the same prayer every week.

"Dear God, this is Emily Quinn. Bless my family and Reid. Help me remember the rules and be a better girl. Look after Penelope, and tell her I love her. Keep me from sin so I can be with her in Heaven someday. Amen."

After the sermon, the adults gathered single file for communion. Father waited in line, looking like every other dad in church as he accepted the body of Christ and did the sign of the cross. He walked back to our pew, nodding to Robert and me as he sat down. I gazed at the crystal rosary and remembered how he shook me before church.

My head ached. I didn't want to think about it, so I found a ray of sunlight streaming through the stained-glass windows. I hid the pain inside spheres of color reflecting on the walls. God's light show danced on the ceiling, forming beautiful rainbows. As the colors collided, my anxiety faded into a confluence of reds, blues, and yellows.

Father chatted about going to a matinee as he pulled the Buick into the driveway. "Let's go see the new Hitchcock movie. I hear it's great."

Mother reached into her purse and took out her compact. "You go with the children, dear. I don't care for Hitchcock films."

"Suit yourself. Robert's going. How about you, Emily?"

My head had begun to throb. I reached up and touched a small bump where I'd hit the table.

"Hey, are you going?" Father asked, puffing on a cigar.

I shook my head "no" and rubbed the sore spot.

Mother touched my knee. "Emily, your father asked you a question."

"I'm sorry. I don't feel good."

Mother checked my forehead. "You don't have a fever, dear. Does your stomach hurt?"

"No. I'm just tired."

Father clicked his tongue. "She's fine, Claire."

Illness infuriated Father. Even in kindergarten, he scoffed if I stayed home from school. So, I have learned to muffle my cough, run out of the room to sneeze, and turn away to wipe the sniffles. I wondered if his agitation had something to do with Penelope. The questions kept going back to her mysterious death because nothing else made sense.

Mother stayed close by as we entered the house. "Are you sure you're okay, dear?"

"Let her be, Claire. For God's sake, stop fussing."

I tapped Mother's elbow. "I'm tired. May I be excused?"

"Of course, dear. It's a shame you'll miss the movie, but take a nap, and you'll feel better. I'll save you some breakfast."

Her dark wavy hair fell around her shoulders as she removed her wide-brimmed hat. I turned away when she opened the coat closet that held the hatboxes.

I clomped up the stairs and into my room. The sound of the door closing relaxed me enough to fluff my pillow and shut my eyes.

*I* woke up to tiny objects twirling in haphazard directions. I touched the bump on my head and sprang up, blinking. I was going blind.

"Good afternoon, goofy!"

I rubbed my eyes, realizing the kooky shapes were the geometric print in Reid's shirt. "Reid! What are you doing here?"

"Waiting for you, sleepy head." Along with his Hawaiian shirt, he wore khaki shorts and rubber flip-flops.

I slid up to the headboard, smoothing my nap-wrinkled dress. "Are you kidding? My father will kill you! How did you get in the house?"

He leaned back in his chair, stretched out his arms, and yawned. "I walked in."

"Reid, my father will flip if he finds you up here!"

He blew out a scoffing puff. "Let him, who cares? You were late coming outside, so I came in. What's the big deal?"

"Well, it's just..." I hemmed and hawed with no clue how to explain the rules.

"What?"

I couldn't tell him that my father would beat me. Way too embarrassing. "Reid, he'll kill me if he knows you're up here."

He puffed again. "So what is this, the White House? I didn't pass any armed guards at the door."

My face felt hot, embarrassed he had made fun of me. Father was probably downstairs with his arms crossed ready to punish me in front of Reid. I eyed the window, wondering if he could jump out.

He pulled a piece of gum out of his pocket. "You want me to leave?"

Only Reid would narrow this down to a simple leave or not leave. I wanted to be angry but was too embarrassed.

He leaned forward. "Emmy, why are you acting like this? I wait on the porch for you to come home from church every Sunday."

I took a breath, hoping not to sound pathetic. "My dad doesn't allow me to have friends in the house."

He stood up with a loud huff and plunked back down, exasperated. "That's dumb. You come in my house all the time! You aren't allowed to see me?"

"No, it's not that...I mean, just not in the house. It's against the rules."

He let out a long exaggerated sigh. "Come on, Emmy, let's go do something."

"How?"

"How what?"

"How will we get out of here without my father seeing you?"

Reid leaned forward. "Emmy, are you serious? Is this a joke? Am I really not allowed in your house?"

I bit down hard on my lower lip wondering how to explain the rules without looking like an idiot. "Uh, well...yes. You always meet me outside. I'm sorry, but I don't want to get into trouble."

"Well, I didn't see anyone when I came in. Is he even here?"

"Shhh." Once Reid stopped talking, I noticed the house was quiet. I peered at the clock—eleven a.m. I had forgotten Father and Robert were at the movies.

My eyes widened. "Let's go! Quick! I'll change clothes and meet you out front in two minutes! Be quiet so my mother won't hear you."

He rolled his eyes and chuckled. "Okay, Agent 99!"

Mother was engrossed in a book as I tiptoed into the living room. "Mother, I'm going out for a while."

"Okay, dear. But you didn't have your breakfast. I saved a plate for you."

"Oh…thank you. I'm not all that hungry. Can I eat when I get home?"

"At least eat the eggs, dear. It's not good to go without breakfast."

I ran into the kitchen and gobbled down the two eggs before hurrying back in the living room.

"Thank you, Mother. I'll see you later."

"Will you be in the street, dear?"

"No ma'am."

"Very well."

Reid waited on the sidewalk, bouncing a basketball. "What took you so long?"

"Sorry…had to eat breakfast."

"Let's shoot hoops at Bailey Park."

"Sure!"

When we arrived at the park, Reid dribbled the ball around the blacktop. "Okay, let's play horse! You first!"

After a few missed shots, I finally got one in the hoop and tossed it to him.

He moved like a dancer, fluid and focused. I loved the way his hands released the ball and how his calf muscles flexed as he jumped.

Reid positioned for a shot and stopped. He left the court and sat on a cement bench with his head down.

Something was wrong, I just didn't know what. I could think of a thousand reasons for his mood change, the main one was seeing me act like a baby back at the house. I stood still, studying his expression.

He finally patted the seat for me to sit next to him.

He wouldn't look at me, not even when I sat down. "Emmy, talk to me."

His tone surprised me, almost like he wanted a confession. "What?"

He faced me, his eyes solemn but tender. "Talk to me."

His somber attitude and question unnerved me. I fiddled with my shoelaces to buy a little time. "About what?"

"What happened at your house?"

There it was. I stared at the ground, biting my lip. How could I tell him my father hated my guts? "I'm sorry."

"So, what's the deal? I mean...is your dad overprotective of you? Does he think I'm a bad guy? Now that I think of it, he never looks at me. That's weird, you know? Doesn't he like me?"

"Of course he does." I hid my smile at his comment about Father being overprotective of me. I couldn't pass it up. Reid gave me an unexpected motive for all the punishments and a lavish donation to my self-esteem. It was an explanation I desperately wanted to believe.

He shot up. "Let's play!"

We played horse, laughing and talking about the game. I watched his long arms position for the basket, in awe of his ability to be graceful and athletic at the same time. After several missed baskets, I waved my arm, dismissing my turn. I wanted to think and consider his explanation for why Father had so many rules.

An hour or so passed. Time to go. Reid stopped playing and turned to me. I walked toward him ready to go home.

He bounced the basketball and shouted, "Tell your dad I won't hurt his little princess!"

I gawked at him. I opened my mouth to respond, but he pointed in the direction of home.

As we walked along the sidewalk, Reid chattered about the latest episode of *Gunsmoke*. I nodded at his chitchat but wasn't listening. I was five minutes back, replaying his suggestion that my father was overprotective of me.

He patted me on the shoulder when we got to my house. "See ya later!"

I lingered on the porch to think. I couldn't stop smiling. Reid had opened a door I'd never considered. I leaned against the house, piecing together the ridicule, the spankings, and the countless rules, applying them to the possibility that Father was overprotective. If he was right, that meant the constant discipline had a purpose—to protect me.

Above everything, I grabbed onto the hope that my father loved me.

# *Seven*

## INVISIBLE DAUGHTER

I bent over to scratch my legs as I got out of bed to look out the window. The scent of jasmine wafted through my window, and dew embraced the grass like tiny glass beads. Mockingbirds warbled in the oak trees in deep, melodic tones. The beauty of nature seemed amplified, like God had given me a magnifier to see the world in renewed glory.

Today was different. Instead of drawing girls and creating characters to hide behind—I drew my father standing next to the Brazilian pepper tree outside my window. Reid's suggestion that my father was protective infused me with a new confidence. Maybe his rules were meant to shield me and keep me safe. Perhaps the torment had a higher purpose.

*He might be trying to protect me like he couldn't protect Penelope.*

I wanted to believe it. Father's relentless punishments and insults left me flawed and worthless. I hated her. Didn't want to be her. Erased her. But if his actions stemmed from love and a need to protect me, I could leave the fantasy girls behind and be myself.

"*E*mily! Come down for lunch!" Mother shouted.

"Coming!" I slid the box of papers under the bed. Father was at work, and Robert left hours ago for a railroad exhibit. I raced down the stairs, anxious to spend time with her alone.

She had set an artful table with a cheese sandwich cut in four equal slices and apple wedges between each piece. The food formed a flower with a maraschino cherry smack-dab in the middle.

"Oh my God! How beautiful, Mother! It's way too pretty to eat!"

She put her napkin on her lap. "Do not use the word 'God' as a vernacular, Emily."

"I'm sorry. I didn't mean anything…"

I shifted, uncomfortable because she wasn't talking. Her gaze drifted between the plate of food and the kitchen. I hated the silence—always have. I nibbled on the melted cheese sandwich and noticed her smooth, unlined skin.

"Mother, when do girls wear makeup?"

She cut a corner of her sandwich. "At fourteen."

"Oh, really?"

"Yes. You can start wearing makeup in a month."

"What kind? Can I wear red lipstick like you?"

"No, dear. That would be inappropriate. You can start with pink lip gloss."

"Oh, okay." I raised my voice to sound more enthusiastic. "What about mascara?"

"No. It would be unrefined for a fourteen-year-old girl to wear mascara."

Mother finished her sandwich and dabbed her mouth with her cloth napkin. She excused herself and started clearing the table.

I wrinkled my nose, wondering how to engage her. "I'm sorry. I didn't know…"

"Please stop talking and eat your lunch. Look…you've barely touched your food. Finish eating and run along, dear."

My mouth dropped open. She had pushed me from a ten-foot ledge, not enough to kill me but enough to leave some pretty big bruises. I watched her, dressed in a pink shirt and form fitting slacks, as she loaded the dishwasher. She was impeccably groomed and seemingly ready to engage in life but not interested—especially in me.

I moped for a few minutes as the invisible daughter. I would pull the fiery sun from the sky and dance on the boiling surface to get her to talk to me.

"I'm going to Reid's house now."

She didn't glance up from her obsessive need to align the forks at an equal distance. "Okay. Will you be playing games in the street?"

"No, ma'am."

"Fine, dear. Be back before dark."

Dismissed. I did an about-face.

I walked outside to search for Reid, dragging my weighed-down body behind. I leaned against the railing, trying to make myself comfortable on the porch steps—as comfy as one can get on a slab of cold cement. Somehow it seemed appropriate. Reid's explanation for Father's wrath gave me optimism, but Mother—that's another story.

I felt neither loved nor hated. The absence of both was nothing. Being around her was always the same. I have tried to reach her, touch her, and engage her. I have left my sketchpad open to my latest drawing, shared a teacher's compliment—anything to impress her, but nothing. After my one-person show concluded, I was left with the aching pain of wanting someone who doesn't want me.

⁓

"Hey, Emmy!" Reid shouted.

Reid stood over me wiping his forehead after his baseball game. He wore blue jeans, a plaid cotton shirt, and tennis shoes. Sweat clung to his hair, forming spiral curls along his thick neck and around his ears. He rubbed the towel through his locks, making a full mess of it.

I cupped a hand over my eyes to get a better view of him. He was the perfect antidote to jump-start my bad mood after being with Mother. "Hi, Reid!"

He stuffed the sweaty cloth in his pocket. "How about we go fishing at Mallard Lake? We've been there dozens of times, and you've yet to catch a fish."

"I know. I guess I'm not much of a fisherwoman."

He crossed his arms. "You aren't getting off that easy. Today you're gonna catch a fish. Let's go!"

"Sure thing." I jumped down the steps and onto the walkway. I had no interest in holding a stick in the water but couldn't wait to sit on the banks with Reid.

"I'll be back in a minute." Reid fetched the fishing gear from his garage, and in no time, we arrived at the lake.

I started to sit down when Reid touched my arm. "Hold on! I'll be right back. Wait for me."

He ran into the brush. I flinched at the possibility of another Reid prank and wondered what creepy reptile would be coming out with him. I kicked the ground, watching dirt clouds form around my feet. I heard the crackling of dried plants, which made me kick harder.

He emerged from the foliage cradling a pile of greenery and beaming like a happy hunter minus the prey. Sprigs clung to his sweaty hair, and he held a bunch of leaves and branches in his bare arms. I couldn't help notice how manly he looked with muscular biceps and a prickly shadow on his lower face.

The sight of him juggling an overflowing pile of vegetation was enough to make me laugh, but judging from his determined face, this was no joke to him. I pressed down on my lips to stifle the giggles.

He set the green heap down and dusted the ground with his hands to form a flat surface. "Now you sit here, Emmy," he said, brushing pine needles and eucalyptus leaves from his hair. "It's softer, and you won't get your clothes all dirty." He sat down and patted the spot for me.

I smiled down at him, touched that he went through so much trouble to protect my old pedal pushers. I started to say something but stopped when he sniffed and fiddled with his bait, which I took as a sign not to fuss. Even so, the guy made me a feather bed twelve feet off the ground—symbolically, anyway.

He handed me a pole. "Today you're going to catch a fish."

"I'm not so sure. I still don't have the hang of it." I didn't want to tell him I wasn't interested in fishing—just him.

He placed his hand on top of mine. "I'll teach you. You have me, Emmy. And I'm not just talking about fishing neither."

I nodded, thrown off by his touch and sweet admonition. The words "you got me" played in my head like the Song of Solomon.

Reid kept a tight grip, rattling on about different lures. I only half-listened with a few "a-ha's" thrown in to keep his hand on mine. The sun beat down on us; the temperature was probably over eighty degrees, but my arms were riddled in goose bumps.

"You got one!" Reid shouted, pointing to the fishing rod bobbing up and down in the lake.

"Oh my God! What do I do?" I jumped up, nearly dropping the pole. I felt the distinct tug Reid had talked about for years.

"Play with him, Emmy…remember the stuff I taught you. Don't pull your line up! Leave it there! Let him bite!"

"He's tugging super hard! I think he should come in!"

Reid squeezed his hand over mine. "No, slow and easy. You don't wanna scare him off. Pretend you're a worm. Keep it steady! Keep him biting!"

He released my hand, leaving me with the jerking pole. "Reid, why'd you let go? I need help!"

"You can do it! You're doing great! You'll land him. Stay cool!"

The pole twisted and tugged as I struggled to hold on. "It's breaking! Look!"

"Keep going! You're gonna bring this tiger in. That's my lucky pole, remember?"

I was unexpectedly excited. "Are you sure?"

"Yeah! You got him, Emmy! Roll him in!"

"What? No, he's too big!"

"You can do it! Ease up, don't jerk him, just stay calm and reel him out of the water!"

My hand trembled from gripping the pole, and my eyes bugged out waiting to meet Moby Dick. Reid spoke in a steady voice, repeating, "Ease him up." Finally, I brought up a big, angry fish.

"You got him," he shouted. "It's a big trout!"

Reid grabbed my fish, removed the hook, and held up the slippery creature by the tail. He threw him in a container with his slimy body flapping against the sides.

"I told you today was the day!" His hands clasped my waist as he lifted me off the ground. We twirled, sharing in a victory dance. We laughed so hard we didn't realize how dizzy we'd become until we landed on Reid's leaf chair.

He landed on top of me. His lips touched mine. In an instant, we froze—the laughter, the catch, everything. The world paused for our first kiss—a grazing kiss lasting a few seconds. Fleeting. Unexpected. It was monumental, exciting, and scary.

Reid cleared his throat and stood up, pulling me with him. He turned and began gathering the fishing poles and buckets.

I trembled more than my flailing fish. My chest heaved up and down from shallow breathing and the realization that Reid had kissed me.

He tapped my nose. "Emmy, I think the sun's getting to you. You don't look so good. Maybe I should take you home and get you some water."

My legs shook and my heart pounded. I wanted to pass out and blame the heat for looking like a buffoon. "I'm kind of dizzy," I said. "I'm sure…"

He dropped the poles and rushed to me. "Put your arm around me, Emmy…that way, I can catch you if you start to feel woozy. You don't want to be falling on this hard ground and rock."

I tried not to cringe. "Okay."

As we walked home, Reid had the poles tucked under his arm and the other arm firmly around my waist. I knew he believed I had succumbed to the heat, and I'd probably blushed enough to mimic heat exhaustion. My mind raced in a hundred directions, embarrassed that I had fallen to pieces over a kiss.

I hadn't realized we were in front of my house until he stopped walking. "Sit here on the porch," he said, guiding me to the first step. "I'm going to get water. Don't move."

"Oh…okay." I moaned under my breath as I watched Reid run to his house in search of life-saving water. The only thing missing was his white horse as he galloped back to me with his miracle cure.

"Here you go…drink this," he said, panting. "Not too fast."

I finished the whole glass. "Thank you."

"Do you feel better?"

I nodded. "Yeah…yeah."

He sat next to me. "I'll stay here until you're sure. Don't get up right away."

I couldn't stand the rouse any longer. "I'm all better. Thank you."

I thought he would jump up with a nod like he always did; instead, he stared off into the distance.

After a few minutes, he took my hand. "Thank you, Emmy," he whispered.

"For what?" I asked. I mean, he was the one that made me a leaf chair, taught me to fish, saved me from a fake heat stroke—and kissed me!

"For a great time and a fun day," he said, drawing the words out to emphasize he meant more.

I smiled at the boy I would spend the rest of my life loving. "You're welcome."

Reid headed down the sidewalk toting his fishing gear and my prize fish, walking with more swagger than usual. When he was halfway home, he spun around, looked at me and waved.

I nodded back with a brief wave. The nod was more of a hello than a goodbye. Hello to the beginning of "us."

I touched my lips, thinking about my first kiss and the excitement of being in love. I couldn't wait to feel it again, to chase the sensation, determined to experience it over and over—with Reid.

*ran downstairs and swung the front door open, hoping to see a Blue Chevy Impala parked in Reid's driveway.

I groaned for the umpteenth time today. Reid left for Yosemite National Park five days ago on a camping trip with his parents.

I rushed back upstairs to wait another thirty minutes before trying again. For the last five days, I hibernated in my room contemplating the "new me." It started with the hope that my father was harsh because he loved me and ended with a kiss from Reid.

I reached under the bed and grabbed the Bloomingdale's box filled with my sketchpads. All my despair, anxieties, and hopes bled out on the pages. I ran my hands across one of the pads and wondered what it meant, how I got here, and why I could never accept myself. How had I felt?

Deformed. Like I had a defect pushing on the walls of my body festering to get out. So, I have fought the only way I knew how, erasing the deformed girl and pretending to be someone acceptable and even likable.

I shut my eyes. "Please...God. I don't want to do that anymore."

Something told me to see the drawings with fresh eyes, maybe God, or perhaps common sense. I turned each page, determined to unravel the mystery. The earliest pictures were simple and optimistic with ear-to-ear smiles, an oversized sun in every picture, and flowers in every corner.

I chewed on my thumbnail as I turned to a picture of our little house surrounded by daisies, neighbor kids with jump ropes, and a dog and cat. The pictures were joyful. That made me frown, caught off guard. I couldn't remember being happy, but the picture told a different story. I looked like a typical four-year-old whose days consisted of lollipops and seesaws.

A jolt sucked the air from my lungs. *My world changed because Penelope died.*

After the sick sensation subsided, I flipped through my later drawings. With each page, the sketches matured to landscapes, flowers in vases, but mostly girls. Lots and lots of girls created from my imagination.

I turned to the next page and stopped—it was a picture of my dead sister, Penelope. The drawing was titled "Penelope at Ten," odd, because she died five years earlier. She had long wavy hair and big gloomy blue eyes. She took my breath away.

Her eyes held a secret. A family secret. I sensed it right away.

Her melancholy eyes held me; I grew weak and dreary, like her. "Penelope, where are you? Can you see me?"

My connection to her was stronger than to my living family. She was my twin, someone I barely remembered and an unmentionable family secret. Maybe the sadness was a necessary pain. Did I owe her my despair?

I traced the outline of her face, mesmerized. "What happened to you?"

I tried to pull myself from her spell. She was dead, but I was alive. But only half-alive because I kept creating characters to play the role of Emily. That changed five days ago when I started drawing my own life. I spent a glorious day at the lake with Reid freed from the bondage of inventing someone Reid might like.

"Okay," I muttered. I took a deep breath and stared at the enemy in the room—the mirror over my white colonial dressing table. Most girls loved to primp, but not me. I had ignored it and pretended it wasn't there. Pretended *I* wasn't there. My drawings were my reflection—a mixed-up game to avoid being myself.

I stood up, knowing what to do.

# *Eight*

## THE LONELY BOY IN THE SHINY SHOES

I sat on the edge of my bed like a fledgling ready to fly. I stood up and began walking toward the mirror.

Stars danced in front of me until I realized I had been holding my breath. An alarm beeped in my head warning me to stop.

"Keep going," I said to myself.

My knees knocked together as I stood in front of the dressing table. My fear was ridiculous. The only thing in front of me was wood, glass, and my image.

I sat down on the stool, resting my elbows on the table. I covered my eyes with my hands. After a few seconds, I spread my fingers. I saw a young girl with smooth skin, rounded features, blue eyes, and full lips. Her dark brown hair hung in waves just above her waist.

I put my hands down and faced her. She moved her fingers along her cheekbones and lips, tracing the outline of her mouth. I did the same. We held our eyes on each other and eased into an affectionate smile. I followed her as she ran her hands through her hair, feeling the silky texture fall through her fingers. She was a young, beautiful girl on the precipice of life.

But she wasn't me.

"Geez!" I pushed back from the table, realizing how ridiculous it was to deny my reflection. If I wanted a fresh start, I needed to leave the mythical characters behind and acknowledge my existence.

I threw on a yellow blouse and capris, determined to view the world with "real" eyes. The clanging of dishes downstairs meant Mother had breakfast ready. That was a perfect place to start.

I stood outside the kitchen. Father had already left for work, and Robert sat at the table scooping Cheerios into his mouth. Mother stood at the cupboard putting the drinking glasses away with the etched pattern facing out.

"Son, slow down. You're going to choke eating so fast. Also, it's bad manners."

"Sorry. I'm in a hurry. Remember the science fair today?"

I put on a smile and practically bounced into the kitchen. "Hi, Mother! Hi, Robert!"

"Good morning, dear. Have a seat."

Robert glanced up from his speed eating. "Hi."

I restrained a grin as I sat across from him. His blonde hair was slicked back with some gooey product, and he wore a starched white dress shirt, creased pants, and shiny black shoes. Under his chin, a red bow tie stood out like a silly-siren. Only Robert would go to a science fair on the hottest day of August.

"So, Robert...do you have an exhibit?"

"No, just the college kids. But anyone can go. It's pretty cool."

"Will Father be there?"

"I don't know," he mumbled.

"Won't he be back in time?"

He shifted in his chair and didn't answer me.

I studied his face. He seemed about as enthusiastic as a quarterback with a broken arm. "Well, I'm sure he'll go if he can."

He shrugged. "Guess so. Anyway, see ya," he said, as he pushed his chair in and left.

Mother moved the glasses back and forth like a game of checkers. I wanted her to notice the "new me."

"Mother, thank you for the lipstick and nail polish. I found them on my dressing table this morning."

"I put them on the bureau five days ago. You're fourteen now, so you can wear pink lipstick and pastel polish."

"Oh, well...I'm sorry." I didn't know how to tell her that today was the first time I'd used the dressing table.

As for turning fourteen, my family doesn't celebrate birthdays. I hadn't thought about it until I attended one of Reid's birthday parties. His mom put on an all-day party complete with games, prizes, and a ten-foot table loaded with sugary snacks. The only thing missing was a lion tamer with a bullwhip.

I understood. I think it was because of Penelope. We came into the world together, and I supposed celebrating my birthday would be a bit like commemorating her death.

Mother continued to align the dishes; she used her index finger to measure the distance. "Can I talk to you, Mother?"

"What's on your mind, dear?"

"I want to talk to you about the next school year," I said, twisting my hair.

She turned and removed the white apron from her green shift dress. "What would you like to know?"

"I wondered about the ninth grade. Will it be a lot harder?"

She sat down. "Ninth grade is much harder, dear. You'll need to settle down if you want to be a good student like Robert."

I felt like she'd jammed a "like Robert" rag down my throat. Of course, I probably deserved it. I made fun of him earlier instead of going with him to the science fair. "Will there be a lot of homework?"

"Yes, you'll have five classes. Your instructors will give you assignments to complete at home, and you must turn them in on time. If you need help, I can hire a tutor for you. It's important you take school seriously."

"I will. I promise. I'm going to be a good student. You'll see. I'll make you proud of me."

She patted the table and went back to arranging the glasses as I got up to leave. I found myself smiling, satisfied we had a conversation. I just needed to talk about something she thought was important.

I stepped onto the porch and grinned at the sight of Reid's family sedan parked in his driveway. I was ready to play the "real me." No more imaginary girls. I smoothed my hair and tucked in my yellow blouse. I leaned against the porch beam and waited for him to barrel down the street armed with camping tales of giant fish and grizzly bears.

A sense of doom surged through me. Abrupt. My stomach churned. A strange buzzing invaded my head, my skin turned cold and damp, and my fingers tingled. I tried to run but stumbled. Dizzy. My heart skipped like a car running on gas fumes as my surroundings tilted. I fumbled to the concrete; my chest heaved as my hair fell around my face.

I was having a heart attack. Jumbled thoughts raced through me, snippets of fear. I'm only fourteen. What do I do? "H-help," I moaned, panting.

I got to my feet. Had to run. I stumbled across the front lawn, doubled over. Terrified to die. Staggering in no direction, desperate, wheezing.

I spotted black pants, shiny shoes, and a red bow tie. "Help," I mouthed. "I'm dying." My breaths were short gasps, straining for air.

Robert put his arm around me. "You're not dying...I promise. You're having a panic attack...I'll help you, don't worry."

He gripped my arms and led me back to the porch steps. "Easy now."

He handed me a plain paper bag. "Breathe into this, slowly."

I inhaled and exhaled, watching his face.

He squeezed my hands around the paper sack. "You need to keep it tight so your oxygen stays inside. Just breathe in and out, don't over-breathe."

Robert kept his hand on my back as I continued to inhale and exhale into the bag. After a few minutes, my fingers stopped tingling and the clamminess faded. I felt stable enough to remove the bag.

He took the sack, folded it, and handed it back to me. "Keep it with you. If it happens again, you'll know what to do."

We sat in silence sharing something impossible to understand. I was lost in thought, or perhaps just lost. "Thank you," I whispered.

Robert stared off. "It's not easy...is it?"

"No, it's not."

We glanced at each other and shook our heads at the same time. We understood a truth we couldn't talk about.

"Are you okay now?"

"Yeah...I'm fine, thank you."

He slapped my knee as he stood up. "I'll see you later."

"Bye, Robert...and thanks again."

I studied him as he walked by himself to the science fair. With his notebook tucked under one arm and his steady gait, he seemed smaller and vulnerable, almost lonely. He had a sensitivity that enabled him to understand my fear, and he treated me with a calm tenderness. That made me wonder whether his life was really so easy and perfect? Why couldn't I see this before?

As he turned onto North Elm Street, I understood. He was different because Father wasn't with him. Father overshadowed him and cut off my ability to see Robert. Without Father, Robert was my brother.

And I loved him. I loved the sweet, lonely boy in the shiny shoes and red bow tie.

"Penny for your thoughts?"

Reid stood above me dressed in a blue tee shirt and white shorts. The trip to Yosemite had tanned his skin to a copper brown, accentuating the muscles on his arms and legs.

I rubbed my hands together, unexpectedly shy. "Hi!"

"What are you thinking?" Reid asked.

"Uh, nothing."

He sat down and nudged me with his shoulders. "Shoot! I thought you were daydreaming about me."

I giggled, warming up as our skin touched. "How was the camping trip?"

"Fantastic. I fished every day with my dad and caught more fish than he did. Mom made s'mores at night over a campfire. You know, those graham cracker things with marshmallows?"

"Um, yeah...I think so."

"My dad says she should enter the Pillsbury Bake-Off and win fifty thousand bucks."

I nodded, trying to concentrate with his shoulder pressed against mine. "Sounds good."

"Yep, my mom's always making up new recipes. She watches that Julia Child lady every day. Dad says she's trying to get him fat."

"Oh, yeah?"

"For sure, she bakes all the time. She'd probably win the bake-off if she entered."

"Do you think she will?"

"Nah, no way. Mom just loves to cook for us. She'd never enter a contest."

Poor Mrs. Wagner. She doted over her family like the mother of a newborn. She rarely left the kitchen except to go to the grocery store. Her house was spotless, and she cooked everything from scratch. She even handpicked her meat from the butcher. I supposed she believed the way to a man's heart was through his stomach. Of course, it was all in vain because every night he prowled the bars looking for women. I heard Father telling Mother that, anyway.

Reid nudged me and raised his eyebrows. "So, did you miss me?"

"Sure did." Flashbacks of the "kiss" turned the thermostat up to 120 degrees.

"So, how about we walk over to Bailey Park?" Reid asked. "There's a festival going on...or art show. I don't know...something."

"Sure, that sounds like…"

Father careened into the driveway, pulling on the parking brake before he made a complete stop.

"Where's Robert?" he shouted, barely out of the car. He slammed the door, checking his wristwatch as he charged in my direction. Still in his summer white navy uniform, sweat rolled off his face onto his stiff collar. Everything about him spelled tension from his clenched fists to his pulsing jaw muscles.

He stood in front of me, jingling the keys he'd stuck in his pocket. "Did you hear me? Where's Robert?"

"He went to the science fair," I replied, as fast and even as I could.

"When?"

"I don't know. Maybe fifteen minutes ago," I said, trying to sound nonchalant in front of Reid. As soon as the words were out of my mouth, I cringed. Casual answers annoyed Father when he was in one of his jumpy moods. It was like pouring water on a grease fire; it ignited him more.

He rolled his eyes and grunted. Without a word, he rushed back to his car, no doubt heading to the science fair to find Robert. He abruptly stopped and glared at me.

"Why aren't you in the house helping your mother?"

My spirit went into free fall. His barbed comment was spoken to humiliate me. Mother never allowed me to help her with housework. She clued me in years ago, after too many failed attempts to dry the dishes right, or vacuum the carpet with the nap smoothed in the correct direction. And Father knew it.

I opened my mouth to say something, but he had already waved his hand dismissively. He swung the car door open and got in, shoving the key in the ignition.

"You're useless!" He slammed the door and backed out of the driveway, clipping a handful of leaves off the shrubs.

The pride I had felt this morning, poised for the "new me," withered with Father's reprimand. I wondered how to pitch an excuse.

Reid's mouth gaped open. "What the heck was that?"

"Oh nothing, really. I forgot to clean the kitchen. He's upset because my mother needed help."

Reid smirked. "He was in a big tizzy to get to Robert! What's with that?"

"Robert didn't feel good this morning. I think he was worried about him."

"Humph!"

We sat together in awkward silence. The sound of my labored swallowing was audible, so I covered my mouth to muffle the embarrassing noise.

"Come on," he said, pulling me up.

"Okay," I said, relieved the subject was closed.

"Let's head out."

"Okay," I repeated, embarrassed my vocabulary had dwindled to a mere "okay."

As we walked, it was hard to let go of my shame. But it could have been worse; I have seen my father a lot worse. At least it was over.

"So, what's with your dad anyway?"

I didn't have a comeback. I couldn't say my father was overprotective of me—Robert, yes. "What do you mean?"

"Why's he so rude for God's sake? Geez, what are you, Robert's bodyguard or something? I don't get it...it's weird."

"He's not always that way. Mother says he's under a lot of pressure in the Navy, and he needs quiet when he's at home...you know, to calm down."

He sneered. "Are you kidding me? He's the one all huffy-puffy acting like Robert was a kidnap victim. He wasn't looking for calm. He was out for blood!"

"No..." I stumbled for words. "Well, like I said...the Navy and all."

"Oh, bullshit. Come on! The Navy isn't a torture chamber. I mean, my dad's the Deputy Chief of Police. That's *real* pressure! He sure doesn't act like that."

My heart sank. Reid might as well have said, "My dad loves me, and your dad hates you. Oh, by the way, he loves Robert so what the hell is wrong with you?" It all boiled down to that.

I spotted the merry-go-rounds and hoards of kids. The band playing "Johnny Be Good" flipped off his interrogation.

"Hey, this is pretty cool, huh?" Reid lapsed into party-mode and did a quick twirl and a few dance moves before turning to me.

"So, you want to listen to the band or check out the rest of the stuff?"

"Whatever you want," I shouted over the music.

"Let's walk around and check it out."

The festival had something for everyone. There were clowns making animals out of balloons, game booths, crafters selling macramé purses, and a Ferris wheel filled with smiling couples. The smell of hot dogs, cotton candy, and corn on the cob gave the air a sweet, greasy scent as folks strolled the grounds eating almost anything cooked on a stick.

"You wanna ride the Ferris wheel?" Reid asked.

I stared at a huge striped canopy packed with artwork. Rows of easels displayed watercolors, penciled sketches, and oil paintings. "What?"

"Ah-ha. You want to check out the art, right?"

"Well, yeah. If that's okay with you."

"Of course. Then the Ferris Wheel?"

"Sure," I agreed. "Then the Ferris Wheel."

Each artist had a booth, some with beaded curtains that tapped together when someone walked in. Others had Moroccan blankets or hand-painted screens outlining their creative space. They displayed their work on beech wood easels with small placards. Artists mulled about garbed in striped tunics and casual slacks, or colorful shift dresses.

I stopped to admire a bold abstract painting with swirls of reds and yellows. "Wow...look at that."

Reid laughed. "Yeah. Pretty kooky, huh?"

We continued browsing cityscapes, abstracts, watercolors, and pastoral scenes. Reid chatted about each drawing, dismissing some art as weird and complimenting the seascapes. He viewed the art with his eyes, but

I didn't see it the same way. I could feel the emotional embrace of the painter's brush and the passion.

Reid stared off at the carnival. "Wanna eat?"

I pretended not to hear him until he patted me on the shoulder.

"Hey, you want some cotton candy or a corn dog?"

"Are you hungry?" I asked.

"Sure, and I gotta get you on the Ferris wheel! It's humongous… check it out!"

It was big all right, like a gigantic bicycle with suspended cars along the edge. "Yeah," I said, raising my voice to match his excitement. "Sure is!"

"Let's grab something to eat and then we'll ride."

After a plump greasy corn dog and a buttery corncob perched on a stick, we waited to board the big wheel.

Reid's eyes were like saucers as he admired the trailing lights and tippy carts. "This is cool, huh? I hope we get stuck at the top!"

"What…why?"

"We can see all the way to the San Francisco Bay Bridge from up there! We'll be able to spot our houses!"

"Oh, yeah…neat."

The wheel paused as fair workers unlatched smiling kids and adults, leaving swaying cars for the next round of anxious carnival-goers. The last boarders were in front of us, so we would have to wait for one more go-around. That gave me a chance to study the crowd of people.

Laughter roared through the festival. Children pulled on their parents begging for another ride on the kangaroo train. Dads threw darts at balloons hoping to pop enough to win a trinket for their child, shelling out two dollars to win a prize worth a nickel. Moms bought cotton candy and snow cones for their sugar loaded kids. The carnival was chirpy, merry, and chaotic, full of color and the smells of fried food and cotton candy.

I found myself frowning and even jealous of the happy carnival-goers.

Reid nudged me. "Our turn! Hey, you okay?"

I shook off the melancholy. "Of course! Sorry, just...spacing out at everything."

"Well, come on! It's our pick!"

"Oh, sure...let's go."

We didn't get to choose our car, but Reid announced it was the one he wanted anyway. The Ferris wheel rotated upward providing a picturesque view as Reid promised. My stomach tensed until Reid put his arm around me. He pointed out all the landmarks and claimed to find my house. After several rotations, metal scraped with a loud screech.

"What's wrong?" I shrieked.

"The ride's over and guess what? We're at the top!"

I started to ask him how long we'd have to wait, but his lips on mine stopped me. He kissed me longer than the first time. It was sweet and warm and more thrilling than any ride I could imagine.

He ended the kiss with a soft peck. "Emmy, I want to tell you something."

"Sure," I whispered.

He stroked my hands. "I want you to know I really like you."

I pursed my lips to keep from giving him a silly monkey grin. "Me too."

He turned silent. His neck muscles tensed and worry wrinkles formed between his eyebrows. He stared straight ahead, squinting. When the wheel started moving again and the carnival worker unbuckled us, he couldn't leave fast enough.

We walked in awkward silence. Reid kept his head down with his hands in his pockets.

He stopped and glared at me, not saying anything.

"What's wrong?" I asked.

He crossed his arms. "Emmy, I'm serious and obviously you are not."

"I don't understand. What's wrong?"

He pointed to a birch tree several feet away. "Let's sit, away from the racket."

We sat several inches apart. I hugged my knees to my chest, trying to read him. He stared at the ground, flicking fallen leaves. His audible sighs and headshakes told me he was brooding and not happy with me. He didn't even react when the band started playing his favorite song "Jailhouse Rock."

After an awkward minute, he turned to me. "Emily, do you understand how I feel right now?"

I opened my mouth and shut it. "Well…not really."

"I told you how I felt, which was a big deal to me. All you said was 'me too,' like it meant nothing."

Hearing my words sounded ho-hum, even cold. But I'd spent years pretending to be someone else—so which Emily did he like? "I'm sorry. I didn't have the right words, but that doesn't mean I wasn't thinking them."

He continued to flick leaves, his eyes blinking fast. "How am I supposed to know how you feel if you don't tell me? I don't think you like me as much as I like you."

I studied him, realizing for the first time he was sensitive and even a little insecure. "I like you a lot, Reid. More than anything."

"You don't have to say that," he mumbled.

"I'm not. I like you more than you know. I'm sorry I didn't explain it that way on the Ferris wheel, but I would have told you later."

He took a long look at me and sighed. "Really?"

"Yes, really…you mean everything to me."

He pulled me into his chest. My head rested against his shoulders as a sinking sensation coursed through me. I had felt it before, a vague feeling of hopelessness. Sorrow. I doubted myself and didn't know if I could kill all the characters I'd created over the years. Now I know that Reid's suggestion that my father was overprotective of me was nothing more than a fool's dream. I would need those damn disguises to navigate through Father's hatred of me.

Children played tag in front of us, twisting and turning behind sycamore trees. The young boy and girl appeared to be about five years old.

The boy teased the little girl and dared her to catch him. He was energetic like Reid. She trotted after him; her dark curls bounced up and down as she tried to keep up.

"Just think, Emmy. That used to be us!"

The girl giggled and kept her eyes on the boy as she maneuvered around the park. Her giggles triggered memories of Penelope.

"Emily, what's wrong?"

I couldn't take my eyes off the girl, as a stream of tears poured down my face.

Reid grabbed my shoulders. "Emmy, what is it? What's the matter?"

I sat up straight and pressed my hands over my eyes. "I'm fine, fine…I'm just happy! I always cry when I'm happy! God, I must look stupid!"

He frowned. "Are you sure?"

"Yeah, yeah, yeah," I blurted out, sniffing. "I'm happy!"

He flicked away a tear perched on my chin. "You're not sorry about what you said, are you? You know…about liking me?"

"Heck no! No way!"

"Well, you can't take it back. You're the one for me."

"You're the one for me too." I caught myself, realizing my response sounded automatic, like before. "Always!"

"Come on girl…we better go. It's getting late. I wouldn't want your dad ticked at me."

The late afternoon sun cast our silhouettes on the dirt path. The shadows fascinated me, elongated figures walking together like dancers in unison with their fingertips touching. Strange, my murky shadow seemed more defined than the reflection earlier this morning in the mirror.

We arrived home. "I'd kiss you goodbye, but your dad might shoot me."

"Hmm," I mumbled, knowing my father couldn't care less.

"Oh hell…I'll take the chance." He put his arms around my waist and pulled me into his body. His mouth touched mine as he drew me closer, parting his lips. The kiss was wet and tasted sweet and fiery. He stopped and gazed at me, caressing my face. He kissed me again.

My body tingled as I tried to catch my breath. "Wow!"

"Bye," he whispered, with a last kiss below my ear.

"Man," I muttered, watching him strut home. *Now that was a kiss!*

I sat on the porch to mull over the day. Touching the dusty steps, I realized I was back where I started this morning with Robert. I patted my pocket, listening to the rustle of the paper bag. At least I made it through the day without inventing a mythical character Reid would find interesting.

"Where the hell have you been? Your mother's been worried sick!"

I turned to find Father's white slacks and white shoes standing inches from me. "I'm sorry, I..."

He kicked me in the small of my back. I lunged forward and fell to my knees on the cement walkway.

"Goddamn it! Get up!" he shouted.

I lifted my head and scanned the neighborhood.

"Dumb ass! Get the hell to your room before I knock you down again!"

I charged up the stairs and dropped on my bed. Father's angry voice buzzed in my head like a vicious intruder, as I tried to catch my breath. The prospect that someone saw me sprawled on the cement smacked me down harder than his kick.

I turned to my side and pressed my legs to my chest. Had anyone seen me? My hands felt sticky, so I held up my hand to find fresh blood on my palm. I straightened my legs, transfixed by the contrast between my bloodied knee and smooth one. Damaged on one side and healthy on the other. Just like me.

Enough. I walked to the bathroom, rolled off three damn squares of toilet tissue, and patted the wound clean. I grabbed a Band-Aid and stuck it on my scraped knee. Done.

I trudged back to bed, patting the dressing on my wounded knee. I shut my eyes, trying to think about the kiss and not the kick, surrendering to the exhaustion of my mind and body.

⌒

### San Francisco County Jail, July 17, 1966. End of Session Two.

I looked around the small office and the watchful eyes of Doctor Lieberman.

Remembering my life left me worn out and sad. The memories were fraught with the tension of Father's anger but also the kindness of Robert and my budding romance with Reid.

The officials informed me beforehand that my post-session with the doctor would be shortened because he had to testify in court. He pulled his gray jacket over his light blue shirt. "How are you feeling?"

I managed a half smile, at least enough to mollify my sorrow. A gaping hole was growing inside me, expanding with each reclaimed memory. I would spend the next week dwelling on the bond that had developed with Robert on the porch and the excitement I felt when Reid kissed me. Love and regret—two emotions that should not be experienced at the same time.

"Emily, the pain of regaining your memory is inescapable. Our journey has just started, and we have a long way to go. Try not to pre-determine what your life will become. Can you do that?"

I nodded in spite of my doubt. The growing sorrow of a lost life routed me in the direction of despair, but I had enough respect for Doctor Lieberman to promise him I would try.

# Nine

## LOSS AND VIOLENCE

*San Francisco County Jail, July 24, 1966. Beginning of Session Three*

Doctor Lieberman looked up before returning to his thick pile of hand-written notes. "Good morning, Emily."

"Good morning, Doctor." I chewed my thumbnail, savoring the sound of my name. The guards all referred to me as "Quinn."

It was hard to regain an identity in a place that strips you of your individuality. Prisoners wore identical jumpsuits, resided in the same austere cells, and ate the same food day after day.

"How are you this morning?"

I started to answer "fine" but stopped, knowing he would call my response trite. "I guess okay. I mean...sort of." I squirmed in my chair, knowing how stupid that sounded.

"I have a few more pages of your journal to go over. I'll be with you in a few minutes."

I glanced around the small office, pausing at a black and white clock above the file cabinets. You don't find clocks in jail. Time seemed endless. Cells don't have windows, so the best way to tell the time was by the routines—when the lights come off or on, cell checks, and meals.

The doctor poured a cup of black coffee. "At the conclusion of our last session, I encouraged you not to predestine your life and to keep an open mind so this process can work. Were you able to accomplish that?"

I rubbed my eyes and kept them shut until I pictured Grandma, my family, and Reid. At first, the memory of Grandma's warm hand, Robert's love, and Reid's boyish passion soothed me. But then came the sting of regret, knowing I had destroyed their faith in me and had no way to atone for the damage.

"I'm trying, I am. It's not easy. I wish that I could go back and do things differently. I think about what my life could have been if..." I stopped, knowing I had failed his request.

He leaned forward with his elbows on the desk. "For the time being, I want you to suspend the inevitable thinking that results from incarceration. Consider two things. First, there are different kinds of imprisonment. As you uncover more details of your life, your opinion may change. Second, I ask you to be open to the possibility that your future may offer more freedom than your past. I'm asking you to free yourself of the anxieties of remorseful thinking. Remember, under hypnosis, you are uncovering your past. The future is unknown. When you slip into negative thinking, keep in mind that your future is ahead of you. No matter where you are, you will have control over your mind which is the essence of real freedom."

"I'll try harder." His words stemmed from an enlightenment I lacked. Even so, I understood the general significance. I needed to stop terminating my life at nineteen years old. As he led me into a state of hypnosis, one word stood out—possibility.

The house had an odd stillness. The usual smell of bacon sizzling on the griddle, coffee percolating, and the buzz of Father's electric shaver was absent. One sound echoed through the quiet—Mother crying.

I tiptoed outside my parent's room to listen, peeking in for a second to see Father beside her as she wept into his shoulder. Every so often, I heard the gentle tug of a tissue being pulled from the Kleenex box. Father didn't say much other than "I know." Mother continued to whimper.

The bed squeaked; I hurried back to my bedroom. Father walked past my room; he went into Robert's bedroom and closed the door. I sat and listened. Father spoke too softly to make out a single word.

Something happened. It had finality, important enough to bring Mother to tears, and a closed-door discussion with Robert.

I covered my mouth to silence a gasp and clamped down on my lower lip to squash my excitement—yes, excitement.

I geared-up for the announcement—my parents were getting a divorce.

I had readied myself years ago. My response was visceral. I didn't need to ponder the news or weigh the pros and cons. This was great news. Life-changing news. Fate had opened the door to my torture chamber and screamed, "You are free!"

I kicked my feet back and forth. "Yeah!"

I took a deep breath and steadied my excitement. I would need to feign remorse in front of Robert, Mother, and even Father. I would have to pay penance to God for rejoicing over divorce. Still, I couldn't wait for the gavel to drop and to hear the judge utter the words, "divorce final."

Robert's door closed. It was my turn for "the talk." I held my breath, clutched the bedspread, and turned my lips inward to hide a smile. I sat up straight, ready for him.

Father stopped at the doorway and leaned against the casing with his arms crossed. "Grandma died. There's a viewing Thursday at 7 o' clock. Wear black... Oh, and don't bother your mother. She's very upset."

*I* fluffed my pillow for the fifth time, trying to sleep. For the last two days, I stayed in my room, only going downstairs to grab some fruit or a glass of milk. I didn't want to hear anyone repeat what Father told me. It was a lie.

⁓

*We* pulled up to an austere gray building, an oblong structure with no signs, no picture windows, just a plain brown door. Everything about the place indicated that the public was not welcome except for one thing. It had a huge parking lot with painted white stripes on the blacktop outlining where to park.

Father got out of the sedan and opened the door for us. Cars drove in and parked, and people filed out. Some I recognized from Father's work, most I didn't. They all did the same thing. They quietly embraced my parents.

The building had a long corridor that led to rooms with closed doors. Pictures of Jesus and the Virgin Mary lined the walls; the paintings were somber, not comforting like Saint Mary's. We walked silently down the carpeted hallway with our footsteps marching in unison.

When we reached the end of a long, dim corridor, a miserable-looking man in a black suit greeted us. He had ghostly pale skin with blonde hair and white eyelashes, which made his light-blue eyes almost disappear. He whispered something to Father. His mouth moved but the rest of his face appeared frozen. Father must have understood what the man said because he nodded.

The sallow man opened a brown arched door and gestured for us to enter. Mother and Father came first, followed by Robert and me. Morose organ music played but when I searched the room, I couldn't find anyone playing an organ. I turned around to see the pale man guarding the entry like a sinister gargoyle.

Mother guided Robert and me to high-backed chairs made of dark, hard wood. The room pretended to be a church by displaying a wooden cross above the door with a brass Jesus, which added dispassion to the setting. The gray floor was scrubbed, but filth still clung to the grout. The room reeked of bleach, which surprised me because it didn't look all that clean.

People filed in and took their seats. They stared straight ahead. Mother's eyes were expressionless, and Robert gazed at the floor. I wanted to run out of the room but the insipid man stood in front of it. His face remained blank and unmoving. He didn't seem like a real person.

Mother nudged me. I thought we were leaving, but she guided me in the opposite direction.

She stopped after we walked a few feet. I craned my neck, my eyes widened at the sight in front of me.

Grandma was posed in a white metal box with brass handles and a half-open lid. A blue tufted blanket was draped over the side. Someone had painted her face with thick gray makeup, painted black lines over her eyebrows, and round pink circles on her cheeks. Her long soft white hair that she always wore loosely tied in a bun had been cut to form horseshoe curls around her chin. Grandma's hands, the hands that squeezed mine, were folded lifeless in her lap.

An unpleasant sensation flowed through me, like blood draining through my body too fast. The world around me constricted to shapeless forms and then blackened. Sound ceased. Time ran out. Hope ended.

As my emotional state crumbled, my intuition took over. I sprang forward to help her; my heart and mind buckled with the realization that Grandma had died. I crashed through the procession of viewers, shoving the stranger-guests aside. Grandma didn't belong in a gloomy building put on display for people she didn't know. She belonged in Seattle among the towering pine trees, the rose gardens, and the meandering trails leading to her forest home.

I reached into the casket and tried to cradle her in my arms. I nestled her body into mine, shut my eyes, and moaned softly into her ear. "Grandma, Grandma..."

Tears streamed down my face. I caught them on my fingertips, wiping the chalky makeup from her beautiful face, smoothing the black lines over her natural brows, and the pink circles on her cheeks. I ran my hands through the tight curls to loosen her soft white hair.

I heard myself sobbing as I embraced her, kissing her forehead and cheeks.

Father grabbed me around the waist and pressed his fingers into my flesh. I tightened every muscle to create a shield over Grandma, grabbing the handle of the casket with one hand. He jerked and twisted my body as I hung on, weeping—long, lamenting cries to keep her with me. I ached for her to squeeze my hand and to hear her French-laden accent telling me she loved me.

The gloomy statue-guard surged forward; he motioned commands with his frigid hands. As Mother sobbed in the background, I pleaded with Father and the grim doorkeeper to let me go as I strained to break loose. In one quick jolt, they pulled me a few feet away. Father tossed me over his shoulders as I continued to cry out for Grandma.

Father marched out of the room and into the hallway. He kicked the steel doors open, emitting a shrill echo throughout the dreadful building—announcing that not one, but two people died. I winced at the feel of his nails digging into my flesh. His firm grip covered my mouth to smother my tortured screams. The mantra "we will leave the world together" played in my head like a maudlin torch song.

A cold wind swept through my black crepe dress. I listened as his heavy footsteps and labored breathing carried me away from the death building. He dropped me on the graveled parking lot next to the car.

"You goddamn bitch!"

I felt a hard kick to my side, and then came another—a brutal strike to my ribs. The blow propelled me against the tire of the car, wedging me helplessly as he struck me again. His foot felt like a stake impaling my organs. He reared back and kicked me again. He kept coming—a cease-less agony drawing the oxygen from my body. I recoiled from the searing pain and prayed for him to finish.

He kicked my side again. The pain multiplied with each blow, shooting burning bullets of agonizing pain. With each strike, my head bounced against the rubber tire. I moaned with each blow. I tried to count, remembering his routine was to strike me until he reached twenty, but the pain was too intense to concentrate. Besides, I knew he'd already surpassed the number. He wouldn't stop. He *couldn't* stop.

I wanted to die and end the unbearable suffering. I couldn't endure the pain much longer. Liquid trickled down my chin; I wondered if it was blood. He continued to assault me. I knew bones were cracking because it was hard to breathe and impossible to move.

"You bitch!" he screamed, drawing back with endless blows.

With each kick, he grunted. I was a glob of bludgeoned flesh, broken, shredded. The violence was too intense to defend; my instinct to scream was silenced by the torture. I began to wither and fade into stillness like the silent suffering of approaching death. I stopped feeling the blows and surrendered to the abyss.

Time became interminable. A chilling numbness replaced my physi-cal pain. I let the tears seal my eyes closed and waited to die, using the last moments of my life to ask God to take me to Grandma and Penelope.

My face twitched involuntarily; I struggled to open my swollen, wa-tery eyes; the world was so distorted, like looking through a cracked window. I couldn't move or defend myself.

A brilliant globe floated in the starless sky, swaying as a lure to keep my eyes open. The glowing celestial sphere floated down like a danc-ing moon—a glimmering carriage illuminating the darkness around me. The gilded door opened, and Grandma rushed to me.

"Open your eyes," she said softly but with subtle urgency. Her skin was smooth and her hair the color of snow rippling down her shoul-ders. Her blue eyes glistened like the morning sun at Mallard Lake as it touched the water.

"I can't," I mouthed.

She moved her face closer to mine. I felt her warm breath on my cheek. She smelled like fresh-baked bread, and the sweet scent of lilacs permeated around her.

As I jerked with each blow to my side, she grazed my cheek and whispered for me to stay awake and keep my eyes open.

"No..." Living meant never seeing her again, and I wanted to go with her. *It was better than this.*

She lifted my chin, as I watched her mouth form the word "live." She stroked my hair, comforting me.

"...Die...same time..." I murmured.

I began to float away, hovering inches above my battered body. Grandma caught me and pushed me back into my beaten body with both hands. Even as she pushed me inward, she embraced me like a wounded baby.

"Live, ma chérie. Mon bébé, I will always be here," she whispered.

My swollen eyes filled with tears; I tried to shake my head, to tell her no.

She picked up my scuffed hand and squeezed it. I closed my eyes and sobbed. A deep in the gut cry because I knew that I could not go with her. I wept—a primal whimper borne from ruinous pain. I begged God to let me go with her. My wish was hopeless because when I opened my eyes for a moment, she was gone.

My sweet, loving Grandma had willed me to survive, but with her plea came the inevitable sorrow that now I had to live in a world without her.

# Ten

## BRUISED

"Jacob, we should take her to the emergency room." Mother kept her eyes on the road with an occasional nervous glance at me, lying in the back seat in a fetal position.

I pressed my hand against my mouth to smother my agony. My body throbbed, especially my sides where he'd kicked me until I lost count.

"No, she's fine. She's okay, really. Did you see how she disrupted your mother's memorial service?" He spoke fast in a hushed voice.

"Of course I did. How do you think I felt? I'm horrified, but you didn't have to hurt her that way. She looks awful. Exactly what did you do to her?"

"I yelled at her about ruining the service, and I kicked her a few times. She's making a big fuss to get your goat."

Mother turned around to view me. "Emily," she whispered. "Please say...I mean, are you okay?"

The question was ludicrous and felt like another kick, but from her this time. I managed to nod and closed my swollen eyes to shut her out.

"Jacob, you shouldn't have..."

"I had to," he said, his voice soft and pleading. "She was out of control. Good God, she deserved to be punished after humiliating you like that."

"Still...you went too far. You did. She may have a broken rib."

"She doesn't, Claire. She does *not*. I only kicked her a few times. You know Emily. She's a liar and a big baby. I'm telling you she's faking. I had to protect you when I saw what she did to you at the service. Good heavens, she threw herself on your mother in front of everyone. Claire, we'll never live down the shame."

"I know, but..."

"Darling, please listen to me," he continued, his tone growing desperate. "I had to defend you. Think about it, she'll be fine but you'll never be able to re-do the beautiful memorial you spent night and day planning."

"Ma..." she whimpered.

"Exactly. Your mother was a beautiful person inside and out. Emily disrespected her memory, and I couldn't let her get away with it."

She gave a prolonged sigh signaling she accepted his explanation.

We arrived home. Father slammed on the brakes and jumped out to shut the garage door. Three doors opened but not mine.

"Come on, Emily," said Father. He kept his voice steady but the uneasiness was apparent. "We're home."

The slightest movement sent spasms throughout my body. I wondered if my ribs were sticking out of my chest or dangling from my ribcage.

Mother opened my door. "Let's go inside...please, dear. I'll help you."

For some reason, I decided to shield her from the intensity of my pain. Maybe I believed Father's story too, that I had ruined Grandma's memorial. Besides, she said as much. "I will...soon," I muttered, fighting to keep the pain out of my voice.

I heard the house door close and released a drawn-out yelp like a wounded dog. I felt like someone had placed me in a compactor. I took short, shallow breaths and worried that my bones had pierced my lungs.

The torment along with the stench of cigar smoke made me want to vomit. I strained against the impulse, sending tortuous stabs through my body.

"Owe," I moaned, trying to sit up. The pain was like a thousand blades piercing me. Impossible.

All I could do was gaze at the inside roof of the car. The tufted pattern made me queasy as the objects twirled in front of me.

Someone widened my car door. "Emily, don't move. Wait for me to help," said Robert.

My body jerked with contractions. I turned my head and vomited on the garage floor.

"Garage," I moaned.

"That's all right. I'll clean it up. Now do exactly as I tell you."

"Okay."

"Don't try to move, only when I say so." Robert grabbed my ankles and slid my legs in the direction of the door opening.

I groaned as the pain pierced through me like a combat sword.

"It'll get better, I promise. You're going to have to bear the pain for now. Do whatever I say and don't move on your own. All right?"

"Uh-huh." My legs were out of the car, but I was still laying flat on my back staring at the car roof. The other car door opened.

"Okay…I'm going to sit you up, and I want you to grab the seat. All right?"

"Uh-huh."

He put his hands on my back and pushed me forward. Every raspy breath made the pain worse, but I held onto the seats. I bent over, gritting my teeth to endure the misery and not scream.

He ran to the other side. "At the count of three, grab my hands so I can pull you up. It's going to hurt, so imagine a peaceful place. You can do it."

I thought of Seattle and Grandma.

"One, two, three," he said. I grabbed his hands as he pulled me out of the car.

I winced, experiencing the throes of Father's violence again.

Robert shut the car door with his hip. "Hang on...we're almost there."

The slightest movement seemed impossible. I slumped, knowing the door and the stairs were ahead of me. I wanted to drop to the cement floor and black out. The pain was *that* bad.

With a short grunt, Robert lifted me into his arms. He eased down to maneuver the doorknob and carried my limp body up the flight of stairs.

He lowered me to my twin bed, folding the coverlet around me. I released my pain into the stillness, relieved I didn't have to move anymore.

Robert patted my hand. I watched him leave and wished I had the strength to thank him.

Shortly after, he came back, plugged in a heating pad and positioned it against my battered side. "Lift your head a little, Em. You need to take these," he whispered, handing me two aspirins. "Your ribs are bruised, and you'll need them every four hours. I'll be right here."

I swallowed the pills and forced my puffed-up eyes open. My face was too numb to form even a pitiful smile, so I promised myself I would thank him later. He grabbed a throw pillow from the bed and placed it on the floor beside me.

I stayed in place, trying not to move a muscle. I thought of Grandma, the sound of her loveable voice and gentle touch, as I tried to push the horror of the memorial out of my troubled mind. I didn't know how to live in a world without her.

Tears trickled down my face, but I was too immobilized to wipe them. I let them flow like warm mineral water, cleansing my weary face. The spilled tears brought clarity when I noticed Robert next to my bed.

In the unspeakable sorrow of losing Grandma and being savagely beaten, I discovered a treasure. I found a guardian, a strong boy, and an angel—my brother.

*I* rolled over and stared at the calendar. Ten days ago I lost Grandma. Days and days with nothing but bathroom breaks. I knew the number of bumps on the textured ceiling and how many cracks were on the walls.

Mother stopped by every morning and evening. The second day, Father came by on his way to Jack in the Box and asked me if I wanted a burger, which I declined. They hadn't talked about Grandma's death or the beating I took at her memorial. One more family hardship shrouded in secrecy.

*Except for one thing—this time I knew exactly what happened.*

Robert had been my devoted caretaker; he checked on me hourly and brought me painkillers and soft food. He covered for me with Reid by telling him I had the flu. He made time every few hours to check my mobility and assess the damage to my ribs. He always reassured me with a soothing smile, but then his expression turned contemplative, serious.

One expression on Robert's face surpassed the others—anger. At the sound of Father's voice, his eyes narrowed, his muscles tightened. That dark, dreadful night changed Robert. He became a devoted brother, watching over me, spending all his free time with me. He was more of a parent to me and no longer a dutiful son.

*And Father had no idea.*

I managed to shift my body enough to toss back the covers. Time to get up and stay up. I moved my legs to the edge of the bed and sat up. My legs trembled and were surprisingly thin, but I chalked it up to staying in bed for ten days. I wiggled my toes and moved my head side to side. Next, I rotated my upper body, encouraged the stabbing pain was gone, leaving only a general soreness. I put my head down and took a deep breath to prepare myself.

I shuffled to the dressing table to get it over with. The plan was to view my body and leave. No emotion, and no poor-me thoughts.

"Okay," I said, lifting my head. My skin was pallid, and my eyes held a malaise and smudgy darkness in spite of spending so many days in bed. No surprise. My dark hair spun out in all directions like a spider web. A hairbrush could handle that problem. I turned to the side and lifted my nightgown, gasping. Nothing could have prepared me for the sight.

My skin was blackened and engorged with red and purple blood. The bruises traveled from the middle of my chest to the small of my back and ballooned in clusters of bloody splotches. My skin was stretched out with reddish streaks scattered across the assaulted area.

I dropped my nightgown.

I walked to my bed and crawled back under the covers, pulling them around me like a cocoon. I shut my eyes and let the warm tears flow.

"I can't do it, Grandma," I whispered. "I'm sorry, but I'm not ready."

### San Francisco County Jail, July 24, 1966. End of Session Three

"Okay," said Doctor Lieberman, tossing the stubby pencil. He rolled his shirt up to his elbows and leaned on the desk. "We've learned a lot today, how do you feel?"

"Awful," I answered, not needing to think.

"Why? Please explain."

I twisted my hair. Open-ended questions un-nerved me, I didn't know how to respond.

He removed his glasses and rubbed his bony hand through his white hair. "Emily, under hypnosis, you say exactly how you feel. It's natural. I notice when you are fully awake, you tend to censor everything before speaking. Please try to say whatever comes to your mind without measuring it first."

"I...don't know how. I've never done that."

"All right. Let me ask you specific questions, and we'll see where that will take us."

"Okay."

"When you came out of hypnosis, what did you feel?"

"Um...pain."

"Pain from what?"

"Well, physical pain in my ribs and mental pain from losing my grandma."

"What about the mental and physical pain of your father's assault against you?"

I massaged my temples. "I don't know. Well, yes. But I messed up her memorial."

"So, you deserved to be beaten by your father?"

"I'm not sure. Maybe I did."

He walked to the file cabinet, picked up the carafe, and poured black coffee into his chipped mug. He returned to his desk and sat down. I waited, listening to his squeaky chair as he rocked back and forth.

"Emily, I need you to understand something. I'm doing a controlled, detailed, and guided therapy with you. This is not psychotherapy in the traditional sense. I'm looking for specific issues as we recover your memory. I cannot influence your reasoning or re-direct your thoughts as you respond to the recovered memories. Do you understand?"

I bit my lower lip and wondered if I'd said something wrong. "But I thought you asked me not to censor my thoughts."

His hands formed a steeple. "I want you to understand why I cannot editorialize what you say to me. I cannot deflect my purpose here, which is to recover your memories and determine how you felt at the time, and provide your attorneys with a plausible defense. And most importantly, I want to guide you to your own understanding."

"Oh." It all came back to the same thing—a defense for murdering my father. Smoke and mirrors paid for by my mother.

A hefty male guard burst into the room. "Let's go, Quinn. Time's up," he said, as he grabbed my arms and cuffed me. "I got her, Doc."

I wrinkled my nose, perplexed at the thought of escaping from the giant brute loaded with a Billy club and huge fists.

The doctor held his hand up. "Hold on," he said, in a voice surprisingly intense.

The fleshy guard paused, his jail keys dangling against his thunderous thighs, waiting for his cue.

The doctor let out a deep sigh. "Emily, you didn't…I'll see you next week."

I started to ask him what he meant but stopped. I'd have a week to sit in my cell and think about it. One last look in his eyes and I didn't need to—I already knew.

# Eleven

## THE BLUE HOUR

*San Francisco County Jail, July 31, 1966. Beginning of Session Four*

Doctor Lieberman was at his desk when the guard led me into his office for our fourth session. He tipped his coffee mug over his lips, gulping down the entire cup. His eyes had raccoon-sized circles and his gray suit was more wrinkled than usual. I glanced around the small office and noticed a plaid flannel blanket and crumpled pillow on the brown leather couch.

"Donut?" he asked, holding out a row of powdered donuts.

I looked at the wedding band on his left hand and wondered if he ever had home cooked meals. "No, thank you."

"I've been going over the results of the tests I sent over Wednesday. Keep in mind, I cannot give you the MSO test until we have finished our regression therapy."

"MSO?"

"MSO stands for 'mental stability at time of offense.' I won't be able to assess that particular test until you remember the preceding events leading to the killing. All your other tests were negative."

"What does that mean?"

"You do not meet any of the criteria for mental disease. You tested negative for personality disorders as well as neurological diseases such as schizophrenia."

"Oh," I said, stroking my palms. Since the murder, I had rubbed my hands continuously—trying, I supposed, to remove Father's blood. The constant friction left them a chafed shade of red, which stood out against my pale skin.

"You have anxiety as we know from your panic attacks, but that appears to be situational. You have been able to control them with your breathing exercises."

"Yes…that's true."

The doctor leaned forward. "There is one area I want to study, which may influence your case. I can't explore it with you now, as I don't want to alter the momentum we have developed in recalling the details of your upbringing."

"But…I would like to know." I hoped for a blackout, sleepwalking, or something to minimize stabbing my father twenty times.

"I understand this is difficult for you. We are walking through this process together. I'm asking for your trust. I don't want to give you a suggestion that would impact your memory."

I trusted him. This probably wasn't the first time he had slept in his office, a space not much bigger than my jail cell. He was a crafty old wizard hooked on sugar, caffeine, and finding out why I murdered my father. "Okay, Doctor. I understand. I'm ready to continue."

*⤸*

I rolled a pencil back and forth on my lips. The air was hazy and humid, worse than usual for August. The fog in San Francisco thinned out in late summer and hovered over the city like a caravan of ghostly drifters. Seven days of hot weather brought the stench of rotting animal carcasses from the Hunters Point slaughterhouses. I looked up from my sketchpad and shook my head.

Grandma died exactly one year ago. After her death, a semi-sheer curtain dropped around me. Nothing had been the same since.

After her passing, Mother put her pictures and mementos away. I only had my sketches. But I missed the tone of her voice, the feel of her hand squeezing mine, and the scent of vanilla on her peach cotton apron. I couldn't get that from a drawing. As I said, nothing had been the same since that night.

That included Father. During the beating after Grandma's memorial, a part of me died. Maybe because that night I wanted to die, my battered mind and body wanted to go with Grandma and not experience pain anymore.

The beating also freed me. I stopped trying to be the good daughter. I ended my attempts to impress him, cut the cheerful smiles, and gave up on good deeds hoping to win his approval. Hope perished during that brutal beating, and unlike my ribs, my spirit never healed.

But the freedom had a flip side. Once I made the decision to give up, I became angry. Not the kind of anger that spilled superlatives, or slapped and stomped, but a silent anger and motivated belligerence. I also vowed to hide my pain in the hollowed out hole inside me. I promised myself he would never see the sorrow in my eyes.

My decision had consequences. Father's insults worsened, his slaps intensified, and his hatred for me deepened. He no longer had a punctuation mark signaling him to stop and lost the satisfaction of knowing he hurt me. There were times the torment became too much, so I came up with a strategy.

Every day, I listened for the sound of his footsteps and called death to my door. Death became a friend, the only thing capable of stopping the pain he continued to inflict on me. I gave myself the option to kill myself. It was no different than a combat soldier carrying cyanide as an alternative in the face of an inevitable and agonizing death. I used the strategy to get through the day. I probably would never commit suicide, but it helped me to cope.

I fought off the sinking sensation of hopelessness. I hated the coping game but it was my only weapon.

"*H*ey!" Reid grinned, wiping the sweat from his bare shoulders. "We won! We had a no-hitter until Montego got up to bat. I had to walk the guy. He's impossible to strike out."

I nodded, smiling as he went on to tell me inning-by-inning about the game. Reid was the starting pitcher and a star athlete and scouted by big-name colleges. But my smile had nothing to do with baseball and everything to do with watching him wipe a white towel along his muscular arms and the back of his thick neck.

He pulled a striped polo shirt over his head. "So, I searched for you. Why didn't you come to the game?"

"Oh, I'm sorry...I was, you know, busy doing things for my mother."

Not true, of course. Mother never let anyone help her; she wanted everything "just so." At a young age, I watched Robert make his bed, tucking in the sheets and making sure the bedspread didn't drag on the floor. When he left, Mother came in and tore off the pillowcase, bed sheets, blankets, and the coverlet. She ironed his sheets and spent thirty minutes fluffing his pillow so the sides were even. Eventually, we all stopped trying.

"Let's go to Mallard Lake," said Reid. He pulled me up and waggled his eyebrows.

As we walked, I noticed he had a skip in his step and a mischievous smile.

"Are you ready?" he asked.

"For what?"

"I have a surprise."

"What is it?"

"If I told you it wouldn't be a surprise."

I raised my eyebrows. "A-hah."

We walked along the dusty path leading to Mallard Lake. We officially ordained it "our lake" a while back. I went from best friend to girlfriend on the top of a Ferris wheel one year ago.

"We're almost there."

"Where?" I asked.

"Stop with the questions! It's a surprise, remember?"

Reid led me in the direction of the treed area surrounding the lake. Dried leaves crackled under our feet as we trudged through the thick underbrush. "Reid? Where are we going?"

"Uh-oh! One more question and I'll have to blindfold you!"

"No, you don't! Okay. My lips are sealed."

We slowed down as we hiked deeper into the wilderness. Reid marched a little in front of me to pull the lower tree branches aside before they smacked me in the face.

He stopped. "Now. Close your eyes."

"Huh?"

He squeezed my hand. "Trust me."

He walked behind me, guiding me with both hands on my shoulders. "Still closed?"

"Yeah," I said, shuffling through dried up leaves. "How much further?"

He moved to the side of me. "Okay, you can open your eyes now."

I rubbed my eyes and stared at a scene out of a romance novel with a Reid twist. He had cleared the trees and crafted a romantic setting in the middle of the wilderness. The centerpiece was a huge dark-blue blanket placed on the forest floor and secured with rocks. There were two pillows on the blanket and a folded white coverlet in the right corner. To the left, was an ice chest. A single rose graced one pillow.

"What do you think?"

I put my hand over my mouth and gazed at the scene. "It's beautiful! I can't believe you did this!"

"Do you like it?"

I glanced at his beaming face and then back at his creation. "Like it? I love it, Reid!"

"This is our place—ours. Just you and me. So, do you really like it?"

"When did you...?"

"Yesterday. I cleared the trees during the day, and last night I put on the finishing touches."

Reid led me to the spot, holding my fingertips like a princess being escorted to a gilded veranda by the handsome prince. The setting was nature's canopy of living trees, forming a protective shield around us. The branches formed dancing shadows on the blanket as the leaves whispered a soothing melody.

"Emily, this is our first place. Someday, I'll build us a beautiful big house in this spot."

I didn't have the heart to tell him it was county land. "That's so nice, Reid."

He ran his hands through my long hair like a sensuous comb, letting it trickle through his fingers. "You are so beautiful."

He held my face and kissed me. Deep. Intimate. My body warmed and tingled. I loved the feel of his hands caressing my body and hearing his breath quicken as he touched me. I stroked his muscular arms and legs, pulling him closer. It was like flying and melting at the same time. I never wanted it to end.

He stopped kissing me, lifted my chin, and gazed at me with his dark, dreamy eyes. "I love you, Emmy. You know that, right?"

"Yes. And I love you, too."

He turned on his back and drew me into his chest. I listened to his heart beating and the sound of his long sigh telling me he was happy. He kissed the top of my head as he pulled me closer.

Part of me couldn't accept what was happening. Doubts tampered with my mind like arsenic hiding in a bowl of sweet, creamy butter. At times, the experience of being in love seemed unreal, like I was enjoying the experience but it was happening to someone else. It made no sense.

The sun started to fade. "Promise me something," Reid whispered.

I snuggled closer. "Of course."

"Promise we'll never change."

"Change?"

"Yes, change. Promise me we'll always be 'us'. That we'll be together like this forever."

I thought about telling him he was my reason for breathing but figured it sounded abnormal, although true. "I promise."

The shadows of our wilderness home faded into subtle darkness. Reid stood up, taking me with him.

"It's time," he whispered.

I opened my mouth to protest, but he was already packing up. As we headed back, my muscles tensed, and my stomach tightened. Reid had promised our love was forever, but until I turned eighteen, our time was merely a snippet of pleasure surrounded by a snake pit.

We arrived at my house. He kissed me and smiled. "I'll see you tomorrow?"

"Yes," I said, fighting the urge to beg him to take me anywhere but home. "Oh, Reid…thank you for the beautiful day. I loved it."

When he left, I sat on the front steps, watching the reddened sunlight and orange blush of sunset yield to twilight. After Reid's declaration of love, I should be dancing in the street but instead, I felt empty. The joy of being with him made his absence equally painful.

I leaned against the porch pillar, experiencing the sinking sensation that always signaled dark thoughts and melancholy. After my beautiful day with Reid, I fought the unwanted downward pull with all the vigor I could muster. *What was this?* The gloom hung on, refusing to release me, pulling me into its murky hole. The feeling brought a pervasive wave of hopelessness. I closed my eyes and called the darkness forward, asking the depression to reveal itself. I wanted to dispel the atmosphere of darkness that continued to chase me.

After several minutes, an answer came—vague, like the faint flicker of a spent candlewick.

I was lonely. My happiness depended on Reid; it didn't come from within me. At home, I felt like a defect in an otherwise exceptional family. Mother had her beauty and breeding, Father, an outstanding career and wit, and Robert attended college at only fifteen. I had nothing special or unique. Eventually, Reid would figure it out and leave me. I would be an empty locket with nothing inside.

I let out a long exhale and pressed my palms against my eyes to thwart my self-pity. Enough, already.

The last of the sunlight scattered in the sky as the sun dipped below the horizon. Grandma always called it the blue hour—when the red light passed into space covering the sky in luscious, spectacular blue tones. The unrivaled beauty held me in its splendor long enough to erode most of my melancholy. I continued to gaze at the sweet light, wondering if Grandma might be close by, reminding me that I was special to her.

I hung around, thinking of Grandma, for the forty minutes it took for the blue hour to surrender to dusk. I told myself whenever I felt depressed and hopeless, I could spend those forty minutes with her enjoying the brilliance of the blue hour.

# Twelve

## Kisses and Daggers

It was a great day for a run. The marine layer dulled the sun, and the wind moved enough to keep the sweat from sticking to my face. September would be here soon, sucking the air into a stagnant misery. I rocked back and forth to loosen up for the long run.

I walked into the kitchen and found Robert leaning over the sink. His face was pallid, and his chest heaved up and down as he struggled to breathe. He wore a plaid bathrobe instead of his usual pressed white shirt and pants. Beads of sweat clung to his forehead.

"Robert? What's wrong?"

He turned his head and patted my hand. "Can you cover for me?"

"Sure...of course. How?"

"If you see Father, tell him I went for a run," he whispered, glancing at my tennis shoes.

I wondered if he realized he was still in his bathrobe. "Okay, but where will you be?"

"I'll hide in the backyard until he leaves. I don't want to deal with him." He cupped his hands over his mouth; I understood the signs all too well. Panic attack.

"Sure, no problem. You better go. Don't worry."

He wiped his brow and went outside. I stared at the closed door and wondered what made Robert so anxious.

Robert had left just in time. Father strolled into the kitchen dressed in a green golf shirt, beige shorts, and loafers. His skin was a dark tan, helped along with bottles of spray tan, leaving some spots a rusty orange.

He leaned against the counter, dropping two sugar cubes in his coffee. "Where's Robert?"

"Hmm?" I asked, buying time.

"Robert. Where is he?"

"Robert? He said he was going for a long run."

"Yeah?" He continued to stir his coffee, clanking the sides of the mug with his spoon.

"Uh-huh."

He raised his brows, a sign he was either in a playful or caustic mood. "So, you look like you're going for a run. Why didn't you go with him?"

"I wasn't quite ready, that's all."

"Ah-ha." He cocked his head, his eyes fixed on me. "So, you're wearing makeup now. The whole works, mascara, blush, and what's that? Blue eye shadow?"

"I guess," I mumbled, resisting an eye roll.

He took a few steps closer. "Hmm. Well, I think there's a problem with your makeup. Do you know what it is?"

The suppressed chuckle in his voice made me cringe. I bent down and tightened my shoelaces, determined not to take the bait.

"You can still see your face! Even Max Factor can't hide that!" He leaned back against the counter, chuckling.

I stiffened and bit my lower lip. The longer he laughed, the harder I clamped down on my mouth.

He continued to chuckle as he left the room.

When I unclenched my lips, I tasted blood. As I touched my mouth, I saw my fingertips were moist with fresh blood. I winced, realizing the force I had used to hold my emotions from Father.

It would have been easy to wallow all day and pout. "Run," I muttered.

I bolted out the door, not bothering to warm up. Mother's repetitive warning about "the street" didn't faze me; I picked up the pace. The air had a musty odor mixed with the scent of fresh cut grass. I kept running, in no direction other than "away." My chest started to hurt from breathing muggy air. I didn't care. I ran faster.

I ended up at the edge of a grassy knoll about three miles from home. I collapsed on the grass, panting. Not wanting to think, I concentrated on the patchy clouds moving into each other and out again. The aroma of bluegrass and the shapely puffs brought back memories of my time in Seattle. One summer, Grandma taught me how to tell one cloud from another. By the end of my month with her, I could name every one.

The clouds drifting over San Francisco were Cirrocumulus, which meant bad weather was on the horizon. I shook my head as I got up to walk home, hoping it wasn't a premonition.

I clomped up the stairs, brooding. Reid was gone, and Robert was heading to the library. I sat down on my bed to wait for Reid to return home and excise the poison of Father's words. His verbal insult had infected me with melancholy, and my only antidote was spending time with Reid.

Father did it again. Used his best weapon on me—the joke. It went like this: humor couched in cruelty with a hurtful punch line. If someone within earshot objected, he would say, "I'm just kidding." He was absolved, and the put-down weighed me down like a two hundred pound weight on a strip of cardboard.

An hour passed; the blues left me groggy and unmotivated. Weighed down. I forced my weary body to get up and search for Reid.

I found Mother in the living room engrossed in her latest novel. I could have snuck out, but instead, I stopped to watch her.

She was stretched out in her chair with her legs resting on the otto-man. Her face was unlined; she looked a decade younger than her forty-five years. She only had one flaw, her fingernails were worn down to the nail plate from the cleaning chemicals she used daily to scrub the house. Other than that, Mother defined perfection.

My brows pulled together, and my body tightened. She looked like a woman without a care in the world, but I knew better. Her mother had passed away, her daughter had been beaten and bedridden for two weeks, and her other daughter died a tragic death years ago that no one was al-lowed to discuss.

Her calm infuriated me. I wanted emotion—anger, sorrow, some-thing; the frustration stored in my head like a topped off gas tank inches from a flame. I glared at her, desperate for answers to how Penelope died, and why my father hated me.

"Emily, is that you?" Mother asked.

I stepped back. "Uh, yeah. I'm sorry. I was just going outside for a while. I didn't mean to disturb you."

"Oh, no. It's fine. Please come here for a minute. I want to talk to you." She grabbed her padded footstool and gestured for me to sit.

"Yes?" I searched her face for a clue; Mother never started a conver-sation unless she had something to say.

She put her book down. "The Navy transferred your father to New York, so we'll be moving in two weeks. They will pack our things. I'll be supervising them and making sure everything is packed correctly."

I stared at her. She continued to chat about clothing, but I remained stalled on the word "moving."

"We'll go through your clothing and dispose of the items that don't fit you anymore. The weather will still be warm when we arrive, but you'll need warmer clothing for winter. I'll shop when we get there, where they have more appropriate clothing for the colder climate."

"Wait…what?" I asked. "What did you say? Moving?"

She raised her eyebrows. "Your father accepted a transfer to New York City, Emily. We're moving in two weeks."

I waited for her to take it back. Tell me it wasn't true, that I misunderstood. The words floated in the room like a string of profanities.

"So, we're clear?" she asked.

My mind stopped the words from infiltrating my mind. "No…I don't understand."

"We are moving to New York City in two weeks."

I shook my head.

"This is a great move. Look at it as an opportunity. New York is the cultural center of this country. This will open up a new world for you. You'll experience the arts, museums, history…subjects you can't find in San Francisco."

The words took hold. "I don't want to move, please Mother! I don't want to go to New York. Please…please, don't make me go! I'll do anything…."

She clicked her tongue. "Honestly, Emily. You are acting ridiculous. We are moving to New York."

"No, please. You know Reid, right? I can't leave him. Please, he means a lot to me. I don't want to move." By the third string of "pleases," I started crying, running the words together and gasping for air.

"The transfer is settled. We're moving in two weeks. Now please, pull yourself together. Your reaction is absurd and your demands to stay here are pointless. Be grateful. This incessant crying is inappropriate," she said, her voice even.

For her, the move was a gift. For me, it was a death sentence. I ran upstairs and away from the verdict; I cried until my mind shut down into nothingness.

⌒

*I tilted my face to the afternoon sun. The warmth felt like soft butter, and the sea breeze wafted through my hair and tickled my skin. I strolled along Golden Gate Park, breathing in the white wisteria along the botanical gardens.*

*I smiled when I passed the Japanese Tea Garden and found Reid and Grandma. They rode on a gilded carousel of animals. Grandma rode a lavender horse with a carved golden mane, blue glass eyes, and a harness of pink roses. Reid traveled on a bronze lion with chiseled teeth and fire agate eyes. They both waved when they passed me and smiled.*

*I stopped in front of the merry-go-round and listened as the band organ played "Over the Waves." The carousel stopped, and Grandma and Reid cheered to me. I jumped on, excited. The carousel started moving again; I staggered on the platform to find an animal to ride. When the ride sped up, I cried out for Reid and Grandma.*

*I stumbled into a stationary cart. I no longer heard Grandma or Reid. I rode in circles in my cold metal cart, not moving up and down, with no one next to me.*

I opened my eyes. Sweat trickled down my face, my heart punched on my chest like warning shots from a sniper. I listened to the wheezing sound of my labored breathing, trying to outrun my dream. The meaning was inevitable.

I was moving to New York City, and there was nothing I could do about it.

<hr />

Reid knelt on the striped beach towel and pulled off his tee shirt. "Man, what a hot day! How about a swim?"

I shaded my eyes to get a better view of him. "Hmm?"

He jumped up and down like a prizefighter. "What do I have to do to get your attention, Miss Quinn? You're always in your head!"

I bristled at his words. Since Mother dropped the big news on me three days ago, I'd filled my head with everything except the move to New York City.

"Sure...I mean, about going for a swim." I stripped down to my two-piece orange bathing suit and let out a deep sigh. We'd been laying on the beach towel for over an hour, the ideal time to tell him. I sighed again, knowing there was no perfect time.

"Last one in!" Reid shouted.

The rocky surface pressed against the soles of my feet as I strolled into the cold water. I wasn't willing to jump in, any more than I was ready to leap in with the news about the move. My stride was sluggish; each step was like walking into a sinkhole. It was no different than my death-march to New York City.

He sprayed me with cold water. "Got ya, Emmy! Come on chicken, the water's not that cold!"

"Yes, it is," I shouted, making a half-hearted attempt to spray him back.

His chirpy mood was in stark contrast to my misery. Reid plunged into the water, and then shot up, swinging his wet hair to the side. "Dive in! The water's great!"

"I'm coming!" I inhaled and ducked underwater, came up, and swam out to meet him.

We frolicked, splashing water and laughing. The wall of water hurled at me masked my downtrodden face. I continued the silly game until Reid shouted for us to swim to shore.

He threw me a beach towel. "What'd ya wanna do today?"

I patted my skin, stalling for time. "I don't know."

He rubbed the towel through his dripping hair. "How about a show? *Night of the Living Dead* is playing at the Granada."

"Sure," I mumbled.

"Or?" Reid grinned. "Okay, you wanna see *The Sound of Music*, right?"

"What?" Reid's cheerfulness made it hard to tell him about the move. His joy also kept him from sensing my bad mood. I had rubbed the towel on my dry legs for ten minutes and he hadn't noticed.

"So, what do you think? *Sound of Music* or *Living Dead*?"

"I don't care...*Night of the Living Dead* sounds good."

"Oh, you're scared, aren't you? You're afraid I'll turn into a zombie!" He lunged forward and tickled me into involuntary laughter.

We sat on the towels waiting for our swimsuits to dry. Reid chatted on about horror films, as I tried to break the news. Between haunted houses, vampires, and werewolves, I couldn't find an opening. Maybe I didn't want to.

⁓

Twenty minutes later, we sat in a movie theater watching *Night of the Living Dead* with a box of buttered popcorn between us. My preoccupation with telling him blurred our time together—for me, anyway. I felt like an animated corpse going through the motions of the day without connecting to anything. While Reid watched creepy cellars and zombies, I viewed *Romeo and Juliet* with ill-fated kisses and daggers. The plot was tragedy and loss, whether in the form of a tattered zombie or rosy star-crossed lovers. It was all the same.

I admired Reid's profile in the darkened theater and wondered how to survive without seeing his face or hearing his voice. I wanted to memorize everything about him. I listened to him gasp at the horror scenes and then laugh. I noticed he grabbed more popcorn during the gory scenes and grabbed my knee every time something surprised him.

The lights came on, startling me out of my bleak tragedy. I sat up straight, trying to shake off my maudlin thoughts.

"Wow! What a neat flick!"

"Yeah, really good," I muttered.

Reid grabbed my hand and led us out of the dimly lit theater. "Did you like the show?"

"Of course," I answered, hoping he'd leave it at that. I'd stared at the screen for two hours and had no idea what happened.

"Do you wish you'd seen *The Sound of Music*? We'll catch that one next time."

I cleared my throat and wondered if he'd picked up on my glum mood. "Sounds good. I'm just thinking about stuff."

"Me too," he said, swinging our arms as we held hands. He walked with a lift like he had the world in his pocket. His exuberance made telling him inappropriate, like crying at a child's birthday party. Even so, I had to tell him. The truth loomed over me like a giant mallet waiting to shatter my life.

"Yeah?" I asked, wrinkling my nose. I studied his face and wondered why he was so jubilant.

"Yep! I've been waiting all day to tell you."

"Oh?"

He pointed to a bus stop bench. "Come on, let's sit. I can't wait any longer!"

"What is it?"

He grabbed both my hands as we sat on the bench. He turned me, so we faced each other. His giddy expression became serious. I gnawed on the inside of my mouth, worried about what was coming.

"Emmy, do you remember when we were young and we played tag?"

I felt myself frown. "Well, sure..."

"We played tag all the time. Do you remember?"

"Yeah." I wanted to add "and so" to hurry him along. Reid liked to draw out the story before he reached the punch line.

"Well...I've been thinking about it."

"You have?"

"A dozen kids on the block played with us, but I always tagged you."

"Uh-huh." Part of me wanted to blurt out my news and end his riddle. My news was earth-shattering, and he sat me down only to give me a long wind-up and pitch about a kid's game. I swallowed an exasperated sigh and waited.

"Do you know why?" He squeezed my hand, so I guessed the punch line was next.

"Uh...no, I don't."

"I tagged you because I wanted to say 'you're it,' that's why." His lashes blinked slowly; the revelation seemed like a big deal to him, but I couldn't say the insight bowled me over.

I forced a smile. "Thank you, that's so sweet."

"I meant more than that though," Reid whispered. "Even as a kid, I knew you were the only one for me. When we played tag, I loved to say the words 'you're it.' And now, look where we are!"

"Yeah." His words were corny but that was Reid. He made a big deal out of small things. He knotted his fingers through mine and stared into my eyes. I decided to sit back and just enjoy myself, knowing our time was marked on the calendar.

"I wanted to give you something to remind you of me." He reached into his pocket and pulled out a small heart charm with a single red rhinestone in the center. "I bought this birthstone for you, but someday, I'm going to buy you a ring."

I smiled and mellowed at the sentiment. We had seen the charm in the Coronet Drug Store window last week. "Aw, that's so sweet of you! It's beautiful!"

"I wanted to give you something...you know, to remind you how much I love you."

Those three words eclipsed everything. Tomorrow, a hurricane could sweep me out to sea, a bolt of lightning could send electrical currents coursing through me, or my parents could exile me to New York City against my will. But right now, the words "I love you" obscured all of it.

I admired the sweet charm. "I love you, too."

"I'll always love you." He kissed me; it was different somehow because it carried the provenance of love and a future.

I was startled back to reality by the sound of a rattling engine, blasting air, and the loud clunk of a bus door opening.

"We're not going!" Reid shouted to the driver, as he grabbed my hand and pulled me from the bench.

The rest of the day played like a love story minus the tragic conclusion. I told myself Reid's words, "we're not going," were a premonition that no matter what happened, we would always be together.

I needed to tell him about New York—but not now. Today was enclosed in a gilded frame and kept safe in a ruby-studded hope chest. The day was untouchable and impervious to whatever harm the future might hold.

# *Thirteen*

## CRACKED AND DAMAGED

"Emily," Mother called out from her room. "Are you going through your clothes?"

I put down my pencil and waited for her question again. A row of moving boxes marked "New York" and "Goodwill" stood in my room like snarling dogs.

I glared at the empty containers and stuck out my tongue.

"Emily, did you hear me?"

Mother stood in the doorway with rolls of brown packing tape around her wrists like bracelets of doom. "Why didn't you answer me?"

"I was sketching," I said, squeezing Reid's heart charm. "I just finished a picture of Grandma. Do you want to see it?"

"Why in the world are you drawing when we leave in one week? You haven't even looked at your clothes!"

She shook her head as she walked to the closet, eyeing the color-coded clothing. I cringed at the sound of the metal hangers as they rubbed along the steel rods.

"I'm sorry," I said softly, knowing I wasn't all that sorry. I wanted to keep my clothes where they were—four doors down from Reid.

She gave me a long stare. "Okay, we'll start with the blues." She placed the moving boxes on the floor next to the bed. "We'll go through them together. If something doesn't fit anymore, it goes in the Goodwill box. We're going to get this done today. No excuses."

"Yes, ma'am." I put Reid's charm in my pocket, noticing an imprint on my hand from squeezing it so tightly.

"Here," she said, handing me a button-down shirt. "Take them off the hangers."

Removing the clothes was like packing the remains of a deceased relative. With each one, I sank a little deeper. I was an unwilling participant in what felt like a crime. And I hadn't even told Reid.

Mother laid each piece on the bed and flattened her hands against the garment like a makeshift iron. "What about this one?" she asked, holding up a blue angora sweater.

"It doesn't fit anymore, but I want to keep it. Grandma bought it for me the last time I stayed in Seattle." I supposed my admonition had been more of a protest, knowing she removed all reminders of Grandma after her death.

I studied her as she held the sweater—a standoff of sorts, waiting to see whether she would discard the sweater in the Goodwill box.

Mother hand-ironed the sweater and smoothed the nap. "Emily, I left a pen on my nightstand. Can you please get it for me?"

"Of course."

I hurried back to my room with the marker but stopped in the doorway. Mother held the sweater against her cheek, cuddling it like a baby blanket. Her eyes were closed, and her black hair fell against the blue angora like silk ribbons floating in a pool of water. She caressed the sweater, singing a lullaby from long ago.

*"Hush-a-bye, don't you cry,*
*Go to sleep my little baby.*
*When you wake you shall have*
*All the pretty little horses."*

I crept back and put one hand over my mouth, listening. Her tone was maudlin, like the overture of a tragic opera. Was she singing to Penelope? Grandma? Me? It didn't matter. What mattered was that my robotic, measured mother showed emotion. I soaked it up.

After a time, she stopped singing. I walked back to the room like nothing had happened.

She placed the sweater in the "New York" box, once again deliberate and detached.

She continued to fold and unfold each garment until she was satisfied the sides were evenly aligned. I longed to embrace her, to be the blue angora sweater she held in her arms. Guilt gripped me, but I didn't know why. When our work concluded, she left without a word. I stared at the space and wondered if, behind her beauty and perfection, my mother was broken.

⌐

I pulled back the curtains and opened the window for the third time. The marine fog that typically lingered over the bay had been absent for days, leaving the air sticky. Storm clouds hovered over the land like black rain.

My stomach tightened, adding ache to the queasiness. Today was the day. No more excuses. In three days, a big Mayflower truck would be parked in front of my house like a giant billboard telling Reid I was moving and didn't have the guts to tell him.

After six clothing changes, I settled on a white blouse and green capris, the same outfit I picked the first time. I chewed my fingernails and stared at my bedroom door, trying to get up the nerve to go outside.

I ran downstairs without thinking and jumped onto the porch. The porch seemed sterile, hardly the place I had welcomed Reid over the last fourteen years. Black mushroom clouds billowed in the sky, ominous plumes sulked over the Earth like the aftermath of a nuclear explosion.

"Hey!" a voice shouted. "You seen Reid?"

I jumped and gasped at the same time, startled out of my apocalyptic state.

Tom, one of Reid's friends, carried a baseball bat in one hand and a mitt in the other. Tom idolized Reid and for good reason. The red-haired, freckled face boy was barely five feet tall and was born with a clubfoot. All the team members called him a water boy, but Reid always called him his backup pitcher.

"No, I haven't seen him."

"Well, when you do, can you tell him I'll be down at the field? There's a game at one."

"Oh sure, I'll tell him," I replied, noting the paradox of the words, "I'll tell him."

He left. I leaned against the porch pillar and rehearsed how to tell Reid. "Reid, there's something I hate to say, and it kills me, but my parents are making me move to New York...Reid, you mean everything to me," I whispered under my breath.

"Geronimo!" Reid broad-jumped from the sidewalk to the porch, right into my arms. He looked sporty and adorable in blue cut-off jeans and a red polo shirt. "Did I scare you?"

"Oh...yeah...you did."

He grabbed my hands. "Let's go to the lake and watch the rainstorm over the water. It'll be better than the Fourth of July!"

"Oh, sure. But wait... I almost forgot. Tom came by earlier looking for you. Isn't there a game today?"

He leaned back, his eyebrows raised and smiled. "Yeah, and?"

His expression told me the guys would need to limp along without their star player. "And nothing."

He held out his hand. "Shall we go, my lady?"

We arrived at Mallard Lake in what seemed like a minute. Clouds loomed over the lake like monsters prowling the lagoon for foolish swimmers.

We sat near the water. Reid was playful and spunky, hardly the mood I needed for a serious talk. "This is so cool!"

He pulled me into his arms and kissed me with long, wet kisses. I went through the motions but didn't find it all that enjoyable. I couldn't experience anything but the repetitive departure speech that played in my head.

He pulled back and began rubbing my arms. "Are you cold?"

"Nah," I mumbled.

"Babe, your arms are full of goose bumps."

"It's not that, really." Actually, the damp sand felt good against my clammy skin. The goose bumps were fear, he just didn't know yet. "Reid, I need to..."

He interrupted. "We need a run. Come on, let's go!"

I had no time to react; we sprinted along the shore in what seemed like a high-speed marathon. I struggled to keep up.

"Over there! The sand is better!" Reid shouted, pulling me down.

His energy was wearing me out, and his happiness had become annoying. I wanted him to be miserable like me and pick up on my despair. It would make telling him much easier. "What do you mean, better?"

He didn't wait for an answer. He gave me a long, sensual kiss. Then came another, and another.

He jumped up and grabbed a long stick. "Okay, a contest! See how far you can throw it into the lake. You first."

I glanced at him, expressionless, not wanting to play a stupid game. I threw the darn thing, which landed a few feet from the water.

"Babe, you can do better!" He ran for the stick; I wondered why in the world he fetched it when hundreds of sticks surrounded us.

We had played a few minutes before he started moving in circles, dragging a stick along the sand. I only half-watched him, as I rehearsed how to tell him about New York. I rested my head in my hands with an occasional glance his way.

He stopped. "What do you think?"

"Hmm? About what?"

"Take a look!"

I walked to where he was standing. He had carved a big heart in the sand with "E and R" written in the middle. I glared at the epitaph.

"Too dumb?" Reid asked.

The inscription crumbled my reasoning. I fell to the ground. "I love it."

He dropped beside me, putting his arms around me. "What's wrong, Emmy?"

I pulled away. "I'm moving to New York."

"Whoa! Was the drawing that bad?"

I stared at the letters drawn in the sand. "No," I muttered.

"What?" His voice had a lull, confusion.

"The Navy transferred my father to New York," I said, sounding like a tape recorder. "We leave in three days."

"What? Wait...you mean this isn't a joke? Come on, you're kidding, right?" He cocked his head to the side and stared at me.

"No, it's not a joke. It's true."

He picked up a twig, broke it in half, and continued snapping until it was too short to break. He took another stick and did the same thing. We sat in rigid silence, as he broke one stick after another.

He stared at the sand. "When did this happen?"

"About two weeks ago."

He turned to me and squinted. "Hold on. Wait a minute. You knew weeks earlier?"

"Well, yes. I tried to tell you...I did."

"When? Yesterday? The day before? You let me spill my guts to you every day, telling you how much I loved you when all along you knew you were leaving?"

"No," I said, turning to him. "That's not true. I just didn't want to spoil everything."

His eyes narrowed. "Bullshit! You could have told me, but you let me go on and on about how you are the only one, and we'd be together forever. I even bought you a charm but did you tell me? Hell no! Saying all those things was a big deal to me. You were laughing behind my back the whole time!"

I put my hand on his elbow. He snapped his arm up.

"No, Reid! I wanted to believe what you said. It's not my fault that my father is being transferred. I don't want to go. You must know that!"

He glared at me. "You played me for a damn fool!"

"No! I didn't!"

The sticks that he had ceremoniously snapped in pieces were piled on the sand. He scooped them up with both hands and rose to his feet. He released his grip and watched the broken bits fall to the ground. Without looking at me, he turned and started in the direction of home.

"Reid! Wait! Please!"

He stopped without turning and held his hand up.

I jumped up and ran toward him. "Reid! Come back! Just stop!"

He put both arms up like a Herculean stop sign.

"Reid! Wait!"

He started running—fast.

I collapsed on the sand and wrapped my arms around my shaking body. I watched him disappear, wailing, willing him to return. It was hopeless.

The engorged blackened cloud that had held its reign all day unleashed its rain like gunfire. I put my head down and let the downpour pelt my body. The watery bullets were a welcome distraction from my internal anguish. The angry storm was nothing compared to the damage inflicted by Reid walking away.

⟷

"Emily! Did you hear me? We leave for the airport in thirty minutes!" Mother shouted from the bottom of the stairs.

"I heard you!" I tied jute string around my Bloomingdale's box so I could carry it on the plane. I couldn't take the chance of losing every sketch of Grandma, Penelope, Reid, and my imaginary girls. I ran my finger along the edges feeling like it was my only friend. The gold-leaf pattern had worn down, but the old box was still sturdy.

I glanced around my empty bedroom, thinking about Reid. I hadn't seen him in three days. I'd walked the streets, combed every corner of Mallard Lake, and even sat in the bleachers of the baseball field until nightfall.

Of course, I blamed myself. I should have told him right away.

I ran my hands along the pleats of the gabardine suit Mother had picked out for the occasion. It seemed as though winter had arrived three months early, she dressed me in a navy blue ensemble with a nautical collar and pleated skirt. The suit was hot and scratchy; a rash was starting to form on my neck. She ordered it from a catalog along with other east coast fashions. They would never sell suits like this in California.

"Emily! Get the hell down here! Time to go!" Father bellowed from downstairs.

I took a last look at my bedroom. Without the furniture, the space was an off-white rectangle, but still, I hated leaving in spite of the misery I'd endured here. This was where I had written to Grandma, sketched, and once giggled with Penelope.

I moaned, thinking about all the times I'd daydreamed about Reid and waited for him to come home.

I stood above the creaky third step. I pressed the toes of my white shoes down, emitting a barely audible squeak. My full weight would send off a pleasing screech, like relieving a tummy aching belch. But I couldn't commit that final act of defiance. I rolled my eyes, fearful of twelve inches of wood and Father.

Mother appeared from the kitchen, breathless from rushing around checking to make sure all the cabinets were shut, the locks turned, and the curtains lined up with equal folds on both sides. "Emily! Why aren't you in the cab?"

I shrugged, not trying to hide my misery.

Mother patted her hands through her hair, pulled back in a French twist. She belonged on Madison Avenue, clad in a pink and gray suit, a pillbox hat, stiletto heels, and a gray handbag draped over her forearm. "We need to go, dear."

"Sorry. I was on my way."

She touched my elbow. "Emily, this will be a good move. The east coast will enrich your life and give you more experiences. This is the best part of your father being in the Navy, being able to see different parts of the world. If he makes Admiral, he could be stationed in Europe. Imagine living in France or England."

I started to object but stopped. "Yes, ma'am."

We walked outside, my head craned in the direction of Reid's house. How could I leave this way? How could he let me? My legs weakened as I stared at his house.

Mother put her arm around my shoulder. "Our taxi is here, dear."

My stomach took a jolt at the sight of our ugly yellow cab. Father sat in the front seat giving an olive-skinned cab driver with a Cantonese accent driving directions. The poor man bobbed his head up and down signaling he already knew how to drive to the airport. Robert was in the backseat dressed in a light blue suit doing a crossword puzzle.

Mother tapped my shoulder. "Emily, dear…Mr. and Mrs. Hemet are here to say goodbye."

I had been too dazed to notice them. "Oh, hello…and goodbye." I cringed, knowing how rude that sounded.

"Take these oatmeal cookies I baked for you all," she said. "Airplane food is terrible! Not that I've ever flown in one, but my niece is a stewardess and she tells me the meals come from a can."

"Thank you," said Mother. "I'm sure Emily and Robert will enjoy them."

"You have a safe trip now," said Mr. Hemet.

As they walked away, I thought about how much Mrs. Hemet reminded me of Grandma. Open. Friendly. Mrs. Hemet and Grandma stood a little closer to God than the rest of us.

Mother slid next to Father in the front seat. My hand held the door as I took one last look up the street. I couldn't believe I was leaving without talking to Reid. I placed one foot in the cab and the other on the sidewalk, suspended between my urge to keep looking for him and forced expulsion.

*That's when I saw him.*

Reid leaned against the side of our house with one hand in his pocket and the other upraised in a stagnant farewell. His beautiful brown eyes were wistful with an air of gloomy acceptance.

I bolted from the cab-crypt. "Reid! I'm sorry, I'm so sorry!"

"I didn't say it right...I should have told you earlier. I'm so sorry! I didn't know how...I love you more than anything. I've been looking for you... Reid!" I became breathless from talking so fast. Out of control. My passionate pleas collided with fallen tears. "Reid...forgive me," I said, panting.

His arms tightened around me. "It's okay, babe. I'm sorry too."

I nuzzled my face into his chest and wept, pathetic and emotional, but I didn't care. I wanted him to understand what I had failed to express at the lake.

Someone grabbed my arm. I swung around to find Mother. Father cursed in the background, but I was crying too loud to make out the words, nor did I care. Mother kept one hand on me and the other stretched like a stop sign toward Father.

She kept her hand on my arm. "Emily dear, we have to go."

Reid glanced at Mother and then loosened his hold. "It's okay, Emmy."

I pushed back into him.

"I love you, and we are not over. I promise you," he whispered in my ear.

Mother led me to the cab with one arm around my shoulders. I kept my eyes on him, unable to control my spontaneous outbursts.

As I slid into the backseat, Robert patted my hand. Mother hushed Father, and the cab driver cleared his throat and started the engine.

I pressed my hand against my mouth as the car turned the corner. Mother reached back and locked my side of the car door. Father cursed a blue streak under his breath as Mother continued to shush him. Robert kept his eyes on me as the driver pushed the gas pedal to sixty-five miles per hour on the freeway and took the off-ramp marked "Airport."

$\backsim$

*M*other pointed out the window of our rental car. "There is the Metropolitan Museum of Art! They call this area the Museum Mile because it has more culture in one mile than anywhere in the world!"

Robert and I nodded with an "a-ha" as she pointed out the Empire State Building, the opera houses, and Lord & Taylor. Father cursed nonstop as he tried to navigate around all the taxicabs and pedestrians in New York City.

Mother's hair had loosened from its French twist and fell in gentle curls at the nape of her neck. Her blue eyes widened as she leaned forward, pointing out the landmarks. I wondered if leaving San Francisco had lifted her spirits, after all, Penelope died there. The house, parks, and even the local stores must have been a constant reminder.

I settled back on the bench seat and gazed out the window. I felt gutted, like someone had scooped out my heart but somehow I managed to keep breathing. A few hours ago on the airliner, I overheard my parents talking. Father's commitment to this Naval Station was three years. On top of that, if he made Admiral, we could be off to a foreign country—a ticket to cultural Heaven for Mother, but Hell for me, at least until I turned eighteen and could return to Reid.

Father cranked up the air conditioner and lit a fat Cuban cigar. The perfumed deodorizer the rental-car agency used to mask the odor of cigarette smoke and baby diapers spewed a foul odor from the air cooler vents. I fiddled with the metal ashtray on the door handle to distract me from my nausea.

"Knock it off!" Father shouted.

"Stop tapping, dear," said Mother. "Your father's never driven in New York City and the noise is distracting."

"Goddam moron!" he yelled. "I've told you a hundred times!"

She interrupted his diatribe. "Keep your eyes on the road, please Jacob. Look! There's Rockefeller Center!"

I knotted my hands in my lap, trying to sense the beauty of New York as Mother pointed out the splendor of the city. I didn't feel the same way. Sure, there were lots of fancy stores, museums, and landmarks, but it was hard not to see the adversity. Trees lined the streets but were stuck in cement instead of dirt. People tossed their trash on the cracked streets; every corner had soggy candy wrappers and cigarette cartons piled over the gutters. The historic buildings Mother marveled about were beautiful but years of speeding cars and cabs had coated the facades with filth. Every other street had a wrecking ball poised to tear down an old structure in favor of a sky-reaching glass box or concrete office tower.

This was not the elated handshake to New York Mother had predicted. I closed my eyes to stop the onslaught of cracked and damaged images. Once I shut my eyes, I still saw the ruinous scene because *I* felt cracked and damaged. The city was a reflection of my malaise and disappointment in being here.

The familiar sinking sensation settled into my bones, muscles, and mind. I steadied myself with a cleansing breath. This was going to be a very long three years.

*San Francisco County Jail, July 31, 1966. **End of Session Four***

I opened my eyes and listened to loud buzzing coming from the hallway. Bleach charged through the single vent in the room, trapping the odor in the small office.

"Sorry. Buffing!" He put the last period on his notes and shut the binder. I wasn't sure if he was waiting for the worker to move the buffer down the corridor or thinking about our session.

"Just a few minutes. They don't use mops anymore. The buffers are faster but loud, I know!"

I nodded and wondered if the cleaning crew ever came in his office. Dust covered the file cabinets, his desk, and everything seemed to be old and dirty. I supposed he didn't trust the prison workers around his confidential documents and the sordid details of the capital cases he studied.

"Good session!" Doctor Lieberman yelled above the racket.

I studied the doctor and waited for the noise to lessen. He was interesting, beyond his idiosyncrasies. His desk was frenzied except for a pair of framed pictures. He dusted them regularly— like now.

He wrapped the corner of a handkerchief around his index finger, rubbing the wood to a shine. I could only view the back of the pictures and wondered whom he cared about enough to keep them tidy and honored. A wife and children seemed the logical choice, although I wondered why his wife would let him out of the house in a shabby suit and coffee-stained tie.

As he picked up the second picture, the holder broke and dropped flat on his desk. It was a young girl, about five years old, with her arms around a much-younger Doctor Lieberman. He leaned the framed picture against a metal tray on the corner of his desk.

The loud buzzing dwindled to a hum. "I'll have to fix that," he said, his voice trailing off.

"Your daughter?" I wondered why he didn't have a more recent picture, but it made sense considering all the old belongings in his office.

His eyes softened, and he let out a long sigh. "Yes, my daughter."

"How old is she?"

He removed his glasses. "Five. She was five when she died of Tay-Sachs disease."

He had probably shared the tragedy a hundred times, but I had a feeling the heartache was brand new. He picked up the second picture and placed it beside his daughter's photo. "My wife," he said. "She passed two years after my daughter, Rachel's, death."

I hated seeing the pain in his eyes but felt honored that he had shared something so personal. He seemed to have no one. I looked at his lined face and wondered if he was in his own form of solitary confinement.

The doctor flipped through his file of papers. "Emily, you've been progressing nicely in hypnosis. Between our sessions, do you find your memories returning with more clarity?"

"Yes. The flashes I experienced when I first came here are becoming...well, more like real memories, I guess. It's kind of like one memory leads to another."

"That's good. In your journal this week, I would like you to expand on how you were feeling in New York in addition to your activities. Write whatever comes to your mind. It will help you get in touch with your memories on an emotional level. You are ready for that."

I stared at him and frowned. "What do you mean exactly...when you said, I'm ready?"

He patted the papers. "You are ready to face your feelings. Recalling what happened provides a level of information but understanding why you did certain things gives you clarity."

"Oh," I mumbled. I hoped he was right, although the thought of learning my motivation for murdering my father terrified me.

"I am confident that you can handle whatever comes out, and I will be here to help you."

I found myself smiling, having come a long way since my first meeting with him. "Okay. I can do it."

He smiled back. "I'll send over some new notebooks."

A guard stood next to me. "Time to go, Quinn." She was a young officer with carrot red hair and about my age. Her hands trembled when she snapped the handcuffs on my wrists. I winced, knowing she feared me.

"I'll see you in a week," said the doctor.

He tucked the picture and the broken frame into his tattered brown leather briefcase. Something told me he wouldn't waste any time replacing the frame and returning it to its rightful place. The pictures held the only spot of clarity and prominence on his old muddled desk.

"Thank you." As I gazed at him, my heart sank. His daughter, Rachel, died at exactly the same age as Penelope.

# Fourteen

## Fresh Paint

***San Francisco County Jail, August 7, 1966. Beginning of Session Five***

The officer removed my handcuffs and chained me to the chair, as usual.

Doctor Lieberman glanced at the officer. "No ankles, please."

The young redhead guard blushed. "Um, it's regulation, sir."

"The shackles impede my hypnosis, please remove them."

"But..." The poor guard's face turned as red as her hair. "It's the rule, sir. I mean, Doctor."

Doctor Lieberman shoved the papers to the side. "I'm sorry, what is your name?"

She touched her badge nervously. "Jennifer...Jennifer Payton."

His expression softened. "Jennifer, it's a pleasure to meet you. Please don't worry about the regulations. Once she is in my care, she is no longer your liability. I take full responsibility."

She shifted from one foot to the other. "Oh, okay. I appreciate that. I didn't know."

"Of course."

She started walking out the door, leaving me shackled to the chair.

126

"Jennifer," he called out with a quick point to my ankles.

She blushed and leapt to undo the shackles. I felt sorry for her; she seemed too timid to work with inmates.

Doctor Lieberman nodded. "Thank you, Jennifer."

"You're welcome," she said, as she scuttled out of the room.

He picked up the stained carafe and poured black coffee into his mug. "So, Emily," he said, lowering himself into his swivel chair. "How was your week?"

"Good."

"Good tells me nothing. It's a banal adjective at best."

He finished his coffee in one long gulp and poured another. I scanned the room as I tried to think of something. The old photos of his wife and daughter were now encased in matching pewter frames.

"Emily, in reading over your journal for the time you lived in New York, I noticed the entries are sparse. Can you tell me why?"

I sighed, realizing I had few memories. "I remember a lot about New York and my time there, but there was a real gap of sorts."

"What do you mean?"

"I just waited for the time to be over. I knew I'd be in New York for three years, so I bided my time. Mother would take Robert and me to plays and stuff, but I remained in my room most of time. Robert stayed with me a lot, talking…keeping up my spirits. I prayed the Navy wouldn't make my father an Admiral so I wouldn't have to move to Europe."

Doctor Lieberman tapped his index finger on his mouth. "I see. You were depressed. You postponed your life."

"Yeah, I guess I did."

"We may or may not go back to your time in New York, but right now, I would like to take you to the time when you moved back to San Francisco."

"Oh…okay."

"Are you ready?"

"Yes, I'm ready." I already understood the drill, as I sat back and closed my eyes, prepared to retrieve the memories that led me to jail.

The jetliner landed on the runway with a thump followed by a rougher thump. I flipped the armrests down and braced myself as the airliner skipped to an abrupt arrival. Judging from the open mouths and gripped hands of the other passengers, I wasn't surprised to hear audible sighs as the pilot announced, "Welcome to San Francisco."

I sighed, but not because of the rough landing. The three-year pause in my life was finally over. Reid's last words, "I love you" and "we're not over" had been my constant invocations.

But I needed to find him first. We exchanged letters every week for nearly two years but then his letters slowed to an occasional short note. Six months ago, they stopped. I continued to write, but he never wrote back. I came up with a lot of plausible reasons but only glanced at the possibility that he forgot about me. It would have made my loneliness in New York unbearable.

After a twenty-minute taxi ride, we arrived at a stately home on Orchid Lane in Pacific Heights. The new house was miles from the old house and miles away from Reid. I lagged behind to get a better view of the new place. The mansion was hardly the tract house we lived in before. I walked into a massive living room with well-placed windows and a stunning view of the city. The fog had cleared enough to see the Golden Gate Bridge.

The kitchen had teak countertops and turquoise appliances. The cabinets were ceiling-high with glass inserts displaying fine crystal. A garish chandelier hung above a wood and glass dining room table. The black and white marble floors were slick, and copper pans hung on yellow domed pot racks.

I leaned against the teak counter, taking it all in. A captain's salary could never pay for this mansion. *Grandma's money.* Mother inherited a truckload of cash and stocks following her death. Grandma's breathtaking estate, artwork, and everything else had been liquidated with a huge deposit into my parent's bank account. Not a single picture hung of her, but the opulent house was a symbol of what her death had done for my parents.

"Humph," I said, under my breath. Grandma would have hated this place and I do too.

Mother stood in the doorway. "Emily, come see your bedroom."

Mother hadn't changed a bit in three years; if anything, she was more beautiful. Her chestnut brown hair was now shoulder length and fell around her face in feathery waves. With her blue eyes and full red lips, she was still the most striking woman I'd ever seen.

My mouth formed a spontaneous "wow" as I gazed at my bedroom. It looked more like a grand master bedroom suite than a spare room. Mother spent months pouring through the catalogs of Ligne Roset for the right furnishings to ensure everything was "just so" and delivered before our March twentieth arrival date.

The ceilings were twelve feet high with painted beams that matched the crown molding along the base. The plush taupe carpeting was thicker than my old twin mattress, and a massive walk-in closet was about the size of my earlier bedroom. The décor was professionally designed, from the sophisticated white Italian linen drapes and matching bedspread, the modern Scandinavian furniture, and the original Nicolas Carone abstract painting on the feature wall. Every dresser, wall hanging, clock, and pillowcase oozed money.

"The room is so pretty," I said to Mother. Father stood behind her and tossed me a dirty look.

"I'm glad you like it," she said.

Father walked off, pounding his feet on the hardwood floor for added drama.

Mother gave me a conciliatory smile that said, "Oh well," as she followed Father.

I kicked off my shoes and stretched out on my new double bed, wondering what Mother would be like without Father.

The three years in New York helped me understand my relationship with her. She was livelier in New York and wanted Robert and me to experience the culture of the city. She took us to operas, and we dined in the finest restaurants. She tutored us in the arts and provided us with advanced books to read. We spent a lot of time discussing the French Revolution, the art of Cezanne and Renoir, the war in Viet Nam, and the assassination of President Kennedy.

But we never laughed, cried, or shared anything personal. It was like reading a newspaper but craving a love letter. I longed to talk to her about boys and how to make friends. So, I was grateful for all the cultural experiences but would have traded it all to sit on the sofa with her watching a soap opera with a box of Kleenex and popcorn.

"Cool room, huh?" Father leaned against my door casing with his arms crossed. He had traded his traveling clothes for beige slacks, a sage green button-down shirt, and a tweed jacket.

I sat up straight. "Yes, very nice." I gave him a fast glance and began putting away the pencils and various odds and ends packed in a small box on my end table.

"Your mother hasn't organized it yet."

"Oh, yeah," I said, placing the tablet and pencils back in the box. After seventeen years, I was still awkward around him.

"This is the biggest spare bedroom, you know."

"No, I didn't know," I mumbled. "Mother said this was my bedroom."

He took out a nail file and began filing his manicured nails. "She feels sorry for you."

I knew he wanted me to ask why, but I had learned long ago to avoid that snare. Besides, I'd already been injected with his sardonic toxin directly into my self-esteem.

He casually swept the file along his nail. "She thinks you're a retard."

I stiffened as my resolve not to show him my anger rang out in my head like a war cry.

"I'm going to talk to her about Robert taking this room."

"Go ahead."

"We'll see how far her pity for you goes. This room should be Robert's."

"Fine." I dug my nails into my forearm and waited for him to leave.

He stuck the file back in his pocket. "You're such a bitch."

He finally left. I let go of my arm, now imprinted with nail marks. I surveyed the room, wishing the doorway had bat-winged gargoyles that would attack Father when he tried to hurt me.

"Err," I groaned, pulling my hair in front of my face. The violent image triggered the memory of me laying face down on the gritty black-top being pummeled by Father. The beating remained in my soul as a reminder of his brutality and hatred.

I closed my eyes, trying to escape the negative thoughts. I couldn't let Father ruin me, not if I wanted a life with Reid. I opened the Bloomingdale's box under my bed and flipped through one of the sketchpads. So many drawings of Penelope, my imaginary girls, places I wanted to see. I settled on a sketch of Grandma and traced her face, asking for strength.

A pounding on the door interrupted my thoughts. "Em, open up!" Robert called out.

"Robert, get in here!" I ran to the door and gripped his arm. "Robert, we're back!"

He grabbed the desk chair and sat down. He already seemed like a doctor in the rolling chair, greeting his patient.

"Really! We're back in San Francisco!"

"Yeah?" he asked, drawing out the word.

"Yeah! I know you'll be going to college soon, but aren't you glad to be back? Where do you think you'll go?"

"Well, I'm looking at colleges. Hopefully, Harvard."

"Harvard? But that's so far away. Isn't there a medical school in San Francisco?"

"Yeah, Stanford. We'll see."

"Okay, but I hope you pick Stanford. You'll be a great doctor."

"I hope so."

Robert had matured into a handsome guy. Not the killer good looks like Reid, but attractive and confident—the kind of looks that wins votes if you're running for Senator. His features were well proportioned and his eyes were gentle, even a little sad. He wore nice clothes but never faddish.

He leaned in closer. "So, why is my sister happy to be back in San Francisco?"

"Well...you know. I hated New York. Plus, I have friends here."

"Friends?"

"Yeah, friends. You know."

"Like, Reid?"

"Yes, he's everything to me. But it's been three years since I've seen him. What if he doesn't think I'm pretty enough?"

He raised his eyebrows. "Come on. Have you looked in the mirror? You're a knockout. Any guy would think so."

"Oh, you're just saying that because you're my brother."

"Are you fishing? Do you think Mother is pretty?"

"Duh—yes."

"Well, you look just like her...so, there you have it."

"Oh, Robert! You say the sweetest things!" I drawled in my best southern belle accent.

He laughed. "Okay, so what's the deal with Reid? What do you mean when you say he's everything?"

"Well, he just is. He's everything."

He spoke to me in his usual calm and patient way. "Everything?"

"Yeah, everything." I shrugged, doubting Robert understood the crazy feeling of being madly in love.

"He can't be everything."

"What do you mean?"

He rolled his chair forward. "Okay, listen. It's not good to focus on one person. You should develop your own identity. Have a purpose that's unique to you. Centering on one person will only set you up for disappointment. We talked about this a lot in New York, about our goals and starting over. This new beginning should be about you, not someone else."

It was hard not to smile at him. He had become in every way, my parent. "I know, Robert…and those talks in New York helped me a lot. I'm just happy to have a new start. Sometimes I wondered if we'd ever leave New York. And here we are—finally!"

"So," he said. "What does this new start look like?"

I tried to think of a good response to impress my genius brother. "Well, it's like the walls, Robert. They're freshly painted, right? All the grime of the past is gone, and they're brand new again. I can be new too and see what life brings me."

He slumped, a sign he didn't like my answer. "Okay, Em. I better go. I have a lot of college forms waiting for me. Be careful, okay?" He stood up to leave.

"Oh, sure."

Robert whirled around. "Don't do it!"

I threw up my hands. "Do what? Don't do what?"

"Wait to see what life brings you. Come on! Isn't it time you take control of your life and not let other people decide what you can or can't do? I don't want you to get hurt again."

"Reid's never hurt me," I said.

"I'm not talking about Reid. I'm talking about life. Get in the driver's seat and write on your own wall. Don't wait around for someone to draw you. You're better than that!"

"I know…"

"Listen, I'm leaving for college soon, and I'm worried about you. I hate leaving you alone."

I didn't want him to worry. He'd spent the last several years checking on me, encouraging me. His face had worry lines at only eighteen years old, and his eyes held a sadness that never went away. I wanted him to follow his dream without fretting about me.

"It's okay, Robert. I'll be fine."

His worry lines deepened. "You'll call me if you need me? You know I'm always there for you, right?"

"Of course I do…always."

"Okay, Em. You'll get there! Just remember, you have a lot going for you and don't let anyone tell you otherwise!" He winked and darted off to his college applications.

I grabbed the fluffy white throw-blanket folded on the bed and wrapped it around my shoulders. Robert's words left me uncertain, puzzled. He understood so much more than me. I stared at the blank walls trying to figure out the meaning of his words. The best I could do was remember his last words "you'll get there," hoping someday I would figure out the meaning.

# *Fifteen*

## TRAP DOORS

*I* tossed back the covers. "Today," I muttered, putting my bare feet on the floor. It was pointless to stay in bed worrying about my reunion today with Reid. I'd slept two hours, tossing and turning between elation and dread.

I had already chickened out three days in a row. The first day, I dressed and primped and sat in my bedroom chair praying for the nerve to board a bus and find him. The second day, I had a panic attack walking down my street. On the third day, I made it all the way to the bus stop before turning back.

I held a cool glass to my face to tame the anxiety rash running from my cheeks down to my neck. I rolled my eyes, knowing my face was a dead giveaway for my insecurities.

"Try, try again," I told myself.

My walk-in closet was loaded with new clothes, all picked out by Mother. She'd spent months studying *Glamour* and *Seventeen* magazines to make sure I'd look like all the other twelfth graders. Time to pick out another "perfect" dress.

As I sat on a cushioned footstool, I rubbed my bare feet back and forth on the thick carpet. "Focus," I muttered. "Get up and stop thinking."

I pushed the dresses down the wooden rack, checking out the paisley prints, corduroy jumpers, and the floral shift dresses.

"That's it," I whispered. I picked up an ice blue sweater dress with long sleeves and a rounded neck. The color reminded me of our lake. I slipped it on and added the black shoes that Mother had paired with the dress.

My heart started to skip along with the familiar "run or die" sensation. I grabbed the paper bag from my purse and sat on my bed breathing in and out like I'd done a hundred times.

My respiration evened out but not my insecurities. I sat up, rocking back and forth, wondering how to muster up the courage to travel to the old neighborhood to see Reid.

"Draw something," I said aloud to myself. My fingers trembled as I outlined the face of an imaginary girl. I kept going, making her confident and pretty, telling myself I could be her. After another thirty minutes, I convinced myself that I was a self-assured girl who had the guts to find Reid.

∼

I stared at Reid's front door. "Focus on the door, Emily," I mumbled. "Keep your eyes straight ahead. You've waited three years. Don't move. Reid's door will open, and you can begin your new life."

My heart pounded. "You can do this."

It hadn't helped walking by my old house. The new owners changed the paint from blue to a sunny yellow and planted flowering rhododendrons up the walkway. Even the new color and lovely flowers couldn't mute the queasy sensation in the pit of my stomach.

"Err," I mumbled, remembering the torment I endured in that house of horrors.

I shook off my troubled thoughts and remembered Reid's last words, "we're not over."

I ran my fingertips through my hair. "Okay." I reached up to ring the doorbell.

Mr. Wagner, dressed in a green tee shirt and white shorts, swung the door open. He eyed me up and down, stroking his massive muscles. "Well, young lady...hello."

"Uh...h-hello," I stuttered.

"My, my. Aren't you a pretty thing."

I pretended not to hear him. Reid's dad was the same man I remembered before I left for New York but three years creepier.

Mrs. Wagner appeared and nudged her way in front of him. "Emily," she said, smiling. "What a lovely surprise. Please come in, dear."

"Thank you." I glanced to her side, half-expecting Reid to jump out.

Mrs. Wagner escorted me to the sofa. She sat next to me while Mr. Wagner sat in an armchair across from me. The living room was simple but tidy, with early American furniture, flowered wallpaper, and a brick fireplace with a mantle filled with pictures of Reid.

Mr. Wagner raised his eyebrows. "So, you're little Emily. Not quite so little anymore."

"I'm seventeen." I pressed on my trembling knees and listened for Reid's voice.

Mrs. Wagner glanced at her husband. "Just a few years younger than Reid."

Reid's poor mom wore a beige housedress and the same pink and white crocheted apron she had on three years ago. Her brown hair was still styled in a short bob, and she wore no makeup other than pink lipstick.

"Emily," said Mrs. Wagner. "Can I get you something to drink?"

I started to agree but didn't want to be left alone with her husband who was checking out my legs. "No, thank you." I pulled the hem of my dress and put my hands firmly on my lap.

"It's so good to see you, Emily," she said. "Did you enjoy your time in New York?"

"It was nice, but I'm happy to be back," I said, louder than needed, hoping Reid would hear me and come running down the stairs.

Mr. Wagner grabbed his keys. "Good seeing you, Emily." He left, probably uninterested in playing pervert to Pollyanna.

Mrs. Wagner scooted closer to me. "Are you sure I can't get you some iced tea? I made a fresh pitcher...it's very good."

"That would be nice," I answered, hoping to remove the gravel from my throat.

She returned with a tray of chocolate chip cookies and raspberry tea. If I didn't know better, I would think she had expected me. Reid's mom was June Cleaver minus the fancy clothes and glamour.

Sipping tea and munching on cookies relaxed me enough to pop the question. "Is Reid home?" I asked, as nonchalantly as I could manage.

"No, Reid is away at college. He's going to Colorado State. He got a full baseball scholarship." She pointed to the framed pictures of Reid on the fireplace mantle.

"Colorado?" My body went limp, unable to focus or form more words.

She put her hand on mine. "But he will be home this summer and will be so glad to see you."

The last thing I wanted was to be rude to her. "Oh, good. I moved back four days ago. I thought he might be home."

"Of course, dear. Reid will be so delighted to know you came back to San Francisco. He was so disappointed when you left."

I searched her face, hoping she wasn't just being polite. "He was?"

"Oh, yes. He's very fond of you. He talked about you a lot. You kids have known each other for so long..." Her voice trailed off. "I miss him so much." The poor lady had no one to fuss over except her philandering husband.

"Yes, I've known Reid since...well, always."

"Oh, yes," she said. "I remember how he would push you around in his red wagon. You were just a tot, not even in school yet."

I couldn't hide my disappointment much longer. "Well... I better be going. Thank you so much for the tea and cookies."

"Anytime, Emily. Reid will be so disappointed he missed you."

"Would it...I mean, would you mind if I left you my address? Just in case he would like it?"

"Oh yes! Please do," she said. "Let me get a paper and pencil."

After a few more niceties, we said our goodbyes. She assured me she would tell Reid I came by and give him my address.

With the paneled door behind me, I stood on his porch to compose myself. It never occurred to me that Reid would go off to college in another state. It was hard to picture him anywhere but San Francisco.

I walked to the bus in limbo, not thrilled but not devastated either. I just needed to get through the next three months of high school. Reid would be home in June. In the meantime, his mom had my address so I was sure he would write.

*I* fumbled with my key, ready to sleep off the rotten day. Not only had I learned that Reid was away until summer but also had to put up with his horny dad. Then, I got stuck next to a sweaty drunk on the bus who reeked of beer and collided into me at every stop.

I stepped into the front room and rolled my eyes, recognizing Father's Pierre Cardin slacks underneath a newspaper. I tried to sneak past him.

I cringed at the sound of paper crumpling.

"What are you doing?" he asked. He smoothed the newspaper and placed it on the coffee table.

"Not much." The question and the folded paper told me he wanted a confrontation. I didn't. I decided to do my time and leave quickly. Indifference was my best weapon. Of course, it's play-acting because every word he had ever said to me was like stepping on dog feces; no matter how hard I scraped the bottom of my shoe, it still stunk.

He looked like he'd just returned from the stylist; his hair was short on the sides and wavy on top. He wore a fitted yellow shirt, slacks, and a two-toned belt, which matched his expensive Italian shoes. I chewed the inside of my mouth to prevent the scowl that begged to come out. He enjoyed Grandma's money, and all he ever did for her was change a few light bulbs and beat her granddaughter.

He gestured to one of the chairs. "Sit down."

I sat on the edge of the chair, trying to read his face. My mask of indifference changed to uncertainty. He lounged on the sofa with his arms resting on the back as though sitting with me was a typical occurrence. He smiled and his left eyebrow tweaked slightly, signaling he was in a good mood. I wondered what I'd walked into—first Mr. Wagner and now him.

"So, are you glad to be back in San Francisco?"

I stared at him and waited for the eventual putdown.

"Isn't it great to be back here?"

"Yes," I answered. I tried to remain calm, but he talked in a language I didn't understand. We never engaged in casual conversations—ever.

"Me too. A lot of changes in three years, huh?"

I wondered if this was a trick question. He seemed as relaxed as a man sprawled in a hammock, while I was on a three-legged chair on the edge of a cliff.

"Yes...a lot of changes."

"Did you notice the new game park?"

He talked much louder than necessary or maybe my brain had turned up the volume. "Yes."

Robert walked by carrying an empty glass from his bedroom to the kitchen.

I started to get up. Father waved me down.

He leaned forward. "Let's go sometime. Wouldn't that be fun? How about tomorrow?"

I stared at him with my mouth open. I didn't try to hide my bewilderment.

"So, Emily," he said with a raised voice. "How about it?"

I was sure Robert heard him from the kitchen. It was strange, not only was Father talking to me, but he *wasn't* talking to Robert.

I glanced between Father and the kitchen, trying to figure out what was going on.

"How about it?"

"Well...sure, okay."

Father sprung up once he got the answer he wanted and grabbed his keys from the coffee table. With a few words about filling up the car for tomorrow, he left.

I stared at the front door, dazed.

Robert came out of the kitchen. He shrugged. I understood his body language; I'd seen the look before. He always followed the expression with "too weird" which he said as he headed for his room.

What just happened? Nothing seemed real. Why would it? Father hated me; I spent every day dodging his venom. Had someone convinced him to start over with me? Mother? Robert? God? Could my new beginning include a relationship with my father?

I shook my head. "No way."

I headed to my room with a fleeting hope that Father wanted to start over. The hope was fraught with trap doors, and I didn't know if I wanted to risk the danger for a chance to have a real father.

⌒

I glanced at the clock and set my pencil down. My hand ached from drawing for nine hours. At five in the evening, I was still in my pajamas. I took a deep breath and exhaled. This was New York again, staying in my room, trying to blunt the tiring effects of depression.

"No," I muttered. It was three months not three years. Doubts crept into my thoughts. Why did he go away to college? Why had he stopped writing to me?

I went to the closet and began flipping through the neat pile of sweaters on the shelf. I'd never been to a department store or picked out my own clothes. Mother enjoyed shopping, close to a hundred brand new sweaters were stacked on the shelves. Not ordinary cardigans, expensive designer brands from Saks Fifth Avenue and the finest stores. I picked up a navy blue cashmere sweater and gasped at the price tag of two hundred dollars. The sweater had a cowl neck and was softer than a blanket. It might as well be itchy wool; I hated navy blue. I tucked the pullover in with the others, knowing I would have to wear it someday. What a waste of money. Grandma's money.

Someone knocked—a fist knock. That meant one thing. Father. I cracked the door open.

"You ready?" Father asked, wearing a Hawaiian shirt, beige pants, and loafers. He smiled, a bit forced, but a smile.

"What?"

"The game park, remember?"

I held back my gut response: *are you kidding and did you really mean that yesterday?*

"Uh..." I stuttered. Speechless.

"Don't you remember? The new game park?"

"Oh, yeah."

I stared at the stranger out of uniform, this casual man in penny loafers and a Hawaiian shirt, and wondered if all the cruelty and sadistic badgering had been sewn into his Navy uniform or something. The man in front of me was someone I'd never met.

"Fifteen minutes?" he asked.

"What? Oh...sure."

I closed the door, clutching the waist of my cotton pajamas, fighting stomach pains. Nothing made sense. Father's change toward me was too radical and lacked a transition. My head swirled with confusion, so I went into autopilot. I dressed in a hurry, trying not to think or keep him waiting.

When I grabbed my purse, I caught my reflection. I thought about the little girl that would sit in her room thinking of ways to win her daddy's approval. But years went by and his hatred for me intensified. I gave up. But looking at my seventeen-year-old self, I still saw a remnant of that little girl who wanted to be loved by her daddy.

I walked outside to find him. Confused, afraid, and kind of hoping.

# Sixteen

## GOING IT ALONE

*F*ather leaned against a porch pillar tossing his keys up and down. "There you are! Let's go have some fun!"

The word *why* screamed in my head. Why are you taking the daughter you despise on an outing?

We stopped at a new red Corvette. The old saying "money can't buy happiness" didn't apply to Father. Since retiring from the Navy and inheriting Grandma's money, he splurged on designer suits, Rolex watches, and now a fancy hot rod.

He swung open the passenger door. "Cool ride, aye?"

"Sure." I got into the car thinking how his new haircut, suntan, and casual clothes made him appear younger than his fifty years.

He stepped on the gas. "Here we go!"

"Yeah," I said, cringing at my one-word vocabulary.

He chatted about the car, from the V8 engine, the chrome grill, the convertible top, and the top-of-the-line options. He drove ten miles over the speed limit, which made the cabin roar. I nodded with a steady stream of "wows" and "cools." If he rattled off car features all night, right down to the top stitching on the seats, that would be perfect because we had nothing in common, and I wouldn't have to talk much.

He turned down an isolated road. I glanced at him and wondered why he stopped talking. The road had no streetlights. No porch lights. In spite of the unlit street, he did not slow down.

My muscles tensed. The headlights on his sports car beamed like dull flashlights into the darkness. The road was narrow with shadows of vegetation on both sides. No other cars were on the road. Father drove in silence with his eyes straight ahead.

The wind whipped through the ragtop as adrenaline pumped through my body. I had to think fast. Clues I hadn't thought of before now seemed obvious. He had never taken me anywhere alone before tonight. I'd never seen the car before so he probably rented it. He drove fast. Too fast to survive a fall.

He had planned the outing for one reason. *He's going to murder me.*

It only took a few kind words for me to walk into his snare, like a farm animal crammed into a truck headed for the slaughterhouse. He was going to shoot me in the head and leave me in the wilderness to rot.

Air continued to whip through the tiny cracks between the ragtop and metal door. He drove at least fifty miles per hour. My fingers searched for the door handle. I had to jump. It was my only chance.

He turned down a busy street with store lights, lamplights, and pedestrians.

I let out a relieved exhale and glanced at Father. Why had my mind gone to such a crazy place?

We pulled into the game park. "We're here!" he shouted, jumping out of the car.

As we walked along the outside festivities, the night sky sparkled with dotted lights from the Ferris wheel and roller coasters. The colored lights of the carnival rides flickered on his smiling face. He seemed like a regular dad, not the murderous mobster I envisioned five minutes ago. I realized this was the father Robert knew.

The arcade was animated with flashing lights and the sounds of pinballs as they ringed and dinged their way into the sounds of children laughing.

Father opened the arcade doors for me. "Pretty noisy, huh?"

"Sure is," I said.

He pointed to a machine vacated by a young couple. "We got one! Let's go!"

"Okay," I replied, cringing again at my one-word vocabulary.

He threw a few nickels into the machine. "Blast off!"

He pulled the flippers and screeched as they hit their targets. I tried to shake off the guilt of believing he invented a murder plot instead of a fun night out. I still found it unfathomable that he could turn from a dictator to a normal dad.

He put more coins in the slot. "Your turn, Emily! Give it hell!"

"No, I'd rather watch you play."

"You sure?"

"Yes, definitely."

Seeing him in a lively setting showed off his playful side. He cracked up, danced a jig at his high scores, and shared a funny story about playing marbles in the gutter when he was a kid. I felt bland in comparison.

"How about a Coke and some fries?"

"Okay," I agreed, still unable to move beyond a one-word answer.

The tables were jammed, but Father managed to find one next to the kitchen. "Fun place, huh?"

I sat up straight. "Definitely."

He scanned the arcade. "I suppose Robert is too mature for this kind of thing."

"He is?"

"I think so, he didn't want to come tonight. I guess it's not cool to spend time with his dad anymore."

I chewed my fingernail, wondering what to say. "I think he's busy... that's all."

He took his eyes off the crowd. "What does he say to you?"

I opened my mouth to say something but couldn't think of a thing.

"Why do you think he would still want to spend time with me?" Father asked.

I bit my bottom lip, trying to think of something. "Well, I'm sure he appreciates all the fun places you guys go."

"I'm not so sure. He's been turning me down a lot lately."

"He's just busy getting ready for college, filling out the forms and all."

"We used to do things every weekend," he said, his voice trailing off.

"I'm sure," I said, flicking my straw. Talking with him was unnatural and almost unbearable.

He stared into his glass and ran his fingers along the brim. "I've given this a lot of thought. Going to Harvard is a mistake. He should stay here and go to Stanford. Robert is barely eighteen. I don't think he can handle the shock of a big Ivy League medical school so far away. He went through college way too fast. I was there to support him, but I can't if he leaves."

I stared at him, speechless. Robert could handle any medical school in the world. He started college at fifteen and sailed through in less than three years. Still, for some reason I wanted to cheer him up.

"You might be right."

He bent his straw as he stared down at his coke. "Will you help me with this?"

My heart skipped, and my hands started to sweat. "Excuse me?"

He put his hands in his lap, "Will you help?"

I rubbed my sweaty palms on my pants. "How?"

He leaned forward. "Get him to stay. Your mother and I disagree, she'd come unglued if she found out we were talking. You'll keep this between us, right?"

I gazed at the stranger. "I guess so."

"Please, Emily. It's important."

"All right."

"Good. She thinks Harvard is the only decent school in the country. I'm the one looking out for Robert. I understand him better than anyone. He's more sensitive than people think."

"Uh-huh."

"You don't want Robert to make a mistake, do you?"

"Of course not."

"I knew I could count on you," he said.

"Excuse me," I said, turning my head. His remarks were ludicrous and his words flowed too smoothly, like talking with me was an every day thing. *When had we ever counted on each other?*

He took a long sip out of his drink and set the glass down slowly. "This is important to me and to Robert. Do you want to help me?"

I struggled to keep a straight face. "Sure."

"Thank you. Here's what I want you to do. Tell Robert you over-heard me talking to Mother about her being sick...that she didn't want him to know, but she wished Robert wouldn't go away right now."

"Wait, what? What's wrong with Mother?" I shouted over the noise.

"No, no, no! Nothing! It's only a story! There's nothing wrong with your mother. She's perfectly fine."

"Then, why?" Telling Robert a lie about something so tragic seemed cruel and unthinkable.

He grabbed my hands. I recoiled, I couldn't help it. Throughout my childhood, I feared his hands, they were a symbol of violence and hatred. *Even though our hands touched, I could not feel them.*

"Please listen. There are all kinds of illnesses, like the flu, diabetes, heart disease, right? But what about the sickness of the heart? She's not even aware how devastated she'll be if Robert moves to Boston. Telling Robert a white lie will save them both from a terrible outcome."

I studied his face, trying to find a hidden message. Was he thinking of Penelope? Another loss could devastate Mother.

"You would be doing me an enormous favor and one I won't forget."

"Oh?" I asked, buying time.

"Yes, I wouldn't ask you if I didn't believe it was the right thing to do."

"Well..." Telling Robert a lie was wrong, good intentions or not, but I needed time to consider the connection between Robert leaving and my sister's death.

"Emily, I've thought this out on every angle. I will be so grateful to you. And we had fun tonight, right?"

I swallowed hard. "Oh…sure, of course."

"Will you help me?"

I took a deep breath and slowly exhaled. "Okay," I said, knowing he wouldn't give up.

He slapped the table. "Good!" He threw down a five-dollar bill and stood up to leave.

We left. The abrupt departure made me question his motivations. As we drove home, he didn't talk, which left an awkward silence. I shifted in my seat and stared out the window as the car raced down the street.

At least I didn't think he planned to murder me on a dark road, so that was a beginning.

⌒

April in San Francisco was beautiful. A hint of dew from the cool night temperature left a glisten on the manicured lawn and bead droplets clung to the fan palms. The Forsythia that lined the driveway showed a spectacular bloom of bright yellow flowers. I leaned back in the chintz porch chair and thought about starting school in a week. High school was bad enough but starting at the end of the year brought a payload of obstacles.

I moaned and covered my eyes. The drive to the game park crept into my thoughts, along with the guilt. How could I have imagined Father capable of murdering me?

Cluttered thoughts began to weigh me down, so I grabbed my pencils to plot a story. Each stroke eased my worries as I escaped into a drawing of a girl with raven hair. She strolled through an orchard of apple trees wearing a simple white dress and slip-on shoes. The morning sun sent beams of light through the trees.

My reverie was broken when I heard a noise.

"Excuse me. Hello, I'm Stella Cushman. I live across the street."

I dropped my pencils. "Oh, I'm sorry. I didn't hear you at first." She was a pretty elderly woman with blonde hair combed in loose curls around her chin.

"No, don't apologize," she said. "First of all, welcome to the neighborhood. I also wanted to tell you the city is repaving the street tomorrow. They're asking us to move our cars off the road by eight tomorrow morning."

"Thank you. I'll tell my parents."

"I'm sorry to have startled you."

"No, you didn't. I mean, that's okay."

She leaned forward. "Oh, my. That's beautiful. Did you draw that?"

I folded my arms across the picture.

"Do you mind if I sit down and look closer?"

"I'm sorry, of course," I said, embarrassed I hadn't invited her to sit down. I moved the picture closer to her.

She held the drawing longer than I had expected. "What's your name, dear?"

"Emily Quinn."

"Emily, this drawing is beautiful. I love the way you used the different colors to catch the imagery of the orchard...and your shading is excellent. You're an artist, aren't you?"

I smiled like a goofy cartoon character. "Not really. I just like to draw."

She patted my arm and smiled. "Oh, this is much more than a drawing. This is art. You have a gift, my dear."

"Wow," I blurted out. "Thank you so much."

"You're very welcome. I'd love to come to your gallery opening someday. It was a pleasure to meet you."

I wanted to throw my arms around her and kiss her. "It was nice meeting you, too."

She got up to leave. "Keep drawing, Emily!"

"Thank you! I will!"

I couldn't stop smiling. For the first time, I felt special. I thought my art was just a way of coping, but if what Mrs. Cushman said was true, that meant my art had a higher purpose. I closed the sketchpad, wondering if a chance meeting with a nice lady had changed the course of my life. I couldn't wait to talk to Mother.

I entered the house. Father was huddled with Robert on the couch extolling the virtues of Stanford. I found Mother in the kitchen scrubbing lunch plates, tuned-in to the conversation in the living room.

I sat down to a chicken sandwich and a small bowl of grapes. "Hi, Mother. I'm sorry I'm late."

"Hello, dear. Please eat your lunch."

"I met one of our neighbors today, Mrs. Cushman. She said we needed to move our cars by eight because the city is repaving the streets."

"I know, dear. There was an announcement in the paper."

"She's a friendly lady."

"Yes. She greeted me yesterday and seemed pleasant."

The small talk was getting me nowhere. "Mother, do you think I can draw?"

She leaned in the direction of Father's voice. "What do you mean?"

"I was sketching, and Mrs. Cushman came by and went crazy over my drawing. She said I had a gift."

"That was nice of her, dear."

My approach was not working, or she was too distracted by the conversation between Robert and Father. I started to show her the drawing but stopped. I'd witnessed too many headshakes over my "C" report cards. Still, I had to ask.

"Mother, do you think I'm an artist?"

She stopped eavesdropping and sat down at the table. "Why do you ask?"

"Mrs. Cushman thinks I'm talented. Maybe art can be my career."

She moved her lips to the side and squinted. "Well, no one draws for a living. Artists have a passion. It's not a career they pick out of a college catalog."

I dismissed her response as a general answer and not at the crux of my question. "What I'm asking is whether you think I'm talented at drawing."

"Of course you can draw, dear. Anyone can draw but drawing doesn't make you an artist. Art is extremely competitive, and most artists don't make a decent living."

"But I could study art in college and get better, right? I could learn how to paint and sell my paintings at shows and stuff?"

"There are other ways to use art, dear. You can study art history or become a librarian. If you want to use your hands, you can go to beauty school and become a hairdresser. There are many careers you can choose if you like art."

I gawked at her, speechless. She delivered the verdict and the punishment at the same time. She might as well have said, "No, you have no talent, and put away your sketchpad and do my hair."

She smiled and returned to the countertop. She picked up a can of Pledge, polishing the wood to a yellowish-brown patina. I watched her shine the teak counter to perfection, but she had thrown enough muck on me to sully a landfill. I retreated to my bedroom.

Robert leaned against my doorframe with his arms crossed. "Spill it."

I glanced up and shrugged. "Spill what?"

He sat down with his hands clasped behind his head. "Are you going to talk?"

I had no intention of reliving my talk with Mother, especially with the Harvard/Stanford protégé. "About what?"

"Come on, Em."

"My name is Emily!" I snapped, remembering his childhood "I'm Robert" period.

"Okay, I'll let you call me Rob if I can call you Em. What'd you say?"

"No, I want to call you Robby, not Rob," I said, unable to control the smile forming on my face.

We both laughed. The absurdity of our dialog was hilarious. We both stood in the doorway of adulthood negotiating which names we should call each other.

Robert laughed and then turned serious. "What's upsetting you?"

"I don't know," I mumbled.

He leaned forward. "Emily?"

I glanced at him and shook my head. "I talked to Mother about me being an artist someday."

"Okay. So, why did that upset you?"

I shrugged. "It just did. A neighbor liked my drawing, so I wanted her opinion. That's all."

"What did she say?"

"She said anyone can draw but that doesn't make me an artist. She suggested becoming a librarian or going to beauty school." I recited, in a singsong fashion.

"A dream killer, huh?"

I smirked. "Yep!"

"What do you think?"

"About what?"

"Do you want to be an artist?"

I wanted to tell him "enough already." I felt myself getting mad. "What difference does it make?"

A silence followed. "Let me see it."

"See what?"

"Let me see your sketchpad."

I shot him a blank look.

He put both hands out in a "give it to me" posture. "Under your bed. Hand it over."

I tugged at the bedspread. "Huh?"

"Do I have to fight you for it? I'll win. Come on, I want to see it."

"Ugh. You never give up, do you?"

"Not where you're concerned."

I reached under the bed and handed him the sketchpad.

He turned each page and studied the drawings. I felt like he was studying x-rays trying to find a disease. I glanced at him long enough to see the sensitivity in his eyes. I resented him at that moment.

He closed the book and sighed. "Emily, she was wrong."

I grabbed the sketchpad off his lap, tearing one of the pages. "I know! Mother already told me!"

He held my wrist. "Stop it! You don't understand!"

"Err!" I hid my face in my hands, my body jerked as I welled up.

"Mother was wrong! Dead wrong! Damn it to hell! Just listen to me!"

I glanced up and wiped my eyes.

He grabbed my shoulders and turned me so I could see him. "Listen! Mother was dead wrong! She's never even bothered to look at any of your art! I've always loved your drawings! They blow me away! Don't let her shit on you! She doesn't know what the hell she's talking about!"

The words "she was wrong" rung in my ears like a siren at midnight. Mother being wrong never occurred to me. One thing I understood for sure: I had gone to the wrong person to validate my art.

I snickered. "Robert. You said the words hell and shit."

"I had to say something to get your attention, goofy. Don't tell Father Flanagan."

We both laughed—the kind of laugh that puts a period at the end of a conversation. "Robert..." I whispered, trying to find the right words to tell him what he did for me.

"I know." He touched me on the shoulder and got up to leave. He walked to the door and stopped. "Believe in yourself, okay?"

I bit my lower lip, which had started to quiver. "Yeah, I will."

I heard Robert grab his keys and leave the house. I pressed my palms against my eyes to snuff out the tears. I felt happy and sad. I was happy he'd convinced me my drawings were good but sad because I knew in my heart he had chosen Harvard.

I couldn't tell him a cockamamie story to trick him into staying. It would have benefitted me, but I couldn't do that to him. When Father put the negatives in my head and Mother gutted me with disinterest, Robert had been there to fill my head with mirthful sonnets to breathe hope into my tired soul.

Now, I had to go it alone because my sweet brother would be moving to Boston.

*San Francisco County Jail, August 7, 1966. End of Session Five.*

I felt hollow when Doctor Lieberman brought me out of hypnosis. I missed my brother and wanted to see him.

The doctor glanced at me without releasing the grip on his pen. "One moment, please."

It amazed me that such a frail man could write with such vigor. I looked forward now to our weekly visits, to some extent because it gave me a break from solitary, but also because I'd grown to like him. He never treated me like an inmate and, in spite of the murder charge, he managed to make me believe I had some good in me.

He took off his glasses and rubbed his eyes. "Are you okay?"

"Yes," I answered. "I was just thinking of my brother. I miss him."

"That's understandable. Your relationship with him was close, and he played a parental role in your life."

The hollow sensation expanded with the word "parental." Robert's role changed from brother to guardian the night of Grandma's memorial with "angel" mixed in. "I can't see anyone until I'm done with therapy?"

"I understand it's difficult, but right now it's necessary in order to gain an unbiased depiction of what happened. Your memories are quite clear, Emily. I'm happy with your progress."

"I'm sorry," I blurted out.

He set down his coffee mug. "Why are you sorry?"

I tugged at the rubber band in my hair. "I'm just sorry...you know, I'm not helping you."

"In what way are you not helping me?"

"Well, my memories...they aren't helping you with my case."

He clasped his hands under his chin. "While it's true I am helping you recover your memories in order to find mitigating factors, that is not my primary role."

I cleared my throat and wondered if I had stepped into confidential territory. "I don't understand."

"My primary goal is to bring you to an understanding so you can rebuild your life. Are you worried about whether or not your memories can be applied to your case?"

"Well, partly. Mostly I'm thinking about the people in my life. But I thought you were looking for mitigating circumstances."

His glasses had slipped to the edge of his nose. He held his expression, calm but serious. "Your mother hired a team of attorneys to strategize your case. I'm here to help you."

"But I thought she hired you to help the lawyers find excuses for why I did what I did. Aren't those mitigating circumstances? Isn't that what you write in those papers?"

He took a long gulp of coffee. "My intentions are clear. To retrieve your memories and find the defining moments that changed the trajectory of your life. After that, I want to help you rebuild your life. It won't be the life you had before, but I am hopeful it will be a life you can shape into something worthwhile."

"Oh, I see. Thank you." I could have pushed the subject because a worthwhile life in prison seemed unlikely. But I left it alone because his words sounded encouraging, even empowering. I didn't want to mess with that.

Doctor Lieberman poured himself another cup of coffee and unwrapped a vending machine offering. I put my head down so he couldn't see me grin. The man never ate anything that didn't come with a plastic sound.

"Emily, there is something I want to explore with you."

The door opening interrupted him. It was the young guard, Jennifer, holding my restraints.

"Jennifer." He got up and engaged her in quiet conversation. She shifted from one leg to the other and listened. Whatever he said must have reassured her because she nodded and left the room.

"Now," he said. "Can we explore an issue that came up in one of our sessions?"

"Sure."

"When you look in the mirror, what do you see?"

"Well, me...I guess."

"But you step back and become a stranger before you look at your reflection. Why?"

I shifted in my chair. "I don't know."

"Take me through the process."

I paused for a few seconds. "Okay, well...I don't like to look in the mirror. I never have. I don't feel connected to her."

"Why do you refer to your reflection as *her*? Explain that."

I took a deep breath, unsure how to explain. "I don't feel like she's me...exactly. I mean, I know it's me, physically. But she makes me feel uncomfortable. So I draw someone else, I think."

"I want you to close your eyes and relax." His voice became rhythmic. "Go back to the mirror, and tell me how you feel."

I closed my eyes and tried to replay it in my mind. My heart started to race and my palms began to sweat. "I always see a girl. She's scared. She makes me feel bad...guilty, I guess."

"Who is she?"

"I know she's me," I answered. "But I have to avoid her."

"Why do you have to avoid her?"

"I don't want to be her. I've never wanted to be her."

"Okay, Emily. Open your eyes and tell me who you want to be."

I opened my eyes and lowered my head. "I pretended to be the girls I sketched every day. That's how I felt strong enough to...you know, be close to people like Reid. Drawing helped me feel better. I felt normal when I could be them instead of the girl in the mirror."

He nodded and jotted some notes on his pad. "Okay. Thank you for your honesty."

I realized my explanation was abnormal.

As Jennifer led me back to my cell, I had a sick feeling in the pit of my stomach. My life had been mired in problems and despair, and I feared it would only get worse.

# *Seventeen*

## ONE FRIEND

*San Francisco County Jail, August 14, 1966. Beginning of Session Six*

My rubber shoes squeaked with each labored step as I climbed the stairs for my sixth appointment with Doctor Lieberman. It was an incongruous sound mixed with the steady tow of iron chains dragging along the cement and the questions inside my mind.

My memories advanced with each session, like enemy troops creeping up on their target. Could I have tried harder with Father? Should I have talked to Mother about Penelope? Had I shown Grandma how much I loved her? Had I done enough for Robert? For Reid?

The doctor was already at his desk when I arrived. "Good morning, Emily."

He seemed livelier than usual or my malaise just made it seem that way. "Good morning."

The doctor glanced at me. "Are you troubled today?"

I rubbed my aching wrists and shrugged. The answer was obvious in light of killing my father, being incarcerated, and the loss of everyone I loved.

He didn't flinch, nor did he seem surprised at my silence. "Tell me what's on your mind."

I gnawed the inside of my mouth to disguise my emotions and not cry.

"Please talk."

I rubbed a spot on my jumpsuit with my fingernail. "I don't want to continue with this."

"Continue with what exactly?"

"Therapy. I don't want to know any more about my lost memories."

His face didn't move. "Why?"

"Remembering makes it worse and I can't change anything," I explained, avoiding his eyes. "My life is over."

"Finish your thought."

I made eye contact for the first time. "What?"

"Is there another reason you want to stop your therapy?"

I clutched the arms of the chair to ward off the falling sensation that accompanied dread and hopelessness. "I'm scared of what's coming."

"Please go on."

I took a deep breath. "I'm afraid of what's coming...the murder. I'm terrified to learn the details of what I did."

Doctor Lieberman walked to the corner of his desk, nearer to me. "Clinically, I must tell you your memories will surface anyway and it's better to uncover them in a controlled setting."

My stomach tightened. "God, I can't even imagine that...remembering the murder sitting in my cell alone."

"I would like you to understand the importance of therapy on a more personal level."

"Okay," I said, my voice breathy.

He paused, rubbing his finger down his cheek. "The hopelessness and pain you've expressed, disregard those emotions for now and tell me the root causes."

"Guilt and regret," I blurted out.

"Yes. Now, although I cannot hypothesize without jeopardizing our sessions, I can give you the most important reason to continue."

"What?"

He cocked his head to make sure I saw his face. "You need to uncover the secrets."

I sat up straight, feeling like a breeze had blown by in the small office. I nodded for him to continue.

"You grew up with secrets all around you. Secrets carry crushing guilt. I believe those unknowns tainted your identity. Once the secrets are revealed, you will have a clearer understanding of who you are, and how the secrets led you here."

"I understand," I mumbled. Like it or not, the secrets would be unveiled, spread out like a disemboweled animal, exposing the damage those family secrets had inflicted.

I settled back as the doctor led me back to the day Robert left for college.

⟋

It was a day of distinction and not in a good way. Today was my first day at a new high school, and Robert was leaving for Harvard.

I sat on the sofa like a dazed orphan and listened to the occasional thump of Robert gathering his suitcases. Mother was in the kitchen, shouting reminders to Robert. Father clomped up and down the hallway.

Mother oozed with parental pride knowing her son was leaving for college, and not just any college—Harvard. I listened to her excited utterances and wondered if she would have been this thrilled if he had picked Stanford.

Her jubilance made me mad. I scowled, remembering the day she shot down my hopes of becoming an artist. I wondered if there were beauty schools on the east coast.

Mother burst into the living room. "Time to go!"

Dressed in a pale green suit, she looked like she was going to his graduation ceremony instead of driving him to the airport. Even her monotone voice was rhythmic. I regretted pouting, I mean, this was her moment too. She certainly had no bragging rights with me; my last report card was barely average.

"Robert, time to go! You don't want to miss your flight!" Mother shouted. I half-expected a quartet of trumpet players to march in and announce his departure.

"I'll be right there!"

Robert entered the room wearing tan pants, a white shirt, casual leather shoes, and a black carry-on bag slung over his shoulders.

Mother examined him up and down. "You don't have to wear a tie. You look fantastic!"

I snickered. That was her way of saying "you should have worn the tie I put out, but it's okay because you're going to Harvard."

"Thank you, Mother." Robert smiled at me and winked.

Father entered the living room. I quickly covered my mouth to keep from gasping. He walked with his head down, dragging his brown leather slip-on shoes. He had puffy circles under expressionless eyes, and he'd barely run a razor across his beard. He wore baggy beige pants and an old sweater, the kind of clothes the gardener wore when he mowed the lawn.

They stood around Robert. Mother hugged him more like a greeting than a farewell, while Father kept his head down.

Robert pulled him to the side. Robert talked and Father nodded. The words "you didn't try to stop him" played in my head as they huddled in a final goodbye.

Mother waved me over. "Emily, come say goodbye to your brother. We're leaving for the airport."

I forced a smile as I walked to him. "Right on, Robby! You're looking good! Off to college!"

"Yeah," he said. "This is it."

"You'll do great!"

We stared at one another, reading each other's eyes. He stepped closer. "Are you going to be okay?"

I coerced my face into a grin. "Of course, I'll be fine!"

He held both of my hands. "I love you."

"I love you more."

He grinned. "No, I love you more."

Mother checked her wristwatch. "We must go. It's time."

The only thing left was a finger wave; she ushered him out the door with Father hobbling behind.

I watched the car drive off and went back to the sofa. Miserable. Empty. I wasn't much different from Father, disheartened that Robert had left to start a new life. I had never considered Father's ploy to keep him here. I knew he would have stayed if I had asked him; Father's deceitful plan wasn't necessary.

The brother that had been my parent and protector for so many years was off to follow his dreams. "Good for him," I whispered, proud I had let him go with a smile and a promise that I would be okay.

⁓

I stood behind a lamppost reading the sign on the sprawling grounds: Laughlin High School. The three-story building seemed more like a museum than a school with its chiseled columns, sharp green steeples, and arched doorway.

Kids walked in groups or pairs as they chatted on their way to class. The camaraderie drew me behind the lamppost even more; I could already feel the initial sting of the new-girl syndrome.

I inspected my black dress with tiny bluebells for the hundredth time, hoping the simple line and small print would help me blend into the crowd. The slip-on flats were fine and didn't add inches to my five foot seven height.

The bell rang signaling school would start in three minutes. I fumbled through my book bag for a hand mirror to check my face. I gasped at the red anxiety rash strewn across each cheek; the stripe stood out like a red light against my pale skin.

"Ugh," I groaned, tossing the mirror back in the bag. I already felt the bite of the first bully calling me blood-cheeks or some other dumb name. They called me the same thing at my high school in New York, and I still couldn't think of a comeback.

I stayed behind the lamppost waiting for the crowd to thin out. I figured I had about two minutes left, so I used the time to imagine a girl with confidence and poise. After a moment, I took the first step toward the brick building in search of my homeroom.

I rubbed my sweaty palms on my dress as I walked through the arched doors. The corridors were jam-packed with boys and girls in all sizes and forms. The rebellious types mulled around their friends in no hurry to get to class, the social kids huddled at the doors talking about who-knows-what, and the studious kids slammed their lockers and ran to class.

I unzipped my bag and found the paper where I'd written all the classroom numbers. Room 18. I was relieved it was on the first floor, so I wouldn't need to run up and down the hallways. I jutted my head straight ahead and avoided eye contact with the other students.

The bell sounded a few seconds after I cleared the threshold of my homeroom. Most of the kids were already settled in, with no assigned seating. The front rows remained empty other than a few studious types. I spotted an empty seat next to a girl with round glasses and short ash brown hair combed in a bob. I quickly sat next to her, hoping she wouldn't tell me the seat was saved for someone.

I glanced around the room, noticing how all classrooms are alike. They had the same black chalkboard and a bulletin board that no one reads. A bulky projector stood in the corner for the occasional boring slide show and a gray clock hung on the back wall.

The cliques were also predictable. The chatty girls giggled like they were at a soirée instead of school, and the studious kids sat still and waited for the teacher. The popular girls sat near the cute boys and wore bright sweaters, lively plaids, and dangle bracelets. They twisted their hair and pretended not to notice when the boys ogled them. The sports guys were the easiest to read. They wore blue and white letterman jackets in spite of the warm weather and clamored about sports teams, dropping names and swapping football stories. They probably couldn't name the Vice President of the United States, but I bet if you asked them who won the winning touchdown two years ago, they could tell you.

The brisk greeting of the teacher jolted me out of my thoughts. "Hello, students. Please pass your homework forward. Today we will continue our discussion of the Reconstruction Era."

The teacher was fiftyish with brown hair, average size, and indistinct clothing. Even his name, Mr. Carter, was ordinary. I was a little surprised at his lack of distinction, guessing fancy neighborhoods hired from the same teacher's pool. I opened my notebook and struggled to pay attention.

The lunch bell rang, a welcome relief from the humdrum facts on the blackboard. Students scurried out the door like mice to a big chunk of cheese. My stomach churned, remembering what lunch had been like in New York, searching for a place to sit only to hear the dreaded words "it's saved for my friend."

I sighed, knowing I hadn't had time to find my "one friend" yet—someone like me that needed a "one-friend" to feel less awkward and alone.

I entered the cafeteria, grabbed the gray plastic tray, and stood in line for green beans and meatloaf. I chanted the "you'll get through this" song to calm my nerves, telling myself it would be over in one hour. I took the "I'm okay" posture as I searched for a place to sit.

I found a spot next to a chubby boy eating alone. I took slow bites to pace myself. The last thing I wanted was to stand alone in the courtyard, staring off into the crowd.

Nibbling on the green beans, I worried Reid had found a girl in Colorado. The uncertainty was killing me.

I scanned the cafeteria for the cute girls. They sat at the same table near the football players. They exuded confidence, even at seventeen. Their hairstyles were teased at the top with the bottom flipped out; they wore dark pink lipstick and black eyeliner with a wing on the end. Their cardigans were unbuttoned at the top, and their pleated skirts appeared to be within a centimeter of the touching-the-knee dress code.

I stabbed the meatloaf and worried I wasn't pretty enough for Reid. I tossed the last green bean on the plate and wrinkled my nose at the cute girls.

The bell buzzed telling everyone lunch was over. I gathered the leftover scraps of food for the receptacle. The chubby boy leaped in front of me, apparently more anxious than me to get out of the cafeteria.

I couldn't help but stare at him. He had an odd shape, short with narrow shoulders and a large behind. He wore a white shirt and blue twill high-waist pants, which accentuated his thick midriff. His flabby arms swung back and forth as he waddled to class. I felt a connection to him along with pity. The poor boy had no chance in high school; it seemed inhumane to make him go. I felt sorry for him as I watched him turn a corner; I never even talked to the poor kid.

The time neared three o'clock. Kids began shoving books in their bags, bracing for the mad dash out of the classroom. I relaxed, knowing I made it through the day. Nothing awful happened other than the expected awkwardness in the cafeteria. Finding a spot next to a chubby boy turned out to be a decent shield because no one sat near us.

I grabbed my books from under my desk. Nothing bad happened, but nothing good happened either. I was a girl pretending to be okay, hiding from the truth that I was alone. My struggle to not get noticed was exactly what hurt me. If no one noticed me, that meant I had no friends, no one to sit with, and no one to talk to. I was invisible.

The bell sounded. I fell into line, making my way out the door when someone tapped my shoulder.

I spun around to find a guy wearing a letterman jacket. He had sun-drenched hair, tanned skin, and a broad smile. "Hey! You're new, right?"

I glanced around, expecting to find a group of his buddies snickering. "Yeah," I said.

"Where are you from?"

"Um...I lived in New York for the last three years."

"Cool! Well, cold. Is this your first time in San Francisco? Why'd you move here?"

I wondered if he was making fun of me. I started to say something when a bouncy blonde cheerleader shoved past a few students and grabbed his arm, ranting about some mutual friend. I used the diversion to exit, dodging around students toward the arched doors.

I was almost out the door when I heard him shout. "What's your name?"

I turned and saw him with his hands cupped around his mouth. "What's your name?"

"Emily!" I shouted, before a throng of kids came out of a classroom and blocked my view.

"Hmm," I mumbled. I put my hand over my mouth to hide a smile as I headed home.

I kicked a rock down the sidewalk, wondering what my parents would be like without Robert. I doubted Father believed the apple of his eye would move to Boston. I reeled back and kicked the rock as hard as I could and smiled. "Go Robert!"

The unseasonable April heat lulled me to a park bench. I draped my arms across my back, closed my eyes, and tilted my face to the sun, thinking about the last three Aprils in New York. The gloomy skies had matched my depression, making it harder to wait out the three years. Oh, the first snowfall in November was magical, transforming old cars to white sculptures and barren trees into willowy shapes. But by February, speeding cars and rain had pushed the snow into piles of dirty sludge.

By the time I reached fifteen, I felt a connection to the seasonal changes, like my optimism had drifted to hopelessness. But now...

I flinched as something smacked my knee. I opened my eyes to see the same guy that talked to me earlier.

"Sorry! You okay?"

I sat up straight and tossed him the football. "Yeah."

"You sure? My buddy won't make quarterback throwing like that."

I wondered how dumb I'd looked sitting on a park bench with my eyes closed. "I'm fine, really."

He stood over me, tossing the football up and down. He didn't have a shirt on, making it impossible not to notice his muscular build. "Yeah?"

I tried to keep my eyes on his face. "Sure, sure."

His friends hollered for him.

"Take a break!" he yelled back.

He sat next to me. "So, do you play?"

I scooted to the side so our bodies wouldn't touch. "Play what?"

"Football. We haven't started yet and need a good running back. That is, if you don't mind being tackled, by me of course." He scooted closer and nudged me with his elbow.

I rolled my eyes and shook my head.

"Oh, I'm just kidding. Sorry, bad joke."

His bare arm was touching mine so I inched to the side.

"Come on, Emily. See? I remembered your name, so you can't be mad. But I'm heartbroken because you haven't asked me my name," he pretend-whined.

I glanced at him and smiled. "Okay, what's your name?"

He straightened up and reached out his hand. "Mark. Mark Hodges," he announced in a fake British accent.

I smiled as we shook hands. With his blonde hair, blue eyes, and tanned skin, all he needed was a surfboard under his arm to star in a beach flick.

"Okay, glad to meet you," I said, wondering why an attractive boy was talking to me.

He spun the football in his palm. "So, new-girl-in-town, what do you do for fun?"

"I'm not the new girl in town. I've lived here before," I replied, hoping to avoid the real question. I couldn't think of a single fun thing.

"Oh, right. You lived in the Big Apple. So, what'd you do for kicks in New York?"

I cleared my throat and wondered if frolicking in the snow would constitute as fun to a San Franciscan.

His friends' laughter distracted him.

Mark cupped his hand around his mouth. "Hey, fatso! Where you going? Bob's Big Boy or KFC?"

His friends laughed in unison, along with a few indistinguishable snide comments, followed by more laughter.

I squinted and saw the chubby kid I sat next to in the cafeteria. He kept his head down as sweat poured down his face.

"Don't forget the hot fudge sundae! Hey! Can ya bring me back one?"

More laughter.

He swung his arms to gain speed. His puffy face appeared feverish as he huffed his way beyond the bevy of football players.

I wrinkled my forehead and glared at Mark.

"What? No big deal. He likes it. At least we talk to him!"

He tossed the football to his friends and got up. "I'm sorry, I forgot you New Yorkers don't get our sense of humor."

I shot him an indignant frown. No words necessary.

"It's no big deal. He's our buddy!"

I smirked. "Right."

His friends continued to beckon him, so he ran off to relieve them. He stopped suddenly. "We're cool, right?"

Surprised he even cared, I nodded. "Okay. We're cool."

I began walking home, thinking about the cafeteria boy. Nobody had asked him if he was cool. I spotted a rock and kicked it, wishing it could land in the face of one of the tormenters.

# Eighteen

## FOOLED

Walking in the door was like entering the Tomb of the Unknown Soldier. Mother sat on the sofa reading her latest novel while Father paced between the living room and Robert's bedroom. He hadn't changed his clothes or combed his hair. Neither glanced up when I entered the house, so I decided not to interrupt their silent vigil. I slipped into my room unnoticed.

I tucked my sketches in the box after drawing for an hour. The house was eerily quiet: no television, radios, nothing. The silent vigil for Robert continued, proving silence was the loudest sound.

I stretched my legs out on the bed and thought about the school day. Getting attention from a cute boy had been flattering, at least until he bullied the cafeteria boy. I cringed, remembering the poor boy rushing past the football players and their rude slurs. I understood his torment; I'd felt it a thousand times at the hands of Father.

"Whew," I muttered, hoping all the brutality was over. With Robert gone, maybe he would try harder to have a relationship with me.

Thinking about school, Father, and Robert's move to Boston left me sleepy. I found myself drifting off, caught between the sorrow of the past and hope for the future.

⟋⟍

*I strolled along the dirt path at Mallard Lake. I sensed a shadow behind me and turned to find a hooded gravedigger walking toward me with a shovel. He held a knife in his other hand, which shone like a sword. I walked backward to keep an eye on him. Rattlesnakes flanked the path and hissed when I tried to run. The villain chanted "no evidence" and guided me to the edge of a cliff. I heard laughter as I fell from a thousand-foot crag. My body began to shut down in a slough of blood as I watched a coroner write " suicide" on my death certificate.*

"No!" I shot up, gasping for air. I flung the sheets and blankets, wet with sweat, to the floor. I rubbed my head, trying to stop the incessant buzzing that always followed my recurring nightmare.

They started three years ago in New York. I had hoped moving back to San Francisco would end them. Apparently not.

I grabbed two aspirin from my nightstand. I had hours before I needed to get ready for school, so I flipped on the radio.

Someone pounded on my door. "Open up," said Father.

I turned down the radio. "I'm sorry, Father. I'm coming!"

I swung the door open. "I was..."

I put my hand over my mouth to stop an automatic gasp. The military man clad in over-starched pants was gone. The carefree Hawaiian-shirt dad was gone. The sad, disheveled father who stalked Robert's room yesterday was gone. The man standing in front of me was a merger of all three.

The blended man wore a beige cashmere suit, alligator shoes, and a fitted cotton shirt worn open with a gold serpentine chain around his neck. His hair was slicked back, his face shaven. His eyes were bloodshot and twitched like he'd downed shots of alcohol. He reeked of English Leather cologne.

I searched his face. "Um...I'm sorry about the door."

"Why didn't you open it right away?"

"I'm sorry. The music was too loud."

"You locked your door. That's against my rules."

I started to say something lighthearted but stopped when I looked into his impassive eyes. "I know, I didn't mean to. I apologize."

He stood in place, glaring at me.

I wanted to turn him back into the arcade-dad. "Are you okay? Can I help?"

"Help?"

I forced myself to smile. "Yes…is there something I can do?"

He backed me up. When he cleared the threshold, he kicked the door closed with his foot. He turned and locked it.

I glanced at the door. "What...?"

He crept toward me.

I kept my eyes on his expression as I walked backward. I couldn't read him.

He continued in my direction.

My heart thumped erratically like it had forgotten how to beat. "Father?"

He walked me into a wall and put one hand around my neck. His bloodshot eyes drilled into mine. He remained silent. He grabbed a chunk of my hair, twisting it around his index finger.

He yanked—fast and violent.

The agony sent pain-tears to my eyes.

He kept his face inches from mine. He smelled of whiskey and cologne.

I turned my head to keep from vomiting.

He whispered inches from my ear. "Never *ever* cross me. Do you understand?"

I nodded. *I hadn't stopped Robert.*

He jerked my hair again. His face was expressionless as he released me. He swaggered from the room and hummed like we'd just finished a friendly chat.

I stood in place, waiting for the humming to stop before I closed the door.

"No," I moaned, sliding to the floor.

I got to my feet, pushing the violent attack from my mind. I didn't want to be a victim, and I didn't want Father to be a villain. I told myself nothing happened.

I turned up the radio, lip-syncing the lyrics of "My Girl" as I dressed for school. I couldn't push the pain away for long; it would be like trying to ignore the wreckage of a plane crash. I zipped up my plaid dress and sat on the bed to brush my hair.

My body went into free fall so fast it sickened me.

A wad of dark brown hair stood like a beacon against the cream carpet. I stared at the glob and bit down hard on my index finger. I hated myself. Despised myself for being so stupid and foolish and gullible and unlovable. I could go on.

I closed my eyes and pushed myself away from the scene. After a minute, I picked up the hair, ran to the bathroom, and flushed the evidence down the toilet.

The heat wave was over along with my foolish dream of a new start with my father. Marine air mixed with light fog blanketed Laughlin High School, but it wasn't thick enough to disguise the kids walking in pairs. The laughter was deafening, magnified by the chill in my soul. I gazed at their silhouettes and wondered why they were laughing. The spontaneity seemed unnatural to me. Of course, it wasn't. I just didn't know what free and easy felt like; I had to invent a character and fake a smile just to get through the door.

My heart did its usual tap-dance against my chest and sparks flittered in front of my face. Panic attacks were routine by now, so I pulled out my paper bag and found a bench.

Someone shook my shoulder. I turned to find Mark with his letterman jacket draped over his shoulder. One of his football buddies stood with him.

"Hey. You okay?"

I shot up and stuffed the paper bag back in my purse. "I'm fine!"

He stared down at me. "You sure?"

I fiddled with the zipper on my purse. "I was just looking for something. That's all."

"Really? You don't look so good."

I ran my hands through my hair and glanced around like I was waiting for someone. "I'm perfectly fine!"

He stood over me, squinting. "You sure?"

I pushed down on my shaking legs. "Yeah."

His friend grabbed Mark's shirt. "Come on, we'll be late, man."

Mark jerked his arm up, releasing his friend's grip. "Emily, you coming?"

"Oh sure, sure...in a minute, I mean. I'm waiting for someone."

"Okay, see ya." He turned and headed to class with his buddy. As soon as he disappeared in the crowd, I took a deep breath and followed him, knowing I was minutes away from a tardy slip.

Spring gloom created a barely visible drizzle, sending the outside-eaters into the cafeteria for lunch. I surveyed the crowded room for space, but every time I ventured to a spot, an arm went up as a student yelled "over here!" to a friend.

The milk carton and Sloppy Joe on my tray teetered; luckily, I spotted a girl leaving and quickly claimed the seat. The girls at the table barely noticed me as they chatted about the movie, *To Catch a Thief.* I still didn't want to think about what happened with Father, so jewel thieves and the love story between Cary Grant and Grace Kelly were a welcome distraction.

"You're new, aren't you?" a girl asked.

I wondered if I'd been staring. "Oh," I said. "Yes. This is my second day."

"Where'd you move from?"

"New York. I was born here but lived in New York for the last three years."

"Wow, that is so cool. I'd love to live in New York. It's so metro and all the top fashion designers live there."

I nodded, noticing the chubby kid that Mark bullied yesterday was sitting next to her.

"I would give anything to live in New York," she continued. "When I graduate, I'm going to apply at Parsons."

One of the girls interrupted. "Come on, Judy. We gotta get to the library and finish that home economics project."

Off they went, leaving a big gap in front of me. I scooted closer to the chubby kid, so I wouldn't stand out as the girl eating alone.

It was rude to stare at him, but I couldn't help it. The kids at the school wore trendy clothes and mop-top hairstyles. The students who had a license drove Ford Mustangs or Plymouth Barracudas and the ones that didn't were chauffeured to school in a Bentley or Cadillac. The class of Laughlin High School exuded wealth but not this kid. He wore a starched beige shirt and sturdy pants. His brown hair was combed to the side, and his face was splattered with acne. He tried to conceal the pimples with Clearasil, which made the bumps stand out more.

As I worked my way through the drippy sandwich, the bun collapsed, sending a stream of meat and red sauce down my dress.

"Ugh," I muttered. I picked chunks of ground beef off my dress and flung the mess back on the plate. The sauce had tinted the top of my dress to an embarrassing red.

I wiped the dress with my napkin, smearing the stain and making it worse.

I saw a hand in front of my face and turned to see the chubby boy holding a drenched napkin.

"Thanks." I took it and began rubbing. "I appreciate…"

When I glanced up, I saw him standing at the soda fountain. I continued rubbing the fabric.

He was back with another napkin. "No, try this."

I lingered on his face. "Huh?"

"Soda water. It'll take the spot out. Also, it's better if you blot the stain instead of rubbing."

He handed me napkin after napkin until the stain was almost gone.

"Wow! Thank you so much. You can barely see it."

The boy smiled. "You're welcome."

I figured I should know the name of the boy that saved me from looking like I'd wrestled with a switchblade. "What's your name?"

"Pudge."

"I'm sorry, what?"

"Pudge. Everyone calls me Pudge. It's short for Perry Unger."

I closed my mouth and tried not to look shocked.

"It looks good," he said.

"What?" I asked, still wondering why he called himself "Pudge."

"The stain. It's gone."

"Oh, yeah. Thank you. How'd you learn that?"

"My Mom."

I had to ask the obvious question. "Why do you let people call you Pudge? Why not Perry?"

He shrugged. "It's my nickname."

I stared at him, wondering why it was okay with him considering all the teasing he endured. "Oh, okay."

I jumped at the piercing buzz of the lunch bell. Kids hopped up and scurried out of the cafeteria, creating a pyramid of crammed students trying to get through the double doors. I wondered why the big rush to get back to class until I remembered a pep rally was scheduled in the gym.

"The school is holding a rally at the gym," I said.

His face reddened. "Oh, yeah."

"I guess we have to go."

He fumbled with his books. "We?"

He seemed to be waiting for an invite. "Yeah, let's go to the rally, okay?"

"What?"

"The pep rally. Do you want to go?"

He brightened as a smile formed on his face. "Oh, sure. Thanks."

We pushed our way into the packed gymnasium. The students had enough pep to take the high school team to the Super Bowl. I resisted the urge to cover my ears at the sound of rubber soles hitting the polished floors, rants from megaphones, and screaming kids. I groaned, confident no one could hear me amidst the racket.

Pudge leaned forward with his hands on his knees, fixed on the cheers, the band, and the waving pendants. I wondered if this was his first pep rally, which seemed impossible as every school held at least one rally a month.

"Pudge!" I hollered over the crowd.

He turned to me, waving his arms as he followed the group-led cheer. "Yeah?"

"Pretty loud, huh?"

"Yeah! This is amazing!"

I studied him, pretty sure it was his first pep rally. When the band played "Peter Gunn," he squealed with delight and cheered along with the crowd. This was not the boy that had waddled past Mark and his cronies; he was downright joyful.

When the rally concluded, kids lingered in their seats in no hurry to return to class. Pudge continued to hum, still caught up in the hoopla.

I understood how he felt. He was a part of something and walked through the door like everyone else without being ridiculed.

"Pretty good rally, huh?" I asked him.

"Fantastic!" he agreed. "Wow! I loved the songs, and the bands, especially…"

A roar interrupted him from across the room.

"Emily, over here!" Across the gym stood Mark Hodges shouting through a megaphone. "Emily! Let's hear it for Emily!"

I waved, embarrassed but flattered at his brazen use of the cheerleader's megaphone.

After a long giggle and another wave at Mark, I turned back to Pudge. The pep had drained from his face as he looked around the gym. He clicked his tongue in a muted tune.

"That was a cool pep rally," I said. "Hopefully, they'll win tonight."

His face crimped into a smile, as he turned toward me. "Yeah!"

As we chatted, he hung on every word, nodding in agreement over the simplest comment. I understood. I'd been in that situation too, staking my claim that I was with someone. But Pudge didn't try to disguise himself; he clearly starred in the role of the fat kid with no friends. I guess that's why I felt comfortable around him; I didn't have to pretend to be someone else.

We filed out of the gym. He stayed close to me, not like a toddler clinging to his mommy, but a boy next to a friend.

We reached the lockers. "Thank you for the pep rally," he said.

I smiled at the sentiment, knowing the rally wasn't an invitation-only event. "Oh, sure."

I got it though. I felt a kinship as I watched him walk to class with a little more swing in his step.

"Hey, Emily!" This time I recognized the voice, minus the megaphone.

Mark nudged my shoulder and jumped back, pretending to be offended. "Why didn't you come sit with me? Do you know how much I had to bribe a cheerleader to use her megaphone?"

"No," I said, giggling.

"I saw you sitting next to Pudge. How'd you get stuck next to tubby?"

I gazed at Mark with my mouth open, at a loss for words. After a few hems and haws, I shrugged.

"Next time sit next to the leaderboard. I might even let you sit next to me," he said with another nudge.

I stared at him, speechless. Thankfully, a bevy of friends swarmed him, rambling on about the upcoming game. I inched my way out of the Mark Hodges fan club, ashamed I hadn't stuck up for Pudge.

⌒

" *I* hate weekends," I groaned as I got out of bed. Saturday. No school. No Robert. No distracting homework. No Reid. The one "yes" in the batch of "no's" was Father. Father was home.

I grabbed my sketchpad, anxious to get Father out of my mind. Father and fear—they go together. I tapped my pencil on the paper, wondering how he would have treated me if I'd gone through with his plan. I wouldn't have had my hair yanked out, but I wouldn't have earned the title of "daughter" either.

I continued to sketch freestyle as my imagination guided the pencil. The weight of Robert's departure sank in, along with the "what's next with Father" question. Robert had kept Father occupied and away from me. So, whether I liked it or not, I would have to listen to his footsteps, examine his eyes for signs of pending violence, and keep my guard up until Reid returned.

Reid was another uncertainty. Surely, by now his mother told him I came by. I thought he would have written by now, but so far, not a word.

I put the sketchpad down and stared at my reflection. Darkness circled my eyes, and my blackish hair formed straggly waves over my bony body.

I shook my head, knowing the vision originated from my depressed mind.

It was New York all over again. I only had my fantasies, inventing a world where people talked to me and things happened. It got me through the interminable days.

Here I was again. A dumb girl sketching pictures no one would ever see and fantasizing about a life that would never happen.

I studied the picture I'd drawn of my dead sister, Penelope. She sat on the beach, staring at the ocean. She wore a long dress, which formed ripples around her ankles. She appeared content and peaceful. Or maybe depressed. I couldn't tell.

A familiar knock shook me out of my thoughts. "Emily, open up, please."

"Come on in, Mother."

"'Emily, we're attending an important dinner party tonight. You need to be ready at seven."

I tucked the book under my bed. "Why am I going?"

"Your father's not in the military anymore, dear. We've talked about this before. He works for a large manufacturing company. Tonight we're going to dinner at the CEOs house. He's a very important man."

"What's a CEO?" I asked.

"Chief Executive Officer. As I said, he's an extremely wealthy and influential man. The party is important to your father, so you need to be on your best behavior. I'll be picking out your attire for the event."

She appeared agitated; the party was obviously important to her. I wondered why Father allowed me to go. "Are you sure you want me to go?"

She rolled her eyes and huffed. "This is not a question of wanting or not wanting you to go. Your name is on the invitation. Now, please... no more questions. I'll be back at five to pick out your clothes," she announced before she left.

"Hmm," I muttered. I glanced at the clock, noting I had five hours. I returned to my artwork, hoping Mother would knock on the door and tell me I didn't have to go after all.

*I* walked into the living room wearing a fitted blue taffeta dress: tailored in the front and zippered in the back. My hair was swept up on the sides and secured with a jeweled clip. I wished Reid could see me all dressed up.

Father came out of the kitchen wearing an Italian suit, holding a crystal goblet. He checked me up and down like I was wearing dirty clothes I'd fished out of the hamper. "Why are you all dressed up?"

I said nothing and waited for Mother. I learned a long time ago to wait. Waited for him to stop, for someone to walk in the room, for God to intervene, for a swat team to storm our house.

He came closer, exuding a mixture of hatred and swagger. He swigged the last of the Vodka and leaned into me. "You think you look good? Well, you don't. You make me want to gouge out my eyeballs."

I twisted the end of my dress and avoided his eyes.

He chuckled hoarsely as he slammed down the goblet. "Now take my goddamn glass back in the kitchen."

Robotically, I grabbed the glass, more to get away from him than anything. I tried to erase his words from my head but I couldn't. The insult scorched me like a branding iron placed on my skin. I stayed in the kitchen until Mother shouted it was time to leave. I dug my fingernails into my wrist to hide the mental pain. It was going to get worse. *A lot worse.*

# Nineteen

## A Real Home

"My dress is caught!" I shouted as I maneuvered into the backseat of our Lincoln Continental.

I opened the door and grabbed the trapped dress.

Mother flipped on the car light. "It's only a little wrinkled, dear. Smooth it with your hands."

Father started the engine. "It's your own damn fault! You move like a goddamn snail."

"Shush, Jacob. Please calm down."

"Fine," said Father. "By the way, Claire, have I told you how beautiful you look tonight?"

She patted her upswept hair with a gloved hand. "Yes, three times... but thank you, darling."

Mother was gorgeous in a strapless black gown with a tiered diamond necklace and drop earrings. Father wore a black tuxedo and satin bow tie. And I was the clumsy misfit sitting in the backseat. I crossed my arms, wondering why I had to go to this obviously stuffy shindig.

He took the third freeway exit to a neighborhood of impressive mansions. They all had massive front yards and well-lit exteriors. The estates were larger than ours on Orchid Drive, but I heard Father tell Robert a while back that anything over eight thousand square feet qualifies as a mansion. So, our house was a mansion but the estates on this street were bigger mansions. I rolled my eyes at the absurdity, and I'm sure Robert had too.

We started up a long, steep road. I grabbed the armrest and tried to see through the darkness. Heights made me nervous, especially knowing the driver hated my guts and consumed more than a few glasses of Vodka.

He finally stopped the car. The place took my breath away; this was no mansion—it was a palace. The estate sat on a bluff surrounded by palm trees, a waterfall with gold lions spewing water into an open pool, and gothic iron statues amidst manicured hedges. It was the kind of place where tourists slammed on their brakes to take a picture to send back to their home folks.

We pulled up to a gate with a uniformed guard. "Good evening. May I have your invitation, please?"

Mother smiled and handed the man the invitation.

"Thank you. A valet will drop you off at the front grounds and park your car."

Father stared at the man as he turned the engine off. The car began to roll down the steep driveway.

"Jacob," Mother whispered. "Put the car in park."

He started up the engine again, drove several feet forward, and handed the man the keys.

After a short drive, the valet stopped in front of a flight of flagstone stairs. "Have a pleasant evening."

Father adjusted his tie as he walked up the steps. He kept a firm grip on Mother's waist.

My palms began to sweat and my heart raced. Mother glanced at me and nodded an "all is okay" signal. I gawked at the white lights lining the entry and the massive columns framing the mansion. *Father must have landed a very good job.*

A well-postured man with a British accent greeted us at the door. I wondered if he was the CEO until he announced:

"Ladies and gentleman, I introduce to you Mr. and Mrs. Jacob Quinn and their daughter, Emily."

I felt like I'd stepped into a scene from *The King and I*. The guests nodded in unison. People mulled about dressed in formal attire. Well-coiffed guests held crystal goblets, chatting in small groups. Servants with silver trays and white cloth napkins draped over their arms offered hors-d'oeuvres to the guests.

I gazed at the splendor of the foyer. The floors were made of shiny ivory pearls with a medieval mural encased in the entry. A golden chandelier hung from a three-story ceiling with scattered inset lights, which made the room seem like a starlit galaxy. Wrought iron staircases graced both sides of the entryway, leading to a sweeping curved balcony set off by massive gold pillars. The foyer had a tufted red velvet fainting couch, no doubt for girls like me that forgot to breathe when taking in such opulence.

A tall man with brown eyes in framed glasses extended his hand. "Jacob," he said. "Thank you for coming."

"Thank you for asking me...us...to your dinner party," Father stuttered.

The man shook his hand and smiled at Mother and me.

Mother grabbed Father's elbow when he started to salute him. "What a great place," said Father.

Mother jumped to his rescue with an extended hand. "Mr. Unger, I'm Claire, and this is my daughter, Emily. Thank you for inviting us."

"So pleased to meet you, Claire and Emily. Please, come over here, I would like to introduce you to my family. Emily, this is my son, Perry."

The distinguished Mr. Unger stepped me into the Land of Oz. With three steps that seemed like shoe-clicks, we stood next to Mrs. Unger and none-other than the chubby kid who sat next to me at the pep rally, Pudge.

"Jacob, Claire, Emily. I would like you to meet my wife, Nancy, and my son, Perry. Emily, I understand you and Perry go to the same school," said Mr. Unger.

I glanced at Pudge. "Yes, sir."

Pudge and I raised our eyebrows at the same time. It was an "Oh my God—can you believe this?" expression.

Mr. Unger made a polite exit. Father, Mother, and I stood next to Pudge and his mother.

"Mrs. Unger, you have a beautiful home," said Mother.

"Thank you, and please...call me Nancy. Make yourself at home. I'm so glad you're here."

Mrs. Unger was a cute lady, not stunning like my mother, but friendly and open. She was short and stocky with an ample bust, thick waist, and narrow hips. Her face was round and soft, and she smiled easily.

She turned to her son and put her hands on his shoulders. "Perry, would you like to show Emily the game room? I'm sure she would find it a lot more enjoyable than staying with the adults."

"Sure," he said. "Sounds good."

I stifled my grin into a polite smile. He looked like a munchkin dressed in a black tweed suit and argyle tie.

Mrs. Unger turned to my parents. "You have a delightful daughter. I'm so glad Perry has someone young here to talk to."

My parents nodded and smiled. I eyed Father, surprised he didn't roll his eyes at the "delightful-daughter" comment. I supposed he couldn't in front of the wife of the CEO. Appearances, appearances.

"Let's go, Emily. Follow me," said Pudge.

I was more than thrilled to get away from Father's watchful eyes. Pudge loosened his tie and led me into a game room. The room was large but casual compared to the grandeur of the foyer. I glanced around, wondering if he'd given anyone else at Laughlin High the tour but dismissed it knowing he had no friends at the school.

We rounded a corner to a group of pool tables with colorful stained glass lamps. "This is the billiard room."

"Cool," I said. The room was sectioned off by different themes and was larger than the school gymnasium. A framed picture of an older man with Pudge shooting pool hung next to a small table.

"Who's that?" I asked.

"That's my grandpa."

"Oh, nice."

He led me to the next section, a darkened room with graduated seating. A yellow and red popcorn machine stood in one corner and movie posters hung on the wall.

"Television room," he said. "This is where we watch home movies. Last week we watched my dad's trip to Japan."

"Japan?"

"Yeah, he travels a lot. During the summer, we go with him."

"Oh wow...that's neat."

The next section was an action room with arcade games, neon signs, and a flashy juke box. A white laminated table with bright blue chairs surrounded a long bar with a giant soda fountain. Cute, red-colored tufted vinyl stools lined the bar waiting for customers.

"This is so cool!" The bright surroundings and flashing lights screamed, "let's have fun." I couldn't have imagined a better place to spend time and figured we'd stop, but Pudge kept walking.

We walked into the final section, the music room. "This is my favorite place," he said.

The walls were painted in three shades of brown with guitars up and down the walls. The guitars were not ornaments; they appeared played, and a few lingered against overstuffed chairs. I thought about my wall analogy and wondered how the menagerie of guitars defined Pudge's life.

I glanced at Pudge. "Far out."

He motioned to a leather chair. "Would you like to sit down?"

"Sure."

Pudge ran to a refrigerator. "What would you like to drink?"

I grinned at the clang of bottles moving around. "Anything...a Coke?"

He popped off the cap. "Here you go."

"You have a lot of guitars. Can you play them?"

"Oh, sure," he said, pointing. "Those are my favorites. The electric guitars."

"Hmmm. How interesting. What's that one?" I asked, pointing to a black guitar.

"That's a Gibson. I call it Lucille. It's like one named after a song written by B.B. King. They played in old wooden halls in Arkansas and would light a barrel of kerosene to keep warm. A fight broke out one night, and someone knocked over the kerosene...the whole building burned down. Later, he wrote the song about two guys fighting over a woman."

"Wow, you sure know a lot about music. How about that one?"

"That's a Fender from the early 50s, it's made of maple wood. The newer ones are veneer and not as good." He touched the guitar like it was a beautiful girl.

I put my hand over my mouth to hide my smile. "Do you play?"

He shrugged. "A little."

"Play something!"

"Nah. I'm not that good."

I clapped and swooned like a fan. "Come on! Play something! Sing a song for me!"

His face turned bright red as he grabbed a guitar. "Well, okay."

I started to tell him I was kidding but stopped when he began tightening the strings and holding the pick-guard. I winced, embarrassed for him.

He strummed a few notes. I didn't recognize the melody, but it was obvious that he could play. I settled down, my embarrassment was long gone.

He paused and set the guitar aside. "Would you like to hear a song?"

"Of course...I would love that."

He walked to the piano. He slumped over a bit, resting his hands on his knees. Seconds later, his eyes closed and his fingers danced on the black-and-white keys, composed and confident. After a few notes, he sang the Nat King Cole song "Unforgettable." His voice was exquisite with a distinct tone and perfect pitch. Beautiful. Melodic. Tiny chills ran through me, I was swept away by the unexpected power of his voice. I understood why this room was his favorite.

When he finished, he stared down for a moment and smiled. "I love that song. Nat King Cole is a favorite."

"Wow," I replied, barely above a whisper. "That was incredible. I had no idea you could sing." His talent defied words, he was that good. His awkwardness disappeared; all I saw was a good friend with an incredible gift.

Pudge broke the silence. "Let's eat!"

"Eat?"

"Sure, Mom will be bringing down some food any minute…just listen."

On cue, Mrs. Unger came into the room rolling a tray full of enough goodies to feed twenty people. Her face lit up when she spotted Pudge at the piano.

"Oh, good, Perry! You showed your friend what a beautiful voice you have! Isn't he wonderful? Now come over, kids, I brought your favorites. Emily, I hope you like them too. Now, if you need anything else, you tell me."

Mrs. Unger didn't talk—she bubbled. She treated us like this was our party instead of the formal soirée outside our doors. The tray held recognizable delights, not extravagant hors de 'oeuvres. There were kabobs threaded with chunks of chicken, pineapple, and red peppers, a platter of cold cuts and cheeses with Kaiser rolls, potato salad, and fruit.

"This looks fantastic, Mrs. Unger. Thank you!" I jumped up to help her set the table.

"No, dear. You're our guest! Now, sit down and enjoy yourself. Are you sure I can't bring you something else? Do you need another soft drink?"

"I'm fine, thank you."

Pudge reached up and gave her a quick hug. "Thanks, Mom."

I was mesmerized—almost in a trance. The bond brought back memories of Grandma and my time with her in Seattle—natural, loving.

"Okay, kids. Let me know if you need anything else."

I placed the finger food on my plate, thinking how different he was from the bullied boy at school. "Your mom seems nice."

"She's the best."

"So, what's it like living here?"

"What do you mean?"

"Well, you live in a mansion…a palace. You have a butler and maids. I can't imagine what that's like."

"Hmm," he said, cocking his head. "Well, I don't think of it that way. I mean…they're not just butlers and maids. They have names. They're like friends."

"Really?"

He took a bite of pineapple. "Yeah. They've always been here, so I suppose I don't know anything else."

"That must be something. And your parents…they don't seem, you know, uppity. They're so nice…normal."

"Of course they're normal. They're just regular people living in a big house. That's all. They're no different from your mom and dad."

I raised my eyebrows at the "no different from your mom and dad" comment.

Pudge furrowed his brow. "What?"

I shrugged. "Oh, they're different. That's all."

He picked up a chunk of pepper cheese. "How so?"

I put my fork down. "My mother's not like your mom. She's not interested in me. And my father…he doesn't like me."

"What do you mean he doesn't like you? How can your father not like you?"

I hesitated. "He just doesn't. I don't know why." I had no idea how to explain why he beats the crap out of me and calls me names. I didn't even know.

"What does he do to make you think he doesn't like you?"

I heard the concern in his voice. He talked faster than before and louder. "Emily? What does he do?"

The question shone like a spotlight in my face. I stared at my hands, thinking. Answering his question meant I had to abandon all the characters I'd invented to keep the truth at bay.

I decided to tell him the truth. "What does he do? He tells me he hates me, that I'm ugly and stupid among other things, and he beats me."

His hand reached across the table and grabbed mine. The warmth felt like someone had poked a hole in a wound filled with poison, allowing the venom to escape. I experienced a physical release.

"How bad is it?"

I straightened up a little before looking down again. "Complete torture," I said.

"Torture?"

"Yep. Torture."

I continued to stare at my lap, pulled down by the weight of my own words. The truth wasn't a cry for help or the introduction to a discussion. I didn't want pity and talking would only prolong the agony. I answered his question and stuck the truth out like my heart on a stake. But now, I wanted to forget it.

"Emily? What...?"

I slapped my knees and faced Pudge. He looked like he'd been stricken with the bubonic plague, and I wanted to take the weight away from him. "Are we ever going to play pinball?"

He stared at me. "I think we should..."

I cut him off as cheerfully as possible. "Come on! I've been waiting to play all night! Let's go!"

"But...?"

"It's okay," I assured him, touching his hand. "I just want to have some fun."

After a delayed reaction, he agreed. Off we went to the pinball machines and played every single one. At first, the sound of the bells ringing and dinging reminded me of the fateful night at the arcade with

Father, but after a while, I put it out of my mind and had fun. Pudge was a terrible player and a funny loser. Every time he lost he pounded the pinball machine and blamed the loss on bad luck and a rigged machine. He kicked and pleaded with the machine only to lose over and over. I laughed so hard my sides hurt.

Amidst the laughter, I hadn't noticed that Mr. Unger had walked in. "Emily, I see you are a good pinball player," he said, with one arm on Pudge's shoulder.

I stood up straight. "Yes, sir."

"That's wonderful. I'm glad you kids are having fun. We are about to serve dessert, and Perry's mom wondered which dessert you would prefer Cherry Jubilee or Crème Brule?"

"Oh Dad, how about chocolate cake?" he whined, playfully.

Shocked to hear Pudge question his father, I stepped back.

"How did I know you'd say that?" Mr. Unger said, chuckling. "But we must ask our guest. Emily, would you like a little of each?"

"Pick the cake! Pick the cake!" Pudge chanted.

"Oh," I stuttered, thrown off-guard by the lighthearted banter. "Anything is fine, sir."

"All right," he said. "I'll have Mom bring a sample of each and two big pieces of cake, okay?"

"Yeah!" Pudge cheered.

I stared as Mr. Unger left the room. He was nice. He didn't have to be or even try to be—the man was very, very nice.

The desserts arrived on a silver tray, a virtual smorgasbord of sweet delights. Each selection had a glass plate with a colored paper doily. There were glass shooters with layers of ice cream, whipped cream, and syrups to add to the chocolate cake. A silver tiered tray held blueberries, shaved chocolate, coconut, and maraschino cherries. It was like being at an elegant tea party with the flashing lights of the pinball machines as the backdrop. Pudge and I made a sweet ruin of the scrumptious display of desserts, enjoying each one as we made a game out of trying to pronounce the names of the fancy ones.

A servant peeked her head in the room. "Miss Quinn, your parents are leaving."

We stopped laughing and stared at each other. "Darn," I said.

"I know," said Pudge. "It seems like you just got here."

We entered the foyer and stood among the guests bidding farewell to Mr. and Mrs. Unger.

"Well, thank you," I said.

"You're welcome," said Pudge.

He shot Father a dirty look. It was almost comical watching the five foot four boy stare down the six foot two former Naval Captain. I half expected him to shout, "Step outside!"

I lined up with my parents as they extended a proper goodbye. I was nearly out the door when Mrs. Unger called me back.

"Emily, I hope you'll come again soon." She smiled and gave me an unexpected hug.

"I will, thank you."

As I waited in silence for the valet to bring the family car, I stared up at Pudge's house. Three hours ago, I arrived at a palace. But now, as I looked up at the mansion and all its grandeur, I only saw a home. *A real home.*

# *Twenty*

## A GODLESS PRAYER

I poured milk over my cereal, shaking my head at the picture of Bart Starr sprawled across the Wheaties box. The football player reminded me of Mark Hodges and how the kids at school considered him a big shot just because he could toss a ball fifty yards into the end zone. Big deal. He was no hero when he bullied my new friend, Pudge. He didn't know the boy I spent time with Saturday night.

I sighed, thinking back about how much fun it was to be with Pudge. I rested my hands under my chin, reliving the sound of his voice as he sang "Unforgettable."

"Ewe," I moaned. The flakes were soggy and as appetizing as a bologna sandwich left in a lunch pail for three days.

I tipped the bowl, watching the swollen mess trickle into the sink. As I reached for a fresh bowl, I heard familiar footsteps behind me. I turned to see Father.

"What are you doing?" He rubbed his prickly face. His eyes were bloodshot, and he reeked of alcohol.

Father drank every day now; he went from social drinker to heavy drinker the day Robert left for Boston. I knew when he was home by the sound of the crystal topper chiming on the scotch decanter. He used mouthwash and aftershave to disguise the odor but the stench still oozed from his pores. He smelled like rubbing alcohol mixed with rotten fruit.

"Nothing. The cereal got soggy, so I'm getting a fresh bowl."

"And why did the cereal get soggy?"

"The flakes turned mushy. That's all."

"I asked you why?"

"I was thinking and forgot, I guess."

"Thinking of what? I asked you a question."

I remained calm, matter-of-fact. "The party, that's all."

He scowled. "You think you're hot shit now because you know the son of my boss?"

The conversation was ridiculous and there was no reasoning with him. He apparently wanted to fight with me. I started to leave.

He gripped his hand around my arm. "So, you're too good for cereal, aye? What do you want, eggs benedict? Ya gotta eat, remember?"

I glanced at his hand and the box of Wheaties.

"Tell you what. I can fix that for you."

He staggered to the sink, grabbed my bowl, and waved it over his head like a murder weapon. "See this?"

I stared at his unshaven, half-sloshed face. Something was coming. I saw it in his face.

He crossed his arms and pointed to the basin and the limp cereal. Most of the milk had trickled down the drain, but the damp waste stuck to the sink like fresh spew. "There's your breakfast, pick it up. Eat it. We wouldn't want to waste food with all the starving kids in the world, would we?"

My hands formed tight fists, and I clenched my teeth. "No, I don't want to."

"You don't want to?" he mocked.

"No!" I yelled. "No!"

He leaned forward. His dry mouth made a clicking sound like someone chewing with his mouth open. "Why are you shouting? Your Mother left a few minutes ago for the store."

I stood up straight. "I won't eat it."

"Okay. Well, let's see. How about I bring the cereal to your school? You can eat it there."

I hit my fists against my thighs, thinking.

He lifted his brows. "Fine. I know when you take lunch…I'll bring it to your table."

I swallowed hard. "You wouldn't do that."

"I wouldn't? Did you forget I was in the military? I've done far worse. You need discipline just like the dumb wimps who couldn't cut it in the Navy. They'd eat their shit if I told them to. So eat it, moron."

"You wouldn't," I said, lowering my voice.

He smirked. "Lunch at twelve. I'll be there."

I examined his face, considering what to do. I couldn't let him disgrace me at school. I picked up each flake and flung it back in the bowl.

Father leaned against the counter and motioned for me to sit at the table.

I stuck a pile of soaked flakes in my mouth and swallowed. I gagged spontaneously.

He wiggled his index finger. "Keep going, soldier."

I spaced out. I jammed another group of mushy scraps down my throat, tasting nothing but Ajax cleanser. I kept going.

When I finished the filthy act, Father smacked my back. "You look kind of green. At ease, slug!"

I listened to his coarse laughter as he stumbled down the hallway and back to his bedroom. I grabbed a clean glass and gulped water until the urge to vomit disappeared and I could go to my room.

I had thirty minutes to get ready for school, but first, I needed to draw. My pencils and sketchpad were like a tourniquet to a gushing wound. I put aching thoughts to paper, hearing the sound of pencils hitting the desk and the rapid movement of my hand rubbing across the sketchpad. Frenzied thoughts poured onto the page. Spots floated in front of my eyes until I realized I had been holding my breath.

I caught a glimpse of the sketch and gasped. The picture showed a man standing next to a young girl. She stared at the man with her mouth open like she was screaming. She was alive but dismembered, her limbs were aligned but suspended in mid-air.

I slammed the book shut. Sweat rolled down my face, and the room twirled as I struggled to get up. I patted my body as I staggered to the bathroom. I plunged my face under the running faucet, trying to break loose from the terrifying image.

"Emily, are you okay in there?" Mother shouted.

I swung the door open. The wood smacked against the plastered wall with a loud thump. My body buckled, water dripped from my face, as I struggled to breathe.

"What's wrong with you?" she said.

I patted my body again and tried to form words. Impossible. I stooped in the doorway and listened to the steady whistling of my labored breaths.

She put her arm around me and guided me back to the bedroom. "What happened?"

My chest elevated up and down, panting. Tingling. Spinning. I doubted I could outrun the terror.

Mother touched my forehead. "I think you're just having a panic attack."

The word "just" sounded ludicrous considering I couldn't breathe, and my body was partially numb. I grabbed the paper bag out of my purse and began the breathing exercises. She kept her hand on my back as I heaved up and down.

After a few minutes, I could breathe easily again. "Yeah," I mumbled. "I've had them before. The bag helps. I'll be okay."

"You're going to be late for school," she said. "Freshen up and I'll drive you. I'll meet you outside in five minutes." With an audible sigh, she got up and left the room.

After I towel-dried my face and brushed my hair, I rushed outside. Mother was already in the car with the motor running when I crawled in next to her. She flipped on her classical music station. The volume was too loud to talk over, so I stared out the window in a stupor. The experience with Father, the horrifying picture I'd drawn, and my panic attack left me worn out. But the fatigue calmed my anxiety and enabled me to think. My life was out of control. The pain in my head hissed to get out, like a pot of water placed on the stove to seethe. Father kept the heat on "simmer" so I would eventually evaporate from the constant heat. My fear was that he would turn up the volume, detonating my mind and igniting everything in my path.

Mother pulled to the school drop-off curb. "Here we are."

I pinched the skin between my eyes and tried to get the disastrous thoughts out of my head. "Thanks."

"You're welcome, dear. Are you okay now?"

I got out and bent down to look at her through the open window. My eyes welled up, desperate to tell her everything. The words pressed against my head like an explosive begging to get out.

It was too late. She adjusted her rear-view mirror and placed her foot on the gas pedal. I watched her drive in the direction of home until she stopped at a red light.

I took a deep breath and started running before the light turned green. A few students gawked at me, but I didn't care. I sprinted to catch up with her and tell her everything. The details might shock her, but I desperately needed her help.

I stopped, as a hollow pain shot through me. I couldn't tell her. *Because she already knew.*

The truth was cloaked in secrecy, like not entering a room when Father insulted me or staying out of earshot when he assaulted me. The obscurity made me question whether she understood the depth of his hatred except for one inescapable fact. The night of Grandma's memorial, she knew he had beaten me to unconsciousness and she did nothing. I couldn't run to her. It would be like running for aid to a comatose patient.

I began walking to class. My throat gurgled when I swallowed, a reflux response from eating dirty cereal, no doubt. I looked down and saw

I had dug my nails into my forearm hard enough to draw blood. I wiped the red away and put on my "I'm fine" face. The words "I'm fine" played in my head like the sound of a siren from a lost ambulance.

Mark strutted toward me. "Emily! You waiting for a tardy slip?"

"I guess so," I answered.

He raised his eyebrows up and down. "You wanna play hooky? Your place or mine?"

I smirked and put my hand over the nail marks on my forearm. His dumb question warranted no answer, which was fine. At least he was a distraction. The horror of the morning dissipated a little under the auspice of Mark's dumb banter.

I got to class as the final bell sounded and settled into my seat. I listened to the teacher discussing the war in Viet Nam. The controversy sparked a heated debate, which kept me distracted until lunch.

The cafeteria lacked the usual clamor of chitchat; the sunshine enticed most of the kids outdoors to enjoy the lunch hour. I combed the small crowd for Pudge but couldn't find him.

I took the last bite of my sandwich when Pudge walked over. "Hi, Emily!"

"Hi! Where've you been? Where's your food?"

"I had a doctor's appointment and then lunch with my mom," he replied. "How are you?"

"Okay," I said.

"Can I sit here?"

I grinned, knowing I didn't own the cafeteria. "Yes, silly."

I thought about how different he seemed. Last week, I pitied him and regarded him as a hopeless loser. Little had I known he was a talented guy, fun to be with, and bright. To top it off, he was the son of a billionaire.

He viewed me pensively with his hands resting on crossed arms. "Are you sure you're okay? Because you seem upset."

I felt like I had cereal clinging to my teeth. "I'm all right," I insisted, with a passing glance. "Just great."

He eyed me and bent forward. "Are you sure?"

I decided to change the subject. "What'd you do at the doctor?"

"Allergist. I have asthma."

I avoided eye contact with him. "What a bummer having asthma."

I spotted Mark and his friends coming my way.

"Hey, why aren't you outside? We have a game of bocce going," said Mark.

I turned to him and smiled. "Oh?"

"Yeah. It's a lot more fun than staying in here, or are you quirky?" he chuckled. "Hey, Pudge. Where's your plate? Did your mommy put you on a diet?"

Mark turned to me. "You coming, Emily?"

"Sounds like fun. I don't think I've ever played."

"Well, come on!" A few of the girls joined in and told me they'd teach me.

I wanted to be normal and away from the watchful eyes of my new friend and his questions. "Sure, sounds like fun!"

I left Pudge at the table with his arms crossed.

Confiding in him about my dismal life had been cathartic at the party but not here. At school, I wanted to play the role of a regular kid. Pudge knew about my miserable life and how it affected my self-esteem. But dear God, I didn't want anyone else to know. I didn't want to live in misery all the time.

So I learned how to play bocce with the popular kids and pretended to enjoy myself. I laughed in the right places and mimicked the other girls. I pretended to be playful, engaging, and connected. The act was phony. I was as fake as a Godless prayer.

The lunch bell blasted. I relaxed my forced smile and dropped the charade. I scanned the crowd, desperate to find Pudge. The guilt gnawed at me. I had to find him.

Mark bounced the bocce ball up and down. "You going tonight?"

"Where?" I asked, looking around for Pudge.

"The football game, where else?"

"Oh, sure..." I blurted out, knowing he wouldn't find me among the onlookers anyway.

His friends shouted him over, so I broke away to find Pudge. I scanned the cafeteria, the grounds, and trotted down the halls but couldn't find him. The final bell blasted. I walked into class just as the five-second buzz sounded.

The time seemed to lag; my mind vacillated between finding Pudge and the dread of going home. When the bell finally sounded, I grabbed my book bag and bolted out the door to get to my friend. The reality of how rejected and alone he must have felt when I went off with Mark killed me. I had to find him.

"South side," I said under my breath. His mother had dropped him off, so I headed to the south curb. I elbowed my way through the kids, eager to apologize and tell him he was not alone.

It was too late. A large white sedan pulled up, and Pudge slid in the seat next to his mother. She leaned over and kissed him on the cheek. They both smiled and began talking—a mom and son happy to be to-gether—and fine.

My body slumped, weighed down by misery. I sat on a small cement bench, bent over, and buried my head in my hands. Two parallel roads ran through my mind. On one side was my mother driving away from me this morning. On the other side were Pudge and his mother driving off on exactly the same road. In the middle was the realization that Pudge was not the one alone —*I was.*

# Twenty-One

## Hold On

The warm weather enticed the kids to dawdle around the school grounds. I searched their faces for tension, a dazed expression, a frowned pause—something. Surely, someone had a parent who drank too much or slapped a kid for not meeting curfew. I needed to find one person to make me feel less alone.

"Stupid," I muttered. I hated myself. Seeing Pudge with his mom dispelled the myth that we were hapless victims clinging to each other. He wanted to be my friend because he was nice—period.

I pulled myself up for the walk home. Burned out. Sick of everything. Father's tyranny had accelerated since Robert left, fueled by his ramped-up boozing. The hope that my father and I would re-connect now seemed like a cruel prank, leaving me morose and pessimistic. Not a good combination for a seventeen-year-old.

The sight of 12438 Orchid Drive sickened me. I stood on the corner and watched a blue jay beat its wings against one of the arched domes, trying to land. Mother had the gardener install bird spikes to keep them from landing in her precious yard and dropping bird crap. After a few failed attempts, the bird flew off for friendlier surroundings. If only I could too.

I turned the key carefully to avoid a click sound and get to my room unnoticed. Tiptoeing through the foyer, Mother and Father sat on the couch in the living room watching an episode of *Perry Mason*. Father was engrossed in the drama; Mother sat a few inches away organizing her files with an occasional glimpse at the show. I put my head down and started down the hallway to my room.

I paused. Anger swelled in my gut, snapping me out of my submissive demeanor. My fists tightened, remembering Father relishing the sight of me cramming dirty cereal down my throat. I could smell his alcohol breath and hear his raspy laugh as my torment tickled his sadistic funny bone. I made myself look at him.

I slapped both hands over my mouth to stop a gasp.

Mother was focused on *Perry Mason*. Father sat next to her— dead. His skin flaked off and dropped like bone ash on his Pierre Cardin suit. His once-meaty hands were small and tight with remnants of flesh clinging to the bones. His lips receded into his mouth and his orbital bone protruded as his eyes disintegrated.

Perry Mason's secretary, Della Street, handed a note to Perry. It read: "The killer is Emily Quinn."

I looked back at Father—alive. He leaned forward, flicked his cigarette into the ashtray, and picked up his Martini.

I ran from the hallucination. My hands trembled as I shut my bedroom door. I clutched my throat, choking on fear. Strange noises buzzed in my head as I fell to the floor. Terror clamped down hard, freezing my ability to reason. I wondered if my sanity was snapping and if the hallucination had been the first sign.

I stumbled into bed and prayed for God's mercy. If insanity was my fate, I pleaded with God to not wake me up.

"Emily! Wake up, Robert's on the phone!" Mother hollered.

I squinted at the table clock. It was 4 a.m.

She opened the door, dressed in her nightgown and slippers. "Wake up! Robert's on the phone and wants to talk to you. Hurry up. He has classes in an hour."

I pulled back the covers. "Oh, sure, sure…"

I stumbled into the hallway and picked up the phone.

"Hello?" I muttered.

"Hi Em. How are you doing?" Robert asked.

"Fine," I answered. "How are you?"

Mother came in the living room pulling on her robe. Father was already on the couch, dressed in a madras robe. He glared at me, obviously eavesdropping.

"I'm good. Em, just listen, okay?"

I turned my back to Father. "Okay, sure."

"How are you really?"

I couldn't answer honestly with Father's eyes and ears on me. "I'm fine."

"Listen carefully. Since I've been here, I've worried about leaving you. I need you to be honest but only answer yes or no. I'm sure Mother and Father are close by and can hear everything you say. Am I right?"

"Yes."

"Okay, just answer yes or no. Is it bad with Father?"

I moved the receiver closer to my mouth. "Yes."

"Your graduation is in ten days. I'm coming, but I don't want you to tell them. Do you understand?"

"Yes." It seemed like a huge secret was unfolding.

"Okay, I don't want him getting suspicious. Ask me how the weather is in Boston."

I heard Father clear his throat. "How's the weather there?"

"I'm only going to be in town for a day," he continued. "I'll be at your graduation. I want you to carry a small bag to the graduation with only the stuff you must have. Nothing else. Ask me how I like school. Keep it casual."

204

"How's school?"

"I'll be there, and you're going back to Boston with me. You'll be eighteen after graduation so you can legally move."

My mind raced. Robert somehow managed to pick up on my misery without even being here. "Uh..."

I tried to picture leaving San Francisco. The possibility never occurred to me, but Father's persistent tirades and the frightening vision of Father dead collided like life and death. Leaving made sense.

"Em? Are you still there?"

"Yes...yes, I'm listening."

"You must get out. It's only going to get worse. I don't want to scare you, but something bad will happen if you stay. I understand everything more clearly now that I'm away from the house. Will you leave with me?" Robert's voice remained determined, almost pleading.

I thought of Reid. His mom must have given him my address by now, but I hadn't heard from him. The truth was that it had been over a year. My mind scrambled with all the "what-ifs" but I knew Robert was right. I had to get out of here.

I cleared my throat. "Yes, Robert."

"Okay, good. This has to be our last conversation or they'll get suspicious. If you need to talk to me, call Vanderbilt Hall at Harvard. Only use a pay phone. Do not say a word to anyone."

"Okay, sure."

"They probably won't go to your graduation, so after you get your diploma, go to the cafeteria. I'll be at the door. We'll leave right away. And don't worry. I'll take care of everything. Stay quiet and I'll explain everything when we're on the plane. Okay?"

"Yes," I replied. The plan was in place. I needed to get out of the house before something terrible happened.

I hung up feeling like a veil had been lifted. Robert had acknowledged Father's cruelty. I rushed to my room, thinking about the urgency in his voice.

Father stood in my doorway. "What'd you talk about?"

"Nothing…he just wanted to say hi."

He gripped my arm and crouched close to my face. "Liar. What did you talk about?"

His sweat grazed my cheek. I tried to wriggle away. "I told you. It was nothing."

He yanked my arm. "What the hell did you talk about?"

"Nothing," I answered, bending away from him.

I cringed at the sound of wood rubbing against the carpet as he shut the door with his foot. He kept the grip on my arm and placed the other hand around my neck. We stood face-to-face. His teeth clenched, and his jawbone throbbed.

"Tell me what he said to you…*now*."

I told myself he would have to kill me before I would tell him. His hand tightened; his sickening breath turned my stomach.

He squeezed my neck. "Tell me!"

I stared into his bloodshot eyes. "No!"

I heard a toilet flush; Mother was close by so his diatribe couldn't last much longer. He loosened his grip and let go. I thought he'd left, but then he cleared his throat and spat in my face.

He hurried off. Saliva dripped down my eyes, my nose, and my chin.

I ripped off my pajama top and wiped the slime off my face. I rubbed, frantically trying to erase the hurled waste. The dry friction hurt my skin. I kept going.

The bathroom was empty, so I bolted inside and locked the door. I turned on the hot water, grabbed the bar of soap, and began scrubbing. I rubbed my face, followed by hot water, repeating the process over and over. It didn't seem good enough. I grabbed a can of Ajax scouring powder and read: "removes germs." So I poured the gritty powder in my hand, mixed it with the hot water, and rubbed it all over my face. I scoured the pasty substance over my forehead, cheeks, and mouth, careful not to miss an inch of skin. My eyes stung, but I didn't care. I kept scrubbing to remove all traces of the repulsive slobber. My stomach convulsed. I puked in the toilet and flushed. I started the cleaning process again until Mother knocked on the door.

"Are you okay?" she asked.

"I'm fine!" I shouted.

I paused long enough to hear her bedroom door close and then poured more scouring powder and hot water on my face. I repeated the process. Ten times. I rushed back to my room, patting a towel over my face.

The bureau mirror cast a reflection on the wall. My impulse was to keep walking. I stopped. I had to face the truth.

I stood, half-naked, in front of the mirror. I was too tired to pretend that what Father did to me didn't matter or that I could survive his hatred. The power I experienced after Robert's phone call was gone. My resolve to act happy and pretend I was okay had drained out of me when he spat in my face. I questioned whether I could survive the ten days until Robert rescued me from my living Hell.

So, I vowed to face the reflection in the mirror. I put my head down for a few seconds and told myself not to alter the image into something bearable. I sat down ready to face the truth.

The girl's face was rubbed raw and covered in scrapes like a feral cat had mauled her. Some of the scrapes had ripped off the skin, revealing bloody tissue. I winced looking at her open wounds but then caught sight of her eyes. The pain drew me closer to her. I leaned in.

Her blue eyes held a silent plea and an undisguised desperation. Her wounds left her too weak to talk or even moan. She only had the emotion in her eyes to plead with me to stop the unbearable pain. Her despair broke my heart.

It took all of my strength not to gasp or cry out in horror at her injuries. My eyes softened like hers and filled with tears. I moved closer. I pressed my fingers to my lips and held a kiss out to her.

"I'm so sorry," I whispered. " I feel it, too."

I knew I didn't have the power to help her yet.

I couldn't leave the girl without doing something. "I won't let you suffer for long. I promise I will return for you. Hold on."

I fixed my eyes on her until her fear faded. I left, knowing the sad girl trusted me and believed that someday I would fulfill my promise to her.

⌒⟶

### San Francisco County Jail, August 14, 1966. End of Session Six

*I* opened my eyes, and for once I didn't hear the sound of Doctor Lieberman's pencil scraping across his notebook or the sound of him unwrapping a candy bar.

His weathered face was stagnant except for his furrowed brow. Was he fighting with the details of our session? I didn't know. I wanted to take the emotion from him; it probably violated his creed, some code of psychiatrist conduct, or something like that.

"I'm all right," I said, putting my hands in my lap. I'd been stroking my face, not to remove the imagined saliva, but a self-soothing gesture. The girl in the mirror that I promised I'd come back for was still with me.

"Emily, this was a difficult session. It's okay to acknowledge that."

"I know."

He walked to the coffee pot and poured himself his usual jet-black coffee and returned to his desk. "Psychiatry is not an exact science. Many would dispute the field as a science at all," he said, thoughtfully.

"I'm sure," I said, although I wasn't.

"Medical school teaches us not to speak in absolutes, or make promises."

"Yes," I said.

He drummed his fingers on his desk. "Emily, tell me about the girl in the mirror. The one you promised you'd come back for."

I rubbed my hands together. "Okay. I felt her as soon as I opened my eyes. She is still with me...maybe she always is."

He concentrated on my words.

That gave me pause, but I kept going.

"I know she is me...I do. I wanted to help her. Maybe I couldn't face what Father had done to me...I don't know. It doesn't make sense."

"It will...I believe someday it will. And although, as a doctor, I cannot promise you anything, I will do everything in my power to find her, too."

The door opened. From the soft sound of keys jingling, I knew it was the young guard, Jennifer. I had a feeling the doctor had her assigned to me.

She led me to the door; I finally heard the sound of the doctor unwrapping a vending machine offering. I smiled, and we exchanged our usual goodbyes and "see-you-in-a-week" words.

The session was painful, as Doctor Lieberman said. Even so, knowing he was there when I came out of the horror helped. He was more than the notorious wizard I first met weeks ago. I no longer felt like a series of notes scribbled in his case study. He seemed to care about what happened to me.

# Twenty-Two

## EXODUS

*San Francisco County Jail, August 21, 1966.  Beginning of Session Seven*

"I did it," I said to the guard, Jennifer, as I cleared the final step. It was the first time I'd climbed the five flights of stairs without tripping.

She smiled. "Good job."

We walked into Doctor Lieberman's office as he was pulling my case out of the filing cabinet. I still winced seeing my name and the growing stack of papers.

The doctor and I talked about the last session and what we had accomplished. After six weeks, I had grown to trust him. I'd never met my grandfather, but he reminded me of an ideal grandpa. Maybe it was his wisdom or the way his spectacles always found their way to the tip of his nose. The doctor was devoted; he knew every detail of my case and slept many nights in his office.

When his voice softened, I knew it was time to uncover the lost details of my life. The sound of his voice disconnected me from my surroundings as I returned to the last days of high school.

The bitter wind whipped across my face, which made the cuts sting. I had to resist the urge to dig my fingernails into my skin. I'd ruined my friendship with Pudge, Reid didn't want me anymore, and Robert was a thousand miles away. I felt as sliced up as my face.

I ducked behind a pepper tree to check my skin before going to class. In the sunlight, the cuts looked ten times worse and impossible to ignore. Knowing they were self-inflicted made it worse. I could have just cleaned my face once, but no—I had to scour my skin off. I dabbed Cover Girl makeup on the cuts and tossed the mirror and foundation back in the bag. There was not a damn thing I could do and frankly, I didn't care. I had more important things to think about, like apologizing to Pudge and running off to Boston in ten days.

I spotted Mark standing with his buddies. He wore a light blue shirt and jeans and held his football jacket over his shoulder. I wondered what he'd do without his letterman jacket. He carried it around like a cloth trophy. I turned, hoping he didn't see me.

"Hey!" Mark shouted. "Come over here!"

I shook my head. "No! I'm waiting for someone!"

He squinted his eyes. "What happened to your face?"

"Cat!" I yelled.

The school bell sounded. I rushed through the swarm of kids and spotted Pudge.

I ran up to meet him. "Listen, I want to talk to you. I'm so sorry about yesterday. Please, Pudge…I hope you can forgive me. I'm sorry. I shouldn't have gone with those jerks. I don't know what I was thinking. Honestly…I feel awful," I said, talking faster than I could think.

"Hey, it's okay," he said.

"No, it's not. I mean…I know you're mad, and you have every right to be…"

He touched my elbow. "Emily, you don't need to keep apologizing. I already accepted your apology."

Once I shut up, I could see he forgave me. I slouched as the hallway tilted from side to side.

"Hey," said Pudge. "Are you okay?"

"Yeah, I just needed to put my head down. I'm fine now."

"Let's talk at lunch. I'll meet you in the cafeteria. Save a spot for me."

"Okay, thanks, Pudge." I choked down the tears and walked to my homeroom.

⌒

*I* set my lunch tray down feeling unexpectedly shy. "Hi, Pudge."

"Hi! How are you?"

I bit my lip and sat down. "I'm okay. How are you?"

"I'm good. Oh, you chose the meatloaf, huh?"

I glanced down at the oblong loaf. "Oh…yeah."

"You do know they use all the leftovers, right? They take all the un-eaten food, roll the ingredients together and call it meatloaf. Hot dogs, hamburger meat, chipped beef…you name it. One time, I saw a hot dog popping out from the top. I thought it was a thumb from one of the cooks!"

The tension dissolved into giggles. "So, what are you doing after high school?" I asked.

"Yale. We leave a couple days after graduation."

"We?"

"Yeah, my folks are taking me. They like to get the family involved. There's a Parents' Day where they tour the school and have a formal lunch afterwards. A welcome, I guess."

I felt a kick in my gut but tried not to show it. "Oh, sounds good."

Pudge put his fork down. "What are your plans?"

I didn't realize I had been scratching my face. I cringed, knowing the makeup had worn off by now. "I'm not sure yet."

"Well…if you need any help looking up colleges, let me know."

He avoided staring at my face, which judging from the itching and burning had to look dreadful. I put my head down and felt one of the dry patches. "I scrubbed my face too hard this morning."

I stared at the meatloaf. That's how I felt, ground up and disguised in ketchup. I grabbed my wrist to stop the urge to scratch.

He leaned forward. "What really happened?"

"He spit in my face," I blurted out.

I knew he was waiting for the rest of the ugly story. So I told him everything—the cereal, the threats, and the choking. The ugliness spilled out of me like an oil spill on pure water, ripping away the barrier I had built to contain the contaminant. This time I didn't deflect or try to disguise the agony.

"He's getting worse, Pudge."

"Let's go outside," he whispered.

I kept my head down and followed him into the sunlight. I hadn't realized we were sitting under a tree until I caught the gentle movement of shadows dancing on the ground.

"Emily, we need to talk."

I gave him a passing glance not meant to linger but send a quick signal of acknowledgment.

He clenched his fists. "I am so sorry. What your father did to you was abusive."

I took a deep breath and nodded.

"I don't pretend to understand how you feel, but I know a lot about verbal abuse. I get jerked around every day at school. Those dimwits will be gone soon enough, and I don't give a rat's ass what they think of me."

I nodded.

"When someone you don't know puts you down, it hurts, but you get over it. But this is your father, the person that is supposed to love and protect you. This is not your fault, and I hope you get that."

As I listened, the knots in my stomach eased with every word.

"Your father is a monster, and he needs to be stopped."

He continued to rebuke my father and tell me it was not my fault. For years, I had felt like a hostage unable to confront my abuser. Pudge untied the ropes and freed me to view Father differently. I couldn't process everything except the words "it's not your fault."

Tears stung my face as they ran across the raw cuts. I knew the school bell would ring soon, so I blotted my eyes and stood up. "Thank you, Pudge."

"Remember, none of this is your fault. He is abusive, and you don't deserve it. You never did."

"Really?" I supposed I needed to hear it one more time.

"Really. He is a horrible, dreadful human being. This has to end. Do you understand?"

"Yes," I said, along with a long sigh. "And I'm okay." The bell sounded, announcing that lunch was over.

"By the way," he said. "Here, I pillaged these from the cafeteria."

I stared at a handful of packets. "What's this for?"

"It's honey. Dab this on your cuts at night and cover it with tissue. Your face will heal in no time."

I glanced at the honey packets and laughed. "How do you know all this stuff?"

"I read a lot."

We hugged and headed in opposite directions to class. All the vile things I believed about myself had been called into question. The words *it's not your fault* played like a hymn of promise to heal my overburdened mind. I reached up to scratch my itchy skin and stopped. In ten days, I would leave with Robert for a new life. Not born of escapism but the realization that I deserved to live free of endless violence.

⌣

The big day had arrived. I stood near the back of the crowded auditorium in my black robe taking it all in. Pudge was huddled with the honor roll students, and Mark and his buddies were clustered in a corner talking about a post-graduation keg party. The other students talked with their friends about the ceremonious exodus and hugged one another.

My exodus was different. I would be leaving with Robert to a place I'd never been. No goodbyes or farewells.

I felt conflicted. The last few days at the house had been quiet which gave me time to think. Getting away from Father made sense, I would have signed up for front-line combat to get away from him. But Mother was another story. I hated to leave her without saying goodbye, and I still had so many questions that only she could answer. How did Penelope die? Would she be sad without me?

Also, where was Reid? Why hadn't he written? Would he try to find me when he returned home this summer?

Pudge stood next to me, dressed in his honor roll white robe and blue sash. "Emily!"

"Hey, hey! Top of your class and valedictorian!"

He grinned and took a little bow. "Are you ready?"

I wondered if he knew about my plan to leave with Robert. "Ready?"

He raised his eyebrows. "Sure…graduation."

"I need to tell you something important," I whispered.

"Over here," he said, motioning to a quiet corner.

I had to talk fast before they called us to line up. "I'm leaving for Boston with Robert after the ceremony. He planned the move. I'm supposed to meet him at the cafeteria doors. My parents have no idea. He told me not to tell anyone, but I had to tell you. Reid doesn't know because I haven't talked to him. My brother thinks I need to start over, away from my father. But it feels weird to leave without a trace… maybe it's wrong not to tell my mother."

He grabbed my arm. "Do it, Emily. This is your chance! Thank God for Robert. There's no choice here. Remember when I told you your father had to be stopped? Well, this is it. Promise me you'll go!" His words were almost loud enough for others to hear him.

"What about my mother?"

"She'll be fine. Robert left for college, right? Once you're settled, write her a letter. Listen, your father's abuse will only get worse. I guarantee you something bad will happen. Your brother is right."

"Wow…Robert said the same thing."

"And I'll be in New York, which is only a few hours away. We can get together on weekends."

"I would love that. But what about Reid?"

He pulled me closer. "Listen, nothing will work with Reid or anyone else while you're under the control of that maniac. He'll poison all your relationships including Reid. But more important, he will continue to poison you. Man, he'll kill your spirit. Please hear me."

I remembered Father's hand squeezing my neck and his hatred spewing in my face. "Okay," I nodded. "You're right."

The vice principal started instructions for the honor students to line up, so I gave him a quick hug.

I trotted onto the stage following the other graduating students and took my seat on cue. The hushed warnings from the vice principal could not damper the excited chatter. The students chatted, poked elbows, itching to leave behind the restraints of high school. I surveyed the soon-to-be adults with black paper plates on their heads. Most of the kids searched the audience on the sly, eager to find their parents.

I sat up straight as Pudge took the podium to give his commencement address.

"Good evening ladies and gentlemen, friends and family, teachers and administrators. We are gathered together to celebrate the accomplishments of the 1965 class of Laughlin High School. Most of you know me as the fat kid everyone calls Pudge. But today I leave that name behind and assume my right to be treated with the respect that I have earned. Let me introduce myself. My name is Perry, Perry Unger…"

As Pudge—I mean Perry, finished his speech and stepped away from the podium, the applause was deafening. People stood on their feet and clapped for the fat kid that no one wanted to be around. I jumped and cheered and even tried to whistle. All the sneers Pudge had endured for years terminated in a round of applause. He had the last word.

People began dispersing. Kids sought out their parents and relatives for a pat on the back. I removed my cap and black gown and watched as parents and students embraced. It was a celebratory crowd of happy kids and proud parents. I had to look away.

My assignment was to go to the cafeteria, meet Robert, and fly to Boston. No celebration, no goodbyes, no parents. I pushed the disappointment out of my mind and placed one foot in front of the other as I walked in the direction of the cafeteria.

I didn't expect anything. Still, with each step, I imagined my parents behind me. I wanted Mother to call my name and beg me to stay. Crazy as it was, I even wished Father would scream for my forgiveness, offering excuses for all his atrocities.

With each step, I descended into sorrow. I wasn't as ready to let go as I had thought.

Desire and reality collided because desire was so much stronger. I wanted to believe my parents had been in the audience and proud to see me graduate. I wanted my mother to help me pick out my wedding dress someday and shop for my baby's first bassinet. Leaving without a word suddenly seemed like giving up.

Before I knew it—I was questioning everything.

My mind flipped from one thought to another—remnants of memories like a haphazard quilt. I found excuses to stay and reasons to leave. I looked up at the cafeteria and saw Robert. He looked different. He had traded his white starched shirt for a brown sweater and his pressed pants for jeans. His hair was no longer gelled; it was soft and hung just below his ears.

"Hi Robert," I said, quietly.

"Hi, Em. I'm happy you're here. No one knows about this, right?"

"Right," I said. "I'm alone."

"That's good."

My hands trembled, so I crossed my arms over them.

He seemed to sense my anxiety. "Let's sit and talk. We have some time."

I sat next to him but couldn't find any words. I didn't know if the move had gotten to me, or seeing the new-Robert.

"Em, listen. Getting away from Mother and Father was the best decision I ever made and it will be for you, too."

I frowned. Perfect, fun, idyllic, carefree and devoted were the adjectives I would use to describe Robert's childhood. Mine started with Hell and went down. So why would Robert tell me it was his best decision? Even in the twilight, he picked up on my confused frown.

"I can't explain now, there's not enough time. You need to get away from them. They're toxic. They've damaged you. These last few weeks helped me to see things more clearly."

I nodded, still at a loss for words. Something stood between us; I supposed it was my lingering doubts. I searched his face for answers.

He checked the time. "Father will destroy you," he said, grabbing my hands. "He's been destroying you for years. He's chipping away at you, little by little, one day at a time. He'll keep going until nothing is left of you."

The hallucination of Father's rotting body slammed through my brain and switched to *my* decaying corpse. I felt my body soften into a withered mass as I struggled to breathe. I began to tremble and shake. Robert grabbed me and tightened his hold. I knew he was talking because I felt short bursts of air in my ear.

My body slid into terror as I screamed into Robert's chest. I wrenched, feeling myself being bashed in a darkened parking lot. Violence collided, one on top of the next. I tried to cough up filthy cereal and clawed at my face to remove whiskey-laden saliva. Visions of Father's thick hands around my neck and his vicious words ripped into my soul.

Robert pressed a paper bag to my mouth. I panted into the bag in short gasps, feeling the bag rustle around my face. I jerked; each breath felt like my ribs were cracking on the gritty blacktop. I couldn't get away from the monster.

Robert held me closer, whispering. "Think about Seattle in the summer…remember walking with Grandma in her garden…"

I grabbed his voice like an outstretched hand saving me from a rip tide. As he talked, I felt the sway of a porch swing and the smell of lemons and roses on a warm afternoon. I remembered the feel of Grandma's hand as we walked among the tall pines and moss-covered pagodas. I pictured us at her kitchen table and the taste of sweet butter melting on fresh baked raisin bread.

The purity of the memories finally eclipsed Father's toxins, dissolved by the power of a grandma's love.

I relaxed into the safe arms of my brother. He continued to talk as I breathed the last of the anxiety into the bag. The flashbacks of Father's fury the night of the memorial cleared my mind once I came to. It was Grandma and Robert that had saved me that night. I needed a direct hit to see the truth.

My legs were still rubbery. "I just need a minute."

"It's okay. We have a little time. I rented a car; you can stretch out in the back until we get to the airport." Although his voice was steady, I could tell he was rattled.

Poor Robert. This wasn't much different than that fateful night; me stretched out in the car, clutching my broken ribs while Father explained to Mother why beating me up was no big deal.

I straightened up, feeling stronger. "I'm better. I can handle it."

"Are you sure?"

The cool night air had already dried the sweat on my face. "Yep! I'm positive!"

"You have me, Em. You're going to be okay. I promise."

Seeing his tender face choked me up. I wondered why I had ever doubted leaving. "Robert…you've done so much for me. I don't know how to thank you."

"You already have. Are you ready to start a new life?"

I was very ready. The panic attack left me cleansed, refreshed. I had to see the rattlesnake coiled up with his flicking tongue and rattling posterior before I could run like hell to avoid his venomous bite.

"I am more than ready! Let's go!"

He held out his hand. I grabbed on but not in despair—in hope.

We walked through the south parking lot chatting about the coolest rock groups, the weather on the east coast, and what kind of car we wanted someday. Nothing dramatic or even significant. Just brother and sister spending time together sharing idle thoughts. I walked with a lift to my steps, light, and energetic—happy.

I turned to Robert. "Did you hear that?"

"Huh? I didn't hear anything."

"Humph. I thought I heard my name." I said. "It's kind of funny, when I walked to the cafeteria, I wished Mother and Father were behind me, calling me. Like that would ever happen."

He looked down at the ground, silent.

I poked his arm. "Come on! I'm okay! I knew darn good and well they wouldn't show up. Besides, I don't care anymore."

He shook his head. "Yeah, I know. But that doesn't make it right."

It was my turn to cheer him up. "So, what's on your wall since you moved to Boston? I'll bet it's a beautiful girl!"

He raised his eyebrows and shot me a mischievous look. "Like I'd tell my little sister."

"Oh, come on Robby! You know I'll find out! Robby's got a girlfriend!"

We both laughed, like old times but better. Nicer because I didn't need to worry about Father walking in. The move to Boston with Robert was already working.

"What's Harvard like?" I asked, wondering about the clothing requirement. I still couldn't get over the change in his appearance.

"Fantastic. Weird at first living in a dorm but now I love it. There's a huge dining hall in each section so it's almost like a big hotel. The school is very focused on the arts. Right outside my room is a huge statue of Picasso. An interesting character to greet before walking to class!"

"Wow, you seem so different. You know...happy. Not so uptight, not that you were ever uptight," I fumbled.

He laughed and pointed his finger. "You did just call me uptight! You called me uptight and then took it back. Nah, you got it right the first time. Leaving helped me figure out what I wanted…it'll help you, too."

"I believe you," I said. "So…I'm obviously not a scholar like you, where should I go to school?"

"I've checked into schools for you. There's an excellent school nearby called Lesley College. It's big in the arts, plus it's in Cambridge, only seven miles away."

Robert had done his homework. "Hmm, Lesley College. I can't wait to check it out. I never thought I'd go to a real college."

"What'd you mean? Are there fake colleges?"

"No, I only meant trade schools…like beauty schools and stuff. Not that they aren't real schools…just different, you know."

"Beauty school? Are you interested in becoming a beautician? I thought you wanted to study art."

I didn't want to bring up Mother's comments after the neighbor had bragged on my artwork. "No, I don't want to go to beauty school. Never gave it a thought. I'm not a good student like you though, and I've always hated math and science. It's not my thing, so I guess I didn't think I could cut it in college."

"You'll do great! Geez, not everyone likes science. Sometimes when you're gifted…like you are in art, it drowns out everything else. Your talent in art negates the need for other subjects."

I felt two feet off the ground. "I never looked at it that way. Thanks, Robert."

"Sure, anytime. Leave the science to us nerds! Well, we're almost at the car. I parked a long way out. I didn't want to take the chance of anyone seeing me."

I looked at Robert; he was my parent in every way that mattered.

He stopped in front of a Chevy Nova. "Here we are."

I touched my lips, savoring my smile and optimism. My "new life" had begun, and I couldn't wait to see what was next.

We drove to the airport talking about Lesley, Harvard, and life as a college student. For the first time, I believed I had a purpose, a future, something to build on. I had always thought of Robert as my rescuer, helping me with my repetitive failures. But now we talked about college, the most interesting courses, and teachers. We had education in common, which gave us a kinship I never thought possible.

Robert pulled into a parking spot. "Guess what? We're here."

I grabbed my travel bag, which was filled with my sketchpads. "I'm so excited, Robert. I can't believe this is happening!"

I stepped out of the car and giggled at the roar of jet engines. My stomach churned with excitement as I stared out at the airplanes.

Robert grabbed his carry-on from the trunk. "You ready?"

"Heck yeah! When do we leave?" I shouted over the airport noise.

He glanced at his watch. "Fifteen minutes!"

I pointed to an airliner speeding down the runway. "Look! That will be us soon!"

The jet lifted off with a sharp rise into the night. "Fasten your seatbelt, Em! Get ready for a new life!"

We rushed to the terminal singing the Beatles', "Ticket to Ride." We brimmed with silliness and excitement.

As I grabbed the door, I heard my name again. This time I knew it was real and turned.

"Emily! Emily! E M I L Y!!!!"

# Twenty-Three

## IMPOSSIBLE CHOICE

Reid sprinted across the parking lot. "Emily!"

I dropped my bag and stared wide-eyed. My name, mingled with the flight announcement and the runway noise, sounded like dueling sounds in the night. I turned to see the expression on Robert's face; his eyes were fixed on Reid.

It wasn't my imagination. *Reid was back.*

He swept me into his arms. "Emily!"

He set me down, breathless. "Good God! I've been looking everywhere for you!"

He talked like he just returned from a week's trip instead of three years. "Anyway, I knew it was your graduation day but the drive took longer than I thought plus I got a damn flat tire. My spare was flat too! So it took forever to find a tire store that was open this time of night!"

He talked fast and waved his arms as he recounted his story. "So I finally got there, and graduation was over! I ran around the school looking for you and then saw you get into a car. I broke the sound barrier to get here!"

He continued to tell me every detail, which gave me a chance to check him out. He was even more handsome than before. He wore a plaid button-down shirt, corduroy slacks, and athletic shoes. His straight brown hair curled up on the ends as it touched his broad shoulders. One of the parking lot lamps hit his face, revealing his dark brown eyes, square jaw, and crooked smile.

I pressed my fingers to my lips, feeling my smile broaden with each word.

Reid picked me up and swung me in a circle. "Are you surprised?"

I broke out in spontaneous laughter. "Of course!"

He puffed out his chest. I'd almost forgotten how Reid loved surprises. "Babe...you look fantastic."

The word "babe" sounded bizarre, considering I hadn't seen him in over three years. His exuberance made my constant worries seem silly.

He glanced at Robert. "Hey, Robert. Long time no see."

Robert stood with his arms crossed, his eyes focused on me.

Reid studied the two of us. "Emmy, what are you doing at the airport?"

"Well, um...leaving with Robert."

"Leaving? Where to?"

I glanced at Robert, who was staring at Reid. "Boston."

He wrinkled his nose. "Boston? Why would you go to Boston?"

"Um, Robert lives in Boston. He goes to Harvard Medical School."

He turned to Robert. "When does your plane leave?"

Robert stiffened and widened his eyes at me.

"No, Reid," I said. "I was moving to Boston with my brother."

"*Was* moving?" Robert asked. "Emily, our plane leaves in ten minutes. Are you kidding me?"

Reid edged toward me. "You what?"

"I was going to..."

Robert put his hands up. "Emily, come on. Tell me you aren't actually thinking about staying here."

They stood on both sides of me. Neither talked as they waited for me to say something. "I know, Robert."

The loudspeaker announced that our flight was boarding.

Reid put his hands on his hips. "Emily. I came all this way. You can't leave. What about us?"

Robert stepped in front of Reid. "Em, we have a plan and everything is settled. This is your chance. It's the right thing to do...please."

I felt like a horrible person. Torn. I didn't want to hurt Robert, but I couldn't lose Reid. I stared at Reid and nodded in Robert's direction, hoping he could find the right words to make him understand.

He scowled at my brother. "Listen here, man. You can't tell her what to do! She's an adult now so let her make her own decision. Who elected you her damn keeper?"

Robert waved the plane tickets at Reid and started toward him.

I swung my arms. "No, Reid! You don't understand. My brother was helping me! It's not what you think!"

"Yeah?" Reid sneered. I remembered something about him—he fights to win. Reid was as tough as Robert was gentle.

"Emmy...come on," Reid said, drawing out the words. "It's been three years. I came back for you, babe."

Robert put his tickets in his pocket. He stood in place taking long breaths, his eyes closing for a few seconds, as he exhaled slowly. It broke my heart to see him that way. I thought back on my first panic attack and how he helped me. He saved me time after time, and I was letting him down. It wasn't fair.

I walked to him. "Robert," I said, unable to finish my thought.

Reid stood next to me, his arms crossed.

"Excuse us," he said. "My sister and I need to talk."

He led me several feet away. "Emily, listen to me. You cannot go home. It's very dark there. You don't have enough light to fight Father. Please come with me. I don't have time to explain everything, but we can talk on the plane. You can always return to San Francisco later if that's what you want."

His words cut me up in pieces. My mind was already made up and there was no good way to tell him. "Robert, I'm sorry. I can't go. I love Reid...you know that."

"Love! This is not about love! Love yourself!"

"Robert, please..."

"Listen to me. If you don't change direction, you will end up back at that Hell!"

I hung my head. There was nothing he could say to change my mind, and nothing I could say to make him understand. I glanced at our plane. "I'm sorry, Robert. I can't...you're going to miss your flight."

He grabbed my hand. "Please listen. You're making a snap decision. Come with me."

The despair in his voice was agonizing to hear. I looked down and shook my head.

The loudspeaker announced the last call for our flight. The aircraft roared to a high pitch as Robert dropped my hand and ran to the plane. I wanted to scream out as I watched him climb the stairs to the fuselage.

The jet started to taxi. I screamed, "I love you, Robert" even though I knew he couldn't hear me. I saw him for a split-second with a halted wave as the aircraft took flight.

The jet climbed into the darkness. The promise of a new life away from Father, Lesley College, and studying art was gone. My body sagged, overcome with guilt that I couldn't make Robert understand that I had to follow the yearning in my heart. I turned, wiped the tears away, and began walking in the direction of my life with Reid.

I had to turn around. A strange breeze lingered, whispering in my ear, warning me to consider my brother's words. Robert had told me home was very dark and begged me not to go back there. He said I didn't have enough light to fight Father. He would have explained everything on the plane. Now I might never know. I looked up and stared at the empty space where he had flown away. Something in the dark void warned me I lost much more than a promise of a new life.

I rubbed my arms, thinking. *What was he going to tell me?*

Reid put his arms around my waist. "It'll be okay."

I turned and wept into his chest. "I feel awful. Robert's done so much for me."

"He can visit you, babe, or you can visit him."

I shook my head. "You don't understand."

"Yes, I do. It was hard for me to say goodbye to my folks when I went off to college."

"No, it's more than that."

His arms loosened. "I'm starting to think you're not happy to see me, that you wished you'd gone with Robert."

I pulled back, wiping my eyes. "No. I just wish he understood."

"He will someday. Robert's always been pretty black-and-white about things. The guy really needs to loosen up."

I gazed up at the sky, half-expecting the plane to turn around. "He's a great brother," I said. "The best."

He bristled. "I wouldn't know, being an only child and all. So...are we going to talk about Robert all night?"

"Guess not," I mumbled.

He took his arms off me. "Geez, this is not the way I expected you to react. I mean, this was a big deal for me. I couldn't wait to see you. But I can't say the same about you."

"No, it's not that...I mean, I stayed with you, right? Doesn't that mean something? You just don't know the whole story."

He crossed his arms. "Are you happy I came back or not?"

I had almost forgotten how quickly he became offended. I took his hand and held it to my chest. "Can't you tell? My heart is with you. I've waited three years for this day."

A grin spread across his face. He spun me around with the smoothness of a tango dancer and kissed me.

After a long and sultry kiss, Reid held me at arms length and examined me up and down. I tried not to cringe, but I wished I had worn something prettier. The comfy wrap-around dress was fine for an extended plane ride but not for reuniting with my love. I smoothed the pale green dress and twisted my hair.

"Your hair's a lot longer. I like it," he said.

My self-consciousness waned, but he was still checking me out. "Thank you."

"You are still my beautiful Emmy."

I smiled, remembering how I'd fretted about my appearance during the last few weeks of school. He pulled me close again and kissed me, running his fingers through my hair. He followed a kiss with a tender hug.

"Oh, damn," he moaned. "I gotta get home. My folks haven't seen me yet. Mom's probably called the National Guard by now!"

"Yeah. She's probably pacing the floor."

"No doubt."

"How'd you get here?"

"I drove. My folks sent me money for a car when I was in Colorado. It's in the parking lot. Come on, I'll drive you home. Bummer you don't live down the street anymore."

He opened the door to a blue Volkswagen. I climbed in, thinking about Colorado. I didn't want to ruin our reunion, but I had to know what his plans were when September came around.

We came to a stoplight. "Which way is the fastest?"

"That way," I answered, pointing left.

"Okay, thanks," he said. "I'll take the long way."

We talked about simple things, mostly about his car-trip from Colorado. I gazed at his handsome profile, still feeling like a wide-eyed fifteen-year-old and madly in love.

He pulled up to my curb. "Wow! You moved uptown! What a pad!"

"I guess so," I said.

He gawked at the house. "Good God! I'm blown away! Babe, you live in a mansion!"

"Yeah," I murmured. I gawked too but for a different reason. My stomach turned as I stared at the porch lights; the whole damn place could be lit up and it would still be dark as Robert said.

He couldn't take his eyes off the house. "Man! This place is unreal."

Thinking about the house sickened me, and I had to ask about Colorado. "Reid..."

He kissed me before I could utter a word. Then another. With each kiss, the clock ticked its way to September and Colorado. I found a break in the kiss and pulled back. "Reid, please. I want to talk to you."

"Yeah, sure," he said, running his hands through my hair.

"No, please," I said, a little louder. "I'm worried..."

"Don't worry," he whispered, kissing behind my ear. "Will this help?" His lips moved up and down my neck.

"Please, stop," I blurted out. "I need to talk to you."

He pulled back. "What?"

I had to soften my tone so he wouldn't think it was his kisses. "I'm sorry, but this is important to me."

"What's wrong?"

"I didn't go with Robert because I wanted to be with you. But I have questions."

He straightened up. "Go on."

"Well, for the last six months in New York, I wrote you but you didn't write me back. I wondered why."

He turned away. "Oh, that...come on, Babe, try and understand. You hurt me when you split for New York. You didn't tell me until the last minute. Then, in your letters you said your dad might get promoted to admiral and take you off to Europe. Your letters kind of seemed like maybe you didn't want me anymore. I guess I had to protect myself."

I stared at him, offended. I wanted to scream out. *I was sad, Reid! I sat alone in my room for three years thinking of you and praying my father wouldn't make admiral. What you read was depression!*

"I'm sorry, Reid. That wasn't what I meant in those letters at all."

"Emmy, what difference does it make now? We're together so what else matters? When I found out you were back in San Francisco, I couldn't get here fast enough!"

I forced myself to let the six-month gap slide. "What about going back to Colorado?" I held my breath, almost wishing I had kept my mouth shut.

He broke into laughter and hugged me. It felt like a "poor Emily" hug. "Don't you get why I came back to San Francisco? For you! For us! No way am I returning to Colorado. I'm staying right here...with my girl."

"Really?"

"Of course! Babe, don't you know I love you? Do you still love me?"

"Yes! Those three years away from you were horrible. I love you more than anything."

His face softened, and he grabbed my hand, knotting them together. "You'll never love anybody else?"

The question was so preposterous, I nearly laughed. "Never in a million years would I love anyone but you."

"Good, because you're the only one for me." He pulled me closer for another long passionate kiss. His embrace felt permanent, hopeful.

After a few more kisses, we exchanged goodbyes. I left feeling like the happy young girl I had drawn so many times in my sketchpad, except for one thing—it was real.

I turned around to see Reid still in his car waiting for me to go inside. I waved and entered the Gates of Hell. I told myself I could handle anything now that he was back. Thankfully, the house was dark so I headed to my room undetected. I repeated over and over, "Reid came back, and he loves me."

⟋⟍

*I* sprang up, gasping for air. My hair stuck out in all directions and sweat clung to my nightgown. I gripped the damp sheets and searched the room. I recognized Italian drapes, framed oil paintings, and color-coded clothing in a large walk-in closet. Two nightmares collided—one in sleep and the other awake. *I was still in Hell.*

"Damn it!" I groaned, drawing my legs to my chest. "It can't be." I couldn't get Robert's pained expression and his words out of my mind. He had tried to tell me something beyond the obvious reasons I should go to Boston. Whatever it was could not be explained in a two-minute conversation at a noisy terminal.

I flopped down at the dressing table, resting my head on the top. The glass cooled my clammy skin. I tugged my fingers through the tight knots in my hair; I was weighed down by guilt and slowed by worry. Everything was an effort.

"Oh," I moaned, remembering how liberated I felt driving to the airport last night. I was a part of something and believed I had a future. Then came the impossible choice, too fast.

My stomach stirred, replaying Robert's warning that I was going to a dark place and didn't have enough light to fight Father. The exact meaning escaped me but the veracity of his words did not.

"Damn!" I groaned. Robert was gone, and I had a nagging sense that I should be too.

I zipped up my sundress and sat on the bed. There's no going back. My future in Boston was gone, but Reid was here. My fingers pressed into my forearm, leaving four crescent-shaped imprints on my skin.

"Emily!" Mother said, knocking on my door. "Are you awake? Perry Unger is here!"

I jumped up, dragging a brush through my hair. "Okay!"

I paused, confused. Surely, he thought I would be waking up in Boston, and since when was I allowed friends in my room? I rolled my eyes, remembering he was the son of Father's boss.

My bed was a mess, so I tossed the bedspread over the sheets.

"He's right here, dear. Please open up."

I smoothed my hair as I opened the bedroom door. "Hi...um, Perry. How are you?"

"Perry," said Mother. "Can I get you anything, a soda or some coffee?"

"No, thank you, Mrs. Quinn. I'm fine."

"Come on in," I said, gesturing to a tweed side chair.

I decided to ignore the obvious "why are you here" question. "That was a fantastic commencement speech. I loved how you shed your 'Pudge' skin. So cool!" I said, running my fingers through the knots in my hair.

"What do you mean?" he asked.

"Well, you know. The way you introduced yourself. That was clever how you shot down the bullies. I always wondered why you let those jerks call you Pudge anyway. It made no sense to me. You never objected or anything," I explained, stepping on my words, talking fast.

Pudge seemed to be studying me, or maybe my manic demeanor made it seem that way. "It beat the alternative," he said.

"You mean getting beat up?"

"No. I wasn't afraid of being beat up. I got clobbered plenty in grade school and survived. Besides, there's no honor in high school for whipping someone half your size. Letting those bozos call me Pudge was pure strategy on my part. The alternative pejorative was worse."

I didn't want to admit I didn't know the meaning of the word "pejorative", so I shrugged. "What do you mean exactly?"

"What are my initials?"

"P.U." I snickered, unable to stifle my giggles.

"Yeah, that's right! Hey, I'd rather be called pudgy than stinky!"

The tension dispersed into a cleansing release of giggles. After a half-minute, he clasped his hands together and his face grew serious. "Why didn't you go to Boston?"

"How'd you find out?"

"Easy. A guy ran around the high school after the ceremony asking everyone where you were. It wasn't hard to figure out it was Reid."

"Oh, of course," I said, wondering if I could make him understand. "He came back, Pudge. For me! He ran across the parking lot calling my name! I couldn't believe it. It was so romantic."

His clasped hands grew tighter.

"It was like a dream come true. We drove back to my house and kissed. Oh, and guess what? He is not going back to Colorado! He rescued me! The whole night was unreal...like a movie but better."

He leaned forward with his hands on his knees. "Your life is not a movie, Emily. And what do you mean he rescued you? Your brother is the one that came to rescue you, not Reid."

His words stung, like I hadn't been kicking myself already. "You don't understand. Reid is a wonderful guy. We're in love. I couldn't just walk away from him."

He crossed his arms and stared poker-faced. "But you could walk away from your brother?"

I felt like he'd kicked my teeth out. I found myself getting mad like I needed to stick up for Reid. "Of course! I hated walking away from Robert. I still do! But I agreed to leave with Robert before I knew Reid had planned to return to me. The decision killed me, but I had no choice. It's always been Reid. Going to Boston would have meant giving up on the one person that makes me happy."

"If Reid loved you, he would understand the importance of getting away from your father. He should have insisted."

I took a deep breath and exhaled. "Reid does love me and he doesn't know about my father."

"Wait a minute. What do you mean he doesn't know? You've been friends since childhood. How's that possible?"

I avoided his eyes. "I never told him."

"Why?" he asked.

"Because I didn't want him to know!" I pushed my palms against my eyes, holding back my tears.

He leaned back in his chair. For a few minutes, he let the silence linger between us. "I don't mean to upset you. It's just that I'm worried about you. I don't get why you haven't told Reid how your father abuses you. If you guys are in love, he needs to know. He can't help you otherwise. Don't you trust him?"

"Of course I trust him. It's not about that."

"Then what?"

I stared at the floor and took a minute to think but couldn't come up with a reasonable answer. "I didn't want him to think less of me, I guess."

His face remained fixed on me, unblinking. He didn't say a word. I figured he was waiting for a straight answer.

I took a breath and stopped trying to think of a good answer. "I didn't want Reid to see me differently. I wanted to be like everyone else...normal, I guess. His parents adore him. How could I tell him my father hates me and my mother pretty much ignores me? He'd start to wonder what in the hell is wrong with me. I've always felt ugly. I wanted him to think of me as pretty and normal."

"What's normal? Normal is boring. You're unique and beautiful. Your father's ugly. He's a monster. His brutality has nothing to do with you. We've talked about this before. Your dad is violent and must be stopped. Robert tried to take you away from your abuser."

His plea jolted me out of denial. Father's abuse was accelerating, and I lacked the strength to fight him. I think that was what Robert meant when he said I didn't have enough light to fight him. Moving would have given me the insight I needed to heal from Father's brutality.

The recognition sobered me. "You're right. Now, what?"

His eyes were solemn as he observed me. I understood why Yale had recruited my valedictorian friend. He was no longer the awkward chubby kid. He was still built like a fireplug and wore clothes that belonged on someone twenty years older, but his demeanor had changed. Perry Unger was now an imposing figure like his father.

He leaned forward. "You tell me."

I glanced around the room. "I have to tell Reid."

"Yes, you do. And you also need to leave."

I was sure I'd heard him wrong. "What?"

"Your father won't stop abusing you just because Reid's back. Good God, why would you even want to stay here?"

I glared at him, annoyed that my decision to tell Reid wasn't enough. "I don't want to stay here! I hate this house! But come on! This just happened, and I haven't had time to come up with a plan yet!"

"I understand," he said. "But you need a strategy and fast. Listen, I think you should go to Boston as your brother planned. You can still be with Reid. If you're meant to be, he can move back east and live near you."

"We are meant to be. He loves me."

"All right, then he should love you enough to do what is in your best interest."

Everything was happening too fast. "You make it sound so easy."

"I never said telling the guy would be easy. Listen, you need to prioritize your life and put the most important thing first."

"That's Reid."

"No," he shot back. "It's *not* Reid! That's my point. The top priority is your safety. Your brother must have been plenty worried to drop everything and come here to remove you from your situation."

"I know," I said, guilt seeping in. "But can you stop questioning Reid's love for me? It's all I have."

"That's the point, and I'm sure Robert felt the same way."

I got it. It sickened me to remember the pride I felt talking about college with Robert. "Go on."

"I understand I'm pushing you, but I leave tomorrow for Yale, and I can't go until I know there's a strategy in place."

"I'm listening," I mumbled.

"Getting out of here is priority one. Can you talk to your mother? Is she aware of your Father's abuse?"

"Some, but not everything...I guess."

"Can you confide in her?"

"I doubt it. She's different."

"Different, how?"

I hated adding Mother to the mix. "Well, she's quiet and reads a lot. I told you about my sister, Penelope...I think she's guarded because of her death. She gives me advice when I ask, but we don't talk about anything personal. She really doesn't care much about me."

"Would she tell your father?"

"Probably," I answered, knowing she would.

"Then she's out. I'm sure that's why your brother didn't tell her. Okay, then talk to Robert, and he'll handle all the details."

"Okay…But I'll talk to Reid first. I don't know what he'll say though."

Pudge jumped out of his chair. "Damn it, Emily! You are frustrating the hell out of me!"

I recoiled, stunned by his sudden outburst. I welled up and for good reason. I was all too familiar with anger. For me, anger bled into rage, followed by violence. My learned instinct was to duck.

He sat back down, scratching the back of his neck. "I'm sorry. I shouldn't have yelled at you."

I put on a brave face. "Please go on. I want to understand, I do. It's just all happening so fast."

He moved his palms downward like he was trying to calm himself. "You love the guy, I get that. But you can't let him decide whether or not you go to Boston. It's not his decision, it's yours. He's not the one at risk. You need to put yourself first."

"I know. I have a hard time with that."

"It's not too late to go to Boston. If you want to tell Reid, that's fine, but then call the dorm and tell Robert you're coming. I'm sure he'll be happy and make all the arrangements so no one finds out."

"Yeah…you're right. Okay, I will."

"So, you'll do it?"

"Yes, I'll do it."

He collapsed forward in his chair and exhaled. "Good. I wish I had more time to see this through, but Yale's orientation is scheduled for tomorrow."

I studied him, realizing how much he was like Robert. "That's okay. Thank you for coming over and helping me," I said, my voice breaking.

"This isn't goodbye. Just call Yale and they'll come get me. And don't think I won't drive down to visit you in Boston because I will!"

He stood up and put his arms straight out like one of those "hug me" statues. "Come here, best friend."

I crawled into his outstretched arms like the petals of a lotus plant hugging the sunshine. Pudge taught me about friendship. Not the kind of friendship I had with Reid, which was based on passion and conditions. My relationship with Pudge was pure and unselfish—unconditional.

After he left, I sat in his chair, enjoying his lingering warmth. It helped knowing there were people in the world like Robert and Pudge. Their compassion would give me the courage I needed to tell Reid the truth about my childhood and why I had to flee before something terrible happened.

# Twenty-Four

## RIPPED APART

The crisp morning air felt good on my face, and the scent of freshly cut grass masked the smell of mothballs coming from my bedroom closet. I spent yesterday alone in my room followed by a restless night trying to figure out how to tell Reid the truth about my life. I leaned against the window frame and took a few more deep breaths before settling in the armchair that overlooked my backyard.

Colorful finches offered a welcome distraction as they flitted around the manicured yard. A few weeks ago, Mother hired a landscaper to design a structured topiary. The man worked for days shaping the junipers as Mother stood over him pointing left and right to make sure the shrubs were symmetrical. The result was a work of art; cones, balls, and tapered spiral shrubs were placed at focal points throughout the yard. I gazed at the perfect forms and wondered why she hadn't worked harder to shape me. I supposed she lost interest when Penelope died.

The only familiar object in the backyard was a small gardening shed Mother had shipped from Grandma's estate in Seattle. She left the splendid art pieces and furniture behind to sell but sent for the shed. They both loved gardening, so perhaps the shed held fond memories of planting bulbs or trimming the rose bushes. I smiled, remembering the tray of

Lava soap Grandma used to scrub dirt off her hands after planting tulips and daffodils.

The sight of yellow birds and artful greenery didn't match my mood, so I spun the swivel armchair around and crossed my arms over my chest. It hurt knowing that if Penelope and Grandma were alive I would have happy memories to share with Reid instead of a horror show. How do I tell him? I doubted a guy whose youth was filled with laughter and freedom could understand fear and oppression. While Reid played baseball, I hid in my room drawing girls to bolster my confidence. His parents doted on him, while my father despised me and my mother ignored me. His history instilled him with confidence while mine left me unstable.

It wasn't Reid's fault. Even as a child, I hailed him as my best friend and knight in shining armor. What a joke. I never called him to battle, never asked for his help. Instead, I designed fictional characters in my sketchpad, met him on the front porch, and pretended to be his jolly sidekick. I never wanted the cute, popular guy to know my father beat me and called me a moron.

Today was truth and tell, front and center. Robert's move erased all Father's boundaries; my brother had been the equalizer and understood how to balance Father's mood swings. Add the constant drinking, and he had become a time bomb. I grabbed my sketchpad and tiptoed to the front door.

"Emily, dear," called Mother. "Come here, will you?"

I bit my lip and considered bolting out of the house. Too late. I took a deep breath and entered the living room. Mother and Father sat together on the sofa. She appeared relaxed, wearing a navy blue jersey dress and sandals, her hair pulled up with an abalone clip. I ignored Father.

Mother pointed to a chair facing them. "Sit here, dear."

I sat on the edge and eyed the front door.

Father cleared his throat. "So, what was Perry Unger doing here yesterday?"

I searched his face, wondering if he'd eavesdropped on our conversation. "We're friends."

"Yeah? Since when? The party?"

I stirred, still wondering if he knew something. "I guess so."

"Well, be on your best behavior. He's the son of my boss, and I don't want you doing anything to make me look bad."

I bit my lower lip and stared at him deadpan.

"Do you understand what your father is saying?" Mother asked.

I gave her a blank look. "Not really."

"Just be careful how you present yourself," she said. "The Unger family is very influential. Mr. Unger will be featured in the next issue of *Time*. We don't want you to do anything that would reflect poorly on our family."

I frowned. "Like what?" I couldn't think of one thing I had done to disrespect the family. I'd never smoked a cigarette, raided their liquor cabinet, or worn my dresses too short.

Father lit a fat cigar. "Don't back-talk your mother. Are you that dumb or just being a bitch?"

"Don't call her that, Jacob."

"Fine. Let's cut through the bullshit, shall we? Your mother wants you to show some class. Perry Unger was valedictorian of his school. The kid's smart. You're a pea-brain. The Unger kid only gives you the time of day because I work for his father. So, try and act like you can count to ten when you're around him. And none of that teenager shit talk."

I stared at Mother, waiting for her to defend me.

She shifted her position and sighed. "Just be on your best behavior, okay dear?"

"Perry's leaving for Yale tomorrow," I said, forcing the hurt out of my voice. "I probably won't be seeing him much anyway."

"Oh, I see. Well, that's nice." She got up and headed for the kitchen.

Father ground his cigar in the ashtray and grunted. His eyes widened and squinted in a silent "gotcha" code. I winced. Pudge was my secret weapon to fend off Father's brutality, and I gave it away.

"Emily," Mother called from the kitchen. "Can you come here, please?"

Father chugged the last of what looked like scotch. "Aw…" he murmured, smacking his lips with two fingers. He stood up, pointing his trigger-finger at me.

I felt like I'd been stung by a dozen wasps as I walked into the kitchen.

Mother put a skillet down and turned to me. "We need to get you registered at the junior college."

"Yeah, yeah…sure," I said, distracted.

"Okay, Monday," she said. She opened a package of bacon and began aligning the strips in the skillet.

The crystal topper on the scotch decanter chimed from the living room. I couldn't wait any longer. I fumbled in my pocket for the crumpled piece of paper with Reid's phone number and snuck out to find a pay phone.

*I* put down the receiver. In ten or so minutes, Reid would know the disgusting details of my life.

I waited for his car to drive up, rehearsing what to say. Even after a dozen speeches, I still didn't have the right words. I rolled my eyes, knowing there was no perfect speech and this was no dress rehearsal. I tugged at my blue sundress and rocked up and down in my white sandals as I waited for his car.

Reid's Volkswagen made a sharp turn and abrupt stop, thrusting the small car forward. If I didn't know better, I would think his little bug was laughing at me. "Hi, babe!" He leaned over and opened the passenger door.

I barely had the door closed when Reid kissed me. After a long kiss and a few quick pecks, he jumped back and grabbed my hands. "I'm so psyched!"

He was almost bouncing. I sensed it in his kiss, his face, and the way he pulled up to the curb to meet me. I wondered how I could turn my cheery Reid into a somber, listen-to-me Reid.

"Let's go to our place," he said. He had just showered; his brown hair was still damp and his face cleanly shaven. His white tee shirt hung loosely except for the sleeves, which were pulled taut by his arm muscles. He wore green shorts and flip-flops, revealing tanned legs.

I considered whether the lake would be a good place to talk. "Sure," I said, realizing there was no *right* place. "I haven't been to the lake since I left for New York."

"Me either. It would have been pointless going without you." He smiled and raised his eyebrows flirtatiously. His dark brown eyes had a playful twinkle. Not the mood I needed to start a serious conversation.

As we drove to the lake, I studied him, still perplexed that he loved me as much as I loved him. Maybe I shouldn't be surprised, my messed up life was the ultimate diversion. The chaos blunted everything.

He shut off the engine. "We're here!"

Entangled in thought, I was surprised we had arrived at Mallard Lake so soon. "Wow...it looks exactly the same."

We walked through the thick brush with Reid leading the way. "Watch yourself, babe."

I listened to the gentle crushing of dried leaves as we walked together holding hands. The sun sent columns of light through the dense trees. Between the warmth of Reid's hand and the serene setting, I felt surprisingly relaxed. I wanted to keep walking and spare him the truth about my life.

"Okay, stop," he whispered. "What do you think?"

Reid had re-created the magic of our first time together. The blue blanket, an ice chest, cut flowers, a picnic basket, and the words, "I love you" written with rose petals.

I put my hands over my mouth. "Oh, Reid. I can't believe you did this...*again!*"

"Surprised?"

"Almost more than the first time," I cooed, grabbing his hand. "Reid Wagner, you are so sweet."

He led me to the blanket. After a long kiss, he rolled over and crossed his hands behind his head. "This is exactly what I wanted."

"To be here?" I asked.

"To be here with you like we were before."

I closed my eyes and listened to the leaves rustling in the wind. "Me too."

He knotted his hand in mine. "Promise you'll never leave again me. I want us to be together forever, you and me."

Nausea and dread fanned out in front of me. There it was again, Reid asking me never to leave him. I clenched my teeth, waiting for the queasiness to subside so I could drop a grenade into his amorous mood.

He kissed me before I could respond and then sat up. "You hungry?"

"Hungry?"

"Get ready for the feast d' resistance!" He rummaged through the picnic basket and handed me a paper plate. "I made sandwiches. Turkey or salami?"

"*You* made sandwiches?" I asked. "Um...turkey."

He squinted his eyes. "I know what you're thinking...and no. My mother did not make them."

"Okay," I drawled. "You made them."

He placed a napkin over his forearm. "Now, young lady. What can I get you to drink? We have Pepsi and Pepsi."

"Oh, let me think. I'll take Pepsi!"

We laughed, eating our sandwiches. It only took one bite to know they weren't the culinary work of his mom. He must have poured the mustard because the bread was bright yellow and soggy.

Reid pointed to my sketchpad. "What's this?"

I had forgotten that I'd tucked it under my arm; it was like another appendage to me. "My sketchpad. I draw sometimes."

"You do? Since when?"

"Since always, I guess. It's a hobby."

He grabbed the pad and opened it. "There's nothing here."

"Sorry, new pad."

"Draw something for me."

I started gathering the dirty plates. "Nah. Don't think so."

He stuck out his lower lip. "Please?"

I shot him a half-smile and grabbed the sketchpad. "What do you want me to draw?"

"How about the tree above us?" He stretched and gestured to begin drawing.

"I'd much rather draw you."

He gave me a "don't you dare" smirk and pointed at the tree.

I opened the sketchpad and began drawing. After a few minutes, I put my pencil down and handed him the sketch. I was uncomfortable showing him my drawing but had already decided that whatever he said, I would laugh off. Reid was an athlete with an eye for line drives and ground balls not easels and expressionism.

"Babe, I had no idea you could draw like this. It's fantastic!"

"You think so?"

"Heck yeah."

"Thanks. You can keep it."

"Of course I can. You drew it for me, remember?"

I giggled. "Oh, yeah."

He tucked the drawing into the basket. We held each other and kissed, each kiss was more passionate than the one before. It was only when the sun started to fade that I realized the night was upon us. The air became chilly, putting tiny dots on my bare arms. A faint shiver grazed my body.

"Are you cold?"

I wanted to pull the sun back to its rightful place and fend off the night. "No, I'm all right."

He rubbed his hands up and down my body. "You're getting cold, babe. I should have brought a jacket. I better get you home."

The realization that I hadn't told him about Father smacked me hard. "No, please. I don't want to go...not yet."

He stroked my face and kissed me. After a few minutes, he jumped up, pulling me with him. My breathing quickened as I stared at his silhouette and waited for him to say he was just kidding.

He bent down and grabbed the blanket. "Ready?"

I forced a half-hearted smile. "No. We don't need to go yet. I'm not cold at all."

He began folding the blanket. "Babe, actually I do. I promised my dad I'd help him with his car tonight. I guess he needs a wrench-holder."

My heart skipped, but I had to tell him. "I need to talk to you."

"What's up, babe?"

"Can we sit?"

"Well, okay. I don't have a lot of time though. What's this about?"

I stroked my bare arms, longing for a script or letter. How could I explain eighteen years of violence in two sentences?

"It's a long story, do you have to get back?"

"Well, yeah. I can call them from a pay phone. Or we can talk on the ride home? It's just that my mom is a worry wart."

I caught an expression on Reid's face. He stared off with his brows creased. I realized he wasn't going home to help his dad; something was probably up with his philandering father, and he wanted to console his poor mom.

I glanced at the spot where Reid had made a heart out of rose pedals. "It can wait."

He relaxed. "Are you sure?"

"Yeah, let's go."

We drove home, chatting about mundane things. I rested my head on his shoulder, wondering whether I should give him a shortened version of the truth. But Reid would likely jump to the "moving" part, and I needed more time. Besides, I wanted to see his expression when I told him about my life, so talking and driving wouldn't cut it.

Reid pulled up to my house and shut off the engine. He brushed his lips against the back of my neck and stroked my hair. Father invaded my thoughts as I tried to enjoy Reid's touch. I thought of Father's hand around my neck and the stench of his alcohol-laced saliva dripping down my face. When I pulled back to catch my breath, he thought my breathlessness was excitement.

He pulled me closer, so I went through the motions but couldn't feel his seduction. His touch seemed blank, his kisses subdued. I feared that Father's hatred was stronger than Reid's love.

"Well, I better go," said Reid. "I love you, babe."

"I love you, too."

I watched his taillights fade and wondered if something else had stopped me from telling him the truth beyond his need to get home. Reid was more loving and attentive than ever but it wasn't enough.

Robert's warning that I didn't have enough light in me to fight Father seemed all too real.

I kicked a rock. "Damn. It's not fair," I muttered under my breath. Father stood in front of my happiness, and that made me mad. I should be floating on cloud nine, reveling in Reid's return without a twinge of remorse. I shook my head and snuck into the house retreating to my room without stopping.

*I stopped—un-nerved.*

Someone had been here. The eerie presence of a trespasser lurked in the room. I switched on the light and set my sketchpad on the accent table. The art pieces that Mother dusted every day seemed out of place, and the air smelled like Cuban cigars and English Leather cologne. A faint laughter brushed my ear, sending a dark chill through me.

I inched my way around the room inspecting everything like the game of "hot and cold." I rummaged through the drawers and checked the closet but found nothing amiss. Opening the jewelry box, I accounted for each necklace, bracelet, and the charm Reid had given me before I moved to New York. After several minutes, I made a sweeping search of the room again but found nothing.

*Until I lifted the dust ruffle underneath the bedspread.*

The secret vault that held the Bloomingdale's box and all my sketch-pads was empty. Eighteen years of artwork, bleeding my emotions to paper every day, had been raided.

I ran down the hallway and slammed both fists against my parent's door. The wood crashed into the wall and reverberated with an echo against the plaster. Mother was asleep in her leather recliner with a book perched on her lap.

I lunged forward and struck the top of her chair. "Where are they? Where'd you put them?"

She stirred, and her eyes blinked like she couldn't focus.

I glanced at her nightstand and spotted a bottle of Valium. "Tell me where they are! What did you do with them?"

She rubbed her eyes. "What?"

My neck burned, and my muscles tightened like they were locked in one position. "Tell me right now!"

She sprang up and stumbled toward the door. "What are you talking about? Calm down."

A flush of heat spread through my body. "No! I can't calm down until you tell me what you did with all my sketchpads!"

Her eyes narrowed. "Sketchpads? What?"

"Under my bed! They're gone! Hundreds of drawings I kept in the big Bloomingdale's box! Where are they?"

The sedatives made her unsteady. She grabbed the doorknob, mumbling something I couldn't make out.

I rubbed my arm, counting to myself to quiet my anger. After a few seconds, I stood up straight and took a deep breath. "Mother, all my drawings are missing. I would like them back, please."

Her face changed from bewildered to a resigned shrug. "Let's sit. Calm down, and I'll tell you."

"Okay," I said, keeping my voice down and enunciating every word. "I'm sitting down. I need those sketchpads back."

She rubbed her hands together and wouldn't look at me. "I'm sorry, dear. I didn't realize they meant so much to you."

I interrupted her. "Where are they?"

She stared off for a few seconds and then sighed. "Your father's been clearing old things from the house. He found them under your bed and must have thrown them out. He didn't know."

I ignored her excuses. "Where did he put them?"

Her face turned toward the window. "As far as I know he placed them in the trash can with the other things, but I'm not sure. I'm sorry, dear."

I held up my hand. "Trash can?"

"Well, yes. I didn't know they..."

I bolted to the side of the house. I studied the two silver trash cans. The first one was stained green around the brim, so I knew it belonged to the gardener. I walked to the second can and swung the lid off, cringing at the sound of metal as it hit the brick walkway.

My rage gave way to a drowning sorrow. My vision dimmed; my body weakened. I knew the signs, so I clutched the sides of the trash can and steadied my breathing. My head throbbed like fluids were pressing on my brain. I told myself to be strong, no matter what. I took a deep breath and stared into the can.

The sketchbooks were dismembered into hundreds of pieces. The pieces lay scattered throughout the bin and were lodged with household waste. Food scraps and old milk cartons clung to the drawings, bleeding the penciled etchings into blurry images. I could see mangled scraps of paper that once held Penelope's eyes, Grandma's smile, and the sunset I had sketched after a clear day in Seattle. I stared at the wreckage for a few minutes and then wiped my eyes.

My instinct to survive kicked in. I needed composure and strength to save what was left of my life. I called on God to give me the grit I needed to recover my destroyed artwork.

The sidelight near the garbage cans wasn't strong enough to do the job. I walked to the garage, found a flashlight, and returned to the cans. With the flashlight in one hand, I reached in and grabbed a chunk of torn-up paper along with the garbage. The sight stuck a dagger into my heart, like saving a dead baby from a muddy grave. I continued to sift through the trash can for each torn piece. The fragments were mixed with banana peels, coffee grounds, soup seeping from empty cans, and wadded Kleenex. As I held each piece, I whispered, "I'm sorry" to what looked like Grandma's smile or the tallest lemon tree in her orchard. I murmured "I'm sorry" to the little girls that lived in my imagination and soothed me after a vicious beating from Father. I touched Penelope's cheek and promised I would put her back together someday.

After I had collected all the parts, I sat on the walkway and cradled the shredded drawings to my breast like a mother holding a lifeless stillborn. I rocked back and forth and wailed a death cry until my voice ran out. I swallowed hard and grabbed the Bloomingdale's box, which leaned against the trash can, unharmed. I ran my hands along each crumbled memory, smoothing the paper as best I could. The flashlight began to flicker, so I placed the fragments in the box and replaced the lid.

Phantom pains sprayed my body like bones snapping, thrusting their hot, jagged edges into my sides like a serrated knife. My face throbbed with raging tears bent on scalding my bare skin. I winced and bore down against the torturous sensations until they passed into a vacuous numbness. Before the agony overpowered me, I carried the box and vandalized sketchpads to a place where no one would ever find them.

⌒

*San Francisco County Jail, August 21, 1966.  **End of Session Seven***

Doctor Lieberman stood over me when I came out of hypnosis. "Emily, drink this," he said, handing me a paper cup filled with coffee. "You've been coughing. You held your breath a lot during hypnosis."

"Thank you. I guess that's why my throat is so dry."

"Give me a minute," he said. "I don't use a recorder, so I like to finish all my notes following the session."

"Oh sure." I set the empty cup down, noticing how thick the notebook had become after weeks of therapy.

The doctor placed his pen on the desk. "Okay, I'm finished. Sorry for the delay."

"I understand."

"How do you feel?"

I knew to resist the "I'm fine" answer. "I feel…ripped apart. I guess like I did that night…and…"

"Are you remembering something else?"

I looked down and shrugged. "I don't know…"

He removed his glasses and tossed them on the desk. He rubbed his eyes before putting them on again. "Emily, therapy is a process, memories don't return with full insight. Only through reflection can we reach a better understanding. Please share your thoughts."

"I don't know…remembering the horror of that night triggered another memory. I always tried to do good deeds for my father and give him things…trying to get him to love me, I guess. He never noticed, or when he did, he didn't like it."

"Please give me an example."

I remembered a time in elementary school—not a pleasant memory. "Okay, well…I made him a coin jar in first grade. I covered a coffee can with construction paper and wrote "best daddy" at the top and pasted red hearts around the edge. I was so proud of it. But when I was walking home, the paper started coming off. I wanted the hearts to stay on but didn't know what to do."

My stomach knotted up the same way it did that day. "Mother had fixed my hair in braids, so I took out the rubber bands and wrapped them around the jar to keep the paper on."

"What happened when you got home?"

I shifted in the chair. "Mother saw that my hair was untied…she said I shouldn't have taken out the rubber bands."

I took a deep breath. "Father heard everything. He came out of the kitchen and pulled me outside. He hit me, and took out a Swiss Army knife and cut the two loose braids from my hair. He told me that way Mother wouldn't have to go to the trouble of braiding it."

An awkward few seconds passed. "What happened next?"

I lowered my head. "I ran upstairs and cried. Later that night, I went downstairs and saw the jar I made him in the trash can."

"What did you do?"

I paused, holding back the memory for a few seconds. "I remember tugging at my hair and staring at the jar in the trash. I wanted so bad to get it out of the garbage, but I didn't want to get in trouble. It was a mess, anyway. Most of the paper was off; the hearts were all crinkled and trash was piled on top of it...so I walked away."

Doctor Lieberman sat slumped with his arms crossed and his eyes down. "Emily, you told me the details, now I want to understand how you felt."

I rubbed my hands together. "I thought about how hard I'd worked to make it pretty...but looking at the present in the trash, mixed in with old milk cartons and tossed food...it looked ugly—worthless. I felt the same way."

Jennifer came in the door. Doctor Lieberman put his hand up and walked over to her. After a few seconds, she left.

I was ashamed and embarrassed. Those were the kinds of stories I never wanted to tell anyone—not Reid or anybody. Those times made me run for my sketchpad to draw the ache of worthlessness away.

Doctor Lieberman touched my shoulder, which made me look up. He slowly shook his head. He didn't say anything—but his face said everything. I knew what Father did that day was wrong and should never have happened.

# Twenty-Five

## HATRED

*San Francisco County Jail, August 28, 1966. Beginning of Session Eight*

*A*s soon as the guard removed my restraints, I squeezed my arms to calm the shivers. There was an in-house death at four this morning, the news spread fast, even in solitary. The girl twisted her bed sheet, strapped it to her upper bunk, cut off her oxygen and died.

Doctor Lieberman nodded to Jennifer as she left and turned to me.

"Emily, let's discuss this before we get started."

I massaged the knots in the back of my neck. "I'm not sure what to say. It's so sad...awful."

The doctor lowered his head but kept his eyes on me. "She was not my patient, but I am bound by a code of ethics that dictates I cannot divulge the specifics of her case. I can, however, speak in general terms."

I took an unsteady breath. "Okay."

"Suicides occur both on the outside and the inside. This is a sad fact of the human psyche that can be controlled but not eliminated."

"But...did anyone try to help her?"

"Inmates are evaluated when they come into the facility, but this is not a guarantee we can help a suicidal person. Sometimes the inmate will not disclose information about his or her past."

I chewed my nails. His answer explained the suicide from a clinical level, but I still thought about the girl and the finality of it all.

"Aside from the tragedy of the girl's death, what is your fear?"

I rubbed my hands to stop biting my nails. It almost seemed like acknowledging my thoughts gave them more power. "I wonder about being in prison for the rest of my life...I might do the same thing."

Doctor Lieberman took off his glasses. "Self-harm is a deep-seated pathology. I have studied you for seven weeks now, have I not?"

"Yes...of course."

"I haven't seen any evidence of this. You are recovering from trauma and memory loss, and I am confident you will go on to live a mentally healthy existence. This will involve time and work, but we are progressing well."

I frowned at his words, not seeing a happy ending—not even close. "What about being in prison for so long?"

The doctor poured another cup of coffee. He appeared tired and as worn out as his old coffee mug. He put his glasses back on and took a long look at me before answering. "I can tell you something about the girl who committed suicide, which will not violate my code of ethics. I want you to listen carefully and draw a conclusion based on the facts. Can you do this?"

"Yes," I answered.

"The case we are discussing was in pre-trial and not yet adjudicated. This was her first incarceration, and she had only been in jail four hours. The case involved driving with a suspended license. She would have been in the facility for twenty-four hours."

"Oh," I murmured. Sadly, I understood.

He pinched the skin between his eyes. "Let's get started."

I felt sad for the girl who could not be saved and I had a feeling he did too. As he spoke, I relaxed and disconnected from the immediate surroundings and returned to the day after Father destroyed my artwork.

he metal chain that held the tattered phone book made a grating sound as it rubbed back and forth in the telephone booth. I leaned on the dirty glass, waiting for the Yale operator to find Pudge.

"Hello?"

"Hi, it's Emily. Should I call you Perry now?"

"Nah...everyone calls me Perry here. Call me Pudge so I know it's you."

I thought about the first time I spotted him shuffling down the high school corridor. "You're so funny."

"How are you?" he asked. "I'm so glad you called."

"Are your parents still with you?"

"Yeah. They're having a formal student-parent dinner tonight to say goodbye. My mom's been preparing all day, packing her purse with Kleenex."

"I'm sure," I said. "You'll need a tissue, too."

"No doubt," he said. "Enough of me. You never answered my question. How are you?"

"Lousy."

"What's going on? Did you tell Reid?"

"No, I haven't had a chance to tell him yet but I will. It's my father."

"What'd he do?"

"While I was out with Reid, he ripped up all my sketchpads and tossed them in the garbage."

Pudge groaned followed by several seconds of silence. "Unbelievable. What a pig. God, Emily...I feel awful for you."

"Yeah."

"Did you confront him?"

"No, he wasn't around. Plus, I wouldn't be here right now if I'd confronted him."

"What about your mom? Does she know what he did?"

"Yeah, she's the one who told me. I think I scared her."

"She'll live. Throwing away your artwork is like ripping out your soul."

"Yeah," I said. "That's how I feel. I took every one of those scraps out of the trash...food was stuck on top of the pages. It was sickening."

"I would have done the same thing," he said. "Where'd you put them?"

"I hid them. Thank God I got there before trash day. It killed me to see all my drawings destroyed. They'll never be whole again," I said, my voice fading.

"I get it. Art's not like music you can replay. What are you going to do?"

I stared through the grimy glass at kids roller-skating down the sidewalk, wondering if I'd ever been happy. "Nothing, I guess. I hate his guts."

"I hate him too," he said.

I ripped a page from the phone book and crushed it in my hand. "I wish he was dead."

"I understand completely. Listen, Emily...you *have* to get away from him. No matter what."

"I know. I still can't believe my drawings are ruined."

"He's evil. I wish I could have stopped the bastard."

"Nobody stops him. He's too crafty and evil."

"Someone has to stop the him. He's dangerous...I'm serious. Call Robert and tell Reid. Get to Boston and away from the maniac."

"I will," I said. "I knew you'd understand."

"I do," he said. "You gotta hang tough, Emily...and keep drawing. Don't let him kill the artist within you. Do not let the villain win."

"I won't, I promise. He's not going to rob me again. I won't let him."

"Good, I'll hold you to that. Please, tell me you'll get out of the house right away. Your father is poison. He's deadly."

I stared at the page I'd crumpled and set it on the phone tray. "I will. He's out for me, Pudge. I *hate* him. I'm not just talking either."

"I do too," he murmured. "I'm *so* sorry this happened."

"We haven't talked much about you. I don't want to be a selfish friend."

"You're not, and I'm fine. I'm so glad you called me."

"Me too. I feel better now that I've talked to you."

"Good. You hang in there and get out of that hellhole. Keep drawing too," he said.

"I will. Thanks, Pudge. Goodbye for now, friend."

"Bye, Emily. Keep the faith."

I stepped out of the phone booth thinking about his advice to keep drawing. I sat down on a park bench and looked out at the kids playing and young couples holding hands. The park wasn't much different than the park I'd shared with Reid. For sure, the parks were more manicured on the rich side of town. The benches displayed shiny brass plaques, and the grass was like thick green carpeting, thanks to landscapers and automatic sprinklers. But the sunlight kissed the trees the same, and the dirt walking trails meandered amidst the trees and colorful wildflowers just like Mallard Lake. That made me think of the tree I had sketched for Reid. I smirked, knowing Father hadn't ripped that one. I supposed that was where I started over.

⁓

*I*t was still dark when I snuck out of the house to walk to St. Dominic Cathedral. It made sense to be the first one through the double arched doors to pay penance and cleanse my soul.

I entered the small space. The priest sat on the far side, separated by a screen. The mesh was so dense I only saw his silhouette bowed in prayer. I took my place on the narrow kneeler, knotting my hands together. "Bless me, Father, for I have sinned."

"In the name of the Father, the Son, and the Holy Spirit," the priest recited. "Please sit down."

"It has been six weeks since my last confession."

"May the Lord be in your heart to help you make a good confession."

I took a deep breath and hoped the Lord would bleed out the evil thoughts in my heart. "I hate my father and wished him dead."

"Continue," he said.

"He did something to hurt me, and I despise him."

"The Lord teaches us to forgive others so that we may be forgiven."

I looked up at the crucifix hanging above the screen. "I am sorry for my sin."

"Start and end each day in prayer and extend to your father an act of kindness today."

"Lord Jesus, give me mercy, help me to be a better person, for I am a sinner."

"Your sins are forgiven. Go in peace."

"Thank you Father, and thanks be to God," I said, before leaving the confessional.

There was an awkward silence when I walked into the house. Mother looked up from her book and gave me a quick nod but said nothing. Father was on the couch reading the newspaper like every other Sunday. Mother sat across from him. Every-so-often he coughed, but her eyes remained fixed on her book. I wondered if she had voiced her disapproval over destroying my artwork. Without a word, she got up and retreated to the kitchen. Two weeks ago, I would have witnessed the same scene— Father browsing the paper and Mother preparing Sunday breakfast.

Except I was different. I didn't tiptoe past him and escape to my bedroom. His evil act changed me. I was still crouched on the bricks, smoothing the blurry pieces of Grandma's eyes and Penelope's smile. I wanted to get my penance over with, so I sat in the chair across from him.

He peered up from his newspaper and rolled his eyes. "What?"

I didn't flinch. "You ripped up my drawings."

"Yeah? So what?"

"They were pictures of Grandma and your dead daughter."

"Like I said, so what?"

"They were pictures of Grandma and your dead daughter," I repeated.

"Fucking clutter! Stupid ass scribbles! Now get the hell out of here!" He snapped the paper in front of his face.

"What about the pictures?"

He leaned forward red-faced; his nostrils flared as he shook his fist. "I said who cares you little shit!"

"I will forgive you for what you did but I can't forget."

He got up shaking his fist. "I'll goddamn give you something else you won't forget! Right now, bitch!"

My resolve toughened as my defiance mounted into rage. I stood up with my hands on my waist. "What about Penelope? You destroyed pictures of your own daughter!"

A shrill clang came from the kitchen. Mother rushed into the room with her chest heaving up and down.

She got between Father and me. "Stop it! Both of you!" She kept her arms stretched between us.

I stood still, stunned.

"Emily, go to your room, now!" she pleaded. "Go, please!"

She trembled and wept uncontrollably. She came unhinged when confronted with the one word never uttered in this house—Penelope.

I crept forward. "Mother, I'm..."

"Just go! Please!"

I did what she asked. I walked into my bedroom and listened. She continued to sob, a low, mournful cry.

I reclined on my bed with my arms behind my head. Thinking. Questioning. I had always figured her ability to love ended with my sister's death. But now I wasn't so sure. Maybe she hid her pain in obsessive details. Had I fed the delusion by putting on a happy face and never questioning her about my sister?

Today, amidst the shouting and hearing the name Penelope spoken out loud, she crumbled. The wall she built could not survive when faced with the name of her deceased daughter.

As for Father, my conscience was clear. I recited the Lord's Prayer and five Hail Mary's, satisfied I had fulfilled my atonement. Now I hoped I had found an unexpected gift that could change my life—my mother.

"Vanderbilt Hall, how can I help you?"

"May I speak to Robert Quinn?"

"I'm sorry, Robert Quinn is not available. Can I take a message?"

"I beg your pardon?"

"Classes are in session until five o'clock. Would you like to leave a message?"

"No, thank you." I held the receiver for several seconds before placing it back in the metal holder.

I stepped out of the phone booth and sighed. Gone were the days when I could knock on Robert's door to talk with him.

"Shoot," I muttered under my breath as I sat down on a bench. Aside from apologizing for that night at the airport, I wanted to talk to him about Mother's emotional reaction to Penelope's name. Robert had a way of grasping the meaning of everything. I jingled the coins in my pocket, wondering what to do. Reid and his parents were in San Jose visiting his grandparents, and I didn't know anyone in Pacific Heights.

I looked around and wondered why no one was ever outside the mansions on Orchid Drive. Our old neighborhood always bustled with children playing dodge ball in the street, mothers tending their gardens, and dads washing their cars. Not here. I'd only seen gardeners and the postman carting mail to the white gilded mailboxes. They even kept the mailman away; the boxes were on the sidewalk instead of the front door.

I heard the whining sound of a city bus and realized I'd been sitting at a bus stop. The destination read "Cole Valley." The bus squealed to a stop, so I jumped on, anxious to see the neighborhood where it all began with Reid.

The folding doors closed as I settled into the first empty seat. The estates, boutiques, and classy restaurants transitioned to dime stores, warehouses, and finally the tract houses I recognized. The passengers were mostly noisy kids with their moms, returning from a shopping trip to Union Square. The sounds of repositioning shopping bags, children bouncing in their seats, and bursts of laughter was a pleasant change from the hushed existence of Pacific Heights.

The bus screeched to a full stop. I jumped off and stood still, taking in the sights. My old Cape Cod house, with a picture window in the front and two dormer windows on top, looked about the same other than the new yellow paint. The small cement porch was swept and tidy. I remembered sitting on the porch watching Reid play baseball and skipping down the sidewalk on the way to Mallard Lake. I touched the smile forming on my lips, remembering the day he kissed me.

A sudden jolt in my gut startled me along with a loud pop in my ear. My chest tightened and a hollow sensation made me shiver. I steadied my body against a stately oak tree and lowered myself to the curb. The sweet memories stopped. I felt unwelcome. Frightened. Chilled, like something catastrophic just happened. The rows of houses seemed to recede from the sidewalk, leaving only a blurred road. The street, the homes, and the sidewalk led me back to the mystery of Penelope, how she died, and why my connection to the family ended with her death. I rested my head in my hands, haunted by the pervasive suspicion that my life changed when she died.

I covered my eyes to shut out the hallucination. "Please, God...make it go away."

I split my fingers. All was normal again. I let out a long sigh, wondering what possessed me to return to the place where I'd been beaten, terrorized, and belittled every day. Who would want to return to that Hell?

"Emily? Is that you?"

I swung around, startled to find Mr. Hemet. "Oh...hello, Mr. Hemet."

"Well, ain't you a sight for sore eyes," he said. "What're you doing in these parts?"

The man who had disciplined Reid and me for the snake-fiasco now seemed harmless and kind. He appeared older than I remembered, barely a hair on his head, leathered skin, wearing a white shirt and baggy pants held up by gray suspenders.

I brushed the hair out of my face. "I decided to take the bus here and look around."

"Well, ain't that nice. Last I remember, you moved back east."

"Yes, to New York…but we're in San Francisco now."

"Well, good for you. Now, you don't need to be sitting on the sidewalk, young lady. Come on, the wife would love to see you and fix you some lunch."

His warmth surprised me. "Oh, I don't want to impose."

"You ain't imposing. Now come along. You look like you could use a good meal."

"Okay, thank you," I said, hiding a grimace. The idea of spending time with the Hemet's seemed awkward, but I couldn't say no without sounding rude.

My reluctance dissolved as soon as I walked in the house. Signs of everyday activities signaled cozy and welcome. Framed pictures lined the mantle and crocheted Afghans rested on the back of chairs. Dusty plastic flowers adorned the doily-covered end tables. In one corner, stood a tall scratching post with a center landing where a tabby cat stared out the window.

Mrs. Hemet came bustling from the kitchen, a stout white-haired woman with twinkly blue eyes and a button nose. I couldn't help but smile. "Oh, Henry! My, my, my! Who have we here?"

She had a high voice that sounded excited all the time. "Are you little Emily? Well, aren't you all grown up and so beautiful! Now, here, you sit down, and I'll get you some food. Do you like pork chops, dear? Oh, and I have scalloped potatoes, and sweet rolls…. Henry, get the apple cider out of the cellar, would you?"

She rushed back and forth, headed to the kitchen and then turned back as she thought of more food to serve me. It was fun to watch her, and I didn't feel like an imposition seeing her so excited to feed me. "Can I help you?" I asked.

"No, no…you relax. Henry and I were just fixin' to eat anyways, and we got enough to feed an army. You sit a spell. It'll be done in no time."

After ten minutes or so, we sat at her round dining table munching on pork chops and potatoes. Mrs. Hemet's face was cherry-red from cooking and scurrying around her little kitchen.

"Did I forget anything?" she asked, eyeing the table packed with food. "Oh! The butter for the rolls!"

"Sit down, Mother. I'll fetch em," said Mr. Hemet.

"Thank you, Henry. Now Emily, how's the family?"

"They're fine. Robert is going to Harvard."

"Oh, my goodness! Harvard! He was so smart, that one, always studying. Such a sweet boy. He never walked by the house without saying hello to Henry and me."

I put down my fork and fiddled with the napkin on my lap. I took a deep breath and let it out quietly.

She patted the table in front of me. "You must miss him. He'll be back when he finishes his schooling. He'll always be your brother. That young'un had something special in him. He was a thinker, that one. I used to wonder what he was thinking."

I thought about the night at the airport. "Me too."

"Can I get you more potatoes?" she asked. "Oh, and leave room for some pie."

"Sure." I wondered why I hadn't come here for comfort during my youth.

Mrs. Hemet furrowed her brows. "How're you doing, Emily? Mm? You've been through so much in your young life."

I leaned forward and tried to act casual. "What do you mean?"

"Maybe she don't want to talk about it, Mother," Mr. Hemet said.

"Oh, no. It's okay," I said quickly.

It was too late. Mrs. Hemet glanced at her husband and changed the subject.

The meal ended with pecan pie and coffee in the living room. The Hemet's chatted about their cat, Dixie, but mostly they asked about New York and what I planned to take in college. Coming back to the old neighborhood turned out to be a good idea although not in the way I had expected.

They insisted it was getting dark and not safe to take the bus home. Mrs. Hemet wrapped up some pie for me and made me promise three times I would come back and visit her. She treated me more like a relative than a casual drop-in.

As Mr. Hemet drove me home, he chatted about his nine grandkids and the best fishing holes in Louisiana. He was easy to talk to. It was a far cry from the discomfort I had felt driving to the arcade with Father. When we pulled up to my house, I thanked him for the delicious meal and ride home.

"You're welcome, Emily. Now don't you be a stranger, you hear? Drop by anytime, there's always a pie with your name on it."

I choked up at his last words; Grandma used to say the same thing. "Thank you so much, Mr. Hemet."

As I closed the car door, I wondered what Mrs. Hemet meant about my being "through so much." The words made me think of my destroyed artwork. I missed looking at the pictures of Grandma and Penelope. My memories of Grandma were still strong; I thought of her every time I passed a lemon tree or smelled the sweet scent of pastries. But I had nothing of Penelope except the sound of her giggle.

I walked to the fence and unlatched the gate, gazing at the spot where I'd hidden the box. It physically hurt knowing the sketches were hidden, but I promised myself I would piece them back together someday. I had to. The drawings held answers to secrets; I felt it in my heart. Those torn pages held the truth about why my sister died, my mother couldn't embrace me, and Father hated me. Someday I would figure out why I lived a tortured life, half at the hand of my father and half at my own.

An icy wind ripped through me, and the air became bitter cold. I gripped my shivery body and put my head down so the sudden cold wouldn't numb my face. After a few seconds, I lifted my head, wide-eyed. The atmosphere was sultry and warm and the air as calm as a sleeping baby.

# Twenty-Six

## ELITE WARRIOR

The marine fog held on as I walked to meet Reid for our date at Lafayette Park. We'd only seen each other an hour or so a day during the past week, and most of the time we were locked in lusty kisses. He needed time to settle in or as he put it "take care of things." I figured that meant checking out local colleges and finding a part time job.

His busy-work over the last several days had given me time to come up with a plan. Today I would tell Reid about my childhood and suggest that we both move to Boston. Surely, he could find a college back east with a baseball team. After that, I needed to make things right with Robert. I wanted to tell him about my move and begin to repay him for his brotherly devotion.

My knee length red dress was hardly the right attire for an overcast day at the park, but I wanted to appear confident when I spilled the truth about my dreadful childhood. No hand-wringing. I pinched my cheeks to add color to my light skin. I caught myself biting my lower lip, a nervous habit I couldn't seem to break. The wait for Reid's car wasn't helping. I moved closer, searching the rows of oncoming vehicles.

His Volkswagen screeched to a stop with a hiccup. I leaped into the bug and leaned across the stick shift for an excited kiss.

"Reid...you're going to love this park! We can walk up one of the hills and get an unbelievable view of the city, and the vendors sell snow cones and all kinds of neat stuff!"

He kissed me and then held me back with a one-eyed squint.

"Of course, it's not half as beautiful as our park."

He grinned and raised his eyebrows. "We aren't going to a park today."

"Oh! Well, I thought...oh never mind, where to then?" I noticed he wore a white shirt, dark gray slacks, and polished shoes. Not clothes for relaxing in a park.

He winked. "Well, I can't tell you because it's a surprise."

I leaned back. "Okay, but there better not be any reptiles."

"My lips are sealed."

I studied him, wishing Robert could have seen this side of him—the sweet, playful Reid.

He glanced at me. "Why the sad face?"

"Oh, just thinking about Robert. I hope he's okay."

"Why wouldn't he be?"

"No reason, I just miss him and wish we'd had more time to talk that night at the airport."

"I don't get why you'd want to move to Boston. In your letters, you said you hated New York. Boston is pretty much the same thing."

"I guess." I tried to picture his reaction when he learned I needed to flee from a maniacal father.

"So, what're you doing now that high school is over?" he asked.

"Hmm?" I asked, my mind still on the wreckage of my past with Father.

"Any plans now that you're out of school?"

"Oh, yeah. Well, I'm not sure, exactly. Junior college, I guess."

"What will you take?"

"I don't know. I haven't picked a major yet. What about you? Which college did you pick?"

"I didn't. That's one of the things I want to talk to you about...later," he said, drawing out the word "later."

"Huh? What do you mean?"

"Emily," he drawled. "I said *later.*"

I wrinkled my nose. Whatever was going on had him pumped up.

We pulled up to The Swan Oyster, a swanky restaurant I knew Reid couldn't afford. He jumped from the car and opened my door. He seemed oddly formal. I couldn't help notice how funny his beat-up Volkswagen looked next to the Cadillac sedans and Town Cars.

Reid grabbed my hand and whispered, "You look beautiful."

I stared down at my simple sundress. "Thank you," I said, trying not to show my confusion.

We walked hand-in-hand under a covered canopy and through the double arched doors. The room had dimmed lighting, white tablecloths with flickering candles, and a pianist in the corner. It was the kind of restaurant I'd been to many times in New York City.

The maître de showed us to our table. Reid cleared his throat, clearly uncomfortable. I smiled, hoping to calm him. I didn't dare tell him I'd picked up on his discomfort. I wanted my carefree Reid back and wondered if my move to upscale Pacific Heights made him think he had to "keep up." If so, I wanted to squash the fallacy; a picnic in the park would be heaven compared to watching him struggle over the protocols of a posh restaurant.

I reached across the table and took his hand. "This is so beautiful, what a lovely surprise."

He scratched the back of his neck. "Are you surprised?"

"Of course. I can't believe you did this for me." I waited for him to loosen up, but he continued to scratch his neck and jerk his shoulders.

He leaned forward. "Emmy...."

He stopped talking when a tall waiter appeared at the table. "Welcome to The Swan Oyster. My name is Pierre, and I will be your server this evening. May I start you off with Black Mussels Gratinées or perhaps our Loche Etive Ocean Trout Carpaccio?"

Reid stared at the waiter with his mouth open. Fortunately, I'd been to enough of these places to know one was a shellfish and the other was caviar. I managed to catch Reid's attention and shake my head.

"No, thank you," Reid replied, clearing his throat again.

"Very well. Here are your menus and may I suggest the Sea Scallops and Trout Quenelles tonight. What may I get the lady to drink this evening?"

"Water is fine, thank you," I replied.

"And for you, sir?"

"Water's good for me too, thanks." He pulled on his collar, twisting his neck. I wondered if he might rip his shirt off, he looked so uncomfortable.

"As you wish. I will bring you our toasted brioche to get you started and return shortly to take your orders."

As soon as the waiter left, Reid ran his hands through his hair and stared off.

"The fire is sure pretty," I said.

He blotted his forehead with the napkin. "Sad again?"

"No, why would you say that? Listen, Reid, we don't have to stay here. We can leave."

"Why? Don't you like the place?"

"No, it's fine. It's just...well, kind of fancy."

"Well, yeah. I wanted to take you to a nice place. What's wrong with that?"

"Nothing at all. I just don't understand why you are having a hard time talking to me. You've never had that problem before. It makes me think something bad is coming."

"Bad? No. Just the opposite. I'm trying to find the right words to tell you."

I leaned over the table. "Can't you just tell me?"

"I'm looking for the right time, and I want you to be in a good mood."

"I am in a good mood. I'm confused. You seem like you want to tell me something, but you're having a hard time. Is this about me?"

"Well...everything's about you. I don't know what you mean."

I glanced at the lobby and wondered if we could sneak out. "Reid, what is it?"

He shifted his position in the high-backed wooden chair. He took a deep breath and let it out, not talking. I waited for him to talk instead of all the nervous silence.

The waiter brought a plate of toasted brioche and a perched pen. I hastily ordered red snapper, and Reid ordered the same. When the server left, Reid continued his uncomfortable silence. The pianist began to play a Beethoven Sonata, which seemed to relax him.

He reached across the table and took my hand. "You look beautiful tonight."

I studied his face and tried to keep a frown off of mine, but his shtick was bizarre. The plan for today was a picnic in the park not sitting in a swanky restaurant with people twice our age. Plus, it was hardly the atmosphere I needed to tell him about Boston.

"Emily, I want to talk to you about something very important," he said, drawing each word out.

I had forgotten one of the quirks of his personality—the long wind-up before he pitched the ball. "Okay...I'm listening."

"I've been thinking a lot about my future since I got home and about what I want and where I'm going."

I wondered why the "I" wasn't a "we."

He cleared his throat and sat up straight. "I joined the Marines."

I giggled. "Good one, Reid!"

He didn't move. "I'm serious, Emmy. I joined yesterday."

I felt my body heat up. "What? This isn't a joke?"

"No. College is not for me."

"What about baseball?" I asked, ignoring the Marine part.

"My future is not in professional baseball. Listen, I didn't even like the coach in Colorado. The jerk made me ride the pine half the time."

"Ride the what?"

"He benched me, Emmy. So I quit."

"You quit? I thought you..."

His big surprise turned out to be my worst nightmare. My head hummed with jumbled thoughts—Reid at the airport convincing me to stay with him, Robert's plea to come with him, Reid's affection for me. Nothing made sense.

"I didn't want to stay in Colorado on the baseball scholarship. It was going nowhere. I hated Colorado."

My muscles tightened, and I felt queasy. The nausea was close to the surface, I had to leave or throw up on the white tablecloth. "I don't feel good."

"What's wrong?"

I grabbed my clutch purse and got up.

He started to rise before I waved him down. I darted to the bathroom, slammed the stall door, and vomited. After a minute or so, I staggered to the sink to splash cold water on my face. With both hands on the sides of the sink, I caught my reflection. My face was a bizarre combination of white with a bright red rash running down my neck.

"I hate you! I hate you!" I shouted at the image. "How could you be so stupid?"

Beads of sweat formed on my face, and my breathing became shallow and threadlike. My heart raced fast enough to knock me over, and a hundred-pound weight squeezed my chest. The room started to fade. The whistling sound of my erratic breathing, along with the familiar tingling fingers, told me I was in the throes of a full-blown panic attack. I ran back in the stall and stuck the paper bag over my mouth long enough to slow my breathing.

I bolted from the bathroom. A patron entered the restaurant, sending a swift wind against my face. I followed the cold breeze until I was outside. I didn't think, I just ran. "Dumb! Dumb! Dumb!" I babbled. "You fool, thinking Reid left Colorado for you! He ditched you for the Marines! Idiot!"

The barely discernable drizzle turned into a downpour. A speeding car hurled a wall of water on me, saturating my dress in dirty water. I stood still with my arms out, dripping wet, my anxiety blunted by the insanity of racing down a city street in a sundress in the rain. I slowed down to an exhausted walk.

"Emmy!" Reid screamed. "Stop!"

I stuck out my chin and picked up the pace. I didn't want to listen to any more of his "big news."

"Damn it! Why are you running from me?"

I swung around. "Running from you? You are the one running from me! All the way to the Marine Corps! You didn't come back to San Francisco for me! Liar!"

He raced to me and scooped my rain-soaked body into his arms. He didn't say anything, but I knew by the steady motion of his footsteps that he was taking me to his car.

Within minutes, the blast of hot air from his car heater hit my drenched skin. Reid rubbed his sweater over my body trying to warm me.

"Don't touch me!"

"What's wrong with you?"

"What's wrong with me? You take me out to some fancy restaurant to dump me? You joined the Marines? Did you think I'd be happy for you? Did you think a T-bone steak would cushion the blow? I hate you!"

"You hate me, huh?" Reid asked, surprisingly calm.

I wiped the tears as soon as they spilled. "Yes. I have nothing to say to you!"

"You didn't let me finish talking. You ran out without giving me a chance!"

"Humph!" I crossed my arms and gazed out the window. The Cadillac sedan and Lincoln Town Car were still parked next to us—no doubt, enjoying their chocolate soufflés by now.

"You left before I could finish what I had to say."

"Fine. Finish your dumb sermon. I don't care anymore."

"You're making this hard, Emmy. What's with you, anyway? This is not how I planned this evening."

My mouth dropped open; I had to look at him. "You are the one who rushed to the airport and sold me a bill of goods claiming you came back for me! I should have gone with Robert!"

"I didn't sell you anything. I came back for you. Damn, Emmy...my life has always been about you. Why would you want to move to Boston and miss out on our being together?"

"Miss out on being together? I thought you came back here for me! You never said a word about quitting the team in Colorado! You conveniently left that part out. Then, behind my back you go off and join the Marines! Where does that leave me?"

He banged his hands against the steering wheel. "Just let me explain!"

I felt like I would explode if I heard another word. "You know what? Forget it! I'm walking home!" I grasped the handle and jumped out of the car, barely dodging a car backing up.

He darted from the car and grabbed my arm. "Babe...Please listen to me...let me explain."

I wanted to run but his tone convinced me to hear him out. I got back in the car, crossed my arms, and bit the inside of my mouth to halt my tears.

Reid slumped and let out a long sigh. "Emmy, honestly...this has got to be the worst proposal in the history of the world."

I froze. "What?"

He pursed his lips together and blew out a longer sigh. "Okay, get out of the car."

"Huh?"

"You heard me, get out of the car."

His face remained steady and focused. I opened the door and stepped out. He ran over to my side, huddled between the bug and the Lincoln Town Car, down on one knee.

He opened a small blue velvet box with his class ring. "Emily Quinn, will you marry me?"

I put my hand over my mouth and gazed into his brown eyes. "Is this for real?"

He nodded, tearing up. "Will you be my wife?"

I reeled back, catching myself. "Yes! Of course!"

"Will you wear this ring until I can buy you a real one?"

"Yes! Oh my God, Reid! We're getting married!"

We jumped up and down, shaking the little Volkswagen bug along with us. We were like kids again, full of excitement and youthful abandon. Tuckered out from jumping, we got back in the car and kissed, and then snuggled, drained but excited.

He kissed the top of my head. "Are you happy?"

"Deliriously," I answered, snuggling closer.

"You never let me finish, you know."

"I'm sorry. I acted like a lunatic. Forgive me?"

"Yes, silly. You're going to be my wife. You're allowed to act a little crazy once in a while. Well, maybe twice a year."

"Okay," I whispered.

"But I do need to explain everything."

"No, we're fine now."

"Babe, it's important we talk about a few things."

I thought about my plan to tell him about Father but now wasn't the time. "Okay, tell me everything."

"I returned to San Francisco for you. When you left for New York, it was hard, but I believed we'd find our way back to each other. As soon as my mom told me you came by, I couldn't wait to get here. But college wasn't for me. The last several months in Colorado, I thought a lot about what I wanted to do. I'm a man now, and I had to make decisions like a man."

"Okay," I said, wondering when he went from "guy" to "man."

"I came back here to find you and start our future. That's why I decided to join the Marines."

This time I reveled in the word "our" instead of "my" like back at the restaurant. "Our?" I asked, needing to hear it again.

"Yes, there is no Reid without Emily. Don't you understand that after all this time?"

"Yes," I answered, touching the ring.

"Okay, so I talked to the recruiter, and he thinks I'm an excellent candidate for the Marine Corps. Marines are the elite warriors, Emily, and this is my calling."

I looked at him curiously. Calling? Elite warriors? I couldn't help think the Marine Corp recruiter played up to his ego without informing him of the drawbacks. Still, I wasn't about to stick a pin in his manly bubble. Besides, he had already enlisted.

"What about the war? Oh my God, Reid, could they send you to Viet Nam?"

"Babe, if they deploy me to Viet Nam, that is my duty. Communism threatens to take over the world, and America must stop them. When France pulled out of Viet Nam the United States had to step in to prevent Ho Chi Minh from taking over the whole country. Communism is spreading like wildfire."

It seemed like I was talking to the recruiter instead of Reid. "So, what's next?"

"I go to Camp Pendleton for training. They put you through all the rigors to make sure you are strong enough to be a Marine. You have to be in top physical condition and combat-ready. Not everyone passes. After twelve weeks, if you pass, the senior drill instructor stands with you and the platoon and calls you a Marine."

I thought I should salute him right then and there. I wanted my silly Reid back, the guy jumping up and down five minutes ago. But he was serious, so I kept listening and nodding.

"Babe, this is our future. Can you envision yourself as a Marine wife?"

"Of course." I didn't know what the qualifications were for Marine wives, but I had a feeling he'd tell me.

"Okay. I leave for boot camp tomorrow. I won't be able to see or talk to anyone for twelve weeks. Those are the rules. I have to concentrate on getting through the program."

"Tomorrow?" The reality of not seeing him for three months took the wind out of my sails.

"Yeah." He kissed my hand. "As soon as I get out of boot camp I'm going to buy you a beautiful diamond engagement ring. Will you wait for me?"

I wanted a minister in the back seat to marry us right now. "Of course I'll wait for you."

"I love you," he whispered.

I clasped my fingers around the ring. "I love you too."

"Okay, sweetie. While I'm gone to boot camp you can plan the wedding with your mother."

"Sure," I replied, automatically.

"Listen, future wife. You won't like this but I leave first thing in the morning. We're talking 4 o'clock, which is 0400 in military time. We need to say our goodbyes now."

"What? No!" I shouted. "You can't..."

He placed his fingers on my lips. "Slow down, babe," he said, sounding more like the drill instructor than the recruit. "It's only three months. What's that compared to our entire lives? You're going to be the wife of a Marine, so you have to be strong and tough. When I get out of boot camp, we'll get married. You'll be Mrs. Reid Wagner."

"Mrs. Reid Wagner," I said out loud. My mind shifted between being married and the requirements to be a Marine wife.

"Yes, my lady. You will be my wife. Forever. So twelve weeks is nothing compared to our entire future as man and wife."

"All right," I answered. I loved hearing the word "wife" but struggled with the Marine part. I almost wondered if I had to sign something with the recruiter too.

"Get ready for the best adventure of your life, Emmy. Once I'm out of basic training they can send us anywhere. Who knows, maybe we'll be living in Hawaii someday or Paris. For now, babe, I had better get you home. I need to say my goodbyes to my folks. Are you happy?"

"Over the rainbow," I answered.

When we arrived home, we kissed and cried for an hour or so. I didn't want to let him go; I couldn't imagine not seeing him for three months. He kept calling me a "marine wife" so I didn't complain. I held his class ring to my lips as I watched him drive off, repeating to myself that soon I will be "Mrs. Reid Wagner."

The lampposts created a yellow glow against the rain cleansed street, and the air smelled like every day in Seattle. Blissful. I lingered on the sidewalk, swaying to the hum of the bridal march under a haloed moon. I finally found the other side of the rainbow. It was like flying into a cloud of ecstasy far removed from the mortal trappings that dared to threaten my euphoria. I knew my altered state would end soon; no one can stay that high forever. So, I savored the taste of its passion and bathed in the lusty excitement. The other side of the rainbow was an unimaginable ride, and I wanted to hang on for as long as possible.

# Twenty-Seven

## STAY CALM

*A* soft thump roused me from my half-sleep as Reid's class ring rolled under the bed. It's been wrapped in a tissue under my pillow or in my pocket since he left three days ago. I'd barely left my bedroom since my fiancée took off for combat training at a boot camp for aspiring Marines or "elite warriors" as Reid called them.

I bent down and pulled up the bedspread. I clutched the gold plated ring to my chest, trying to recreate the proposal. The ring was cold, and the stone setting scratched my chest. Since that night, I've written "Emily Wagner" on lined paper, worn a lacy slip on my head, and practiced the bridal walk. That evening, I was over the rainbow, and my body vibrated with the elation of being engaged. My euphoria didn't last though because the United States Marine Corps sent him off before sunrise the following morning. I never had the chance to talk to him about Father or going to Boston. So, I was back to Earth and white knuckling the twelve weeks until he returned home and we could get married and move away.

My life consisted of too much waiting. I flipped on my favorite radio station, listening to the Temptations and "My Girl," hoping to elicit an ethereal response—but nothing. I placed the ring in my pocket and slumped into a chair, picking at my light pink nail polish. My engagement was quiet. Instead of skipping on the beach with my fiancée, trying on wedding dresses with my mother, and flashing an engagement ring to everyone in sight, I was sitting in my room alone.

The next song on the radio was "Big Girls Don't Cry." I listened to about half the lyrics before grabbing my stash of coins to call Robert. I held my shoes and tiptoed a straight line to the front door.

I should have checked my peripheral vision. The stench of English Leather cologne turned my stomach.

"Where do you think you're going?" Father asked.

The rasp in his tone made me cringe. "Just out."

He placed his hand on the door. "Don't talk shit to me. When I ask a question, answer me. Don't give me that 'just out' crap!"

"I didn't mean to. I'm going for a walk. That's all."

"Get outside."

I knew the code. Going outside meant out of earshot of Mother. Nothing was ever innocent with Father. Every discussion carried a consequence, either mental or physical. Mental was worse because it fed into my pervasive feelings of failure. I did what I'd learned to do—freeze and detach.

He leaned against the cement pillar with his arms crossed wearing a gray pinstriped suit with a matching vest. I recognized it, an Oleg Cassini design. I heard him boasting a while back about how Cassini designed for the Kennedys. He wouldn't assault me and risk a wrinkle in his precious designer ensemble.

He pulled out a silver cigarette case and lit up. "You know, I never disciplined you for your disrespectful language the other day. Your mother says you're going through a teenager phase, but I don't care. I didn't raise you to talk down to me."

I surged with blood-red outrage at the "raised you" comment. I steadied myself and faced him head-on. "You tore up my sketchpads. The drawings meant a lot to me."

"Are you still crying about a bunch of dumb scribbles?" His head tilted back as he laughed, exposing his fat, bristly neck. I wanted to slit his throat and shut him up. My body shook; it terrified me to know I hated him *that much*.

He continued chuckling. "Your little stick figure drawings were important to you, huh?"

I forced my face into a frozen position. "Yes, they meant a lot to me. The books were private, and you had no right to destroy them."

"No right? Who do you think you're talking to? This is my house, you little shit! You're eighteen. I can kick your ass out any time! I only let you stay because your mother feels sorry for you."

It was no use. He was Attila the Hun, and I was an eighteen-year-old girl without a job, no driver's license, and a fiancée in boot camp for three months. "I only wanted the sketchpads."

"You should have kept your room neater and not hidden crap under the bed. They're gone, so quit whining." He threw down his spent cigarette and stomped into the house.

His words "they're gone" tugged at my spirit. I had to know.

I crept into the backyard, tiptoeing past the trash cans and down the brick walkway. When I reached Grandma's old gardening shed, I unlatched the door and found the box where I'd hidden it behind an old potting table. I fell to my knees, reaching behind stacks of clay pots until I found the Bloomingdale's box. I dusted dirt off the lid and sifted through the scraps, trying to piece them together. My body and mind ached; I closed the box and rested my head on the top, feeling as shredded as the contents. After a few minutes, I re-hid the container and made the sign of the cross.

I snuck out of the yard to call Robert.

⌒

"Vanderbilt Hall, how may I help you?"
"I'd like to speak to Robert Quinn, please."

"Mr. Quinn is unavailable. May I take a message?"

"Not available?"

"Classes are in session until five o'clock. You can call back this evening between seven and eight. No phone calls are permitted after that time. Students are in study until eleven in the evening. May I ask who's calling?"

The telephone dangled on the metal cord as I fumbled for a piece of paper. I could hear the switchboard operator talking, so I stuck the receiver under my chin and jotted down the times on the back of an old ticket stub. "Can you tell him Emily called?"

The failed phone call left me weak and lonely. "Robert..."

I missed Robert even more than I missed Reid. I had nowhere to go but back to the place my brother had begged me to leave.

⟶

*I* cracked my bedroom drapes and watched Father carry his briefcase to his Corvette. As I leaned against the window frame, I listened to him rev the motor and the muted sounds of pebbles crackling under his tires. His car roared as he made a full turn in the direction of work. It was the same drill Monday through Friday.

"Whew," I said, as I sat down. He was gone.

"Emily!" Mother shouted. "We talk to your guidance counselor today and then you'll register for classes. Come and eat!"

"I'll be there in a minute!"

I examined my green jumper, striped blouse, and black leather flat shoes, wondering if this was the proper attire for registering at a junior college. Smoothing the stray hairs off my face, I pulled my long hair back with a wide blue headband.

"Emily! Your breakfast is getting cold!"

I tugged at my knee socks and rushed into the kitchen. The table was set with white placemats, crystal water glasses, and bone china with blue and yellow iris flowers around the rim. Crisp linen napkins were folded into triangles and placed under the forks. In the center, a white milk glass vase held flowers in the exact pattern of the china.

"Wow! The table is beautiful!"

"Thank you. We leave for school in fifteen minutes. Please eat your breakfast."

I studied Mother as I buttered my waffle. She wore a pink suit with black piping, and her chestnut hair was pulled back in a herringbone clip. "You look pretty today, Mother."

"Thank you. You look nice, too. Are you ready for college?"

"I am, definitely!" I answered, elevating my voice to give it more gusto.

She nodded and went back to her food. She cut her waffle into equal pieces, using the prongs of her fork to measure the slices.

I wondered if she was thinking of Penelope, wishing she could register two daughters for college instead of one. That made me overcompensate, trying to fill the void for the daughter she lost. "I'm excited to start junior college."

She smiled. It wasn't the ticker-tape parade she gave Robert when he left for Harvard, but junior college was no Harvard. If only I could tell her about the wedding. That could excite her, fussing over the flowers and table settings. But I couldn't ask her to keep a secret; there were enough secrets in the family. Besides, she would probably tell Father and I couldn't take the risk.

After a rushed breakfast, we headed to the college a few miles away. This was an important day but not because of junior college. I had made up my mind to talk to her about Penelope. I studied her, wondering the best way to bring up the subject. In a sense, we weren't that different. She covered her pain with an obsession to details and indifference, and I hid mine with phony cheerfulness and a need to please others.

We arrived at the college, which was packed with cars. The parking lot was small so by the time we found a space, I was ready. She shut off the engine and reached for her purse.

"Mother, wait. What time is our appointment?"

She glanced at her wristwatch. "In thirty minutes, why?"

"I hoped we might just talk."

"Do you have questions about college?"

"No. I mean...the counselor can answer any questions. I wanted to talk about something else...important."

She crossed her arms over her handbag and half-smiled. "Sure, dear. What is it?"

I took a deep breath. "Can we talk about Penelope?"

I expected her to reel around in shock but she didn't. She stared out the window with the same blank expression I'd seen a hundred times before. "No. Please drop it."

My breathing quickened. I did my best to control my emotions so we could face the truth about why my sister died. I wanted her to explain the guilt and isolation that stalked our family. "Please...Mother," I whispered.

Silence. I measured my breaths to keep from wheezing. Her expression was vacant, and I feared the answer lied within her emptiness. "Please, Mother."

She continued to stare out the window. "No."

Her void gave me chills, like she lived in a dead space between the past and a future that never happened. "Why? She was my sister, and I want to understand things..."

Her shoulders drooped. "Talking won't change anything."

"We've never talked about her. That might do some good...you know, to remember her."

I wanted to ask how she died, but she wilted with each word. Piling on more seemed heartless. "I think of her all the time...wouldn't it help to talk about her?"

A painful minute passed. "It's too late. Stop dwelling on the past."

I slumped, knowing the conversation was over. As the sun hit her face, I noticed lines I'd never seen before. It seemed like her fate had been cast thirteen years ago, and she lacked the desire to climb out of the darkness. What she didn't understand was that her refusal to heal from my sister's death affected me too. The fate she accepted became my fate.

"Let's go register."

"All right, Mother."

We walked to the registrar's office without speaking and deadlocked in the tragedy of Penelope's death.

We drove home in silence. I chewed my fingernails and stared out the window. Her cold reaction to my bringing up Penelope confirmed my worst fear. My sister's death changed her and kept her from reaching out to me. I sulked, weighed down, not understanding why she didn't even want to try.

We pulled into the garage. "I'm going for a walk, Mother."

She nodded without a glance my way. She retreated to the house, no doubt to re-align dishes or polish the counters. Anything to escape the world and me.

I walked along the sidewalk in no particular direction. The hot sun began to thaw the starch on my shirt, which made me itch. I loosened a few buttons and rolled up my sleeves. I lollygagged, kicking rocks, thinking about the day.

Weary, I sat under a shade tree, kicking off my shoes. The tree reminded me of the one I lay under with Reid on our last visit to our lake. But even that couldn't lift my depression. If only I could draw and let my imagination pull me from the loneliness. I knotted my hands behind my head, knowing my sketchpad was back at the house.

The thick grass and warm sun soothed me to a faded state. I turned to my side, thinking of Mother and Penelope, drifting off in the sultry warmth of August.

⌒

*I* woke up and checked the time: 9 a.m. I rolled my eyes, realizing I had forgotten to wind my wristwatch this morning.

A mailman carrying a sack brimming with white envelopes barreled down the sidewalk. "Excuse me, sir, do you have the time?"

"Sure, three o'clock."

"Thank you, sir." I started the walk home, thankful I had four hours before Father returned from work.

I felt better after the short nap. My thoughts flipped between my morning with Mother and my upcoming wedding. My talk with her had been a disappointment, but at least the subject of Penelope was exposed, which was a start. Once Reid returned from boot camp, I could tell her about my engagement.

"Ah," I murmured. In three months, I would be walking down the aisle in a flowing white gown to marry Reid!

Thinking of my engagement aroused my senses. The world seemed more colorful and alive. I listened to the whistle of the automatic sprinklers spraying the vast green lawns and admired the snowberry shrubs and gooseberry bushes that bloom in late summer. The butterflies and purple finches fluttered around the foliage, perching for a few seconds to drink the nectar before flittering off to another ripe perennial. Mourning doves foraged for seeds in the soil, and blackbirds sat on the telephone wires warbling to their mates.

I froze at the sight of my house. My smile faded. I squinted, trying to make sense of Father's car parked in the driveway. It couldn't be past three thirty. I backed up, staring at the hunk of red metal. It was not supposed to be there. *Something was very, very wrong.*

The car portrayed chaos. It was parked askew, and skid marks smudged the driveway. Pebbles from the side path were scattered across the hood. The Corvette was a symbol of Father's newfound wealth and bravado. He must have been too distracted to notice the sharp rocks on his shiny red paint.

The front door was not closed all the way. Could there be a problem with Robert or Mother?

My mind raced with daunting possibilities, remembering Mother's vacant expression this morning when I asked about Penelope and her melancholy on the drive home.

I gasped, dashing into the house. "Mother! Mother!"

She sat on the couch with her elbows on her knees and her hands over her face.

I ran to her side. "Mother, what's wrong?"

Father careened into the room. "You bitch!"

He grabbed my arm and rammed me into the chair next to Mother. I got to my feet, searching her face. "Mother! What's the matter? Are you okay?"

Father lunged forward, pointing his finger. "Look at me when I talk to you!"

His hands balled into fists. He jabbered too fast and garbled to understand. I continued to search my mother's face. "Mother?"

"I said look at me!" He reared up and got within inches of me. He screamed, as spit flew in my face. "Don't talk to your mother, you lying bitch! Face me!"

Mother moaned. "Jacob, please...stop."

"Hell no! Not this time, Claire! I'm not going to keep my hands off this whore for your sake! You know damn good and well what she's done!"

His eyes were blood red, half booze and half rage. He still wore his pinstriped suit but had taken his jacket off; perspiration spots spread all the way down his side. His ruddy neck pulsated and his nose was bulbous. His anger formed a scalding heat around him, and his breath smelled like whiskey and tobacco. I jumped forward and huddled on the couch next to Mother.

"Okay, Claire! You can't protect her this time! Are you going to tell her or am I?"

I'd never seen him this furious, and not just at me, at Mother too. I ran over a list of possible wrongdoings but couldn't think of anything. But then my stomach knotted. Robert. He must have discovered the plan to move to Boston. Nothing gets Father's goat more than my relationship with his imagined protégé. Knowing him, he claimed the plot was my idea and made Robert an unwilling participant. His palpable rage made it hard to think, to reason, or even react.

"Jacob, please. Please calm down. Let me talk to her."

He staggered and caught himself on the piano. "Then tell her! You've coddled this demon long enough!"

She raised her hand like a frantic stop sign. "I'm begging you, Jacob. Calm down, everything will be fine. We can discuss this as a family."

He emitted a guttural chuckle riddled in sarcasm. "A family? She's no member of the family! She's never been anything but trouble! She's nothing! Nothing!"

His anger put me in a maze, trying to figure out what I had done wrong. "What did I do?"

She took a deep breath. "Emily, why did you discuss personal family issues with your friend, Perry Unger?"

Father charged at me with clenched fists. His nostrils flared and his alcohol-reddened eyes bulged out. He moved like a drunken overweight boxer. "You bitch! I'll kill you! Hear me?"

He took a swing at me and tripped over his own feet. "Bitch! Liar!"

I hunkered next to Mother, watching him stumble around the living room.

"Please, Jacob," Mother said in a weak voice. "Sit down. Let me handle this."

He fell into a chair. "Well, do it!"

She turned to me. "Emily, you said some terrible things about your father to Perry," she said, her voice fading in and out. "He repeated them to his father and Mr. Unger fired him."

I froze. This was bad—*very bad*. "Oh my God," I mumbled, remembering my last phone call with Pudge. "I'm...so sorry."

"You're s-sorry?" asked Father, his words running over each other. "You bitch! You ruin my life, get me fired, and you're *sorry*?"

"I didn't know...."

He started to get up but wobbled and fell back. "Don't give me that shit! Get your ass over there and tell him you made the whole thing up!"

I held my hands up. "I will, I will...I promise." Father kept a loaded gun in his nightstand. I would have agreed to anything.

"And another thing," he said. "I'm the only one in charge now! You'll pay for this!"

I glanced at Mother, whose hands were over her eyes.

He reached for his drink, knocking the glass over. "Look what you did! Gimme another one!"

Mother put her hand up. "I'll get it. Please calm down." She straightened his glass, grabbed the decanter, and poured him more whiskey.

I wanted the diatribe to end. "I'll do whatever you want. I'll fix this… I can…I will."

Father swigged the alcohol and slammed the drink on the coffee table, almost missing the edge. "Take care of it, Claire. March the little slut to my boss and make her confess she made the crap up. Or she can sleep in the street or let some John take her in!"

"Please stop, Jacob," she said in a faint voice.

"It's okay," I said. "I'll tell him…I apologize. I didn't know."

He narrowed his eyes. "You're so full of shit. You knew exactly what you were doing! Don't give me that crap!"

I watched him stagger from the room and listened until I heard his bedroom door close. I spun around to check on Mother. She looked haggard. The beautiful contrast in her features, her chestnut brown hair and milky skin, were now her worst features. Her dark hair against her pale skin made her look anemic, and dark circles overshadowed her blue eyes. The thought killed me, but I wondered if she would have protested if he had held a gun to her head. I pictured her reaching up with her long, slender fingers and firing the pistol herself.

I wanted to embrace her, but her spacey gaze told me not to. "Mother…are you going to be all right?"

She got up without a glance my way. "Let's go."

She walked a few steps in front of me. The night air had a bite, and wisps of fog lingered in pockets over the ground. I felt like a child again, following her lead and waiting for instructions. She started the car, not bothering to turn her head as she backed out of the driveway onto the street. She gripped the steering wheel with her eyes fixed straight ahead, expressionless.

I swallowed hard and tried to think of something to say. She seemed like a woman who had reached the end of a tedious journey and had nothing to show for it.

She turned into a parking lot and shut off the engine. It started to rain. Between the darkness and the downpour, I didn't know where we were except that we were *not* at the Unger's. The showers sounded like gun pellets hitting the sedan with an aftermath of raindrops pouring like tears down the window. Mother's hands still clung to the wheel.

The silence was killing me. "I'm sorry," I whispered.

She didn't move from her trancelike state.

"I'll say whatever you want to Mr. Unger."

She remained motionless. Her distance frightened me and made me wonder what she was thinking, or if she was thinking at all. She appeared lifeless.

"What do you want me to say?"

She didn't answer.

After several painful minutes, her mouth opened. "Nothing," she said.

Her stone-like expression gave me chills. "Nothing? What do you mean, nothing?"

"You aren't going to the Unger estate. I'll handle this."

I started to protest but stopped. I'd pushed her this morning with Penelope and didn't want to make it worse. "Please let me do this," I said, quietly. "I can make everything right...I promise."

"Calm down," she said.

It seemed like she was trying to calm herself. Her words struck me as a mixed up euphemism for "don't die." We sat in silence for several minutes. "Where are we?"

"At a hotel. Stay here until I talk to Mr. Unger. I'll pick you up when I finish. I packed you an overnight bag. You'll be safe here."

My mouth opened as I stared at her like a stupid child. She sounded pre-recorded. I wondered how and when she'd managed to pack me a bag. "Mother, let me go with you. I'm supposed to fix this, not you. Please let me..."

Her head shook back and forth as I talked to her.

"Can you at least let me wait in the car while you talk to him? That way, I can help if you need me."

"No."

The temperature seemed to fall with each word. I started trembling. She still refused to look at me. "But...what about you?"

She reached behind her head and rubbed the muscles in her neck. "I'm fine," she answered in a monotone voice.

"Are you sure, because you seem... not good?"

She shifted her body to face me. The space between her cheekbones and her mouth were sunken. I wondered why I hadn't noticed how thin she'd become. "You shouldn't have talked to Perry. You should have known he would tell his father."

"I know. I didn't think." I took an unsteady breath. She was right, I should have known. His father was still with Pudge when I called that day.

She opened the car door. "Let's go. I'll pick you up as soon as I can. You'll be safe, so stay calm."

There were those words again—stay safe and calm. *When had I ever felt safe and calm?*

She checked me into the hotel. I stepped into the small but pleasant room. She did not.

"I wish you'd let me go with you."

She stared at me with vapid eyes. "I'll be back. Stay calm."

I watched her willowy body walk down the corridor leading to the elevator. A sick sensation grabbed me and made me question her well-being. She was married to my father, after all. Did she need protection from him? Were there secrets in their marriage that threatened her safety? She crossed him when she took me to a hotel instead of Mr. Unger's. *What would he do to her?*

# Twenty-Eight

## PENELOPE'S PICTURE

This was my first time in a hotel. I closed the door, sliding the chain across the top. After a long minute, I surveyed the room. Something told me there was some creepy history associated with this place. Many of the hotels on this side of town had been bordellos during the Gold Rush. I wondered if this was one of the places that survived the 1906 earthquake. It still had a transient gold-seeker air.

The space expressed functionality, from the double bed, the veneer side tables, and the matching white lamps. A round clock sat atop one of the end tables along with the telephone. Over the bed hung a faded desert landscape in a cheap frame. The small bathroom had a toilet, sink, and a bathtub with a white shower curtain. A single awning window was next to the bed. I tried to open it with the hand crank but it wouldn't budge.

Every thought in my head screamed, "Why am I here?" Mother was on a preordained combat mission destined to fail. Mr. Unger was brilliant and probably pegged Father as a narcissistic blowhard long before his son confirmed his suspicions. There was no fix.

Mother's pledge to keep me safe placed her in the line of fire with Father. No justification would be good enough to douse his fury when he found out he would never get his prestigious job back.

*Why did you spill the truth to Pudge?*

I didn't blame him. After our last phone call, he must have thought I was in Boston. He didn't know Reid's proposal and deployment derailed my plan to tell Reid about Father.

I bent over, struck with stomach pains. The truth goaded me. I could have told Reid, marriage proposal or not. Didn't matter. I could have said, "Reid, my father is abusive, I am moving to Boston." It was one damn line. I had dozens of opportunities to tell him and chose not to. The reason was simple. I was ashamed and didn't want him to know.

Every decision I made carried a consequence, from not getting on the plane with Robert, my failure to tell Reid about Father, and saying Penelope's name out loud. Uttering her name activated a tripwire that could not be undone. *Why couldn't I just leave it alone?*

I crawled into bed, pulling up the beige bedspread. The stiff underside was scratchy, so I fumbled for the blanket and wrapped it around my body. The clock on the nightstand said 8 p.m.

The clock ticked for each second. I tightened the blanket around me, chilled by the memory of my mother's dead eyes, and her sallow skin. I wondered if the years of depression had finally shown their hand, and she could no longer disguise her sorrow with red lipstick and sable curls around her flawless face. I choked down tears, unwilling to accept such a dismal fate for her.

My arm was starting to bruise where Father had grabbed me. His malice had escalated; his words were crueler, his rage more violent. I knew why. Father was an unwilling loser. He used to be a big shot Naval Captain whose charisma impressed everyone. Not anymore. His drinking left him bloated, muddied his complexion, and slowed his wit.

English Leather cologne and mouthwash no longer disguised his sour stench, and not even his Pierre Cardin suit could hide his flabby paunch. When the distinguished Mr. Unger fired him, he snapped. Finally, his brutality carried a consequence.

There were consequences for Mother and me also. Men like my father didn't repent, they attacked. I chewed my thumbnail, willing Mother to knock on the door. Where was she?

I reached for the phone to call Robert.

"Front desk," an operator answered.

"I would like to call my brother, please."

"What is your room number?"

"I don't know. If you hold, I can check on the door."

"That's not necessary. There's an informational pamphlet on the table with the room number."

I held the phone between my shoulders and chin and grabbed the paper. "I'm in room 102."

"You can dial out locally by pressing the number nine before the phone number."

Her words took a moment to sink in. "But he lives in Boston so how do I do that?"

"I'm sorry," she said. "We cannot make long distance calls."

My chest tightened as I hung up the phone. I rubbed the bruises on my arm—now fully formed. I counted five; they looked like ink blots. I should have gone with Robert that night. He told me something bad would happen if I stayed in San Francisco and I didn't listen.

Hours passed but I couldn't sleep. I grabbed the overnight bag. It was a carpetbag I remembered from my childhood. As I ran my hands over the nubby surface, I heard a click like the snap of a camera, and then another. I closed my eyes and remembered a time years ago playing with Penelope:

*"I'll be Mary Poppins and you be Bert! Go up to Mommy's closet and get the umbrella! Hurry, Emily!"*

Someone knocked on the door. I sprang to my feet, almost knocking over the lamp. "Mother…" I muttered under my breath.

I swung the door open to find a tall man holding a tray and a covered plate. I stared at him with my mouth open.

"Room service, ma'am."

"I didn't…"

He held the tray closer and stiffened. "Your mother ordered food delivered every six hours, ma'am."

I took the tray and closed the door. Food delivered every six hours? I set the food on the end table.

After a few minutes, I raised the lid. Roast beef, mashed potatoes, and pickled beets. Each menu item was sectioned off so nothing touched. I dropped the lid back on the food. Mother thought of everything. She got the details but ignored the meaning.

I returned to the carpetbag, stroking the material, hoping to remember more about my time with Penelope. I closed my eyes, rubbing the fabric like a magic genie bottle, waiting for my sister to return. It was odd to remember now. I thought about what Robert said about things becoming clearer after he left the house.

I glanced at the clock. It was 11 p.m. I unzipped the bag to find pajamas, a blouse, capris, and underwear, all encased in plastic bags. I frowned; how did she find the time to pack clothing with Father there seething?

I reached into the side pocket and pulled out a folded piece of yellow lined paper. It was curled on the edges like it had been tucked away for years. "Hmm," I muttered.

It seemed as though the paper was touching *me* instead of the other way around. My fingers flicked the corners, noticing there were two pieces of paper. I opened the folded square to half-length. On the outside of the intertwined parts, it read: "To Grandma from Emily and Penelope." The handwriting was strained, like a child's writing. I put my hand over my mouth. It must have been written after a stay with Grandma. I opened it all the way.

*Dear Grandma:*

*Thank you for the fun time. You are the best grandma in the whole world.*
*I love you,*
*Emily*

I touched the grooves where my hand had pushed down to shape each letter. I swallowed hard, knowing how long I must have worked to form the words. *Why was it never mailed?*

"Oh," I mumbled, exhaling the word. Mother didn't mail the letter because Penelope died.

Even at eighteen, my heart didn't seem strong enough to absorb the sorrow. My heart paused and strained to beat again. Mother had erased everything of Penelope after she died; and here I was, holding the only known evidence of her existence. I slowly opened Penelope's letter.

A pain shot through me, fast and unexpected, like a sniper's bullet. This was not a letter. Penelope had drawn a picture. I bent over and listened to the steady puffs coming in and out of my lungs as I tried to catch my breath.

My hands trembled; I set the picture on the center of the bed and sat with my legs folded under me. With both hands over my mouth, I let the tears spill down my face as I studied the drawing.

The picture showed stick-figure girls in fancy tulle gowns—Penelope in pink and me in blue. We held trick or treat bags and wore big "U" smiles. The background was covered with both stars and the sun. In the right-hand corner, she had tried to sign her name. Some letters were backward and most illegible. I smiled at her barely-readable name and choked up when I noticed that she must have tried to make up for it by forming each letter in a different crayon color.

I closed my eyes, imagining her showing the picture to me with her little face beaming. I probably giggled, commenting on the pretty gowns. I pictured us sitting at Grandma's kitchen table, kicking our feet with excitement.

The ticking clock seemed to grow louder. Midnight. Mother must have talked to Mr. Unger by now. I folded the precious papers and tucked them in my pocket. Finding part of Penelope calmed me enough to close my eyes. I patted my pocket and whispered my sister's name as my body drifted into sleep.

$S$unbeams fell in crisscrossing patterns on the walls and furniture of the small room. One shape was different: the silhouette of someone behind me.

"You can turn around. I'm behind you," the shadow whispered.

Her voice was thin, low, and pitiful. Agonizing to hear. I kept still, giving myself time to think.

"I'm right behind you. Why won't you look at me?" Her tone was weak and protracted.

My legs trembled violently; I grabbed the end table to steady myself. "Please," I whispered. "I don't want to see you."

"But you have been looking for me for years and I'm here now. I don't think you want to find me. You are hurting me, you know."

"No, I don't want to hurt you," I answered fast.

"Then please turn around." Her voice dimmed like she was shutting down.

"I want to, but I'm scared," I mouthed.

She whimpered like someone in physical pain. "I would never...ever... hurt you."

I glanced at the wall and saw that her shadow had withered. I spun around to find her. "Where are you?"

The room darkened. My eyes squinted to adjust to the sudden darkness. "Please! Say something!"

A dirty-faced gravedigger holding a shovel burst through the door and grabbed the child. He held her by the waist, her curly raven hair hung down, shielding her face. I heard gurgling sounds coming from the girl as she struggled to breathe. Within seconds, blackness enveloped the little girl and they were gone.

I shot up, my heart pounding against my chest like an angry fist. "No! Stop!"

My hands drew back from the sweat-soaked bed. My labored breathing told me I was wide-awake and in the aftermath of a horrid nightmare. The blanket I'd clutched all night lay wadded in a blob on the floor along with the crumpled top sheet.

I remembered Father getting fired and his tyrannical rant, Mother's vacant stare, the creepy hotel. Reality was as ominous as the nightmare.

I stumbled out of bed to the door, running my shaking hand on the chain. I crept into the small bathroom, trying to keep one foot out the door as I pulled back the shower curtain. The vanity mirror was in front of me, impossible to avoid; my hair was a tangled mess, my eyes swollen. I repeated, "bad dream, no one is here," as I removed the white towel from the rack and wiped my clammy skin.

I grabbed the tossed blanket and collapsed on the bed. The clock read 1 a.m. My vision was blurred from crying. I watched the vexing jerks of the second hand as it measured each excruciating minute.

My head ached like an unyielding vice. I picked up the phone to call Robert and then dropped it. My throat scratched as I tried to form words. I rocked, trying to soothe myself. The chorus in my head repeated, "Stay calm, Mother is coming."

Penelope. I reached into my pocket and unfolded her sketch. The paper shook as my hands trembled. I traced our faces, Penelope's and mine, and prayed for strength. Why did it show up now? *It had to mean something.*

I examined the drawing for clues. Penelope had drawn us side by side holding hands. Tears of sentiment and sadness trickled down my cheeks, threatening to shut my eyes completely. I brushed them away as fast as they dropped and tried to shake off the poignancy long enough to be objective and figure out the meaning. There must be an answer here; the picture held a secret if only I could find it.

I pushed the picture back. Strange sensations fluttered through me, pulled down by the truth that she wasn't here.

The pain was too much, so I tucked the picture back in my pocket. I had to stuff the sorrow aside long enough to think. I pulled my knees to my chest and stared at the ticking clock, waiting for Mother. The clock said 3 a.m.

The second hand disabled my hopes with each tick. I wrapped the hotel blanket tighter to soothe my shaking body. My teeth chattered as I rocked back and forth staring wide-eyed at the clock.

Morning finally came. I rushed to the window and managed to free the hand crank enough to see outside. The window overlooked a giant airshaft offering no view. My life felt like an emergency. Mother said she would be back soon but had been gone over ten hours.

I sat up straight with my back against the headboard. The blanket stayed wrapped around my body as I stared at the hotel clock. The second hand pulsated like a beating heart, reminding me that lives were at stake. Mother was out there trying to fix my mistake.

Time hardened and became my adversary. I couldn't sleep or eat. I stayed frozen in one position, guarding the time, and praying for a knock on the door. The only sound was the ticking of time and the tapping of my teeth.

Midnight came again. I pictured Mother's empty stare, Father's venomous words, and the way his face twisted with rage.

Robert's admonition that "something bad will happen if you stay there" was coming true.

Tick…tick…tick…The persistent sound unraveled my troubled brain. I struggled to keep my eyes open as I held vigil. The clock started to blur, leaving nothing but the relentless ticking. The monotonous rhythm ticked in sync with Robert's last words "something bad will happen."

The time ticked faster and louder, and the clock had grown twice as large. My ears buzzed like static from an un-tuned radio. I gawked at the distorted clock, wondering if it was a time bomb waiting to detonate, fulfilling Robert's prediction.

The vigil that kept me fettered to the clock threatened to kill me. I jumped out of bed, grabbing the night bag.

I rushed through the lobby, not stopping to acknowledge the hotel clerk. My swollen eyes stayed fixed on the front door as I ran outside and away from the dangerous bomb-clock. I had to get home to stop something bad from happening to Mother.

# Twenty-Nine

## CLICK-CLICK-CLICK

A streetlight cast a beam through the haze, illuminating a bus. I combed through my bag for coins to take me home and help Mother. Nothing else mattered.

I boarded, throwing all my change into the slot. The sounds of nickels hitting metal made me cringe, reminding me of the dreadful night at the arcade. The potbellied ruddy-faced driver gave me a suspicious look, so I widened my puffy eyes and put on a smile. He waved me on with a dismissive gesture.

The bus had plenty of seats, but I ran like a child playing musical chairs, dropping on the first one. The seats were filled with mostly uniformed factory workers. They stared out the window with blank faces, closing their eyes and opening them again when the bus made a stop.

In spite of only a few catnaps over the last forty hours, I was alert and restless. Adrenaline coursed through my veins like a solar tornado, annihilating the common sense notion that I should be sleeping. The sporadic reverberation of air going in and out as the door opened and closed sounded like a breathing machine hooked to a comatose patient. The ticking clock was still in my brain; the sound mixed with the air pressure, reminded me of a time bomb and its aftermath. I squirmed in the lumpy seat and tried to shake off the sound.

I grabbed the carpetbag to make sure the clock was not in the bag. I removed every item in search of the bomb-clock. After several inspections, I was convinced it wasn't in the suitcase. I patted my pockets, just in case.

"Are you okay, young lady?"

I jumped at the sound of the woman's voice. She looked to be in her thirties with long wavy blonde hair and green eyes. She wore a colorful tunic with ornate flowers with itty-bitty mirrors mixed into the print.

"I'm all right," I replied.

She placed her palms together and bowed. "I'm Gina."

I wondered what the palm gesture meant or if I should return the sign. I shifted in my chair, feeling uncomfortable.

"What is your name?" Gina asked.

She was the first person I'd talked to over forty hours. Maybe it was her casual appearance or her serene expression, but she didn't seem like a stranger. "Emily."

"I sense you are troubled," she said.

It would have been silly to disagree. "I suppose I am."

"You are filled with doubts, aren't you?"

Her assertion was not what I expected given the swollen eyes and the frantic search for the perilous clock. "Doubts?"

She turned her body toward me. "Doubts have plagued you since your early years."

My eyes widened. I wondered if she was a wizard or fortuneteller. "I'm worried about my mother and whether she's okay. That's where I'm going right now."

She gazed at me for a long time. I expected her to take tarot cards or a crystal ball out of her paisley tote bag. "Your doubts are self-inflicted and I do not get a sense that your mother is in danger. What is coming through is that you are tortured by something and seeking answers."

"Are you a fortuneteller?" I blurted out. I started to apologize for my rude question, but she held up her hand.

"No, I am a teacher and a psychic. I rarely approach people, but I had a strong sense you needed guidance."

I glanced around the bus. "Well, yes...I do."

"You are full of doubt and guilt, which keeps you from being the person you are meant to be. You need to seek understanding and truth, or the negative energy will lock you into confusion and despair."

The nebulous lingo was interesting, but my time with her was limited. The bus ride was about fifteen minutes, and I needed answers now.

"How do I find the truth? In my dreams? Because I have bad dreams a lot."

"Dreams are beyond your will and are generated by mental and physical stress and will not offer you enlightenment."

I started to doubt that I would get a straight answer. Her talk was cerebral and laced with too much hippy-lingo for me to understand. "Then how?"

"Quiet your body and rid yourself of the toxins within you. The poison is preventing you from seeing the truth. You are filled with scattered thoughts without direction, am I right?"

I leaned forward. "Yes, very."

"The mind generates what you think about. If your thoughts are full of negativity, you will create negativity in your life. Take the time to meditate, and once you become calm you will become mindful, which will lead to the awareness you are seeking."

There was that word "calm" again. If I didn't know better, I would think Mother sent her here to talk to me.

I sighed. "I don't understand."

She touched my hand. "I'm referring to right thinking. Emily, who do you love?"

"Reid," I answered quickly.

"Does Reid generate negative thoughts within you?"

"Sometimes. It's not his fault though."

"No matter. Who in your life provides you with positive energy?"

The woman waited patiently as I thought of the people in my life. Her head was down like she was praying.

"My grandma. She passed away nine years ago and maybe my brother, but I disappointed him so..."

Her eyelashes fluttered for a few seconds. "I must discount anyone with a maybe for now. Your grandma, does she give you any negativity?"

"No, she was an angel."

It was jarring to watch her put her palms together as her eyes flickered. I wondered if she might be talking to God.

She raised her head. "Is there anyone else you love without conditions?"

"My twin sister, Penelope. She died when I was five."

"You had a twin sister?"

"Yes, I did."

She closed her eyes. "That is a very powerful connection." Her eyes remained closed like she had reached beyond Earth.

"Yes. She's always with me. I think my life would have been different if she hadn't died."

"How did she pass?"

"I don't know. My parents won't tell me or talk about her death. I tried to ask my mother but nothing came of it."

Her lips moved without a voice, her eyes closed. I leaned forward, wondering if she had the power to unlock the mystery of Penelope's death. She finally opened her eyes.

"There is a strong connection between you and your twin. What is your last memory of her?"

"I don't have a lot of memories other than the sound of her giggling. Oh...and earlier, I remembered playing a game with her."

"Do you have anything that belonged to Penelope?"

"My mother put all of her belongings away after she died. But I found a drawing last night that had been tucked away and forgotten. She drew the picture when she was five years old."

"May I see the drawing?"

My body tingled, and a rush of warmth flowed through me as I handed her the picture.

She ran her hands across the paper, opening and closing her eyes. I bit my lower lip and waited.

She handed the paper back to me and furrowed her brow. "Your sister is with you and is trying to find you to give you clarity."

"I know," I practically shouted. "I have always thought so."

"I urge you to seek a quiet place to sit and meditate. Hold this picture, it has positive energy. Pray every day to Penelope and remove all your thoughts and concentrate on your love for her. She will be your spiritual guide and take you to the level of mindfulness you need to reach awareness and eventually calm and healing."

Gina reached up and pulled the rope, signaling her stop.

I jumped up with her. "Can you tell me anything else?"

"Once you clear your mind of the obstacles, the truth will follow." With her last bit of advice, she placed her palms together and bowed before she exited the bus.

I stared out the window going over Gina's words when the cranky bus driver announced, "Pacific Heights."

I got off, still thinking about Penelope. Everything Gina advised seemed eerily true. I believed Penelope was trying to tell me something. *Something no one else would tell me.*

I stood in place collecting my thoughts. My teeth chattered, so I clenched my jaw and told myself it was just the cold air. I wanted to quash the timid thinking that had defined my life until now. It was a mistake to let Mother drop me off like a helpless child so she could fix my problem. No more. How many times had Robert encouraged me to be strong? It was time to test my courage. I stuck out my chin, determined to keep my wits and think strategically to outsmart Father and help Mother.

Fog hung like a translucent sheet over the night. I knew my house was among the mansions, but the haze clung to the street in a milky veil. It would be challenging to navigate the fog in Pacific Heights because there were no sidewalks, only rounded curbs. I edged my feet along the concrete, putting one foot in front of the other. The mist and fog thickened with each passing minute, forming spooky shapes in the night. This was the kind of night trick or treaters love—the perfect backdrop to parade the streets as ghosts and goblins.

A hard jolt stopped me like someone had slammed on the brakes. My body surged with an energy I'd never felt before. Fog floated like vagabond ghosts, and shapeless forms meandered around me. I remembered being outside with Penelope on a similar night.

Once the burst of energy ceased, my body moved like a lead weight, so I lowered myself to the curb. I pulled hard on the memory. The fog changed from cloudy tufts to a blinding wall of chalky bleached murk. The haze of the white night cleared my brain and activated a long-forgotten memory. I remembered the feel of scratchy tulle against my skin and could taste chocolate and caramel. I gazed out at the white canvas as my mind released a memory from thirteen years ago:

*It was a foggy Halloween night. Our costumes looked exactly like Penelope's picture—she wore a pink satin and tulle gown with gold sparkles that fastened in the back with a big bow. My dress was blue, and I had silver stars instead of gold.*

*Mother had spent hours creating tiaras out of colored paper and glitter and wands made of foil. We bustled down the stairs in our costumes, waving our magic wands. Mother beamed as we twirled around the living room in our billowing gowns. We danced and spun in circles until we became dizzy and fell to the floor on top of each other, dissolving in giggles.*

*Our painted wands had lost their foil from wrestling, so I asked Mother to fix them. I ran upstairs to fetch the glue, and when I came* downstairs Mother and Father were quarreling. She was supposed to hand out the candy while Father took the three of us around the neighborhood. He told her it wasn't fair to make Robert wait, and we could catch up with them after she finished fixing the wands. She insisted it wasn't safe to let my sister and I go out alone in the fog. He laughed, and told her to stop treating us like babies. The phone rang, so Mother ran into the kitchen to answer the call. While she talked on the telephone to Grandma, Father ushered Robert, dressed as Batman, out the door.

Mother came back from the kitchen and scanned the room, shaking her head. She simultaneously worked the foil around our wands and glanced at the door, as my sister and I held out our gowns and pretend-danced with Prince Phillip. When she finished the wands we grabbed them along with our treat bags and raced to the door. Mother yelled for us to stop. She told us it was too dangerous to go out in the fog alone.

We couldn't wait to show off our costumes and fill our candy bags. Together, we formed an alliance, jumping up and down and chanting "please," drawing the word out as we begged her to let us go. The more she shook her head the louder we shouted and the higher we jumped. After a few minutes, she rolled her eyes and her "no" changed to a reluctant "okay." She had one condition, which she repeated three times— we were not allowed to cross the street.

A switch flipped. The memory stopped. I heard a click, click, click, like a film reel had ruptured. The night came to a screeching stop. All except one thing.

*I saw a magic wand lying in the middle of the street.*

⌒

The sky spread its billowed white gloom over the houses, lawns, cars, and pathways. A single street lamp formed a beam in the dense clouds like a beacon guiding me to the next step. I sat on the curb, my arms swaddled around my shivering body. I tugged at the memory. The fog seemed to taunt me while the flare challenged me to unlock the secret of Penelope's death. I kept my eyes on the light, but nothing more came to me. My recollection of that Halloween night snapped like a rubber band against my skin.

In my gut, I knew Penelope was lost on a damp, cloudy street on a night like this one. The details of her death were immersed in layers of secrets, confusion, and penalties. My life had never been quiet enough to remember what happened to her. I'd spent every day in combat, dodging the bullets of Father's madness, arming myself with fantasy to avoid the lethal artillery of a battle I didn't understand.

The fog held answers. I had always visualized Mother shrouded in a blinding mist. Still, tonight's memory of her beaming as Penelope and I danced in our costumes remained as clear as a cloudless morning. My central belief was now a certainty.

*My life changed because Penelope died.*

I ached for the animated mother absorbed in the wiles of her twin daughters. I got up, half-dazed, and continued in the direction of my house.

The journey was a sightless walk into Hell. I inched along the curb with outstretched arms. With each step, I prayed I wouldn't touch human flesh. That terrified me far more than the shapeless white ghosts, which now seemed to goad me forward. I imagined Mother's silky voice urging me to keep going. My only roadmap was an occasional porch light and the mailboxes near the lawn. As I came upon each box, I stopped and traced the raised letters of the homeowner. I progressed slowly, careful not to make a sound and arouse suspicion.

The sixth mailbox spelled the name: Quinn 12438 Orchid Lane. I crouched beside the mailbox to think.

I had to know if Father was home. I crawled on all fours along the gravel to check for his car. Pebbles cut into my legs but I kept going. I prayed for an empty driveway. After several yards, I touched rubber and then felt the ice-cold metal of Father's Corvette. My knees knocked against each other as I squatted next to the sports car. I didn't have time to plot a strategy except to help Mother and outmaneuver Father.

I scurried in a stooped position to the corner of the house using my arms to guide me. Potted geraniums lined the walkway, so I hunkered down to keep from knocking one over. I reached the side fence, stood up, and unlatched the gate. I looked in all directions to determine if anyone had seen me, which was pointless because the fog hid everything, including me.

I re-latched the gate and faced the yard. I had to get to the rear of the house to find a window. I took a step, which was like walking through a cloud.

I twisted my foot and recognized the gritty surface of the brick path. No windows faced the sidewalk, so I wouldn't need to worry about Father seeing my silhouette. On my left were the metal trash cans. I touched one and moved two steps away so I wouldn't bang into them. Mother's obsession to line them in a neat row helped. My heart pounded so fast, I could hear the beats in my ears. Instead of my usual self-soothing gestures to control my anxiety, I did the opposite. I tensed every muscle and clamped down on my jaw as I continued to the back of the house.

The gooseberry shrubs to the right, thick and full of thorns, prevented me from using the house as a guide. I inched my way down the walkway, straining to detect the outline of a tree or shrub. I reached out and touched a thorny bush. It drew blood.

Puffs of white smoke came from my mouth too fast. I was overbreathing. I paused for a few seconds to catch my breath and then continued my advance. After several steps, I felt the ridge at the end of the sidewalk. I bent down and touched the soft spikes of grass. Once I reached the oak tree, I would be able to view the back windows.

Creeping on the lawn wasn't as easy as I had thought. I kept my arms out so I wouldn't bump into something. I slowed the pace. What was evident in daylight was unrecognizable in the fog—like waking up at night to scary objects in the room, which turn out to be ordinary things in the light of the day. I stopped again to slow my breathing and calm down.

I waved my hands for any signs of the tree. After a short distance, I heard the sound of crackling leaves beneath my feet. Vague silhouettes of branches peaked out from the mist. I had reached the pinnacle unscathed and leaned against the trunk to consider my next move.

The old Bloomingdale's box was nearby, reminding me of the day Father destroyed my drawings. My chest tightened. I feared the vile memory would unravel my resolve to find Mother, but I didn't know how to stop the agitation in my soul. Crouching like a foot soldier in my yard didn't help. It put an exclamation point on the truth that I was an outsider in my own family. My heart pounded, and the smallest sound in the stillness of the fog made me jump. I stayed down, telling myself to remain strong.

After a minute, I shimmied to the far corner of the house. All was dark except the kitchen. Mother had to be there.

I fell to my hands and knees and began crawling toward the last window. The frosty grass numbed my hands, and my hair hung over my face. I stopped long enough to tuck my hair into my blouse and dry my hands on my jumper. A soft glow formed on the ground as I inched my way toward the lighted room. Since leaving the hotel, I'd been on autopilot, propelled home by a force I didn't understand.

I reached my destination and leaned against the stucco. The visible puffs of white breath quickened. I shivered, realizing my fears were out of control. My knees started to convulse, so I folded my arms and pressed my upper body weight on my legs. It worked. I rubbed my hands together to warm them and inhaled and exhaled to slow my breathing. I rested my head against the house and prayed for the strength to follow through on my plan to find my mother.

I crouched down and peered through the glass, as I tried to adjust to the brightness. The room was empty with no signs of Mother. The dinette chairs were tucked under the table, the counters cleared, the drawers closed, and the cupboards shut. My stomach churned at the sight of the sink. I could still taste the putrid flakes and visualize the sick expression on Father's face as I swallowed them one by one.

Vile visions invaded my mind. I lowered my head and mouthed, "focus" in rapid succession. I bit down on the inside of my mouth, determined to purge the unwanted thoughts. I called on Penelope, Grandma, and God to help me. After a few minutes, I heard the radiant laughter of Mother, Penelope, and me on that Halloween night. I kept them with me as armor to stave off the memory of Father's brutality.

Time dragged on as I waited for Mother to walk into the room. The light remained on like a flare warning me to stay put. My body tensed from bending in one position, and I could no longer feel my feet. The god-awful sound of the bomb clock started ticking again, beating in sync with my thumping heart. I lost track of time and didn't know how long I'd been staring into an empty kitchen. I turned to view the back yard. The fog had thinned. I wondered how much time I had before dawn. In daylight, Father could find me.

"Please God, please...." I muttered, remembering the vacant expression on Mother's face and Father's vicious, drunken threats. "Stop him."

I leaned against the house, clutching my chest, panting. My puffs of breath blended into a long stream, piercing the damp air, reminding me of the hazard of being here. When I opened my mouth to tell myself to calm down, my jaw froze. I twisted and tried to shake off the terror and return to a position where I could reason, but the physical and mental torment was too powerful.

I imagined myself looking at Father's face, first as a child, then as a young girl, and an adult. He transformed from a strict father to a monstrous lunatic like a flip book in my head. The memories spread, ignited, and swelled as they took charge of my senses. Untamed revelations reared up, and I couldn't hold them back.

I cowered under the window, damp and weakened, as I struggled to regain the courage that drove me here. But the untreated trauma of a vicious childhood held a death's grip as I convulsed with agonizing clarity.

Brutality and sadistic acts butted up against pretense. Violence erupted, everything happening at once. I bore down as he ripped clumps of hair from my scalp, and his fleshy hand squeezed my neck. His disgusting spit dripped down my cheek. Chips of bone spattered in my chest as he pounded me against the gritty asphalt. His violence and filthy slurs mutilated my spirit and scorched my soul.

*Why? Why? Why?*

Stepping on a creaky stair. Running in the house. Locking a door. Walking too fast or too slow. Not putting the rake away. Removing rubber bands from my braids. Using more than three squares of toilet paper. Not putting the hatbox away. Singing too loud. Coughing. Sneezing. A dripping faucet. Saying Penelope's name out loud.

My mind exploded with overwhelming intensity; I had to shut off the past. My brain couldn't hold a thought for more than a second or two. I hadn't slept or eaten. My limbs were leaden, my reactions sluggish, and my mind drained its contents into vacuity. A voice in my head took over, telling me what I needed to do. Robert's premonition that "something bad would happen" was unfolding.

The voice directed me to advance. I moved along the edge of the house to the back door, slid my hand up the wood panel, and turned the knob. Open. I crept into the back foyer. The house was dark except for the kitchen. I bent over and walked on tiptoes toward the glaring light to find Mother.

# *Thirty*

## SHREDDED BLACK VEIL

I dropped the bloody knife. It chimed as it hit the kitchen floor. Blood oozed between my fingers as I pressed on Father's chest. He was quiet—so quiet. I gazed with stony eyes at his battered body and then looked away.

*Time shifted in jagged increments so fast I couldn't keep up. When the static cleared, it was a foggy Halloween night. A ghostly fortress draped the street with impenetrable white clouds. I shook my empty treat tag, bouncing up and down, as white vapor swirled in the moonless sky.*

"Come on!" I shouted. "Hurry up!"

"But Mommy said not to cross the street!"

I cupped one hand over my mouth. "Everyone's on this side! There's more candy!"

"But Mommy told us not to!"

"Come on! It's okay!"

"I can't see you! Where are you?"

I held up my arm. "Follow my magic wand! Hurry! Run!"

Two glowing eyes with columns of light beamed through the fog. I opened my mouth to scream, "Stop!" when tires and brakes screeched, echoing like a belated foghorn. A hollow yelp knelled through the night followed by metal hitting a street lamp. Rubber tires spun against the curb. The noise gyrated and stopped and then started up again, emitting high-pitched sounds that reverberated in the night. Seconds later, the car rumbled and sped off with its red taillights fading into the distance.

Plumes of white smoke climbed like spiteful ghosts to reveal my sister lying in the middle of the street. I ran to her, pulling her into my arms. Her head fell limp into my lap, and her hair hung in blood-soaked strands across her face. I tried to scream but only a throttling gasp sputtered in and out. I shook her tiny shoulders but stopped when her head slumped sideways against my forearm. The air smelled like burnt rubber. With one arm around her and the other on the gritty road, I bent my knees and inch by inch dragged us off the street.

We huddled together on the damp sidewalk as the fog formed a ghostly barricade around us. I cowered to the haunting vapor. "Shh," I whispered. My gut contracted as I trembled and twitched, pulling her closer to shield us. I wept and convulsed in terror, praying for the ghosts to go away.

I turned my face to the side, straining to scream. My words slurred and were riddled with choking sounds. My mind could only think "open your eyes," as my body retched on the words. I stroked her head, trying to rouse her. My mouth opened and closed, mouthing "please," and "wake up," gasping, suffocating on fear.

Sirens blared. Long, red trucks and white cars with twirling lights stopped in front of us. The alarms ended with an abrupt screech. Men surrounded us. A uniformed stranger gripped me under my arms and lifted me several feet away.

Men huddled in a circle, calling out. "One! Two! No Pulse! Go!"

They pulled out instruments and wrapped her in white cloth strips.

My fingers began to tingle, and my legs went numb. I felt a tug on my arm and then a strong push. I turned, but no one was there. My body wafted from the scene, carried too far away to see clearly. I struggled to move closer but with each movement, I drifted further away.

The men stopped touching my sister. One knelt on the ground next to her, writing on a tablet. One man put equipment in a large case while the other five or so stood around talking to one another.

Mother ran down the sidewalk, shrouded in white dust, screaming "Penelope!" When my mother reached her, a man grabbed her elbow but she wriggled free. She flung herself on the ground and pulled my sister into her arms. The men gathered around her, shaking their heads with an occasional glance at one another.

Space moved in and out. Seconds seemed like hours as I sat on the sidewalk near Reid's house. The fog hovered over Mother, forming shapes and drifting up and down in the night sky. Mother's body jerked with each scream, and her face tilted upward as she cried out for God.

A man in a dark uniform stooped next to me. "What's your name, honey?"

More sirens clamored in the background, coming closer. My eyes remained fixed on Mother. Her damp hair hung like a shredded black veil over her face. She began to choke on her tears as her body convulsed. Men tried to coax her away, but she held on tight.

The strange man asked me, "What happened here?"

Fog tufts formed around Mother, shaping into alabaster angels, standing around like sacred guardians. Most of the angels floated around her and then drifted off. A few stayed close by.

The man shook my shoulders. "Can you talk?"

I gazed at his hand; his fingers were broad and thick like my father's. I turned back to the sound of my mother screaming.

A graceful, birdlike angel twirled blithely around me. She stretched her feathered wings across the sky, hovering close to my face. I felt her misty breath against my ear as she whispered, "listen," over and over. Her voice was melodic, like wind chimes echoing from Heaven.

I strained to see my mother and sister but the angel moved closer, blocking my view. "Don't cross the street in the fog," she warned. Her words resounded, ringing in waves, touching my skin and bouncing off.

The angel was too late. I had already crossed the street and urged my sister to follow me.

More sirens screeched as men in black uniforms filed out of flashing white cars, yelling. "Clear the Scene!"

Uniformed men shouted numbers to one another. Some of the men placed orange cones on the road, some stood on the opposite side blowing whistles and holding up their hands when cars tried to pass. Their flashlights sent white spheres of light back and forth on the ground.

The angel that had warned me not to cross the street drifted into the heavens. Mother stayed cocooned around my sister, crying into her body. Father was now with her. He grabbed her shoulders and pulled her into his chest. She pushed him off, her face twisted in pain. He tried again. They grappled as she struck him with one arm and shoved him off of her. After a few minutes, he dropped his grasp, rubbing his eyes.

He spotted me. His lips compressed, and his muscles flexed. He ran toward me, shaking his fists. "This is your fault! You crossed the street! You killed Penelope!"

I hunkered down, wailing. When he was inches from me, two police officers grabbed him and yanked his arms behind him. "Easy, sir!"

His head snapped back. "Goddamn, Emily! You killed your sister!"

More officers clustered around Father. They moved him several feet away and let go. Father's mouth moved as officers wrote on tablets. He pointed at our house and the direction of the street where we had crossed. While he talked, the men nodded. One patted his shoulders.

Father turned and glared at me, drawing his face in a tight grimace. "She's the one! She did it!"

I couldn't look at him anymore. My lips quivered as I stared at my hands.

A lady officer squatted next to me. "Emily, I'm Officer Blanchard. You are safe, sweetie. It'll be okay."

I pointed my finger toward my mother and sister.

She patted my hand. "Your mommy's fine, Emily. You'll see her soon."

I leaned forward to see Mother's face, but she was still covered with the shredded black veil. An angel hovered near her as she continued to cry out for Penelope.

Lights continued to flash, radios buzzed, and the uniformed men shouted instructions. Men placed my sister on a flatbed and covered her with a white sheet. My world blurred as I watched them load her in a long white truck. Mother crawled in the truck next to her. I watched them drive off.

The lady officer put her arms around me. "It's okay, Emily. I'll take you home."

I pointed at the taillight of the white truck until I couldn't see it anymore.

"Take my hand," she said. I bowed my head, glancing only at Reid's house. Neighbors stood on their porches silent. I whimpered quietly, unable to hold a thought for more than a second or two. The only sound was the gentle tap of my empty treat bag against my tulle and satin gown. I knew my life had shattered and nothing would ever be the same. I just didn't know why.

I heard the snap of metal binding my wrists together. "Emily Quinn," an officer said. "You are under arrest for the murder of your father, Jacob Quinn."

Two men shoved me behind a metal barrier. They sat in the front seat of the car, talking in halted sentences to a radio voice filled with static electricity. After the short drive, they led me to a small room with a blackened window.

The space had a square desk and a few wooden chairs. The officer removed my handcuffs and directed me to sit. I reached down and touched the chair, surprised, because I didn't feel connected to anything. The room was so cold my teeth chattered.

A uniformed lady walked in and held out a sweater. "Here, Miss."

I pushed my arms into the sleeves, noticing red spots splattered across my jumper.

A man gestured for her to leave. He had a rounded face, brown eyes, and a baldhead. He wore a plain white shirt and gray trousers. "Can I get you coffee or a soft drink?"

"Miss Quinn?" he asked.

His thin lips seemed to disappear when he moved his mouth.

He grabbed one of the wooden chairs and sat next to me. "Can you tell me what happened tonight, Emily?"

I gazed at him, wondering why he called me Emily.

He leaned back and put his hands behind his head. "Listen, Emily. It's better for you to tell me everything. The quicker you get it off your chest the faster you can get out of here."

I pressed on my arm but couldn't feel anything. I pushed again and watched as a white spot appeared and disappeared.

"What were you doing at your house tonight?"

I tried to figure out why he knew my name and I didn't.

"Why did you go to your house?" When he spoke, his mouth formed a circle. "Listen. We got all the evidence we need to charge you with first-degree murder, but I'd like to get your side of the story."

Another man walked in, about thirty or so, with black hair and full lips. When he smiled, his teeth lined up straight and white. "Hello, Emily. I'm Detective Warner. You must be thirsty. I brought you a glass of water. Can we talk?"

He placed the water on the table in front of me along with a box of Kleenex. "Now, Emily. I'm sure you didn't mean to kill your father, there must have been a terrible fight between you. I get how it is with fathers. Mine's a pain in the ass. I've wanted to stab him a time or two. Stuff happens. You went there to talk, things heated up, and one of you grabbed a knife. That's what happened, right?"

I examined my hands, which seemed strangely large.

"He pushed you too far, didn't he?"

I wondered why he was still talking.

"Emily, I don't want you to get blamed for everything. Every story has two sides. If you tell me what happened, I'll help you. Right now, you're looking at first-degree murder. It doesn't have to go that way. I don't see you as a cold-blooded killer. Tell me your side of the story. Things got heated between you. He pushed your buttons and maybe even threatened you, right?"

His mouth stopped moving. I couldn't find his white teeth anymore.

The man with the thin lips bolted toward me. "Tell us! You butchered your father! You stabbed him till your hand got tired! We got your prints! What'd he do, cut your allowance? Not let you drive his fancy sports car?"

He threw gory photos of a slashed body on the table in front of me. "Look at what you did! That's your father! You carved him up like a turkey! Look at him!"

"Easy, Harold," the younger detective said. "Let her talk."

I recoiled and crossed my arms, rocking and shivering.

"Don't try that silent act with me! You knew exactly what you were doing! Do you get what they'll do to you if you don't talk? They'll strap you to a chair like an animal, stick electrodes in your brain and zap electricity through you till your heart stops!"

I pulled on the sweater, wrapping it tighter—rocking.

The young one motioned for the older man to back off. "Emily, I want to help you. I don't think you went to the house intending to murder your father. You seem like a nice girl, but sometimes things get out of hand. It's not your fault. Tell me what happened so I can help you. You might even be able to leave here. Don't you want to see your mother?"

The room narrowed, receding from the side inward. I closed my eyes and opened them again, but the room had only constricted.

The mean one pounded the table with both fists. "Stop playing us! I see girls like you every day. Your rich papa gave you everything! You're spoiled rotten! So, did big daddy finally stand up to you? We already know you got kicked out of the house. That pissed you off, right? You went there to even the score. That's what you did, right?"

His sour breath brushed my cheek. Growling. He slapped the table again.

He puffed and signaled to the blackened window. A door opened. "We're done here! Take her to booking!"

⁓

### San Francisco County Jail, August 28, 1966. End of Session Eight

"*Y*ou are waking up now, energy is returning to your muscles..." said Doctor Lieberman.

I didn't open my eyes. I didn't want to live in a world where I was alive, and Penelope was gone because I urged her to cross a street to her death.

So, I kept them shut. I heard the sound of tires squealing, the muted thump of the car hitting my sister, and the smell of burning rubber. I remembered the primal screams of Mother begging God to bring her daughter back to life. I envisioned Penelope's lifeless body, the fog angels warning me not to cross the street, and Father blaming me for my sister's death.

Doctor Lieberman rested his hand on my shoulder. "Please open your eyes, Emily."

The memory opened a thirteen-year scab, pooling guilt-ridden blood around me. I clenched my teeth to keep from weeping. I couldn't face what I had done nor did I invite excuses to unburden my conscience. I didn't deserve it.

We sat like this for over five minutes. I inhaled and exhaled, clamping down on my emotions, refusing to open my eyes. Doctor Lieberman kept his hand on my shoulder. The intrusive sounds of whistling, shouting, and the banging of inmates in the jail yard permeated to the fifth floor reminding me of my mortal sins.

The years of shame made sense. I understood Mother's rejection and Father's hatred. For thirteen years, I sought the truth of how my sister died, thinking it would rid me of my guilt and insecurities. *Little had I known.*

"Emily, you were only five years old," he murmured.

He'd consulted with Mother early on, so I had to ask. "Did you know?"

"No. I did not. I wanted to learn everything from your perspective, so I purposefully excluded talking to anyone in your family."

I kept my eyes shut and bit down hard on my lower lip. Knowing we had uncovered the truth at the same time made the discovery more intimate. "I killed her...it was my fault."

"No, Emily. A car killed her...a hit-and-run driver in the fog."

"I told her to cross the street," I said, noticing my voice was hoarse like I'd been screaming.

He sighed. "You were a child. A five-year-old does not understand cause and effect."

I had to talk fast, or I wouldn't have the nerve. "Mother warned us not to cross the street in the fog."

Doctor Lieberman put his hand under my chin. "It's important for you to process this with me."

I felt warm tears trickle down my cheeks.

"Please listen to me. Every time you think about that night, remember this. You are not responsible for her death. You were only five years old. The events that transpired that night were a tragic accident. Unfortunate decisions were made before you left the house that night."

The sorrow and grief was unavoidable. My shoulders shook as I fought to keep my eyes closed. "I crossed the street in the fog and begged her to cross too."

"No, Emily. A five-year-old does not see the fog. What you saw was more candy on the other side of the street. Let me repeat...unfortunate decisions were made *before* you left the house that night."

I covered my eyes. "What?"

"Allowing you and Penelope to walk the streets in the fog alone is where the mistake lies. Notice I did not say blame. Mistakes are made without ill intentions. You and Penelope should have had an adult with you. An adult would have kept you from crossing the street. What happened was a tragic mistake. You are not to blame. You will experience the tragedy and the sorrow of losing your sister, but you must not bear the weight of a mistake beyond your capacity to make."

I understood his argument but the fog that plagued me on that night had cleared to a place of gloom. I felt gutted.

"Please, Emily..."

I opened my eyes to the creased, troubled face of Doctor Lieberman. In his watery eyes, I sensed his deceased daughter, Rachel. We shared an unexpected connection, a doctor and his patient congealed in the deaths of precious kin we would give anything to see again.

We talked for another forty minutes or so. I allowed myself to weep and listened to the doctor's words about grieving and memory loss following the trauma of her death. I promised to remember what he said about blame and responsibility.

We never discussed my father's killing. Penelope's death had blocked his murder and erased the horror from my mind. Nevertheless, the night of the murder was coming, probably next week. He devoted the post-session to concentrate on sweet, little Penelope.

*And getting me to open my eyes.*

# Thirty-One

## LONG-HELD SECRETS AND LIES

*San Francisco County Jail, September 4, 1966. Beginning of Session Nine*

The guard un-cuffed me following an RCI, an acronym for "routine cell shakedown." Two guards tore my bed apart, checked inside a wall socket, and the sink receptacle searching for contraband. After about three minutes, they called the "all-clear." I cringed at the sound of metal clinking against metal as he slammed the cell door.

The secret of Penelope's death was now an inconsolable sorrow. I remembered the car crashing into the lamppost, seconds of silence as I waited for the sound of my sister's feet, along with flares flickering in the fog. I heard Mother's screams and angels lingering amid the mist and vapor. Deafening chaos followed by irrevocable stillness.

*The night that changed everything.*

I had to prepare for a therapy session in thirty minutes. I placed one hand on the basin to steady my persistent vertigo, splashing my face with cold water. Didn't help. Nothing helped. Part of me had hoped that hypnosis would have uncovered an extenuating circumstance for killing my father. Just the opposite. He had a reason to hate me. He couldn't forgive me. Now, I would never be able to forgive myself—for two deaths. I rocked back and forth and let the tears spill into the bowl. The memories were like links in a chain now, steering me to the night I murdered my father.

As I shuffled into Doctor Lieberman's office, I found him studying a hefty pile of papers. His index finger trailed the words, as he appeared to rush through the documents. He glanced up. "Good morning. I'll be with you shortly."

I tried to get comfortable for my ninth therapy session. My stomach ached like an open wound pulsating, reminding me of my transgressions. The dreaded day was here to retrieve the details of the murder. There was no going back. Mother, Robert, and even Reid needed to know the truth, and I couldn't let fear cheat them out of learning what happened that night.

"Just a few minutes," said the doctor. He piled the papers, bouncing them up and down.

"No problem." The doctor had stopped by my cell four times since learning how Penelope died. He feigned an excuse, but I knew he was worried.

He grabbed his clipboard and some blank paper. "Welcome, Emily. Please sit down."

I frowned, knowing I was already seated.

"I met with your attorneys to go over the witness list. I would like to discuss it with you."

I gripped my chair. This was the first time we'd talked directly about the upcoming trial. "Okay."

"I was going over a list of character witnesses and need your input."

The knots in my stomach tightened. "Uh...yes."

"Before we get started," he said, moving papers around. "I need to talk to you about your brother. Let me preface this by telling you to relax. He was involved in a car accident but he is fine."

My heart began to skip beats. "Robert? What's wrong? What do you mean? A car accident?"

I had been asking questions in an attempt to postpone the answers, so the doctor cut me off. "Emily, he is fine. I only found out because your attorneys tried to reach him through your mother to testify on your behalf."

My heart rate climbed so fast it vibrated. "What happened?"

"First, let me reassure you again that your brother is fine. He was in San Francisco when the car accident occurred, and he sustained head trauma. He required surgery, which was successful."

"Head trauma? Surgery?" I tried to stay composed so he would continue to answer my questions. It was all an act to keep my skin on.

"Yes, a procedure to drain the fluid in his brain. The surgery was successful. He is on medication and will need ongoing physical therapy. He is expected to make a complete recovery."

I broke in. "Expected? What do you mean expected?"

He sighed, slowing down his explanation. "Physicians don't talk in absolutes, Emily. Your brother's operation was successful."

I needed a minute to absorb the shock and slow down. "Okay. Keep going. I want to know everything."

"Your attorneys found out when they tried to reach your brother to testify on your behalf. Your mother requested that he not be contacted until he's back at Harvard. He's on a medical leave, and she is concerned the upcoming trial will impede his return to school."

I shrugged, trying not to show my disappointment that she put education over me. Poor Robert. She wanted to patch him up quickly so he could get back to test tubes and all-night cram sessions.

"He was in San Francisco? I'm sure, the funeral..." I said, my voice weakening.

"I don't know all the details, but he called your house after you left for the hotel. Apparently, he caught a flight out the same day. As you know, the visibility was difficult that night and not long after his flight landed, his rental car veered off the road several miles from your hotel."

"Oh..." I lowered my head, thinking. I should have known Robert would come to my rescue. The facts piled up quickly. "I left a message with Vanderbilt Hall for him to call me...he was hard to get ahold of. He must have called the house and found out Father had thrown me out."

The doctor nodded. "That would make sense."

"Why wasn't I told this before?"

"I'm sorry, Emily. Your mother didn't want you informed. Perhaps she thought it might jeopardize your therapy."

"Sure," I said, shaking my head. "Harvard."

"Do you have any more questions?" he asked.

I stared off, thinking. The news of Robert's accident left me oddly composed. Robert was my hero, and I wanted to be strong for him. Once the trial concluded, I knew we'd talk again. He'd want the whole truth. I needed to break my pattern of denial and fear and show him his years of love and counsel had finally sunk in. His words "you'll get there" played in my head. This was the time.

I straightened up. "I would like to make sure Robert is okay."

"He is stable and the doctors are optimistic. Your attorneys would like him to testify on your behalf."

"I don't care about that."

He set his pencil down. "It's important you take this witness list seriously."

I thought about what he must think. "Okay, I'm sorry. I'll pay attention."

"Thank you. The first person on the list is Perry Unger. He volunteered to testify as soon as he learned about the murder. He will be an excellent defense witness, affirming the abuse you suffered from your father."

I choked up at the sound of his name, remembering our talks, the party, and laughing in the cafeteria. "Perry is a great friend."

"Your attorneys assure me he is well spoken. Now, the next person is Reid. How do you think he will react? Your legal team will be unable to reach him until he finishes his military training."

Telling Reid terrified me more than anything. He left thinking he would return to a fiancée when, in fact, he would return home to a murderer. I winced, remembering his talk about how to be a "marine wife."

"I don't want to involve Reid," I answered. "He's in the dark about everything. I can't imagine...."

"It's not something you need to decide now."

I swallowed hard. "What about my mother?"

Doctor Lieberman shifted in his swivel chair and pinched the skin between his eyes. "Unfortunately, your mother is being called by the prosecution."

The old sinking sensation hit me. "So...are you saying she's against me? She wants me to be convicted?"

"No, but she doesn't want to be involved in your trial other than hiring your defense team. She was subpoenaed by the prosecutor."

"Oh, okay. But when you said she doesn't want to be involved, are you saying she won't testify for me?"

"Emily, she won't testify for you. I'm sorry."

I felt like someone had knocked me to the floor. Sure, I understood why she had been detached during my childhood, but her rejection still hurt. She was the one person who could help ease my self-hatred over my part in Penelope's death. I longed for the compassion she must have felt for me before that Halloween night. Knowing she refused to stand up for me in court put a period on the end of our tortured relationship.

"Emily, this is a lot to take in. Would you prefer to reschedule our session?"

"No," I said, trying to take the hurt out of my voice.

"We can do this next week."

Something pushed me to proceed. I remembered all the times Robert urged me to think for myself and confront life instead of running away. "I want to continue."

Doctor Lieberman looked at his blank papers and then up at me. His face was lined with doubt; he seemed to be waiting for me to reconsider.

"For this to work, you must be willing to relive every detail of that night. To date, we have succeeded in remembering everything except the murder. I think this is partially due to the trancelike state you were in the night your father died. Your sister's accident was a long-repressed memory and it usurped the killing of your father. It is possible you are unwilling to face the murder. If that is the case, hypnosis will not work."

I wondered if he had given up on me remembering the murder. "So, what are you saying? You don't believe I'll ever remember?"

"This is not within my control. Hypnosis requires a willingness to uncover the truth. So far, you have not been forthcoming in the particular details of that night other than going to the kitchen. For this to work, you will need to be willing to open the door…literally."

"I am willing," I answered. "I've run from reality my whole life… inventing characters to play the part of the happy girl. I know Robert would want me to continue. Besides, I owe him the whole truth."

"Very well. I will lead you through a guided hypnosis. Lean back, allow your body to relax. Listen to my voice and answer my questions exactly as you remember them.…"

"Okay," I said. "I'm ready."

I settled back, listening to Doctor Lieberman's words, embracing the sound of his voice. Willing to face that night and to give the few people that still cared about me the truth.

⁓

*I* huddled inches from the back door, wondering if I'd made a mistake. Ever since Mother dropped me off at the hotel, I'd felt compelled to come home and stop the "bad thing from happening" Robert had warned me about. Now my mind was as murky as the fog I walked through to get here. I began to think. Why was Robert so determined to get me away from Father? What didn't I know? I slunk back against a coat rack, questioning everything.

*Why was I here?* What made me think Mother was in danger? I'd never even heard them argue before the night of his firing. Even during the drive to the hotel, her blank expression wasn't much different than any other day. I endowed her with loving emotions to make myself feel better and recreate her joy that Halloween night. I was trying to take one snapshot and turn it into a photo album of undying motherly love.

Hogwash. I shook my head, appalled at my lack of insight. I was stooping like a prowler in the back entry, knowing I put myself in jeopardy for nothing. I rubbed my numb feet, trying to get them to work again so I could get out of this house of Hell. I released a long-overdue yawn and ran my fingers up to the doorknob, ready to drag my leaden-body back to the hotel.

I touched the knob, and pulled my hand away. A voice in my head told me to wait. I slid to the floor, wondering why I couldn't just leave. Delayed, dulled-out questions plagued me. Something wasn't right. Robert told me on graduation night that leaving the house helped him see things more clearly. I'd been gone forty some-odd hours and now that the smokescreen of helping Mother was gone, I felt it too. I needed answers to the secrets that eluded me and kept me chained to a tormented life.

I rubbed my arms and listened. Wood crackled in the living room fireplace as Father's favorite crooner, Frank Sinatra, played on the phonograph. I rolled my eyes in disgust. It was hardly the sound of turmoil. I pictured Mother sitting in her peach cushioned chair reading a novel and Father lounging on the sofa smoking a fat cigar and drinking scotch.

Between the crackling fire and the lulling melody of "Someone to Watch Over Me," my eyes started to droop. I leaned against the wall—

A clanking noise roused me. The music stopped. I listened to the steady sound of the record player needle scraping on the lead out, knocking back and forth against the grooves.

The sound continued. The adrenaline that waned when I first arrived escalated; I was determined to find out what no one wanted me to know.

The kitchen cast enough light to guide me into the living room behind Mother's chair. I crouched down, hearing raised voices, arguing. I scurried just outside the kitchen. No one was there. They had to be in the dining room. I snuck into the kitchen and crawled inside a tall sideboard cabinet.

I heard three voices—Father, Mother, and Robert.

At the sound of Robert's voice, I raised my arm to open the door. As my fingers touched the wood, the voice inside my head began to talk again. It whispered to halt, stay quiet, think. I pulled my hand back. The wounds that Father had inflicted became septic, poisoning not only me, but Robert too. He tried to tell me something that night at the airport, but I was too beguiled by Reid to pay attention to him. Now was the time.

With a slow, measured breath, I drew back against a stack of linens and listened.

"Robert, dear," said Mother. "Please calm down."

"I am calm, Mother. Tell me where Emily is and I'll leave. Gladly."

"No, Robert," said Father. "Don't leave! Come on Son, you just got here. I haven't seen you in months, for God's sake. Let's sit down, and talk...."

"Where is she?" Robert interrupted.

Father snorted. "Emily? Goddamn, Robert...she's a big girl. You don't need to protect her."

"Yeah?" Robert asked, his voice steady. "Someone needs to keep her safe. You two never did. Now tell me where she is so I can go."

"Robert, dear," said Mother. "How can you say I didn't keep Emily safe? I've always tried to protect you and your sister."

Robert huffed. "How can I say that? Are you really that delusional?"

The putrid stench of tobacco mixed with Father's English Leather cologne permeated the stale air. I could even smell his sweat. The conversation had an air of desperation from Father and determination from Robert. Mother sounded calm and measured.

"Son!" said Father. "Let's get out of here. Please! You know how much I love you. Don't do this!"

I heard an occasional ping, like crystal goblets chiming against each other.

"Robert!" Father shouted. "Listen to me!"

"So, Mother. Are you going to keep straightening those damn glasses?"

I cocked my head. Thinking back, I could barely recall Robert talking to Mother. I thought it was because Father occupied all his time but now I wondered.

"Stop, please." Her voice sounded flat, like a child learning to read.

"Just tell me where my sister is so I can leave."

The sound of the moving crystal became louder, like a pinging gavel telling Robert to shut up. "Please, dear…you need to calm down."

Robert let out a gasp. "Calm down? How many times have you told me to calm down? Do you know how that made me feel every time I tried to talk to you about what Father was doing to me?"

Robert's words sucked the air out of me. I clutched one hand to my chest in an effort to push the air from my lungs. The other hand was pressed against my mouth. I curled up tight. Long-held secrets and lies began to unfold. Far more hideous than I could have imagined. The inside of the cabinet was pitch black, but I could swear a light started to creep into the airtight space.

"Please stop, dear. Emily is fine," said Mother. I listened to the soft clang of glass as she continued to re-arrange the crystal in the buffet.

"Robert," said Father. "Come on…let's get out of here. Don't upset your mother. Let's go somewhere and talk." His tone turned to a high-pitched screech; the words were close together mixed in with labored breaths. "Please, Son."

Robert didn't respond to any of his pleas.

Father panted like he couldn't catch his breath. "Talk to me! Give me a chance!"

I pressed my ear against the door. The voice in my head told me to stay quiet and piece it together. I tuned in to every word and the inflection in their voices.

"Mother," Robert said. His voice held disgust and agitation. "Just tell me where she is."

Mother continued to play with the crystal goblets. "She's at the Pacific Coast Inn. She's fine."

"No, Robert! You're not leaving!" Father pleaded.

Chairs knocked together. They argued. The words piled on top of one another making it hard to understand. The scuffle was pandemonium mixed with the unlikely sound of crystal chiming. I started to open the door but stopped when someone walked into the kitchen.

Mother's stiletto heels tapped on the tile floor. The scent of Chanel No. 5 lingered as she paused at the kitchen counter. She hummed "All the Pretty Little Horses," as I listened to the slow scraping of wood and the gentle thump of a drawer opening. After a few seconds, I heard a soft ping on the teak countertop. Her high heels rapped lightly on the floor as the scent of her perfume faded into the living room. Her hum dwindled to a faint purr as I heard the jingle of car keys. Moments later, the engine started and the electric garage door opener thumped to a close.

I shook my head. My mother, the woman I came to rescue, strolled out of the house like a carefree society lady out for a Sunday drive.

The fray moved to the kitchen.

"Robert, stop! Talk to me! Your mother left to get Emily. There's no reason for you to run off and find her. She's perfectly fine!"

Robert huffed. "Fine? When was she ever fine? Let go of me!"

Father seemed to be pleading with Robert like he was trying to save him. "Listen...leave Emily alone. Nobody can help her! She's trash!"

I felt my eyebrows come together, perplexed. Father was too frantic, too desperate, too everything. He argued with Robert like talking with him was an emergency.

"Leave me alone. I'm going. Get out of my way."

"Goddamn it, Robert! I've done everything for you...you know that! I'm the only one that loves you!"

Robert snarled. "You sick bastard! That's what you said every time you snuck into my room at night!"

Shoes scuffed against the floor. The stench of alcohol and sweat grew stronger.

"Get off of me!" Robert said with a strained voice.

"No, I can't let you leave!"

The ruckus escalated with rapid movements, unraveling too fast for me to understand. I cracked the sideboard enough to see them.

Father grunted and pushed his body into Robert, pinning him against the counter. Robert pushed back, as the two thumped against the teak cabinets.

"Just listen to me!" He put his hand over Robert's mouth. "Listen to me!"

Robert tried to budge Father's two hundred forty pound body. His head jerked back and forth, attempting to get Father's hand off his mouth. He gripped Father's arm, fighting to break free. The other hand banged against the counter like he was searching for something.

I couldn't move. I felt sick to my stomach, paralyzed. My hand was on the cabinet door ready to step in, but the voice inside my head told me to wait.

Robert's free hand slapped the counter as Father's broad hand covered his mouth. "I can't let you go!"

Robert found the utensil Mother had placed on the countertop.

*It was a twelve-inch ceramic knife.*

The "something bad" was unfolding as my brother had predicted. No time to think. I pushed the sideboard to help Robert.

I reared back when I saw Robert plunge a knife into Father's chest. Blood spattered like red spit across the floor as he sliced into his neck, ribcage, and upper body. Father's body bounced with each blow as Robert pierced through his skin, muscle, and fat. Body fluids pooled like crimson twine around his neck. Saliva dribbled down the side of his mouth. He thrust the blade into the center of his torso like he was trying to find his heart.

I pressed both hands against my mouth. My brain and body disconnected, immobilizing my ability to stop him from slaughtering Father. I scrunched up in the cabinet, mesmerized by the bloodshed, wondering why I couldn't stop him.

Robert kept going. He sliced his portly torso, puncturing, slashing his body, shredding ruddy rotund skin, and ripping raw tissue into tattered pieces. Robert continued to pierce his chest, as he moaned and wept. His force weakened with each plunge into Father's butchered body, stab-by-stab coming to the realization that he had finally stopped his heart.

A terrifying ballad played in my head—Mother's "All the Pretty Little Horses," along with the morose sound of Robert whimpering.

Seconds later, Robert left. Father's lifeless body lay on the kitchen floor along with the knife Mother had placed on the counter. His body was twisted, smeared with blood, and his eyes wide open. I wondered how he felt as he watched his son put an end to his vicious and sadistic life. Even dead, he looked as though he could reach up and continue his tyrannical control over my life. The fear I carried for eighteen years oozed out of me in unison with the blood draining from Father's dead body. I gazed at the corpse and thought about the flesh-eating crocodiles I wished on him after one of my visits with Grandma.

*Little had I known that my brother, Robert, needed protection from Father far more than I did.*

# *Thirty-Two*

## INTO THE VAULTS OF HEAVEN

*San Francisco County Jail, September 4, 1966. End of Session Nine*

By the time Doctor Lieberman counted to the number five, I was fully alert. At the count of ten, I listened to the drum of his leather shoes on the floor. His face was inches from the paper as he noted the details of our session.

He stopped and gave me a long look. "It's vital that I get these notes down. Can you hold on a few minutes?"

I nodded. "Of course."

He recorded his official record, which gave me time to think. Over the last weeks, I believed we were rummaging through the chaos of my life searching for evidence. Little had I known my brother's life had been ravaged in ways far worse. I thought Robert had led a charmed life with a doting father. At times, I resented him. Robert spent his childhood with a depraved monster, not a devoted father. All the while, Mother looked the other way. While my brother lived in agony, he still found the strength to keep me safe from Father. He even tried to rescue me from the Hell house, and I refused him.

There were signs of discord, and I missed them. I failed to question the expression on his face when he told me life was hard. I hadn't dug into the cause of his panic attacks. I could have pushed to find out why he was so determined to get me on the plane following my graduation. I allowed my miserable life to blind me from the truth that Robert was being molested. Who was there to help Robert? *Nobody.*

"Just a few more notes," said Doctor Lieberman. "Are you all right?"

"Yes, I'm okay. Please...finish your notes."

Knowing what happened that night calmed me. I was focused. All the years of anguish and turmoil made sense. As secrets unraveled, so did the burden of trying to figure out why nothing ever seemed to connect.

I fixed my eyes on the doctor. As he continued jotting down notes on a pile of loose paper, his glasses teetered on the tip of his nose, a centimeter or so from falling off. He didn't seem to notice. His slender fingers raced across the document, pausing only for a second as he shook his ballpoint like an old-fashioned fountain pen before he turned to the next page.

It started to rain. The wind pelted droplets against the window in rapid succession. The downpour mixed with the doctor's tapping feet sounded like a drum-roll in anticipation of a larger event.

He held up his index finger as he perched the pen over the last page. "Okay. I'm finished. Let's begin."

His tone made it clear he had a lot to say. "Um. Doctor...I don't feel too well. My throat is dry, and I have a pounding headache. Would it be possible to get a glass of water and maybe some aspirin?"

He jumped up. "Oh...of course. I'll go down to the infirmary and get some. I'll be back soon. The clerk makes us sign for everything."

He walked to the door and then turned around. I wondered if he realized he was leaving me unattended.

"Emily, we had a major breakthrough today. Will you be okay in here?"

I rubbed my temples. "Yes, I'm all right. It's just this awful headache."

"We'll fix it." Within seconds, I listened to the receding sound of his footsteps in the hallway.

There was no need to ponder the pros and cons or weigh the rights and wrongs. I had already made up my mind. I put my head down, briefly shut my eyes, and took a long, cleansing breath. I stood up.

I walked to Doctor Lieberman's old desk, seizing the nine weeks of copious notes. They were about three inches high, so I separated them into three stacks. I gripped the first stack, straightened the pages, and ripped them in half. First, down the middle, and with a quick shift, I tore them down the side. I ripped the second stack and then the third. I gathered the torn paper and edged closer to the fifth-story window, tearing them into tinier pieces, careful not to drop any of the fragments.

The world seemed to move in slow motion, but in fact, I moved steadily as I reached the filmy glass.

I unfastened the window, opened my hands, and released the torn pages into the open air. Some dropped on the floor, so I picked up the pieces and did the same thing. Soon, all the evidence had been set free. I beamed with approval, like sending a wounded bird to flight, content in knowing my deed worked. The paper raced aimlessly in the wind, capturing rainwater and smearing the ink as they made their way into oblivion. The late-summer storm battered the scattered paper, dissolving some and shredding others into useless litter. The proof of what happened that night hovered in the storm-filled skies of San Francisco. I watched as the gale-force wind swept the wads of tiny paper into the safety of Heaven and into the hands of Almighty God.

I gazed trancelike at the debris and thought about Father and the shredded artwork in my sketchpads. Except this time, no one could rescue the pages; nobody would piece them back together. They belonged to God now, and He could decide what to do with them.

My body faltered, so I grabbed the wooden ledge and stood vigil over the last tiny bits of tattered documents. The rain slowed to a steady drizzle while the wind continued to breathe its mighty vigor over everything in its path. I leaned against the casing, drained from bloodletting the memories and emotions of a failed life. The truth was out—how my father died, the circumstances of Penelope's death, and the sickening fact that Father had abused Robert for years.

The door opened and closed. I braced myself. "Emily," he stated. "Step away from the window."

I turned to find him holding a glass of water in one hand and two aspirin in the other. He glanced at his desk and back at me. His face went blank.

It hurt to look at him. "I wasn't going to jump."

"I know. Please sit."

He walked to the window and gazed out as he shut it. We both sat down. He rocked back and forth in his swivel chair, saying nothing. The squeak sounded like a cell door opening and shutting. His elation following the session seemed to drain out of him, lost to the wind and my decision to erase the evidence of what happened the night of the murder. After several minutes, he rested his elbows on the desk and studied me without saying a word.

It pained me to know I had destroyed his trust. He had broken a lot of rules for me. Insisting on no shackles. Assigning me a tame guard. *Leaving me alone to get aspirin.*

I sat up straight. "How angry are you?"

He leaned back. "We worked for weeks as a team and yet you independently made the decision to destroy evidence."

His words slapped me hard in the face. For a half-minute, all I could do was nod. I couldn't help but wonder whether I'd broken the law by ripping up the pages but then the truth snapped back at me.

"I'm sorry, but I knew you would not suppress the evidence. As soon as I learned the truth about the murder, I knew exactly what I had to do, and I never questioned it. I couldn't take the chance..."

His face was expressionless. "They teach us in medical school to 'do no harm.' A physician would find murder in conflict with this rule. As a forensic psychiatrist, I study cause and effect. We retrieved your memories to find the prior experiences that led to the murder. I only asked that you trust in the process."

"I understand, and I'm sorry," I said. My voice was so weak, I wondered if he could hear me.

After a long minute, he ran his hands through his frizzy hair. "Why did you tear up the notes that proved you didn't kill your father?"

It killed me to hear the disappointment in his voice. I took a deep breath. "Because...I decided to accept the plea deal the prosecutor offered."

"Second-degree murder will carry a penalty of fifteen to twenty-five years. The evidence proved your innocence. In all likelihood, you would not even be charged as an accessory because you were mentally incapacitated before the murder. Why would you take the plea when you are innocent of the murder charges?"

I found it difficult to swallow. Hearing "fifteen to twenty-five years" wasn't something I wanted to think about. "It seemed like the only choice...it's hard to explain."

"This was an impulsive act on your part. We can go to trial and work out a strategy with your attorneys. I wasn't hired by the state and can testify on your behalf."

Everything in me screamed "no." As soon as I learned how Father died, the choice came easily. I studied the doctor's face and wondered if I could make him understand.

"My mind is made up," I replied softly. "I appreciate your help...I really do. But I won't be going to trial. I realize my decision seems spontaneous...but that's because there was nothing else to consider."

Doctor Lieberman shook his head as he stared off. After several quiet minutes, he sighed. "Do you understand that in taking the plea you are perpetuating one of the factors that negatively affected you during your life? You will be keeping another family secret."

His argument was compelling but not relevant. I glanced at the window, noticing it had started to rain again. "Doctor, I don't have a family. My mother doesn't want me...maybe never did. I spent my life chasing her, trying to get her to love me...but she never..."

I held up my hand signaling to give me a moment. Even now, her rejection pierced my heart. I guessed there would always be a part of me that held out hope for a relationship with her.

I cleared my throat and stuffed down the hurt. "Anyway, my Grandma is gone, and my mother wants nothing to do with me. She was there that night, she must question whether I killed my father...and she put the knife on the counter. What did she think would happen? Who did she want to be killed? Robert or Father? I'll never know because she set this in motion and left."

"There is so much to consider...and you and your brother have a long road ahead in terms of healing. But Emily, you are my patient. I don't want you to take this plea."

"Robert is my only family...he's all I have. He was always...*always* good to me...putting me ahead of himself. When he recovers from the accident I'll tell him everything. Please..." I had to stop again because my heart was racing, and I couldn't catch my breath.

Doctor Lieberman helped me through the panic through guided relaxation. I held on, absorbing his voice and suggestions. After several minutes, I felt calm enough to continue.

"Doctor, can you try to understand why I destroyed the evidence?"

After an excruciating moment, he sighed. "Ethically, I can't answer you."

"But would you have...?" I stopped. I couldn't ask him nor was it fair. I was trying to justify my actions and salvage my relationship with him by forcing him to understand. In truth, his opinion didn't matter, or I would have asked him before I destroyed the documents. Drudging up hypotheticals with his wife and daughter as the subjects crossed the line. So I shut up.

Minutes, which seemed like hours, went by with silence between us. He stared off. I expected him to call the guards or something. The wait was agonizing.

Finally, he faced me. The lines on his face read like a shriveled map, and he appeared withered under the burden of losing his family and fighting for lost souls. He glanced up at the picture of his daughter, Rachel. "Yes," he whispered.

His answer and the sorrow in his face took my breath away. I put my hand over my mouth to keep from gasping. My eyes filled with tears as I thought about his daughter and how he'd lost her at the same age as Penelope.

He took off his glasses and rubbed his eyes. "A lot has happened. What are you thinking?"

I shifted in my chair, trying to get comfortable. "Doctor...do you think my father deserved to die?"

He kept his gaze on me. "What I believe is not important, Emily. What do you think?"

I scratched my cheek, disappointed that he gave me a psychiatrist's answer. "I'm searching for answers...that's all."

"What answers are you looking for?"

"I tried to live by God's word but failed miserably," I answered, my voice cracking. "I mean...I'm only nineteen and my life is over. Sometimes it seems like it never started. I don't know...I wish I understood."

"What are you trying to understand? Break your questions down."

I took a deep breath and let it out. "It's hard to explain."

He leaned forward. "Take a minute and try."

I searched for insight. I could still hear Robert pleading with me to get out of the house before something bad happened. I let my desire for Reid and my selfish need to pretend my life was normal keep me in a destructive place. I knew Robert was right, but I didn't take his advice; in fact, I never did.

I paused, cocking my head to the side. "I'm trying to remember what Robert said to me at the airport. I remember thinking his words meant more...."

I covered my eyes, attempting to re-create that fateful night. "I remember now," I murmured. "He begged me to get on the plane with him and away from the house. Reid stood next to me, and I was torn. Part of me knew I should leave with Robert, but I chose Reid. I'll never forget the heartbroken expression on Robert's face...but he also seemed...afraid. It haunted me afterward. He was going to tell me something. I think he planned to tell me what Father was doing to him."

"What did he say?"

"He said, 'you cannot go back there. It's very dark. You don't have enough light in you to fight Father,' and I didn't understand what he meant."

"What do the words mean to you now?"

"I never stood up to him. For as long as I can remember I felt flawed and unable to think for myself. I hated myself and pretended to be the girls I created in my drawings. I think Robert believed I wasn't strong enough to overcome someone as powerful as my father."

His furrowed brow told me I gave the wrong answer. "Powerful?"

I knew the truth but hated to say it out loud. "No, not powerful... evil."

He nodded. "What else did Robert mean?"

I choked up and took a moment to calm down. "Father made me feel evil. I saw my reflection in him...whatever he said to me...I believed."

"Why?"

I rubbed my palms, letting it all go. "I think because he adored my brother so much. Robert was so good, and well...perfect. I thought because he loved Robert so much I must be damaged and unlovable."

"Emily, your father molested Robert for years. He didn't love him, he controlled and raped him. He took away his childhood."

I heard a gasp drag through my lips, unable to stop the sickening thought of Father molesting Robert. I gazed at the doctor, feeling locked in a painful understanding. "What he did to Robert was worse than his abuse of me."

"Emily, you were severely abused by your father and ignored by your mother. The death of your sister confused you, and somewhere in your subconscious you knew you had witnessed a traumatic event. You had no identity because you rejected the identity your father gave you. You were a lost child clawing your way out of the darkness."

His words reached inside my soul. "Can I find my way out of the darkness, Doctor?" I asked, my voice breaking, wishing I could take the question back.

"Yes, Emily. You have always been walking in the direction of light. You just couldn't find a door in that much darkness."

My body bent forward, strained by all the tough questions and answers. But one question haunted me, and I needed to ask while I had the chance.

"Doctor, do evil people deserve to die?"

He stared off, pinching the skin between his eyes. I wondered if he was considering all the patients he'd counseled over the years. Minutes had passed before he turned to me. "Why did you destroy the pages that proved who killed your father?"

My throat constricted, I made a gulping sound when I swallowed. Earlier, I had given him the factual answer that I decided to take the plea. He was asking for more—the truth, actually. I choked back the tears and held up my finger to let him know I intended to answer him.

"I didn't want Robert to pay for killing Father. I wanted to help him...finally."

"Why?" he asked, without pause.

"Because as I watched him stabbing Father, I didn't want him to stop. I thought my father deserved to die, and Robert deserved to live."

"And?"

My face twitched, unable to hold the tears at bay. My palms brushed away the teardrops. My chest heaved from touching the raw truth with my bare hands. I held my breath, blinked, and did everything possible to contain the agony of learning so much, so fast.

Finally, I felt strong enough to tell him. "Because...somewhere in my soul I believed that I deserved to live too."

Doctor Lieberman nodded. I think he was satisfied that he had guided me to an understanding. I asked him if I could talk to the prosecutor. He somberly agreed, made the call, and handed me the phone. I talked to the district attorney all of two minutes. Done.

He sat on the corner of his desk. I looked at his lined and sorrowful face, trying to speak. The emotions, so close to the surface, held me back. Doctor Lieberman had opened the shades that kept me locked in darkness and helped me find my way into a measure of light and truth.

I searched for words. "Doctor..."

The door opened. Jennifer walked in with her restraints.

"Thank you," I blurted out. My body weakened, making it hard to walk. I struggled to stay strong.

He started to object to the cuffs, perhaps momentarily forgetting I was a prisoner.

I tried to smile. "It's okay."

Doctor Lieberman nodded as he touched his haphazard desk. I nodded too, knowing this might be the last time I would see the wise, long-suffering, gentle doctor. He walked over and embraced me in a final goodbye. His touch left me with a crushing sorrow. His frail bones made me realize he was not long for this world.

Back in my cell, I sat on my cot with my knees to my chest and cried. I looked around at the windowless walls, the stainless steel sink and toilet, and the single ledge that held my sketchpad and pencils. For weeks, the tiny room and thick, gray bars made me feel trapped like a caged animal.

A feeling of peace melded into my sobs.

As I sat alone in the barren cage, I had never felt so free in my entire life.

# Thirty-Three

## REUNITED

*California State Prison in Corona, October 21, 1966*

The clatter of pots and trays weakened to an occasional thump, signaling mealtime. I touched the pen-strokes of Pudge's letter and placed it on the wall shelf with the others. Pudge was still a loyal friend, writing me weekly and planning a visit to the prison on his next college break from Yale. His letters were always upbeat, talking about music and art, avoiding the murder subject. He kept track of my release-date and was convinced my life would have a happy ending. He also checked on Robert weekly, providing me with updates.

Mother had lied about Robert's accident. His injuries were far more severe than she disclosed to my attorneys. The crash occurred on Highway 101, as he was heading to my hotel following the murder. His head trauma required two surgeries, which left him in a medically induced coma to drain fluids from his brain and replenish the oxygen in his blood. The doctors expected a full recovery, but the road back would be long and challenging.

I have accepted the murder and my part in it, except for one thing. I was still haunted by the eerie ping of Mother placing the knife on the countertop and the sound of her stiletto heels hitting the tile as she hummed "All the Pretty Little Horses." I would likely never learn the truth about her intentions because she'd shunned me since Father's murder.

I shook my head at the absurdity, as if her rejection was something new. In a sense, I died on that cold street along with Penelope. The icy stares, the constant dismissals, and the withheld affection continued to hurt. I massaged the tense muscles in my neck, trying to snap out of my never-ending obsession with her. I grumbled under my breath, knowing she left me with one more family secret.

I lined up for lunch with my fellow inmates. The routine was no different from lining up at the high school cafeteria and the food tasted the same. However, this time I would be repeating the routine for the next ten years.

Prison was an alliance, like a sorority minus the classes. The women shared a commonality—terrible childhoods, repeated traumas, along with a few tough breaks. They all had a story, but most of their circumstances were not applied as mitigating factors in their sentencing. My attorneys and Doctor Lieberman were able to reduce my charge to voluntary manslaughter, which carried a penalty of ten years, a light sentence in a capital murder case.

I nodded to the girls at the table as I sat down to a tray of runny potatoes and meatloaf. I listened to a conversation between Peggy, a convicted bank robber, and Cindy, imprisoned for check fraud. The chatter revolved around Peggy's ex-boyfriend, a hardened felon with a James Dean face and the heart of Jack the Ripper. On the streets at fifteen, she got sucked into his illegal shenanigans all in the name of love.

At the end of the row, Cathy, stared wide-eyed after a bittersweet visit with her two school-age children. She spent days excited to spend time with her kids followed by tears in the aftermath. A prison visit was regulated time within the dreary walls of a penitentiary, not a trip to Disneyland. After five minutes, her son and daughter became antsy to return to their friends. Still, she marked her calendar in anticipation of the next lackluster visit.

"You're dreaming again, Emily!" said Doris.

She sat down next to me. Doris, the oldest inmate, had already served twenty-five years of a life sentence for killing her abusive husband. She watched over everyone, especially the under-thirty group. The girls all called her "Mom." Before her arrest, she was a professional ballet dancer and now teaches a prison dance class every Thursday. At sixty-five, she still had the willowy body of a ballerina, snowy white hair, and soft hazel eyes. With her gentle nature and compassion, it was difficult to imagine such a sweet woman banished from the outside world. When an inmate felt down, Doris would get the girl on her feet and dance her doldrums away. Then she would sit and listen and steer her in a positive direction.

I snapped out of my thoughts. "I guess so...I'm a nervous wreck."

Today I would meet with Reid after three long months to explain how I landed in prison instead of in his arms. My nerves were shot. I wanted to cancel, but I owed him an explanation along with the ugly word "goodbye."

Her long, graceful fingers rested on my hand. "Talk to me, sweetie."

"I dread seeing him, Doris. I don't know what to say. I've gone through a thousand speeches but they all seem inadequate. I'm so ashamed. It's going to kill me to see the disappointment in his eyes."

She patted my hand. "I understand. It's going to be hard. But who knows? He might surprise you. From what you've told me about Reid, the man loves you."

"Loved," I murmured.

"You can't predict what he's thinking, sweetie. Aren't you projecting how you think he should feel?"

"Maybe. But Doris, I never told him about my past. He must be horrified that he proposed to me. I have so many regrets. I don't deserve him...never did."

She lifted my chin. "Emily, of course you deserved him. You're a sweet girl. Your words are coming from your feelings about yourself, not his feelings for you. Try to listen to Reid's heart today."

I chuckled. "You must be related to Doctor Lieberman, my psychiatrist. That sounds like something he would say!"

She laughed and squeezed my hand. "Then he is a wise man!"

The bell rang, telling us to return to our cells. The knot in my stomach tightened knowing in one-hour I would be looking into the eyes of the man I had loved my entire life.

*I* bounced my legs up and down, waiting for the guard to come to my cell and announce Reid's arrival. I had brushed my waist-length hair until my scalp hurt, scrubbed my face, and smoothed every crease out of my prison jumpsuit. I bit down hard on my lower lip, trying not to undo all the self-esteem progress I'd made over the last few months.

"Quinn! You have a visitor!" a guard announced.

With her announcement my stomach muscles tensed up. The room whirled as I stood up, so I rested my hand on the wall and waited for the sensation to pass.

"Chop! Chop! Let's go!"

"Okay." I took three steps and placed my hands behind my back with my wrists together.

After a snap, we headed down the corridor to the visitor room. "Don't worry, Quinn. Once we get to the door, I'll remove the cuffs. He'll never see them."

I cringed, wondering how many times she'd said those exact words to other inmates. I felt sick. My skin was clammy, and I panted like a thirsty dog.

We arrived at the plain brown door. "Can I please take a minute?"

She covered a yawn. "You're cutting into your time. Just so you know."

I inhaled slowly as I heard the click-click as the officer removed my cuffs. Questions fired, one on top of the other. What will I find? An angry Reid, betrayed Reid, bewildered Reid, or a "get me out of here" Reid?

The guard led the way. "Okay, Quinn. Sit directly across from your guest and no touching."

I stepped into the stark, rectangular visiting room. Like the rest of the facility, the room smelled of undiluted ammonia. The tiny space held a round steel table and four chairs. The inmates lived to sit at that table, but for me, it was a cold slab of truth-or-tell.

I sensed Reid's eyes on me as soon as I walked in. Reality slugged me in the gut, crippling my resolve to face him. He left engaged to the girl-next-door and came home to a convicted murderer wearing a regulation jumpsuit inside bars and barbed wire. My best attempt to prepare for the visit included a hairbrush and colorless lip-gloss. Living on cereal, bologna sandwiches, and stew left me a scraggy, pale stick-figure. And Reid hadn't been prepared for any of this.

As I sat down, I put one hand over the other to control my trembling. Every nerve in my body wanted to press the panic button. After nineteen years, Reid was seeing the real me, an insecure nutcase. Without my masks, I sat in front of him like a tragic clown. I kept my head down and waited for him to say something. The humiliation cut so deep, I thought I might stop breathing.

Reid finally mumbled something. I strained to listen, but my heart pounded so hard against my bony chest, I couldn't make out the words.

"I'm...so sorry," he said, his voice cracking. He pressed his hand over his mouth.

I could see him from my peripheral vision and wondered how grossed-out he was to see me.

"God...Emily. I'm so..." He didn't finish because his voice dissolved in a muffled whimper as tears streamed down his face.

I sat on my hands, now shaking uncontrollably, and braced myself for his rage.

"Emily...please, can you look at me?"

His voice reeked of grief, which confused me. I clamped down hard on my lower lip, wondering if God brought me to the room to witness the pain I had caused. *Look at what you've done.*

After a tortuous minute, I raised my head. Seeing him sent a sharp pain across my face. He was not the brazen soldier who left three months ago. His eyes were watery and his lips quivered. I saw no anger; he seemed *frightened.* I owed him more than staring at a steel table while he tried to pull words out of my mouth.

I tried to speak, but only uttered, "Uh." It was as if my central nervous system was shutting down.

"Emily...I should have been here..." He placed his head in his hands and sobbed, trying to talk. "Emmy, I..."

I couldn't let him carry a burden he didn't own. "Reid, this is my fault. I did this. I'm so sorry..."

He shook his head. "I shouldn't have left," he interrupted. "Your dad...the fight or whatever happened. I should have been here to help you. I always thought he was an asshole...I should have known something was wrong."

He seemed like a man coming home from war with survival guilt. I examined his face, wondering how I could explain everything in a one-hour visit. I opened my mouth to object but ended up with a woeful sigh.

"Can you tell me what happened? I mean...I read the papers, but can you explain?"

My right eye began to twitch. I couldn't tell him about the murder, but I needed to say something. "There's really no simple answer. Nothing was ever simple..."

"Emmy. Please, this is me...Reid. None of this changes my feelings for you, do you understand?"

His words made me realize I had short-changed him again. None of the predictions I imposed on him were true. With his masculine features and sun-streaked hair, he seemed more like a prince than a soldier. But no happily-ever-after" loomed in my brain. This was a short visit in a barren room with the man I loved needing answers.

"Reid, I'm sorry. I'm not the girl you thought I was...I lived in fear, afraid...all the time..." I struggled to continue, but the words stalled.

He leaned forward. "What were you afraid of?"

The fear in his voice made me wonder whether he could handle the truth. "Mostly my father...but everything, really. Something was wrong with me. I wasn't happy like I pretended to be...I should have told you."

He slumped, rubbing his eyes. "Why didn't you?"

"I was afraid if you saw the real messed-up girl, I would lose you. I never understood why you chose me as your best friend...I never felt good enough..."

"No, that's not true," he said, his voice breaking. "You picked me the first time I saw you."

I raised my eyebrows. "What do you mean?"

He reached for my hand. The guard started to rise, so he flinched and pulled his hand back. He paused for a few seconds. "I'll never forget that day. That movie *Lady and the Tramp* was playing in the theaters, and Penelope decided we should do a play and perform it for the adults. She always came up with these grand ideas. Such a little actress..." His words trailed off, half-smiling.

I frowned, wondering why he'd never talked about Penelope before now.

"Anyway, she told everyone what role they would play...giving me Tramp, of course," he said, chuckling. "I asked her who got the part of Lady and she said it was you. That's when I saw you."

"What happened?"

"I looked at you, and you were staring at me with those big blue eyes. You were so bashful...the opposite of Penelope. We practiced our parts together, I remember you were wearing a white shirt and pleated skirt with a pink headband in your curly hair. Every time I said something, you would giggle and blush. I knew you liked me...and I felt like you needed me. It sounds weird for a six-year-old to think that way...but I did."

I watched him brush away the tears of the memory, realizing for the first time that Reid liked me exactly as I was that day. Evidently, the accident and Penelope's death changed how I viewed things. The biggest shock was the depth of his feelings and how early they developed. I never believed we were fated to be together always; in fact, I worried all the time he would drop me as his best friend.

"Reid...why didn't you ever talk to me about Penelope? You must have known about the accident. Why didn't you say anything?"

"It was a nightmare. My dad found out about the crash on the police radio and called my mom. All she knew was that a Quinn sister was killed in a hit-and-run. An hour or so later she found out it was Penelope. Your folks hushed the whole thing up so fast...I guess they told people not to discuss it...I don't know. The neighbor kids were all scared, I know that..."

I studied the pained expression on his face, but his explanation hadn't explained why he never spoke of her. I mean, kids talk. "Okay...but why didn't you talk about her?"

He pursed his lips, letting out a long sigh. "It was hard to talk about... even now. When my mom first told me a Quinn sister died, I went to my room and prayed it wasn't you. I couldn't imagine not seeing you again. When I got the news that it was Penelope...I was relieved, like God had answered my prayers. A few hours later, I felt so guilty. I mean...your sister was dead, and I was happy. Think about it...I prayed that Penelope had died."

I covered my mouth. "Oh," I muttered.

He rubbed his temples. "After she died, you became so quiet and sad...you seemed lost. I just wanted to protect you and make sure nothing bad ever happened to you again..." He stopped, choked up. "I guess I failed."

"No! You're not to blame for this! Come on, Reid, you weren't even here."

He grimaced. "Exactly."

I signaled to the guard for more time, but she shook her head. So I told Reid over and over that this was my fault, not his. I realized I had underestimated him. I spent my childhood fantasizing that he was my knight in shining armor rescuing me from my wicked life. Hearing him now, that was how he viewed himself. The revelations were too sad and all too late.

The officer gave me the five-minute warning. "Reid, how did you like boot camp? How did it go?"

He wilted in his chair, mumbling under his breath. "Okay...means nothing now."

I knew he meant the life he'd planned for us, a future no longer possible. "Reid, I'm going to be here a long time. I want you to go on without me."

He banged his fist on the table. "No! I won't!"

The guard moved to the front. "Back down! Now!"

He shot her an angry scowl.

I waved my hands to the guard. "It's okay! I'm sorry. Please...everything is fine."

She held her defensive stance. After a minute, she eased up but kept her eyes firmly on Reid.

"Babe, do not do this," he said, spacing out his words for emphasis.

It sounded odd to hear him call me babe. "We have to be realistic," I said, struggling to keep my voice steady.

His squinted and his neck muscles tightened. "Do not do this, Emmy. Listen to me, please. Do not do this."

"Reid," I asked, lowering my voice. "What?"

He glared at me, half indignant and half desperate. "Do *not* tell me we are over. You can't do that to me...to us."

The five-minute clock was ticking, no time for measured words. "I'm going to be here for ten years."

His body stayed rigid and his eyes pleading. "I...do...not...care!" He cupped his hand over his mouth, peering at the guard. "I can get you out."

"No. I don't want that," I whispered. "Please...that will only make things worse."

He leaned back with his eyes steady. "Do you still love me?"

"Of course I do, but things have..."

He straightened up, took a deep breath, and let it out slowly. "Good. You had me scared for a minute. I love you and that means forever. Don't give me the do-the-right-thing speech...I won't accept it." Tears dropped down his face so fast, a few droplets landed on the table.

*And it was killing me.*

I didn't want him to suffer or leave upset. "Okay. I'm sorry."

He opened his mouth to talk when the guard announced the time was up. The officer moved in between us and told him where to pick up his belongings. She led him out the door with no time for parting words.

Reid resisted the departure, straining to see me as she ushered him out the door. "I'll be here next month! And the month after that!"

I nodded as the lady guard cuffed me. I heard him shout, "I love you!" from the hallway.

I listened to my shackles scrape against the gray tile floor as I was escorted back to my cell. The grating sound reminded me that no matter how much he professed to love me—everything had changed.

The officer slammed the cell door, that metal-on-metal swan song reminding me of Penelope's death. I sat down, considering my visit with Reid. I tried to block out the rattling wheels of the laundry cart and the loudspeaker announcing an inmate count in thirty minutes.

Reid was the loving, protective man I had created in my fantasies. Seeing him through the prism of my self-hatred tainted him as much as me. I had used my sketchpad to draw girls and create a fantasy life. So whom did he love? I was a phony. After Penelope died, I pretended to be someone else. It was too confusing.

"Damn it," I moaned, exhausted. It was difficult to analyze my life after-the-facts, and I couldn't make Reid understand in a one-hour visit. I looked down at the dingy floor, thinking about his vow to visit me every month. I'd been here long enough to know that the connection between an inmate and a loved-one grows thin over time. I winced, thinking of Reid's face going from passionate to bored and then resentful over the next ten years.

I pressed on my eyes to thwart the tears close to the surface. If only I had gone to Boston. Robert would have told me about Father molesting him. I would have understood how he had suffered and the extent of Father's brutality. My fake life kept the people I loved away because I never allowed them into my imaginary world.

*Real people cannot survive in a fantasy.*

The buzzer blasted for the inmate count, so I quickly rose and stood by my cot waiting to be counted.

Prison stripped my identity to the core—prisoner 154—the truest identity I ever had.

# Thirty-Four

## UNEARTHED COFFIN

"Quinn! Package!"

I glanced up from the tattered *Good Housekeeping* magazine to see Janice, one of the senior prison guards, and so far the grumpiest. At barely five feet tall, she still managed to lug around a bulky canvas bag stuffed with mail, a clipboard, and a silver chain with keys strapped to her belt. Most carriers used a cart but not Janice; sweat clung to her face after only ten minutes into her shift.

She held up a package. "Quinn! You hear me?"

I felt the blood drain from my face as I gawked at the gold flaking paper, the warped lid, and the worn letters that spelled, "Bloomingdale's."

"Hey! You want it or not?"

I dropped the magazine and lunged to my cell door. "Of course I do!"

"Sign here," she said, opening my door. "It's all yours."

I couldn't write my name fast enough. "Thank you!"

"Don't get why you want the old thing anyway… ain't nothing but torn paper." She rolled her eyes before shouting the next name on the list.

I sat down, holding the box like an unearthed coffin. I jiggled the contents, having held it for so many years I could tell the weight almost to the ounce. The container had been dusted off but was otherwise the same as the overcast day I hid it in Grandma's old shed. I wondered how it got here.

Even after months of therapy, I stroked the crinkled lid sensing a pull and odd loyalty to the old Bloomingdale's box. I shook my head, perplexed that a boxful of torn pages held so much importance to me.

*Why were the sketched secrets and imaginings of my gruesome childhood here now?*

I raised the lid to see the shredded paper. Gripped by sorrow, I remembered the day Father ripped them apart. I touched the fragments of Grandma, Penelope, and the imaginary girls I'd weaved into my miserable life. The drawings were aged with curled edges where the garbage and time had corroded them. Some fared better than others but together they formed my make-believe life.

A plain white legal-sized envelope was neatly taped to the underside.

The sight made me queasy. The envelope was edged with evenly aligned tape. I ran my index finger along the rough area where it had been applied and re-applied. In the center was Mother's perfect handwriting. It read: "Emily."

I hadn't seen my mother since right after the murder. The visit was no different than any other time in my childhood. She had the same vacant expression while I waited for her to say something to alleviate my agony.

And here I was again. I longed for a thoughtful manifesto filled with insight and promises, yearning for a change of heart and a willingness to accept her share of the blame for shattering my life—and Robert's. Maybe she wanted to start over and build a real family with Robert and me.

I rolled my eyes, realizing I had written the letter for her. I reached for the envelope hoping for heartfelt pleas for a new life with me, imagining different scenarios. One thing was sure. The box was here and so was a letter from her. That had to be a good sign.

My stomach churned, knowing this could be the start of a relationship with her. I drew a deep breath and removed the paper from the holder. I mouthed a silent prayer, hoping.

*Dear Emily:*
  *I found this box while packing after the sale of the house. I thought you might want it. I trust you are doing well.*
*Regards,*
*Mother*

The familiar sinking sensation passed through me. Her note was a head butt, reminding me her ability to love died with Penelope. After my sister's death, she ignored me and handed Robert to my father to molest. I clutched my gut, sickened. I threw her message back in the box along with my other fantasies.

I pushed the scraps around, searching for something good to hang onto, like Grandma's smile or Penelope's eyes. As I sifted through the wreckage, I spotted a corner of yellow paper.

"Huh," I mumbled. The paper was stuck under a stack of aged tissue. I slid it out, noticing it had been folded four times.

I glanced at Penelope's earlier drawing. The picture and my letter to Grandma were now encased in a wooden frame I made in a prison craft class. The paper in my hand was also from a yellow lined tablet. That made me pause; goose bumps ran up the back of my neck. Growing up, no one uttered Penelope's name, and yet she was always with me—percolating, begging to come out.

I unfolded the paper. It was a drawing, this time by me. "Oh," I groaned.

A torrent of heat flushed through my veins. It was an epitaph, really. I had sketched the picture following Penelope's death. I turned away, slowly breathing in and out, trying to absorb the shock.

I thought of Robert and how he'd tried to teach me to face life head-on. The truth steadied me enough to continue.

The picture showed Penelope and I dressed in our sleeping beauty costumes. I had drawn Penelope as an angel. She loomed above me while tears flowed like rain around us. You couldn't tell which tears were hers and which were mine; we were as intertwined as we were on that fateful night.

The prison buzzer announced lunch. Next, came the clanging of cell doors opening and the chatter of women as they lined up single-file for the cafeteria.

"Damn," I said, under my breath. Lunch would be thirty minutes followed by two hours of free time on the cellblock. I dropped the picture in the box and slid it underneath my metal table.

All I could think about was getting back to the drawing. The cafeteria worker placed a ham sandwich and an apple on my tray as I grabbed a small carton of milk. I found the first empty spot and smiled at the ladies at the table. Doris was several yards away and too far off for conversation. I welcomed the silence to consider my unexpected arrival. It must be a prophecy, why else would it show up now? I chewed my food and waited for the time to pass.

The buzzer sounded again. Guards organized the inmates five at a time to line up and return to the cellblock. That meant hours playing board games or watching television.

I motioned to one of the guards. "I'd like to go back to my cell, please. I don't feel well."

"You need to go to the infirmary?"

"No, I just want to lie down."

"Suit yourself," she said.

I waited until the cell door slammed and the guard was out of sight before returning to the Bloomingdale's box. As I held the old friend, a pervasive sensation that something was wrong pursued me like a zealous hunter. I ran my fingers through my hair, wondering why the drawings in the box seemed more real than the life I had lived all those years. It made no sense to create an existence through art. It was like playing a role in a movie and getting stuck in the plot and character.

Maybe keeping the box was a bad idea. I gazed off, trying to decide.

After a few minutes, I forced myself out of the stare. Finding the picture now, a link to Penelope, had to mean something.

"You thought you'd seen the last of me, didn't you?"

I glanced up to find Doctor Lieberman standing outside my cell. "Doctor Lieberman? What are you doing here? I'm so glad to see you!"

I giggled like a two-year-old as the officer opened my cell door. The doctor grabbed the only chair in the room. His frizzy white hair appeared freshly washed, and he still wore his rectangular glasses perched on the end of his nose. His face read like a diagram, lined in wisdom, leading back to his soulful eyes. I thought of him as a grandfather, not caring that all his patients probably felt the same way. No matter my surroundings, my life was better because of him. The brooding, compassionate genius with a quirky dependence on sugar, caffeine, and cognition was one of a kind.

He leaned forward. "How are you, Emily?"

"I'm all right," I said, grinning.

In spite of my smile, I knew he didn't buy it. He glanced around the small cell, pointing out the fact that I was behind bars.

I shrugged. "Well, I'm coping. What are you doing here? I'm so thrilled to see you!"

"I'm retiring...maybe," he said. "From forensic psychiatry, anyway. I've been offered an adjunct professor position at Stanford. But I wanted to come and visit my favorite patient. I never thought our work was quite done."

I couldn't picture him anywhere but his cluttered office. "So...you're retiring? How nice."

"I haven't made a final decision yet. I'll know when the time is right."

"So, you didn't think our work was done?"

He rubbed his chin. "No," he said, slowly. "I didn't...I'm not saying this because of your decision to take the plea. He continued to stare off, tapping his mouth. "There seemed to be a few missing pieces...I think."

I felt the same way. It seemed as though I'd put a puzzle together only to discover a missing corner. Still, I was grateful that he helped me understand how Father's abuse and Mother's detachment had destroyed my self-esteem.

"Yeah, I know what you mean. Oh! Doctor! You won't believe what came today! The box! The Bloomingdale's box along with all the drawings!"

He raised his eyebrows. "How did the box arrive?"

I put the box on my lap and sighed. "My mother sent it over after she sold the house. She didn't say much though...well...nothing, really."

His eyes softened. "How did that make you feel?"

For some reason, the extra lines forming on his forehead made me smile. "Awful," I said. "But I'm used to it by now."

He continued his "doctor" stare. "So, how did you feel when you saw the box again?"

"Fantastic! It was like seeing a long-lost relative. I felt like a part of me had returned."

He gave me his "hmm" expression. "I see."

I understood his apprehension and couldn't deny the implication. The box held all my imaginary girls—decoys to keep me away from my real life.

"Oh! I found another picture. A drawing I sketched right after Penelope died. It was stuck underneath a pile of tissue so I guess Father missed it."

"Oh? May I see it?"

"Of course. I'm going to frame it like this one." I pointed to Penelope's picture and my letter. I handed him the drawing with both hands.

He re-positioned his glasses and examined the picture. I knew what he was doing. He was looking for clues to my psyche at the time I sketched it. I curled my lips inward trying not to grin at the sight of him crouched over the drawing like someone peering into a microscope. I'd almost forgotten how his intensity amused me. He was a combination of Sigmund Freud and Dick Tracy with a little Pink Panther.

He picked up the framed picture on my desk. "When did you draw this?"

"Um...well, I guess right after Penelope died." I pointed to the image. "See, we're still in our costumes."

"May I look more closely at the picture Penelope drew and the letter you wrote to your grandma?"

"Sure." I handed him the drawing.

He glanced back and forth between the two pictures like a doctor examining x-rays.

A moment seemed like an hour, so I had to ask. "Is anything wrong?"

He took off his spectacles, pulled out a handkerchief and wiped the lens. "Emily, I need to do something."

I felt my face get hot, embarrassed he had ended our visit so abruptly. "Oh...of course."

"I would like to continue our visit but not here. There's an office on the next floor for attending physicians."

I stared open-mouthed. "Can I ask why?"

He stood up and signaled to the guard. "I would like a session with you."

I made a face. "Now?"

"Yes. I want to take you back to the time where you and Penelope walked the streets trick or treating. It's a narrow period we have not discovered."

I couldn't imagine why. Things were legally settled after I accepted the plea. I opened my mouth to object when an officer opened my cell.

We walked in silence on the concrete floor; it was the first time I'd traveled so far without cuffs or shackles. It reminded me how much clout Doctor Lieberman had at the prison.

My heart went out to him. He couldn't straighten his back, and his strides were short and jagged. His chin jutted out, and his glasses perched on the end of his nose as he clutched the framed picture and newly discovered drawing to his chest. I wondered if he needed a reason to keep going and to continue his routine of caffeine, snacks, and the cases that he brilliantly studied and solved. Something made me think that leaving his patients meant giving up to him.

He had his own key. I hadn't been a resident of the prison long enough to know that physicians regularly visited, and Doctor Lieberman was a celebrity among them.

The room was Doctor Lieberman's office in reverse. It boasted dark mahogany desks, burgundy leather chairs, coffered ceilings, and wall-to-ceiling bookcases with gold bound books. Filing cabinets were disguised as wall units with locked drawers. In one corner stood a steel coffee carafe, a glass decanter, and a bowl of lemons and limes. The room was more like an executive suite than a state prison office.

The doctor pointed to a chair with cushioned armrests and a high tufted back. "Have a seat, Emily."

"Coffee?" The cups were teacups. I grinned as he poured three cups, about the equivalent of the big chipped mug in his office.

"No, thank you." I sat up straight and cleared my throat. "Doctor... why are we here?"

He tipped his teacup to his lips, as he settled down at the massive L-shaped desk. "What do you mean?"

"I thought our hypnotic sessions were over. I took the plea deal. I'm confused."

His eyes softened. His expression said, "you poor little thing," but not in a condescending way. "Your well-being is not a case to me, Emily, and your recovery is still fluid. We have made remarkable progress in our therapy. But remember, memories are pieces of interlocking experiences that together form a complete picture. I want to ensure that you recover enough of the missing links to shape a cohesive understanding. That is your best chance of making a full recovery."

I shifted in my chair searching for the right words. I remained apprehensive. The session seemed important to him, significant enough to drop everything and usher me from my prison cell to this office. I understood what he said about finding the parts to form a picture; there were gaps in my memory of that night, for sure. For whatever reason, some details remained a mystery. Perhaps the specifics were too close to the second I lost my sister.

"Doctor...I appreciate your help...so much. But I don't think hypnosis will work this time. I don't remember much about what happened before the accident. Even the aftermath is fuzzy..."

He politely interrupted. "You will not recall events you don't want to remember. It was painful for you to discover the actual events of your father's murder...but you did. On some level, you knew the truth would eventually surface. You wanted the facts to come to light on your terms in order to give you control over the outcome. You're capable of reaching a deep level of hypnosis, but you have not accessed the events preceding your sister's accident. I believe this is because your subconscious was not ready to face that night completely."

I tried to think of ways to get through to him. "But I remembered the worst part. I heard the sound of the car hitting her, my mother crying, Father blaming me..."

His expression changed, seemingly weighed down by something.

I watched his shriveled face and felt horrible for disagreeing with him after everything he'd done for me. But the thought of going under again and drudging up more pain stopped me from saying, "okay" to him.

"Emily, we all have a section of our brain called the 'hidden observer.' It keeps an eye out for us and keeps us safe. This tells us not to get in a car with a stranger and so forth. Some people ignore their hidden observer and some don't. You possess a strong observer, but at times you have chosen to disregard it. This was especially true when the signal pertained to you. When your father hatched a deceitful scheme to trick Robert, you instinctively decided not to. But when your hidden observer advised you to tell Reid about your father, you ignored the warning. I am asking to lead you through a guided age-regression hypnotic session to recall specific events of that night. What is your mind, your hidden observer, telling you to do?"

That did it. I could just as easily be back at the airport, searching Robert's face for a truth he understood and I didn't. I took a long, deep breath and gripped the armrests. "Okay, Doctor. I want to try...I'm ready."

My surroundings dimmed as I listened to the doctor's voice. "It is Halloween. You are excited to trick or treat..." said Doctor Lieberman. Time became distorted as my body disconnected into a blissful expanse of tranquility.

⟜

*A* numbing cold hit my face, and the nutty scent of hickory filled the air. I jumped in place to warm up. "Come on! Let's go!"

Mother stepped onto the porch and gazed at the sidewalk. "Girls," she said, her voice raised. "Settle down. The fog's dangerous. Do *not* cross the street, stay on our side. Do you hear me?"

I only half listened. My empty treat bag was in one hand and I held out my gown with the other. "Yes, Mommy!"

Mother crouched down, pointing her finger. "Emily," she said, in a stern voice. "And Penelope...I mean it."

"No! We're Briar Rose and Aurora!"

She shook her head. "You need to take this seriously. What did I say?"

We began jumping up and down, chanting. "Trick or treat! Don't cross the street!"

She crossed her arms over her chest as we broke into giggles and continued our cheer. She half-smiled. "Okay...but be careful."

We hurried down the walkway, stumbling on our dresses. "Bye, Mommy!"

Billows of fog lingered midway on the street. The bitter cold pierced through my gown and squalls of cold air stung my face. We uttered "brrr" at the same time as we jumped up and down, trying to warm up.

"Watch this!" I shouted. "You can see puffs of smoke when you breathe! We look like Daddy smoking!"

We giggled and puffed until the game left us breathless. The fog had thickened and hung like a white canopy over the sidewalk, obscuring everything in its path. Our excitement languished in the haze of the vaporous night.

I gazed at my dress, which was blurred by the chalky mist. "Nobody can see our beautiful dresses!"

The fog lingered like a vengeful beast, stealing our enthusiasm and ruining our Halloween. We had worked so hard on the costumes with Mother—satin jumpsuits with frothy tulle skirts, one in blue, and the other in pink. It made me mad that I could barely see the silver sequins that Mother had hand-sewn on the scalloped edges of the netting. The fog spoiled everything.

Except for our magic wands, which she had coated with phosphorescent paint. "Our wands! Look! They glow in the dark! Let's play the fairy game!"

"Yeah! Pink! Blue!"

"I know! Whoever reaches the end of the block first gets to wear the pink gown!"

Bursts of fluorescent streaks and our invigorated voices ripped through the murky night as we hollered, "Pink! Blue!"

*The memory snapped.* I reared back, gripping the arms of my chair, as a blinding globe shot through the fog in my direction. My chest heaved, and I gagged at the smell of burnt rubber. The reel began to skip; a clicking sound followed, like tape flapping against a projector. I kept my eyes shut as my breathing quickened.

Doctor Lieberman rushed forward, like a tourniquet to a gushing wound. I grabbed onto his voice; his tone modulated up and down like rocking on a porch swing.

"Emily, you are safe, sitting here with me and nothing will happen to you. What you are remembering has already happened and cannot hurt you. It is like watching a movie that you can stop and start at your own will. Feel yourself calming down at the sound of my voice. Now, I want you to stop remembering trick or treating. Halloween is over. You are back at your house. Tell me what happened next..."

The fear that held me back vanished with each word until his voice was just a murmur that propelled me back—to another time.

⌒

Robert sat next to me on the sofa dressed in a Batman costume. His body trembled against mine as he stared at the floor. Unfamiliar sounds and images taunted me, flitting through my mind like the rapid wings of a hummingbird, unwilling to take hold. My brain couldn't retain a thought and nothing made sense.

The door opened and Mother appeared. Her hair hung in twisted strands over her face and her eyes were glassy. Her face was so pale; I thought the cold air had frozen her face.

"Mommy! Mommy!" I called out.

She climbed the stairs without a word to Robert or me; she didn't even glance our way.

I looked down at my gown and wondered why the netting was torn; a red splotch coated the front and bits of dirt clung to the tulle. The treat bag on my arm was flat.

Short gasps passed through my throat. There were no sounds in the house other than my labored breaths and the clock ticking on the mantle. Children outside chanted "trick or treat" but no one came to our door. I started crying louder, so Robert looped his arm around my elbow and huddled closer to me.

I listened to heavy clumps striking the ground near our house. Father pushed the door open and stood in the entryway. His face was puckered and his teeth clenched. He kept one hand on the door and the other in a fist as he surveyed the room. He looked like a monster, so I nestled near Robert and put my head under his chin.

He slammed the door with his foot; his eyes narrowed as he searched the living room. The muscles in his neck throbbed, and his face seemed to swell and gnarl. I turned just enough to see him and cringe, as I scooted closer to Robert.

He pointed his finger at me. "Penelope is dead! And *you* killed her!"

He lunged to the couch and pushed me off Robert. I landed on the floor, toppling over a bowl of sweet tarts and caramels. Robert screamed and then broke into a yelping cry.

Father rushed to him and pulled him into his lap, cuddling him. "I'm here, my boy...it's okay. It's not your fault...Daddy loves you."

Robert continued to weep. Father held him close to his chest, rubbing his back. "Now, now...it's all right. I'm here."

I got to my feet and stood in front of them, whimpering.

His face twisted into the monster again. "Get the hell out of here!"

My eyes widened as I glanced at Robert and back at Father.

"You heard me! Devil!"

I gulped and pressed my hand over my mouth.

He pulled my brother closer. "I'm here, my boy."

He cupped his hand over Robert's ears. "Leave! I said go... now! Murderer!"

I ran upstairs to my bedroom and crawled under the bed. Little flecks of gold and silver were scattered across the floor from our magic wands. Muffled sounds persisted from downstairs. Remembering the scowl on Father's face and the feel of his hands pushing me off the couch crept me further back. I wondered what I had done wrong. Indistinct sounds whispered in my ear and then passed away. I cowered, waiting.

Mother walked into the room. "Emily? Where are you?"

"Here, Mommy," I whispered. "Daddy's mad at me."

She peered under the bed. Her eyes were bloodshot and thin streaks of black mascara trailed down her light skin. "Emily, get up. You need to come out."

I started to drag myself from the tiny space and then stopped. I studied her face, worried that she was angry with me, like Father.

"Come on, Emily."

Her face was smooth and not scrunched up like Father's. "Okay, Mommy," I said, as I scooted out.

Mother retreated to the bed. She dabbed her eyes with a wadded tissue and kept her head down. I stood in front of her, wondering why she wasn't smiling or saying much. She continued to blot her face and sigh, looking off. The quiet between us made me tremble. My chin began to quiver as tears trickled down my face.

"Don't hide under the bed anymore...and please stop crying."

"I-I'm sorry, Mommy." My voice cracked, and I began crying harder.

She handed me a tissue from her pocket. "Here, wipe your face."

I did as she asked, but the teardrops spilled from my eyes too fast to stop them. My chest heaved up and down as I hiccupped and tried to talk.

"Stop crying." Her mouth moved, but the rest of her face stayed fixed in one position. The tone of her voice had no highs and lows, and her eyes were blank when she looked at me.

I moved closer so she would hold me like she always did. "Mommy...I'm scared."

She stretched out her arms and held my shoulders, keeping me away. "Sit down," she said.

I blinked through my watery eyes, trying to find my mother. Her vacant stare terrified me. I put my fingers on her wrist hoping she might hold my hand. "Mommy," I said.

She stiffened and moved her hand. "Calm down."

I had never seen her that way and wondered why she was mad at me. "What did I do?"

She stared straight ahead. "Penelope went to heaven. She's not coming back. She's an angel now." She spoke in a series of monotone words, like a flavorless meal that you chew and swallow.

I stared at her, waiting for her to take it back. She wouldn't look at me. "No!" I cried. "I don't want her to be an angel!"

Pressure swelled inside my body like my heart had cracked open, sending splinters of pain through me. Tears flowed down my face as I shook and convulsed. Soon the sobbing changed to a prolonged wail.

She stiffened. "Calm down."

I gagged on my tears, struggling to talk. "I want her back! Please... Mommy! Make her come back!"

She continued her blank gaze. "Calm down...she's with God now."

I tried to speak, but my lips smacked together without a word.

She got up and grabbed a tablet and crayons from the dresser. "Here," she said. "Draw a picture of your sister as an angel in Heaven."

Her body was rigid as she turned to leave. I followed her, sobbing. My mouth was wide open, but all that came out was a barely-audible squeal. My arms were stretched out as I wiggled my fingers at her.

She didn't turn around. "Draw the picture...I'll be back later."

I stood in the doorway and watched her enter Robert's room. Father was with them; his voice was louder than the others. I heard hushed voices mixed with sniveling.

I turned and faced the bedroom. Twin baby dolls sat at a table with their hands posed on pink plates waiting for a tea party. I fluffed their dresses. "Don't worry, Mary Lou and Peggy," I whispered. "The party will start soon."

The paper Mother had given me was on the bed. I grabbed the crayons, wondering how to convince my sister to leave Heaven and come home.

I decided to draw Earth instead of Heaven. I had to make it extra-pretty so she would miss me and hurry home. I sketched our house and the front porch with a flowerpot of daisies. The apple tree on the side of the house was filled with red apples, and the grass was bright green. I put our swing set in the yard so she would remember all the hours we sang "Somewhere Over the Rainbow" as we tried to touch the sky. I drew myself with an ear-to-ear smile skipping rope in my Sleeping Beauty costume.

I placed her as an angel in the sky, still wearing her Halloween costume. Her mouth was upside down, and big teardrops fell from her eyes and touched my shoulders. I colored a beautiful rainbow with arrows to give her directions home. I filled the background with snowcapped mountains because the snow on the faraway hills meant Santa Claus was coming soon. I knew she would want to be home in time for Christmas.

"Pretty," I said under my breath.

I had to sign it so God would know who sent it. I chose thirteen crayons for my name. I gripped my fingers around the red crayon to form the first letter. My hand shook from pressing down too hard. I chose a purple color and tried again, but only managed a dot. I picked up the blue crayon and carved the top with my finger, hoping a sharp point would help. I used both hands this time, moving the tip down the paper. It broke in half.

"Oh no," I moaned. I gazed at the picture, knowing God couldn't give it to my sister because I couldn't write my name. I only managed to write one letter.

*The letter was "P" and it was backward.*

A whimper escaped my mouth. "Please...come home...Emily."

I gazed at the picture and tucked the drawing under the tissue in the Bloomingdale's box. I couldn't send it because I needed my sister's help.

She would always curl her hand around mine and help me form the letters of my name—*Penelope*.

# Thirty-Five

## DEATH COULD JOIN WHAT LIFE DIVIDED

As Doctor Lieberman brought me out of hypnosis, he couldn't disguise the urgency in his voice. "...You are fully awake, completely relaxed, and refreshed..."

His custom following a session was to sit quietly for a moment or two to let the recovered memories converge with the present. Not this time. "You will get through this...I will help you. Tell me..."

The static in my head shut out his words. I didn't know how to react, how to plug the discovery into my brain and summon the courage to appear in person at my unraveling. My nightmares with the gravedigger holding a shovel now made sense. *They were waiting to bury the right daughter.*

My heart, usually racing with panic, was faint and hesitant. I rocked back and forth, staring into space. I held the news at arms-length, unsure whether to accept the truth or not. If Emily was dead, I hadn't mourned her. If I was Penelope, I didn't know her. I was frozen, and deadened at the age of five. My life turned out to be a twisted prank.

"This is a shock...one we will work through. But right now, what do you need?"

The absurdity made me laugh. We spent months searching for significant events and forgotten memories only to find a missing life. I took a breath and exhaled the word, "How?"

He explained how the gowns were switched during the fairy game. My head bobbed up and down as he continued the long explanation. I didn't need it. The answer was simple. The pictures proved everything. Emily could write. I could not.

*The facts left no doubt—I was Penelope.*

My teeth chattered as I rocked, clutching my arms. "Why?"

I sensed despair in his voice and an odd stillness in the room. "Your parents assumed you were Emily, and your father accused you of killing your sister. My theory is that your five-year-old mind thought that if you took on the persona of Emily she was not really dead. You were. Because your parents so quickly eradicated your sister's existence and death, you suppressed the memory of that night. Your subconscious battled for the truth but growing up in a hostile, secretive environment made that impossible. This is a deep-seated trauma, but you can heal from this revelation through therapy."

My heart skipped a beat and then did a double thump. The physical sensations sputtered and snapped back only to break down again. A frenzied collage of disturbing images flipped through my brain, one on top of the other.

The doctor pushed back his leather office chair. "Are you...?"

Terror crashed head first, devouring the air in my body and the good sense I needed to stay put. I jumped up, in spite of the whirling room; flashing green and yellow spots flickered in my face. My knees buckled and the ringing in my ears sounded like a death siren. I tried to grab the desk that stood in front of me, but my arms dangled like dead posts on my sides. I felt myself falling. Next came a sudden snap of pain as my head hit the mahogany desk.

One powerful strike to my skull transported me to an endless space. Free of pain and withdrawn from the restrictions of time gave me the freedom to consider everything. I had fought so hard to get my nineteen years back but doubted I could survive this final revelation. Doctor Lieberman's last words "I will heal" echoed like bells in a hollowed building.

White vapor surrounded me, and a patch of darkness hovered like a black beacon in the distance. I patted my body, figuring I stood halfway between life and death. The quiet was oddly pleasing. I turned in every direction, wondering why there were no birds or trees or signs of life. Even so, I didn't feel lonely. At least I wouldn't need to disguise my remorse with a fake smile or chase away my rampant tears. Guilt didn't seem to exist here. My shame dissolved into the emptiness.

I heard muffled voices and felt fingertips on my chest and head. I supposed that meant I staggered somewhere between life and death, agony and peace. If death was the outcome, it didn't seem that bad.

A shadow grazed my cheek. I held it close instead of flicking it away. I moved my hand from the white mist to the shadow, watching it turn light to dark. When my hand passed through the darkness, my body released the strain of thinking. I relished the sensation and edged closer, making sure I kept half my body in the light. The shadow meant death, and I hadn't decided.

So I staggered between life and death, pain and numbness, truth and lies. Inch by inch, minute by minute. The shadow pressed lightly against my skin. I savored the touch, trying to decide. Death seemed better, so I edged closer to the bleak nothingness. It wouldn't be much different than the life I'd led, living in fantasy and never embracing reality. I hadn't lived at all. Not really.

Death whispered, "Come with me." I moved closer, inviting its fiery breath in my ear. The sound of air pushing in and out and the tight squeeze of a vice around my arm told me I was in medical trouble anyway. Someone put a device over my mouth and nose. Oxygen surged through me, trying to pull me from the flat line I leaned on. That made me mad.

I listened to the machine and fought back. *Who are you to tell me I have to live?* I reared back from the pulsing equipment so I could travel between life and death.

Loud voices merged with Doctor Lieberman's. I would have to scream louder. "How can I live with the death of my sister knowing I caused not only her death but also stole her life?"

I heard nothing and took the silence as my answer. This was my opportunity to make things right and to be with my sister free of secrets and guilt. Like it should have been.

Impending death freed me of fear and gifted me with insight. The secrets were exposed; answers that had so long eluded me flowed free, like an endless shore. But the answers spawned questions, ugly ones, too late to resolve.

My body gave way to the inevitable sorrow. "Why didn't anyone realize I was Penelope?"

We looked exactly alike, but our personalities were different. Why didn't anyone notice that my sweet, shy sister died and the outgoing kid was alive and living the wrong life?

How could my mother erase the daughter she thought was Penelope? Why couldn't she see beyond a Halloween costume? The night Emily died, Mother refused to look at me or take me into her arms. She blamed me. I might as well have died along with Emily because from the time of the accident I was dead to her. She carried her guilt, but her resentment of me was stronger.

I thought of Reid. No wonder I thought he made a mistake picking me as his best friend. He didn't pick me; he chose my sister. He loved her from the moment they locked eyes, that's what he said. He picked the shy curly-haired girl in the background, not me.

Dramatic and extroverted, I was the sister that didn't need protection. On the night of the hit-and-run he prayed for my death. He played a knight in shining armor to the girl he thought was Emily. I followed his lead, wondering in the back of my mind why I felt like an imposter.

Reid's heart was infused with devotion, even after my arrest. Even so, I doubted him, knowing in my heart our love was fleeting and unstable.

My skin suddenly felt hot and pressure formed in my head, remembering Father. "Damn you, Father! I hate you! You hear me?"

I curled up and wept at how I let him abuse me. My self-loathing locked me in anxiety and blunted the insight I needed to recognize what he was doing to Robert.

So my unstable life made sense now. Out of my sister's sorrowful death came two graves. My life was a mistake. Could death lead me to her? Was the darkness enlightenment if I could find my sister? I could make amends for urging her to cross the street and explain how I embodied her life. I could reunite with her.

*The goal was clear and the path unrestricted. Death could join what life divided.*

I listened to the pulse and push of machines trying to fix whatever ailed me. They were too late. I wasn't going back. My choice to end my life was not because of the monotony of prison or the disgrace of being labeled the killer of a parent. I had already made my peace with imprisonment and the stigma of being a murderer. Choosing to die also had nothing to do with the dread of facing an indifferent mother. Her blank stare ripped me apart for years, so the fate had been sealed.

"The girl in the mirror," I said, thinking of the day Father spat in my face. I remembered her pleading eyes and my promise to someday come back for her. That was Emily. I had vowed to return to her. Help her. She deserved to find peace.

With my decision, I found a sobering clarity. The masks fell off; the insecurities all made perfect sense, along with my fanatical connection to the gold Bloomingdale's box. The last of the secrets dealt a deadly blow. The girls in my sketchpad were Penelope screaming to get out. The tortured thoughts of my sister in daydreams and nightmares had been Emily trying to tell me she was the one that died.

The single cloud welcomed me. My heartbeat felt vague and diminished and my breath thin and rickety. The mass grew and turned on its side forming a tunnel for me to walk through. I examined the darkness and found it beautiful. It held no sorrow, just the opposite. It called me to sleep as I did as a baby with Emily. Innocent and pure.

The tunnel widened, and I grinned. I hadn't known that death would be so sublime. As I smiled, the cloud laughed and extended its arms. It howled a sweet, urgent song to hurry and to come inside where all was peaceful. No mental or physical torture. Free of rejection and guilt. I wouldn't have to feel the pain of knowing Mother hadn't looked at me long enough to realize that I was Penelope. That she so quickly expunged the memory of Emily. I wouldn't have to agonize over her indifference or obsess over my desire to make her love me.

A rush of air made my body tremble. It seemed miles away but still strong enough to stir my thoughts. I began to wonder about my mother and whether losing both daughters would push her further into depression. And how would Reid and my brother—

A warning cried out, forcing me to remember what violence felt like. Hatred seeped into me and squeezed the last remnant of joy from my heart. My gut convulsed as filthy cereal was forced down my throat. Saliva trickled down my face, cracking my skin. I winced in pain as hair was ripped from my scalp. Currents of stabbing pain pummeled my sides. I cried out as shards of bone sprayed my insides, nipping at my organs. Shattered ribs pierced my lungs, cutting off the oxygen I needed to breathe. My voice became silenced by the agony, thrusting as blow after blow ruptured blood vessels and shattered flesh.

The tunnel swelled up in protest, promising me an end to my agony. The opening expanded and waved like the banderole on a flagship. The sight tantalized me and stimulated my resolve to die.

"Run!" I yelled. I couldn't wait to die and be a child again with Emily.

Dust and mire whipped through the air as I continued to run. The pursuit to find the end invigorated me. A prolonged chorus of voices urged me to quicken my stride. As I advanced, the chorus grew, adding pulsating vibrato to seduce me into a chasm of endless rest.

My body grew laden and frail as I neared death. The black presence caressed me, waiting to engulf me in my waning moments. My hands and legs weakened. It didn't matter. The tunnel had a fierce energy that swept me forward with little effort. I reached out to the darkened chamber, having gone too far to turn back. The euphony deepened, loud and pulsating, co-mingling with my withering body as I neared the final portal to the end of my life.

# Thirty-Six

## DUELING INTENSIONS

The blackened cloud expanded with a vigorous breath, urging me to push on.

"Just get through the tunnel," I muttered to myself.

I felt ninety. Skin clung to my bones, and my muscles cramped with the slightest movement. Spasms in my back slowed me down as I walked in a stooped position. I moaned in disgust, knowing that staying on Earth had withered my body.

I feared not reaching the end in time. To remain in this abyss would be the worst form of punishment; suspended between life and death was where I lived before. "Keep going," I told myself.

My legs became too weak to lift, so I shuffled forward an inch at a time. I squinted, trying to figure out how far I'd traveled, but there were no landmarks to gauge the distance, just an endless blanket of haze. I trudged along without sound. Every so often, I touched my knee to feel the movement.

I held up my hand; it was nearly translucent with bluish veins and knotty bones. "Excuse me. How much further?"

The mass burgeoned to twice its size, consuming the white that hovered nearby. The sight sent sparks of energy through my failing body, giving me the strength I would need to pass through. I pursed my lips and let out a long exhale.

A faint voice broke into my brain. "No. It's dark."

I paused and turned my head to both sides. The air was stagnant and quiet. After a minute, I pushed my leg forward. I had no intention of giving in to delusional thoughts. Not after I'd gone this far.

The chasm praised me with a sweet taunt of hurried ripples like a flirty finger wave.

I tried to smile but only managed a head nod. Walking sent gripping pain through my calves and back. I told myself a short distance stood between agony and an afterlife with my sister.

The ground rumbled beneath my feet. I stopped, worried I might lose my balance. As soon as I stopped walking, I heard the voice again in a series of indistinguishable words. I cocked my head, trying to make out the message, which sounded distraught.

I started walking again. I was certain my mind was playing tricks on me. My stride shortened; I dragged my feet at barely a toe length with each step. My bones scraped against each other. It would be easier to collapse and die, but I didn't want to live in purgatory and miss being with Emily.

The ground shook, throwing me off balance. "Turn around," the voice urged.

I squinted, trying to recognize something beyond the haze. I didn't want to battle hallucinations in my weakened state. It seemed unfair.

I stopped, cupping my hands around my mouth. "Who's talking?"

The dusk howled in disapproval, blowing puffs of ash in my face. The dusty powder fluttered into my eyes, making them burn and water.

"W...?" I blinked, rubbing my eyes. Hot, dusty tears trickled down my face, stinging the open wounds. Had I seemed ungrateful? I was trying so damn hard, but my limbs were weak. Two steps seemed like ten. My breathing was thin and raspy. It didn't help that ash had settled into my lungs, intensifying the pressure on my chest.

I held up my hands. "Please. I'm going as fast as I can."

The tunnel suppressed its angst and widened the doorway.

I bent my arm, pumping, trying to pick up speed. My arms were pitifully thin and not capable of much. I thought of Emily, imagining the expression on her face.

"It's a trick. Turn around." The voice was clear and familiar.

"Robert? Oh my God! Is that you?"

I stood in place, listening for the slightest sound. Clouds drifted by, easing in and out in silence. The air turned frigid, sending unwanted shivers up my body. My back stiffened from standing in one spot, but I stayed and waited for Robert.

Time seemed like an eternity. The darkness hovered around me, blowing frigid wind in my face. There was nothing on my bones to cushion me from the icy air. The wind began to howl, devouring any sounds in its path.

Spasms immobilized my body from staying in one place too long. The voice, I surmised, must have been an apparition.

I convulsed with grief. If only I could have seen Robert before my skull slammed into the desk. I stared down at my shriveled body, knowing it was too late. I failed Robert in death as I had failed him in life. I winced, rotating my feet to continue the trudge.

"No," said Robert. "Turn around."

The sound of Robert's voice buckled my knees. I stood still, wobbling, holding my arms out like a seesaw. "Robert?"

I scanned the mist, straining to find him. A channel attached to my eyes like an extended telescope, allowing me to see beyond the void. I had to catch my breath.

Robert was lying in a hospital bed. His once-spry body was delicate and immobilized. I gasped at the tubes inserted into his trachea and listened to the steady whisk as screens measured the oxygen in his lungs. Wires stuck out everywhere, taped to his chest and arms, leading back to metal machines. Monitors lit up and beeped intermittently. A chart dangled on the edge of his bed, and everything was a bleached white.

My heart surged, as I staggered in his direction. "Robert!"

I glanced around for ghosts, hoping to barter for a dying wish to be at his bedside. There was no one but the smoky billow whose patience seemed to have worn thin. I put my palms together, begging for a reprieve.

Shadows moved in, obscuring the channel that allowed me to view Robert. White mist co-mingled into the darkness like dueling intensions, forming a circle around me.

"Please. I just want to see him one more time! He's my brother!"

The black cloud enveloped me, revealing an arched opening. The edges had petals of black elderberry, crimson berries, and white baby's breath. The scent of carnations filled the air, sweet and fragrant.

There would be no favor. Death had readied the passage for me to walk through. My body slumped, and it was hard to hold my head up. I turned back for a last goodbye. The white mist pushed the shadow aside.

Robert strained to prop himself up. His face was ashen and glazed with pain.

I pursed my lips and took a deep breath. "No! Stay down!"

He put his hands under his legs, rotating his body. The wires on his skin stretched and pulled as he shifted his weight. The tube on his neck bulged and made him hack.

I cupped my hands over my mouth. "Stop! Stop!"

He paced himself with the influx of oxygen. "Then listen."

I inhaled, noticing how shallow my breathing had become. "Okay... Robert."

He nodded and lowered himself on the bed. I kept my eyes on the machines measuring his heartbeat and the oxygen level in his blood.

I couldn't help but wonder where our youth had gone. We never jumped in rain puddles or laughed until our bellies hurt. Robert took cover at science fairs while I hid behind the girls in my sketchpad. We fretted over rules day and night and lived like sullen shipmates trying to survive turbulent winds in an unworthy vessel. It sickened me to realize we never had a chance.

He reached up and held the tube attached to his throat, which made a gurgling sound.

I cringed. "I'm here...don't do that again."

He turned his face. "Don't go there."

I stared at the wires connecting him to life. He could barely move, and when he did, the physical pain forced him down. His limbs looked rigid like they had started to atrophy. I wondered why he fought so hard to live. I was saddened that my short life had reached its final day, but the afterlife had to be better than this. That made me question whether he might go with me. His body had failed him anyway, and I doubted anyone had come to visit him. His hospital room had no flowers or greeting cards. No "get well" balloons or gift-shop teddy bears.

"Robert? What are we fighting for?"

He turned his head and closed his eyes. His chest moved up and down, like a reminder that he was still alive. He grew tranquil, and tears ran down his face.

I took the deepest breath my lungs would allow. "Come with me, Robert."

"Listen." The word sounded like an answer, and not a prelude. As always, he understood the meaning and I did not. He seemed to be waiting for me to understand something.

"I'm so tired, Robby." I felt guilty saying the words, seeing him vulnerable and fighting to stay alive. "Please. Let's go together."

He shook his head from side to side on the white pillow.

When I opened my mouth to speak, my voice cracked. My body jammed at the slightest movement. But his physical body was diminished too, maybe beyond repair. It occurred to me that he might be holding on for my sake. "You can give up, Robert. It's okay...really."

He didn't say anything.

Darkness called to me like a fervent temptress. I edged closer, savoring its warmth and the promise of healing sleep.

I read Robert's lips. He formed the word "no" over and over.

"Robert," I said, my voice trailing off. I couldn't tell him the despair of learning the ugliness behind all the secrets had crushed my will to live.

He struggled to move only to collapse as he continued to mouth, "no."

The shadow embraced me, soothing the pain in my joints and caressing my aching muscles. I leaned into the dark, accepting that my condition had declined beyond repair.

I raised my head enough to see Robert one final time. "I love you, Robert," I whispered, my voice dissolving into sobs.

His face crimped. "Do *not* go!" The words echoed and grew louder in the narrow channel.

My lungs made a rattling sound with each breath. I moved my mouth, exhaling the word "*why?*"

He closed his eyelids and kept them shut. "Shh," he whispered. "Just listen."

My heart ached knowing he still believed in me. He still believed I could listen to the rumblings in my soul, and all of this would make sense. I didn't have it in me. He did, but not me.

I put my head down and clasped my hands together in a silent prayer. "God. Please don't let him blame himself for anything."

I wiped my eyes with the back of my hand. The irony was inescapable. We were both inches from death, and Robert was still trying to help *me*.

The darkness lingered like a seductress and brushed its velvety smoke against my face. The melody that had enticed me here picked up again; the tempo sounded like a heartbeat. It grew louder. The uproar made it hard to listen, reminding me of the times I tried to hear my inner voice only to be smothered by Father's vicious insults.

I elbowed the shadows. "Quiet...please." I wanted to stay alive long enough to give my brother the respect he deserved.

Robert opened his eyes and gazed at me. He seemed to be waiting for me to recognize what he already knew.

His face was drawn and pallid, but his eyes were intense, determined. The tube in his trachea tugged at his neck, but his mouth quickly formed words. The machines hooked to his body restricted his movement but didn't stop him from communicating through signals and gestures. I studied him and listened. After a time, the wires and machines disappeared. Oh, they were still there but had faded into the background. His mental strength overpowered his physical limitations.

My skin tingled. "Robert. I under..."

I felt a hard smack on my back. As I turned, the black cloud pressed into me. Sheets of my skin sloughed off and dissolved like dying embers. Sharp nails bore into my body, crushing tissue. I cried out in tortuous pain, jolted by the sudden surge of violence. The touch that I thought was tender and soothing became not an embrace but a death grip. I gagged as my throat tightened. Pressure pushed on my chest, squeezing the oxygen from my lungs. The sweet scent of carnations turned to the coppery smell of blood as the pain doubled.

I heard Robert weeping.

I coughed up blood and jerked in agony. My flesh ruptured as persistent strikes battered my sides, my back, and legs. I wrapped my emaciated arms around my head as sharp blows bludgeoned my skull. Rapid kicks split my ribs. The savagery wouldn't stop. Torture silenced my voice. I didn't want to die this way, but the truth came too late.

*I didn't have enough strength to fight it.*

A faint glow appeared in the distance. I fixed my eyes on the sight and waited for the end. The beam flickered and throbbed like a siren on mute, warning me. The orb was a flaxen color, like the lemons in Grandma's orchard. It twinkled and dropped like shooting stars. I shut my eyes and let go.

The globe brightened and flashed, making me open my eyes. Death surrounded me, but the radiant glow was brighter and cast its beam into the darkness, siphoning the gloom from me.

"Listen," said Robert, between sobs. "Listen!"

His words pulsed through me and urged me to pay attention to my surroundings. But then came another strike hard enough to kill me. I curled up tight, as blow after blow crushed my spine and skull. I jerked, tightening the grip around my head. The rage kept coming.

Light continued to flash, faster, and brighter. I thought the radiance might numb me, but it was just the opposite. The beam had energy and a vitality that triggered me to think beyond the violence.

I held death back and listened.

Robert's words "you don't have enough light in you" flowed through me, swift and sure.

The white mist pushed its light into the darkness. The shadows coiled, reared up, and spit gray ash into the hollows. The beams widened and cast its radiance into the dark, illuminating the dank drifts of blackened spirits. It oozed white pearly glares into the gloom and showered death with a cleansing wind. The darkness fought back with feverish heat and taunting screams. It was like lighting a fire in fresh snow.

My eyes widened as the beams of light wrung the truth from the shadows.

*It was Father waiting in the darkness.*

His skin was pitted, his eyes bloodstained, his face distorted with hatred. He shot up with clenched fists.

I faced him, grim and steadfast. I knew what to do.

*I had to fight with everything in me to beat Father with my own light.*

The truth filled me with fervor. I wriggled inches away. My heart pulsed rapidly inside my chest as I turned to Robert.

His mouth formed the word, "Go!" His hands pushed forward, and his body twitched with urgency.

I stared at Father as a forceful puff escaped my lips.

Father's head snapped back, howling. "Moron! Look at you! You're dead!"

"Run!" Robert screamed.

I forced myself to my knees, crawling on wasted hands away from Father.

He screamed, "Weakling!"

My legs buckled, and I collapsed on my stomach.

His hoots broke into rampant laughter.

I scooted, dragging my body an inch at a time.

He belly laughed. "You're too stupid!"

I heard air pushing from a tube. "Keep going!" Robert screamed.

"Err!" I put all my weight upon my hands and pushed myself upright. I teetered from side to side; my limbs turned and bowed as I ran on crippled legs.

"Give up!" Father shouted between the laughter.

I didn't look back. He pursued me with vigorous footsteps. Wicked taunts. My limbs felt like stumps as I plowed on. My waist contorted. I thought my body might snap in half. I kept going.

"You're too dumb to outsmart me!" Father screamed.

My rickety legs earned strength. I pumped my arms to gain speed as death groaned and receded into the background.

"Give up! Goddamn, bitch!"

Even with my diminished limbs, my will to live was stronger. I picked up speed, using all the vigor I could summon and ignoring his taunts.

The air turned misty, washing my wounds. I continued to flee from evil with my inner strength.

The wind swished against my face, and the sweet scent of Grandma's honeysuckle aroused my senses as the word, "run!" whistled in my ears. Grandma appeared next to me, floating blithely as a carefree angel. She cheered me on with twinkling eyes and her French accent, shouting, "live me chéri!"

Robert shouted, "yeah!" as I dashed faster and faster. I started flying through a cloudless sky, racing in the direction of my life. Worries shed like a molting bluebird, a feather at a time, to keep me in flight and give me fresh, beautiful plumage in which to begin my new life.

I laughed, looking down at my body. I thought I had been running into the light, but no—it was so much better. As I raced through the darkness, I became lighter. I gained the light Robert talked about. *I understood!* I flew, shedding the gloom and grabbing the light with my hands. I began to glow, casting off the shadows to laugh, and cry, and experience the pain for as long as I needed to. I would survive as long as I continued to run from the darkness and confront the secrets that shattered my life. The truth that I was Penelope meant I didn't have to hide anymore. I could mourn my sister and find a way to honor her life. I could start over.

*I* opened my eyes and saw the tender face of Doctor Lieberman. His thin but strong hand held mine. I squeezed back to let him know I wanted to recover. He let out a long sigh and squeezed my hand again. I smiled and thought of Grandma.

I moved my mouth from side to side to loosen the oxygen mask. He lifted the device.

My lips formed the words, "Thank you."

Thoughts and passions stirred inside my mortal body. I finally understood what Robert meant when he told me to find my own light. Finding that strength allowed me to live.

I knew what I would tell the doctor when my strength returned.

Thank you for rescuing two little girls on a foggy street fourteen years ago. Because of you, I would no longer be tethered to the fictitious girls in my sketchpad and haunted by shame. My sweet sister, Emily, could rest in peace with the dignity she deserved. I could be a worthy sister to the brother that gave me everything and asked for nothing.

I blinked as tears filled my eyes, and my chest surged with the emotion of gratitude. The last recognition was the one that meant the most.

*Thank you for bringing me to my own understanding.*

*S*ally Saylor De Smet worked as an editor and public relations spe-cialist for dignitaries before writing *Pages in the Wind*. She has a love of poetry, the classics, and any story filled with psychological intrigue.

De Smet was born in Nashville and lived in several states before set-tling in San Diego, California. She has two wonderful daughters.

www.ingramcontent.com/pod-product-compliance
Lightning Source LLC
Chambersburg PA
CBHW051315250626

47155CB00007B/2333